英文商業書信
寫作技巧與範例

Business Writing
Skills, Applications, and Practices

作者 **Michelle Witte**

審訂 **Judy Majewski**

譯者 **羅慕謙**

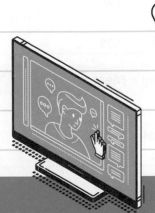

Contents

商業英文書信
Writing Business Letters

active voice 主動語態
動作主詞同時擔任句子主詞的英語語態，例如「The dog bit the boy.」（狗咬了小男孩。）便是主動語態；「The boy was bitten by the dog.」（小男孩被狗咬了。）則為被動語態。

abbreviation 縮寫
單字縮略的寫法，如以 Mr. 代替 Mister。

acronym 字首縮寫
由各個單字的字首組成的縮寫，如以 RAM 代表 random access memory（隨機存取記憶體），以 PT 代表 part time（兼職）。

bold 粗體
粗體字型有突顯的功能，例如本表中的英文詞彙便以粗體顯示。

bulleted list
項目符號和編號格式
列表中的各項目縮排並以列點（・）或其他符號標示。

closing 結尾敬辭
亦作 complimentary close，是書信的結尾用辭，如 Sincerely、Regards 等。

correspondence 通信
個人或公司之間以信件、電子郵件、傳真等進行溝通。

enclosure 附件
信函中除了信件本身以外的附加文件或資料。信件若有附件，需在信中告知對方注意。

functional writing/document
功能性寫作
為了協助讀者、而非為了娛樂寫成的文章。

hard return 段落分隔符號
按 enter/return 鍵跳到下一行。

header/heading 標題
在功能性文件中用以引入新的一段。標題應以粗體標示，並簡要提示接下來的內容。

hierarchy 階層
在書信寫作中，階層指的是文件內容的組織安排，也就是將主要想法放在最上層，下面則是用以支持或相關的想法與資訊。

indent 縮排
把段落中的一行往頁面中央移動，遠離左邊的邊界。

internal 內部的
公司內部的，如可用於 internal reference number（內部參考文號）。

jargon 術語
非常專業的單字和詞彙。

margin 版邊
文章周圍空白的部分。英文商務書信的版邊通常為 1 英寸（2.54 公分）。

postscript 附注
信件結尾補上的內容，以 PS. 標示。

punctuation 標點符號
逗號、冒號、句號等在文字間做為區隔或標示作用的符號。商業書信寫作中，需格外注意各種標點的使用時機。

return address 寄件人地址
寄信人的地址，即信件無法投遞時退回（return）的地址。

salutation 稱呼
信件開頭對收信人的稱呼，如 Dear Ms. Jones（敬愛的瓊斯女士）。

signature 簽名
本人簽下自己的名字；商業文書中用簽名表示文件的真實性或私人性。

signposting 標示
用標題或其他格式指引讀者在文件中找到特定資訊。

skim 略讀
快速瀏覽，只找出主要的內容或特定的資訊。

Tab 鍵；移字鍵
電腦鍵盤上的按鍵，用來把文章開頭向右移，產生的間隔為 2.5 公分左右。

tone 語氣
行文的基本風格和氛圍，展現寫作者的格調和對於讀信者的態度。專業的語氣一般為商業書信所採用。

Unit 1　什麼是商業寫作？
What is business writing?

1　商業寫作是指在商業領域中會應用到的寫作方法，包括：

letter 書信

email 電子郵件

fax 傳真

résumé or CV
履歷表

memo 備忘錄

presentation 簡報

report 報告

other kinds of documents
各種文件

2　商業寫作不是為了娛樂而閱讀的

　　我們閱讀商業寫作是為了得到資訊（information），不是為了娛樂或放鬆。商業寫作的讀者不想跟看小說一樣享受曲折的情節，而是想立刻就看到最後的**建議**（recommendation）或**結論**（conclusion）。

3　商業寫作是功能性寫作（functional writing）

　　商業寫作的讀者會利用該文件去完成工作任務。商業寫作通常用來做出決定，比如說僱用新員工、改變企劃小組的成員、與另外一間公司解除合作關係，或是購買產品或服務，也可能會用來在演講或開會中與他人交換資訊。

4　閱讀商業寫作的人是忙碌的商務人士（businessperson）

　　商務人士通常沒有很多時間仔細閱讀收到的文件，而是會**略讀**（skim），只找出跟自己直接相關的資訊。因此商業寫作應該要有**清楚的格式**（clearly formatted），由簡短的段落、標題，與標有項目符號或數字的列表組成。

5 商業書信須使用專業語氣（professional tone）

　　商業書信不同於私人信件，**使用的語言通常以正式、禮貌用語為主，較少使用太過口語化的俚語（slang）**。此外，私人信件常見的非正式詞彙或片語，若用在商業書信中，在特定情況下可能顯得格格不入。針對這一點，可以參考下方對照表，其中列出了數個非正式、正式用語的例子：

非正式 vs 正式用語	
Informal 非正式	**Formal 正式**
• Hi, John, 嗨，約翰	• Dear Mr. Smith: 親愛的史密斯先生：
• It was great to . . . 能夠……很棒	• It was a pleasure to . . . 能夠……實屬榮幸
• I'd like to talk to you about . . . 我想跟你談……	• I am writing in regards to . . . 此次來信是針對……
• Can you tell me . . . ? 可以跟我說……嗎？	• Please could you inform me . . . ? 能否請您告知……？
• Thanks for . . . 謝謝……	• I very much appreciate . . . 我非常感激……
• I'm sorry to tell you that . . . 很抱歉要跟你說……	• I regret to inform you that . . . 很遺憾要通知您……
• Bye! 再見！	• Yours sincerely, 此致，

　　商業書信雖然通常使用正式用語，然而**正式程度（formality）需視對象、情境（context）、目的調整**，例如寫給地位（status）較高的主管時，用語要盡量正式，對平輩的同事或下屬則可以較不正式。此外，也需考量與收信者的**親疏關係（familiarity）、年齡、性別**等條件，若用過於正式的用語寫給熟識對象，可能顯得疏遠（distant）、冷淡。

　　溝通情境也會影響書信用語的正式程度，例如討論重要公事時，宜採用正式用語，而在推銷信中則可使用較非正式、活潑（lively）的語句。另外，現代商業書信經常使用**電子郵件**，電郵的用語常因講求溝通效率（efficiency）而**漸趨口語化（colloquial）**，追求簡單、直白，反而應避免過多、過於正式的用字。

Unit 2　如何寫好商業寫作？
How do I begin to write well for business?

如何寫好商業寫作？
❶ 了解你的讀者
❷ 預想讀者會提出什麼問題
❸ 回答讀者的問題
❹ 能讓讀者很快在文件中找到資訊
❺ 內容要清楚直接

1 了解你的讀者

要寫出好的功能性文件（functional document），你必須先知道：

◆ 誰會閱讀這些文件？
◆ 他們為什麼要閱讀這些文件？

動筆之前，先想想：

◆ 你的讀者是哪些人？
◆ 他們是什麼**職位**？有何**經驗**和**背景**？
◆ 讀者對你要**提到的主題**有多少了解？
◆ 讀者希望透過這份文件**達成什麼需求**？

　　有關此點，請參考以下信件摘錄，內容取自於一封對於建言信（suggestion letter，參見本書 Part 11）的回覆信。從信中用字遣詞可看出，**收信者 Mr. Jones 為餐飲服務業的資深專業人士**，因此**代表餐廳且相對資淺的寫信者**仔細考量讀者身分和需求後，**以相對正式的語氣**回覆他的建言。

Dear Mr. Jones:

Thank you very much for your suggestion about the service situation in our restaurant. We very much ❶ appreciate the views of people like yourself with many years of experience in the service industry. We will work on our staff training and ❷ hope you will feel more satisfied the next time you visit us.

❶ 展現對讀信者身分的了解，尊重讀信者意見，以及顯示對其經驗和背景的認識。

❷ 預想讀信者需求，在信中提供對讀信者後續行動有幫助的資訊（告知對方可再次來店體驗）。

　　在本章〈Unit 8〉（p. 38）還會再詳細說明如何分析你的讀者。

2 預想讀者會提出什麼問題

想一想：**你的讀者在閱讀這份文件時，心裡會提出什麼問題？**好的功能性文件，會預想（anticipate）讀者有哪些問題，並給予答案。讀者會有的問題，通常都會跟他們後續就此文件要做的事直接相關，所以要考慮到所有他們可能會提出的問題。相關的問題可能有：

❶ 在開會時、研討會上或是活動舉辦過程當中，**發生了什麼問題？**

❷ **為什麼**我在讀這份文件？內容**和我有何關聯？**

❸ 接下來應該怎麼做？**可以採取的措施**為何？

Dear Staff:

❶ Attendance at our monthly meetings has been low recently. This is a friendly reminder that **❷** attending the monthly meeting is one of the major requirements in this company. It is also important for attendees to be there on time. Otherwise, the flow of the meeting will be disrupted. Meetings begin at 9:30 a.m. on the first Monday of each month. **❸** Please set a reminder in your calendars.

❶ 明確告知讀信者這封信件欲討論的問題為何。

❷ 向讀信者表明為何需要閱讀信件討論的內容，顯示信件和讀者有重要關聯。

❸ 告訴讀者接下來可以採取什麼具體措施。

---

3 回答讀者的問題

想像讀者的各種問題並回答問題。這是組織功能性文件內容很好的方式：想好讀者可能會提出哪些問題後，在文件中**一開始就清楚回答這些問題**，而且**重要的問題要一開始就提出回答**。〈Unit 8〉還會再詳細說明如何預期和回答讀者的問題。

We will refund the purchase price. We are very sorry for the inconvenience.

重要問題先回答　　　　　　　　　　　次要資訊在後

---

4 能讓讀者很快在文件中找到資訊

忙碌的商務讀者沒有時間仔細閱讀文件內容，所以務必把重要的資訊以醒目的格式突顯出來，方便讀者找到資訊。方式如下：

❶ 把彼此相關的資訊組織成清楚的段落，前面並**設定醒目的粗體（bold type）標題。**

❷ **以編號或字型大小（font size）顯示文件內容的階層（hierarchy）**，也就是顯示不同的段落彼此存在何種**上下關係**，而哪些資訊又是最重要的。

❸ 在段落中，以**項目符號清單（bulleted list）**列出重要的資訊。

❹ 如果列表中的內容有前後關係，那就用**數字編號（numbered list）**。

❶ ❷ 用粗體標題或字型大小顯示內容階層。

❸ 以項目符號分項列出重要資訊。

❹ 以數字編號將前後有關的資訊，按照順序排列。

❶ ❷ Goals for the next six months

❸ • Reach out to new markets in Mexico.
 • Create an employee handbook.
 • Continue to seek out government contracts.

Lessons learned during the past six months

❹ 1. Allow more time for government bids.
 2. Have our finances checked before making any government bids.
 3. Provide training for staff in the newest design software.

5 內容要清楚直接

句子要簡單明瞭，讓讀者一看就懂。不要用太過正式的語言，想像你正直接（face-to-face）跟讀者說話，用這樣簡單的語言就可以了。動詞語態上，商業文件通常使用**主動句**，較少用被動句。

主動語態 vs 被動語態	
Active voice 主動（常用）	Passive voice 被動（少用）
• We received your order. 我們收到了您的訂單。	• Your order was received. 您的訂單已經收到。
• We decided to . . . 我們已決定要……	• The decision was made to . . . 已有決定要進行……

需注意的是，在部分情境下，主動語態會帶有**批判的（critical）**口吻。此時，則可以採取**被動語態**以維持**中性（neutral）**的語氣，例如可比較以下兩個例句：

❶ You sent the package to the wrong address. (Active voice, critical tone.)
你把包裹寄到了錯誤的地址。（主動語態，語氣帶批判）

❷ The package was sent to the wrong address. (Passive voice, neutral tone.)
包裹送到了錯誤的地址。（被動語態，語氣中性）

1 Review the concepts

➊ What is a functional document?

➋ How do people read functional documents?

➌ Why is it important to make key information stand out visually?

➍ How can you show readers the structure of your document?

➎ When should you use a numbered list rather than a bulleted list?

2 Below is a list of phrases. In each pair, one is informal and the other is formal. Decide which is which. Then copy the phrases into the tables below.

➊
- I would like to inform you of . . .
- Let me tell you about . . .

➋
- I am very pleased to hear that . . .
- It's such great news that . . .

➌
- I'll send you another one right now.
- I will send a replacement immediately.

➍
- I want to know more about . . .
- I am interested in learning more about . . .

Formal language
➊ _____
➋ _____
➌ _____
➍ _____

Informal language
➊ _____
➋ _____
➌ _____
➍ _____

Unit 3 商業信件基本格式與元素
Basic Business Letter Format and Parts

商業書信包含幾個特定的部分，動筆前需學會如何正確使用與安排格式。

下面就是商業書信的主要構成元素，下一頁有細目說明。

信首 Heading
① SENDER'S ADDRESS 寄件人地址
② DATE 日期

Catherine Davies
15 Qingtong Rd.-1011
Pudong New District
Shanghai, PRC 201203

November 2, 2023

開頭 Opening
③ RECIPIENT'S ADDRESS 收件人及地址
④ SALUTATION 稱謂

Ms. Nina Lin
Double Design
Room 205, Building 3
Lane 2498, Pudong Avenue
Shanghai, PRC

Dear Ms. Lin:

I am writing to request an interview regarding Double Design's opening for a graphic designer.

I am a recent graduate of the Academy of Art with a degree in graphic design. For the past six months, I have interned with Studio Design in Shanghai, learning to apply the skills I gained in school. I would appreciate an opportunity to learn more about the graphic designer position and to discuss how I can contribute to your company.

I have enclosed my résumé for your reference. Please feel free to contact me for any reason at (021) 5184-3155 or by email at cath.davies@yahoo.com. Thank you for your attention. I look forward to hearing from you.

正文 Body
⑤ BODY OF LETTER 信件正文

Best regards,

Catherine Davies

Catherine Davies

Enc. (1)

結尾 Closing
⑥ CLOSING 結尾敬語
⑦ SIGNATURE (handwritten) 親筆簽名
⑧ NAME (typed) 姓名
⑨ ENCLOSURE/ATTACHMENT 附件
⑩ COPY TO 副本註明

cc: Flora Lopez

Quality Cosmetics, Inc. ❶
302 Beauty Lane, Suite 5
San Bruno, CA 94066
(650) 656-7000
act@cos.com
[1 blank line]
October 12, 2023 ❷
[1 blank line]
CERTIFIED MAIL ❸
PERSONAL ❹
[1 blank line]
Permissions Department
Harbinger Publishing
309 Ditmas Ave
Brooklyn, NY 11218-4901 ❺
[1 blank line]
Attention Mr. Donald Williams ❻
[1 blank line]
Re: Your letter dated October 9, 2023 ❼
[1 blank line]
Dear Permissions Department: ❽
[1 blank line]
Subject: Illustration: Girl Applying Lipstick ❾
[1 blank line]
May I use one of your illustrations in my in-house report titled "Third Quarter Growth in the Cosmetics Industry"? The illustration is called "Girl Applying Lipstick."
[1 blank line]
Thanks for your time and attention. Please contact me as soon as possible at (415) 748-9852. ❿
[1 blank line]
Regards, ⓫
[1 blank line]
Irina Safarova ⓬
[1 blank line]
Irina Safarova ⓭
Analyst, Quality Cosmetics ⓮
[1 blank line]
IS/jd ⓯
[1 blank line]
Enc. (1) catalog ⓰
[1 blank line]
cc: Flora Lopez ⓱
[1 blank line]
P.S.

❶ **SENDER'S ADDRESS** 寄件人住址

- 如果信紙上印有信頭（letterhead），就不需要再打上這些資料。信頭就是公司專用信紙上印有公司名稱與商標的地方。寫商務書信時，最好使用這種已經印好信頭的公司專用信紙，這樣看起來比白紙要專業。

❷ **DATE** 日期

- **美國的日期寫法**：月—日—年（例如 October 12, 2023）
- **英國的日期寫法**：日—月—年（例如 12 October 2023）

❸ **SPECIAL MAILING NOTATIONS** 郵寄紀錄

記錄郵寄的方式與性質，如：

- CERTIFIED MAIL 掛號信件
- SPECIAL DELIVERY 限時專送
- AIR MAIL 航空信件

❹ **ON-ARRIVAL NOTATIONS** 內部紀錄

記錄郵寄的性質，如：

- PERSONAL 私人信件
- CONFIDENTIAL 機密文件
- PRIVATE AND CONFIDENTIAL
  私人機密文件
- STRICTLY CONFIDENTIAL
  極機密文件

❽ **SALUTATION** 稱謂／稱呼

常見稱謂如下：

- Dear Sir:
- Dear Sir or Madam:
- Dear Mr./Ms. [Last name]:
- Dear [Full Name]:
- To Whom It May Concern:
- Ladies and Gentlemen:

❺ **RECIPIENT'S ADDRESS** 收件人及地址

常見內容包含如下：

- name of person addressed
  收件人名稱
- title of person addressed
  收件人職位名稱
- name of organization 公司單位名稱
- street number and name 號碼與街名
- city, state, and postal code
  城市、州、郵遞區號
- country of destination
  寄送國家名稱（應單獨一行）

❻ **ATTENTION** 致 (指定的受信人)

如果收件人地址上已寫明 (見第 5 點)，就不用加寫這一行。此外，Attention 的對象應與信封上的收件人相同。

❼ **REFERENCE (if any)** 信件參考文號

將信件分類和編碼，以便日後參照。例如註記是求職信、發票信或是回覆某信等。

❾ **SUBJECT** 信件主旨

❿ **BODY OF LETTER** 信件正文

⓫ **CLOSING** 結尾敬語

⓬ **SIGNATURE (handwritten)** 親筆簽名

⓭ **NAME (typed)** 姓名 (打字)

⓮ **TITLE (typed)** 單位或職位名稱 (打字)

⓯ **IDENTIFICATION INITIALS**

(of the writer and typist) 鑑別符號

當寫信人和打字者不是同一個人時使用，各取其姓名首字母縮寫。寫信人的姓名縮寫用大寫放在前面，打字者的姓名縮寫用小寫置於後，格式如下：

- IS/jd
- IS:jd

（指寫信人是 Irina Safarova，
打字者是 Joe Davis）

⓰ **ENCLOSURE/ATTACHMENT** 附件

（常用縮寫：**Enc.** 或 **Encl.**）

⓱ **COPY TO** 副本註明 (說明另寄副件給某人)

cc 是指 **carbon copy**。

⓲ **POSTSCRIPT** 附注

（商業書信應避免使用）

1 信頭 The letterhead

信頭就是公司專用信紙（stationery）上印有公司名稱、地址與商標的地方。寫商務書信時，最好使用這種已經印好信頭的公司專用信紙，這樣看起來比白紙要專業。請看下面例子：

信頭 letterhead

2 日期 The date

由於商務書信的內容往往是與時間密切相關（time-sensitive）的資訊（像是訂單），因此一定要寫上寫信的日期。日期應該寫在**信頭（公司名稱和地址）的下面**，把月分用字母拼寫出來，年分也要寫完整，比如「November 12, 2023」。不要只寫數字（11/12/23），也不要用縮寫（Nov. 12, 2023）。

在美國，日期是按照「**月、日、年**」的順序寫出來，在其他的英語國家，日期多按照「**日、月、年**」的順序寫，還有些人覺得「**年、月、日**」的寫法最清楚，但是這種格式並不常見。

排列順序	✕ 不能只用數字	✓ 年分／月分完整寫出
美式：月／日／年	3/15/2023	March 15, 2023
英式：日／月／年	15/3/2023	15 March 2023
年／月／日	2023/3/15	2023 March 15

3 經辦人 The attention line

attention 就是「**致某人**」的意思，表示這封信的**指定收件人**。可以指定某個特定的人（Attention Dr. Smith），也可以指定某個職位（Attention: Accounting Manager）。在**個人寫給個人**的商務書信中，**經辦人不一定要寫出來**，但是如果是寫**給公司或部門**的信，寫上經辦人可以**增加信件處理的效率**。經辦人的寫法有很多種：

❶ 把 attention 這個字**完整地打出來**： Attention Ms. Jane Harper
❷ 也可以使用**縮寫**： ATTN: Ms. Jane Harper
❸ 可以在 attention 後面**加上冒號**： Attention: Ms. Jane Harper
❹ attention 後面也可以**不加冒號**： Attention Ms. Jane Harper
❺ 也可以打出**完整的句子**： To the attention of Ms. Jane Harper

4 參考文號 The reference number

參考文號跟經辦人一樣，在商務書信中**不一定是必須的**，不過參考文號有助於追蹤訂單和其他的通信。機構之間的商務書信裡，通常會有一個內部參考文號，可以是以日期的形式（如 111223），也可以是字母和數字的組合，以**方便公司找到對應的檔案**。常見寫法有：

- ◆ Ref. No. 111223
- ◆ File number 111223
- ◆ Reference number AR48.
- ◆ Please refer to file number 111223（請參照 111223 號檔案）

不同的公司會有不同的參考文號，因此可以在同一行把雙方的參考文號都寫出來，並標明「本公司參考文號／貴公司參考文號」，如：

- ◆ Our reference 111215 / Your reference OS 234

如果沒有參考文號，最好能夠提一下之前的通信紀錄，如：

- ◆ Regarding your letter of November 12 （有關您 11 月 12 日的來函）
- ◆ In reference to your request of October 3, 2023 （有關您 2023 年 10 月 3 日的請求）

5 稱謂 The salutation

稱謂就是你稱呼收件人的方式，稱呼包含三個部分：

❶ 收件人的頭銜（title）

  ❶ 務必**把收件人的頭銜寫對**。

  ❷ **不同的專業有不同的頭銜**，醫生和博士的頭銜是 Dr.；大學教授可能是 Dr.（博士），也有可能是 Professor（教授）。法官、政府官員和高級職員的頭銜一定要先查清楚。常見專業頭銜縮寫有以下幾種：

頭銜	縮寫	中文職稱	頭銜	縮寫	中文職稱
Doctor	Dr.	醫師／博士	General	Gen.	將軍
Professor	Prof.	教授	Colonel	Col.	上校
Associate Professor	Assoc. Prof.	副教授	Inspector General	Insp. Gen.	檢查總長
Governor	Gov.	州長	Senator	Sen.	（美國）參議員
President	Pres.	總統	Representative	Rep.	（美國）眾議員

  ❸ 寫信給不具醫師、博士或教授等頭銜的**男士**時，要用 **Mr.（先生）**，寫信給**女士**要用 **Ms.（女士）**，除非對方明確要求你使用 Mrs.（夫人）或 Miss（小姐）。

❷ 收件人的名字

根據情境不同，可用不同方式表達稱呼收件人姓名，**常見有以下幾種寫法：**

稱呼方式	範例	使用時機
Dear ＋頭銜＋姓氏	Dear Dr. Howard	**一般情境**皆適用
Dear ＋名字	Dear Jessica	寫信者跟收信者已經**熟識**到可以只互稱名字的地步
Dear ＋先生／女士	Dear Sir（用於男性） Dear Madam（用於女性）	**不知道**對方的**姓名**，但是**知道**對方的**性別**
Dear ＋先生或女士 致先生或女士	Dear Sir or Madam Ladies and Gentlemen	**不知道**對方的**姓名和性別**
Dear ＋名字＋姓氏	Dear Kim Jones	**知道**對方**姓名**，但**不知道**對方**性別**

❸ 標點符號（punctuation）

◆ 最常見的就是在名字後面加一個**冒號**，例如：Dear Ms. White:

◆ 但是也可以完全**不加標點符號**，例如：Dear Professor Bard

◆ 在較不正式的商業書信中，也可以在名字後**使用逗號**，例如：Dear Mr. Howard,

6 主旨 The subject line or heading

你可以加上一行「**主旨**」，作為**信件的標題**。加上主旨有助於讀者立刻了解信件的主題。基本上，主旨要**簡明扼要**。主旨的寫法也有很多種，下面是幾個例子：

◆ Re: Information Technologies Conference

◆ Subject: Information Technologies Conference

◆ SUBJECT: Information Technologies Conference

◆ Information Technologies Conference

雖然「主旨」可用大寫呈現（SUBJECT），但一般來說，**商務信件中應避免在任何一個部分全使用大寫字母。**大寫字母比較不容易讀，而且會影響到信件的語氣。

7 正文 The body

正文就是信件裡**最主要的部分**。正文通常由段落（paragraph）組成，整個正文的長度取決於你有多少資訊要傳達給對方。正文應該要**簡潔扼要**，**內容要有組織**，方便讀者找到需要的資訊。

第一段

在第一段裡，清楚說明寫作這封信的**目的**，如：

* With reference to our conversation of August 3, . . .
  就我們八月三日的對話……

如果你的信會很長，在第一段把信件的內容條列出來，常用的開頭用語如：

* With reference to your letter/email/fax of (date) . . .
  就您於……月……日的來信／電郵／傳真
* Thank you for your letter/email/fax/catalog/etc.
  謝謝您的來信／電郵／傳真／目錄等
* Regarding our meeting on Thursday . . .
  有關我們星期四的會議……

中間的段落

中間的段落應該用來**詳細說明主題**，並給予**重要的細節或指引**。段落盡量簡短，每段只處理一個小主題。如果有重要資訊，不妨用**項目符號**或**數字**編成列表。此外，務必保持內容**簡潔**，讀者會希望你的信簡短扼要。

結論／最後一段

結論的內容取決於信中傳達的資訊。你可以在結論裡**提出推薦、總結想法**，或**表示願意提供幫助**。如果是求職信，最好在結尾加上**如何（how）**、**何時（when）**、**哪裡（where）**可以聯絡到你。

商業書信最後一段常用的說法有：

* Please don't hesitate to contact us again if you have any questions or concerns. 如果您有任何疑問，歡迎再次向我們洽詢。
* Please let me know if I can be of more assistance.
  如果還有什麼我可以幫上忙的地方，請通知我。
* If you need further help, please contact us again.
  如果您還需要進一步協助，請再與我們聯絡。
* We look forward to [our next meeting / working with you].
  我們誠心期盼〔下一次的會面／合作〕。

8 結尾敬辭 Closing line / Complimentary close

在結尾敬辭後面加上**逗號**，並且只有**第一個字母要大寫**。結尾敬辭有正式和較不正式的區別，**常用的結尾敬辭有：**

商業書信常見結尾敬辭	較個人化的結尾敬辭
• Yours truly, • Respectfully (yours), • Cordially (yours), • (Yours) Sincerely, • Sincerely yours, • (Yours) Faithfully,* • Faithfully yours,	• Love, • With love, • Best wishes/regards, • Warmest/Kindest regards, • Your devoted friend, • Cheers, • As always,

* 在英式用法中，(Yours) Faithfully 常用作不確定收信人姓名時的結尾敬辭，此時收信人稱謂常為 Dear Sir 或 Dear Madam；若確定收件人姓名，則會用 sincerely 取代 faithfully。

9 簽名 Signature

商務書信都要簽名，而且最好用好的筆簽。比起大量印刷的商業信函，有簽名的商務書信感覺起來親切多了。在親筆簽名之後，打上你的**名字和職稱**；如果不是很長，那就寫成一行，如果你的名字和職稱太長，那就分成兩行：

* Jackie Smart, President　◎ 寫成一行
* Reginald K. Dahl　　　　◎ 寫成兩行
  Marketing Director

如果是**電子郵件**，在郵件**最下方鍵入你的名字**，並附上一個「.sig」的簽名檔。本書 Part 2 還會再詳細說明如何撰寫商務電子郵件。

10 附件 Enclosure/Attachment

附件就是隨信附上的文件，可能是簡章、訂單、目錄、報告或其他的文件。你**應該在正文就告訴對方你隨信附上了附件**，然後在**頁面底端簽名的下方再提一次**。你**可以採用這些說法告知附件資訊：**

* We are enclosing . . . 隨信附上……
* We enclose . . . 隨信附上……
* Enclosed is . . . 隨信附上……
* Please find enclosed . . . 請見附件中的……

頁尾寫法	範例
Enclosure 完整地打出來，**括號**寫出**附件數目**	Enclosures (3)
用 Enclosure 的**縮寫**（Enc. 或 Encl.）	Enc. (3)
列出全部**附件名稱**	Enclosures (1) Invoice 1029; (2) Return slip; (3) Customer satisfaction survey

Unit 4 書信範例格式套用
Sample Business Letter

[Your Name 寄件人姓名 / 公司名]
[Address: Street → City → State → Zip Code
寄件地址：街名、市名、州名、郵遞區號]

1 blank line

[Phone: Phone # → Fax phone # → Voice mail phone #
電話：市話、傳真、語音訊息]
[Email Address 電子郵件地址]

1 blank line

[Date today 寫信日期]

3 or 1 blank line(s)

[Special Mailing Notations 郵寄方式註記]
[On-Arrival Notations 信件內部註記]

1 blank line

[Recipient's Name 收件人姓名]
[Company Name 收件人機關名]
[Address 收件地址]

1 blank line

Attention [Recipient's Name 經辦人〔收件人姓名〕]

1 blank line

Ref: [What this letter refers to 參考文號]

1 blank line

Dear [Recipient's name 招呼語和收件人稱謂]:

1 blank line

[SUBJECT 主旨句]

1 blank line

(First paragraph) 第一段

1 blank line

(Second paragraph . . .) 第二段等

1 blank line

Sincerely, 結尾敬辭

1 blank line

[Sign here 親筆簽名]

1 blank line

[Your name 寄件人姓名（打字）]
[Your title 寄件人職稱]

1 blank line

[Identification Initials] 鑑別符號

1 blank line

Enclosures: [Number] 附件〔數量〕

1 blank line

cc: [Name for Copy] 副本〔對象〕
[Name for Copy]

1 blank line

PS. 附注

三種商業書信格式
Three Business Letter Styles

1 什麼是商務書信？

商務書信就是公司寫給**公司**、**客戶**（client）、**顧客**（customer）或**合作夥伴**（partner）的信件，使用的語言比一般朋友之間的書信語言要**正式**，並以**商業流程**或**商業交易**等為主要內容。

2 什麼時候需要寫商務書信？

你會用商務書信與顧客、客戶、商業夥伴和其他公司進行溝通。有些商務書信是「公司寫給公司」，有些則是不同公司個人之間的書信往來。商務書信的格式，與學術寫作或創意寫作不同，通常公司會就所有的內部文件和通信採用**固定的格式**。如果你的公司已經有固定的格式，那就按照公司的格式。

3 信的長度超過一頁時，如何安排格式？

如果信的內容超過一頁，那就換一張紙繼續打下去，但是**不要加入信頭**，而是用空白、紙質好的白紙。第二頁起的格式安排有幾種不同的做法，但是都要在頁面頂端寫上**收件人的名字**、**頁數**和**日期**，有些人還會加上參考文號或主旨。你可以把所有這些資訊都靠左對齊，或是把名字靠左對齊，頁數打在中央，日期則靠右，然後空三行，繼續信的內容。

5-1 | Basic business letter formats 商業信件基本格式

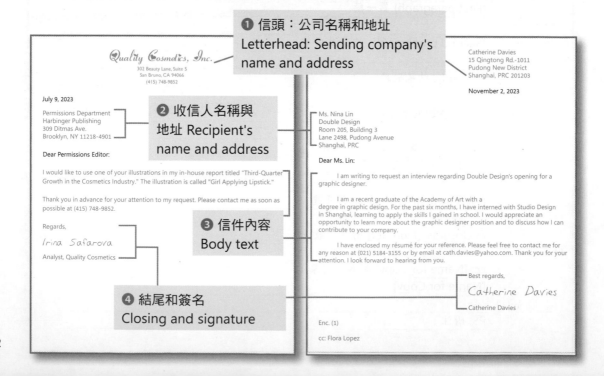

❶ 信頭：公司名稱和地址
Letterhead: Sending company's name and address

❷ 收信人名稱與地址 Recipient's name and address

❸ 信件內容 Body text

❹ 結尾和簽名 Closing and signature

❶ 齊頭式（block style）：
廣受歡迎

❷ 改良齊頭式（modified block style）：亦常見

❸ 縮排式（indented style）：
逐漸式微

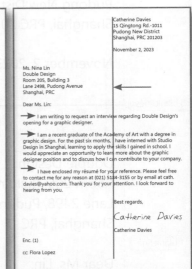

---

4 商務書信之格式 (1)：齊頭式（block style）

齊頭式（block style）是一種簡便的商務書信格式，在齊頭式中，文件或信中的每個部分都從**左邊的邊界**起頭。不同的部分（比如說不同的段落或地址）則以**空行**的方式隔開。齊頭式很簡單，因此非常受到歡迎。其主要格式為下：

❶ **段落齊頭**：在齊頭式中，文件或信中的每個部分都從**左邊的邊界**起頭。

❷ **不同的段落之間要空行**：不同的部分（比如說不同的段落，或商務書信中的地址），則以**空行**的方式隔開。

　　❶ **日期**和**收件人的地址**之間：空一行或空三行
　　❷ **稱呼**與信件**內文**的第一段之間：空一行
　　❸ 信件內文的**段落之間**：空一行
　　❹ **大小標題與隨後的段落**之間：不空行

Catherine Davies
15 Qingtong Rd,-1011
Pudong New District
Shanghai, PRC 201203

1 blank line

November 2, 2023

❶ Every part of a piece of writing begins at the left-hand margin.
段落齊頭：信中的每個部分都從左邊的邊界起頭。

3 blank lines

Ms. Nina Lin
Double Design
Room 205, Building 3
Lane 2498, Pudong Avenue
Shanghai, PRC

1 blank line

Dear Ms. Lin:

❷ Use hard returns between paragraphs.
不同的段落之間要空行。

1 blank line

I am writing to request an interview for Double Design's opening for a graphic designer.

1 blank line

I am a recent graduate of the Academy of Art with a degree in graphic design. For the past six months, I have interned with Studio Design in Shanghai, learning to apply the skills I gained in school. I would appreciate an opportunity to learn more about the graphic designer position and to discuss how I can contribute to your company.

1 blank line

I have enclosed my résumé for your reference. Please feel free to contact me for any reason at (021) 5184-3155 or by email at cath.davies@yahoo.com. Thank you for your attention. I look forward to hearing from you.

1 blank line

Best regards,

Catherine Davies

3 blank lines

Catherine Davies

1 blank line

Enc. (1)

1 blank line

cc: Flora Lopez

5 商務書信之格式 (2)：改良齊頭式（modified block style）

　　改良齊頭式（modified block style）結合了縮排式與齊頭式的特點，外觀看起來跟縮排式很像，而最大的特徵，就是在改良齊頭式中：❶ **段落首行齊頭**，新的一段段落將與左邊的邊界齊頭（flush left）。❷ **寄件人地址、日期、結尾敬辭和簽名都縮排**，如同縮排式。改良齊頭式就跟齊頭式一樣，版面看起來清晰整齊，亦是商務書信經常使用的格式。

5-4 | Modified block style: cover letter 改良齊頭式求職信

❶ Body text begins at the left-hand margin.
信件正文的段落齊頭：從左邊的邊界起頭。

1 blank line

3 blank lines

Catherine Davies
15 Qingtong Rd.-1011
Pudong New District
Shanghai, PRC 201203

November 2, 2023

❷ The return address, the date, and the closing and signature are indented.
寄件人地址、日期、結尾敬辭和簽名需縮排。

Ms. Nina Lin
Double Design
Room 205, Building 3
Lane 2498, Pudong Avenue
Shanghai, PRC

1 blank line

Dear Ms. Lin:

1 blank line

I am writing to request an interview for Double Design's opening for a graphic designer.

1 blank line

I am a recent graduate of the Academy of Art with a degree in graphic design. For the past six months, I have interned with Studio Design in Shanghai, learning to apply the skills I gained in school. I would appreciate an opportunity to learn more about the graphic designer position and to discuss how I can contribute to your company.

I have enclosed my résumé for your reference. Please feel free to contact me for any reason at (021) 5184-3155 or by email at cath.davies@yahoo.com. Thank you for your attention. I look forward to hearing from you.

1 blank line

Best regards,

3 blank lines

Catherine Davies

Catherine Davies

1 blank line

Enc. (1)

1 blank line

cc: Flora Lopez

6 商務書信之格式 (3)：縮排式（indented style）

縮排式（indented style）比其他通用的商務書信格式稍微複雜。縮排式是比較**老式**的商務書信格式，所以很多人都熟悉這種格式。在縮排式裡，每個段落的**首行要**縮排，信件中某些其他部分也要縮排，**要縮排的部分包括：**

- 段落的第一行
- 寄件人地址（return address）
- 寄件日期（date）
- 結尾敬辭（complimentary close）
- 簽名（signature）

採用縮排式時，最重要的就是要**前後一致**，縮排**最少要四至五格**，要縮更多格也可以，只要每個段落縮排的距離都一樣即可。至於信中的其他元素也一樣，基本原則是縮排的距離一樣，彼此上下對齊。

❶ 段落的第一行要縮排

每個段落的**首行**都縮排，與正文的左邊邊界距離 1.5 公分左右，這是最常見的縮排距離，但是大於 3.5 公分的縮排也有人用。不同的公司對於怎麼縮排、縮排多長可能有不同的習慣，關鍵就是要**前後一致**，也就是每段縮排的距離都一樣。要把段落縮排有幾種可行的做法：

- 可以固定按幾次空白鍵
- 可以按一次 tab 鍵
- 也可以利用段落格式設定的功能

通常你會用 enter/return 鍵在段落之間多空一行，但是採用縮排式的商務書信，也可能在段落之間不空行。不過最重要的原則仍舊是要**前後一致**。

❷ 商務書信中的其他部分縮排

商務書信採用縮排式時，還有其他的部分也要縮排：**寄件人地址、日期、結尾敬辭、簽名**。這些部分的縮排方式，應該從**頁面的右半邊**起頭，統一從頁面中線稍微往右的地方起頭。

有些人覺得縮排式是商務書信最傳統的格式，但也有人覺得這種格式過時了，而且縮排式在頁面上看起來不是那麼清晰，要把縮排的地方上下對齊也不是那麼容易，而其他的格式應用起來通常比較簡單。現在大家更喜歡採用其他新的格式，但是很多商務人士還是習慣使用縮排式。

5-5 | Indented style: cover letter 縮排式求職信

Catherine Davies
15 Qingtong Rd.-1011
Pudong New District
Shanghai, PRC 201203

1 blank line

3 blank lines

November 2, 2023

Ms. Nina Lin
Double Design
Room 205, Building 3
Lane 2498, Pudong Avenue
Shanghai, PRC

❷ The return address, the date, and the closing and signature are indented. 寄件人地址、日期、結尾敬辭和簽名縮排。

1 blank line

Dear Ms. Lin:

❶ Indent each new paragraph. 段落的第一行要縮排。

1 blank line

I am writing to request an interview regarding Double Design's opening for a graphic designer.

1 blank line

I am a recent graduate of the Academy of Art with a degree in graphic design. For the past six months, I have interned with Studio Design in Shanghai, learning to apply the skills I gained in school. I would appreciate an opportunity to learn more about the graphic designer position and to discuss how I can contribute to your company.

1 blank line

I have enclosed my résumé for your reference. Please feel free to contact me for any reason at (021) 5184-3155 or By email at cath. davies@yahoo.com. Thank you for your attention. I look forward to hearing from you.

1 blank line

Best regards,

3 blank lines

Catherine Davies

1 blank line

Catherine Davies

Enc. (1)

1 blank line

cc: Flora Lopez

信封的寫法
The Envelope

第一印象在商務領域中非常重要,而**信封(envelope)**就是對方收信時第一個會看到的部分,所以信封的版面務必要清楚專業。信封上最重要的,就是**寄件人的地址**和**收件人的地址**。

1 寄件人地址(你 / 公司的地址)

如果你的地址沒有預先就已經印在信封上,那就把地址打在信封的左上角。**盡量不要手寫**,先打**名字**和**頭銜**,然後是**公司的地址**。地址當中不要有句號,但是逗號、破折號、連字號和表示縮寫的句號,應按正常規則使用。地址當中最長的一行長度,不要超過信封長度的一半,或是信封寬度的三分之一。

2 收件人地址

打完自己的地址後,想像寄件人地址右方空白的部分有一個 1.5 公分寬的邊緣,並將這個邊緣留白,接著在這個邊緣的右方,把收件人地址打在**信封的中央**,但高度不要超過郵票的下緣。先寫收件人的名字與頭銜,接著依照對方國家的習慣寫地址,地址當中同樣不要有句號。

如果你用的是有透明窗口的信封(開窗信封,window envelope,參見下圖),就把信紙折好,讓信紙上的收件人地址正好對著窗口。

window envelope

3 郵寄方式註記

可在信封上的郵票下方處加上**郵寄方式註記**（**special mailing notations**），以註明信件的寄送方式。這項註記可用全大寫書寫，常見的例子包括：

- ◆ CERTIFIED MAIL 掛號信件
- ◆ SPECIAL DELIVERY 限時專送
- ◆ AIRMAIL 航空信件

4 內部信件種類註記

可在收件人姓名旁註記信件種類，以便對方知道信件性質和該如何處理信件。此項註記並非必須，但商業書信中算是標準做法。內部信件種類紀錄和郵寄方式註記相同，可用全大寫字母書寫，幾種範例如下：

- ◆ PERSONAL 私人信件
- ◆ CONFIDENTIAL 機密信件
- ◆ PRIVATE & CONFIDENTIAL 私人機密信件

6-1 | Envelope 信封

❶ 寄信人的姓名、公司名稱和地址
Sender's name and address

郵戳
Postmark

Irina Safarova
Quality Cosmetics, Inc.
302 Beauty Lane, Suite 5
San Bruno, CA 94066

郵票 Postage stamp

POSTAGE
POST OFFICE
TWO PENCE
MAURITIUS
PORTO

CERTIFIED MAIL

❹ 內部紀錄
On-Arrival Notations

PERSONAL
Mr. Donald Williams
Permissions Department
Harbinger Publishing
309 Ditmas Ave.
Brooklyn, NY 11218-4901

❸ 郵寄紀錄
Special Mailing Notations

❷ 收件人的姓名、公司名稱和地址
Recipient's name and address

1 Review the concepts

1. What does "flush left" mean?
2. Which letter format involves lining up each element flush left?
3. In which format(s) will the sender's address be on the right side of the paper?
4. Which is the oldest format for business writing?
5. How does the modified block style combine indented style and block style?
6. In the modified block style, which parts of your letter will be on the right side of the paper rather than flush left?
7. Where should the receiver's address go on a business envelope?
8. What is a "window envelope"?

2 Apply the concepts

1. Label each element in the following letter.

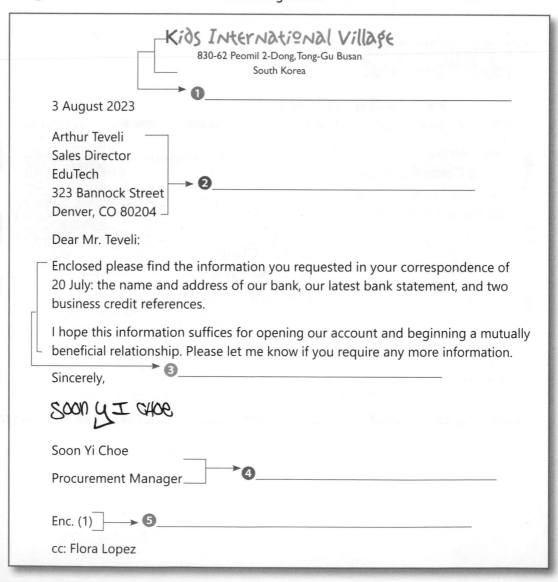

Kids International Village
830-62 Peomil 2-Dong, Tong-Gu Busan
South Korea

❶ _____

3 August 2023

Arthur Teveli
Sales Director
EduTech
323 Bannock Street
Denver, CO 80204

❷ _____

Dear Mr. Teveli:

Enclosed please find the information you requested in your correspondence of 20 July: the name and address of our bank, our latest bank statement, and two business credit references.

I hope this information suffices for opening our account and beginning a mutually beneficial relationship. Please let me know if you require any more information.

Sincerely,

❸ _____

Soon Yi Choe

Soon Yi Choe

Procurement Manager

❹ _____

Enc. (1) ➙ ❺ _____

cc: Flora Lopez

❷ **Please write** your address, the date, the recipient's name and address, the salutation, the complimentary close, **and** the signature **in block style in this "letter."** Use the address of a friend or another business for the recipient's address. The hard returns are marked for you.

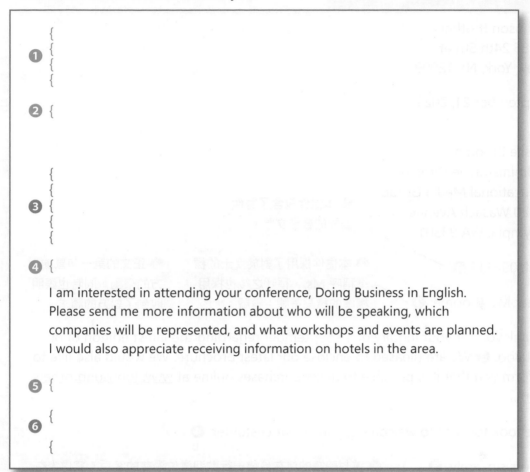

❶ {
  {
  {
  {

❷ {

❸ {
  {
  {
  {

❹ {

I am interested in attending your conference, Doing Business in English. Please send me more information about who will be speaking, which companies will be represented, and what workshops and events are planned. I would also appreciate receiving information on hotels in the area.

❺ {

❻ {
  {

❸ **Address this "envelope." Use your home or business address and a friend's or colleague's name for the receiver.**

❶ {
  {
  {
  {
  {

❷ {
  {
  {
  {
  {

7-1 | Sample 1 範例分析（1）

Johnson Brothers
3486 24th Street
New York, NY 12009

September 21, 2023

Leslie Broome
Administrative Director
Educational Media Group
2620 Wasach Avenue
Olympia, WA 98501

Ref: 092115 ❶

❶ 本信件包含了寄件公司的參考文號。

Dear Ms. Broome: ❷

❷ 本信件採用了對於女士的標準稱呼 Ms.，稱呼之後也採用標準的標點符號：冒號。

❸ 正文的第一句感謝對方的來函，同時也表明收到了對方的請求。

Thank you for your inquiry of 11 September regarding the latest edition of our catalog. ❸ We are pleased to enclose our latest brochure. We would also like to inform you that it is possible to make purchases online at www.johnsonbrothers.com.

We look forward to welcoming you as our customer. ❹

Yours sincerely, ❺

Dennis Jackson

Dennis Jackson
Marketing Director
Johnson Brothers

❹ 這封簡短的信在最後一行歡迎這位潛在的客戶。寫信人在這裡其實也可以請對方有疑問時聯絡他。

❺ 結尾敬辭採用了標準的大寫規則（第一個字母大寫）與標點符號（敬辭後加上逗號）。

Enclosure (1) catalog ❻

❻ 寫信人提醒收件人，本信附有附件，也就是產品目錄。

參考文號：092115 ❶

布姆女士您好：❷

非常感謝您於 9 月 11 日來函索取我們最新的產品目錄。❸ 隨信附上本公司最新的目錄手冊。您也可以在 www.johnsonbrothers.com 線上訂購本公司產品。

誠心期盼您成為本公司的顧客。❹

Nobu Design Company
7-2, Marunouchi 4-Chome
Chiyoda-ku, Tokyo 107-8799

November 16, 2023

Donald Liu
Research and Development Director
TelTech Group
Shin-An Road 5, #43
Taoyuan 330, Taiwan

Dear Dr. Liu:

❶ 本信件加入了主旨一行，使信件的主題更明顯。

❶ Subject: November 2 board meeting summary and minutes

Thank you very much for attending our second board meeting on November 2. We were very pleased to host all of the members of our board, and we were very happy with the board's response to our progress and your advice regarding the future of our company.

As agreed, we have attached copies of the meeting minutes. We would like to present the main points of the minutes in this letter.

❷ 由於這封信很長，因此寫信人加入清楚的小標題，方便收件人快速瀏覽，找到重要的資訊。

❷ **Goals for the next six months**
In the meeting, the board gave us very good advice on how to make our company grow over the next six months. Our key goals are to

❸
1. Reach out to new markets in Canada through our contacts there,
2. Formalize our company policies with an employee handbook, and
3. Continue to seek out government contracts as well as private sector sales.

❸ 寫信人採用編號列表，使重要的資訊更加醒目。

Lessons learned during the past six months
We have had a great deal of success over the past six months. We have also learned how to approach challenges differently in the future. The main lessons learned were

1. To ensure that company files are accessible and compatible with all employees' computers by installing a company server,
2. To allow ample time for government bids and the awards process, and
3. To have Nobu's financial records vetted for the government contracting process.

Thank you again for your valued input on Nobu Design. Enclosed are the full meeting minutes. Please don't hesitate to contact us with any additional suggestions or questions.

We are looking forward to the next meeting of the Nobu Board. We hope to have more great progress to report to you at that time.

Best wishes,
Eleanor Abe

Eleanor Abe, President
Nobu Design Company

❹ 寫信人指出本信附有附件，以及有哪些人也收到本信的副本。此外本信的作者是 EA，而是由打字員pty打出。

Encs.

cc: Kenneth Takahasi, Mitsubishi; Gordon Day, ACER; Penelope Clarke, Sony; Cindy Kimura, Nobu
EA/pty ❹

❶ 主旨：11 月 2 日董事會議摘要及紀錄

非常感謝您於 11 月 2 日前來參加第二次董事會議。此次能夠招待董事會的所有成員，我們感到非常榮幸，也非常高興董事會對於我們的進展感到滿意，而您也就公司的未來提出寶貴的建議。

在此依約隨信附上會議紀錄的副本。以下簡單總結此次會議的討論結果。

❷ 未來半年的目標

在會議中，諸位董事就本公司未來半年的成長方針給予了非常寶貴的建議。
我們的主要目標將為：

1. 透過當地商業夥伴擴展加拿大市場。
2. 以員工手冊的形式確立公司政策。
3. 繼續致力爭取政府合約及私營企業的訂單。

過去半年心得總結

過去六個月來公司的營運相當成功，我們也學到未來該如何以不同的方式面對挑戰。我們主要的心得為：

1. 公司須裝設專用伺服器，方便所有的員工都能從個人電腦上取得公司內部檔案。
2. 對於政府的招標和評選過程須安排充裕的時間。
3. 公司財務紀錄先經過審查，便於承包政府項目。

再次感謝您對 Nobu Design 的重視與投入。隨信附上完整的會議紀錄。有任何建議或疑問，歡迎隨時與我們聯絡。

我們誠心期盼下一屆 Nobu 董事會議的到來，並希望屆時能為您報告公司更大幅的進展。

DISCUSSION & EXERCISE **3**　　Unit 7

1 Review the concepts
  ❶ What is letterhead?
  ❷ When should you use letterhead?
  ❸ Which line should contain a person's name or title—the subject line or the attention line?
  ❹ What does "Enc." mean?
  ❺ What does "cc:" at the bottom of a letter mean?
  ❻ If you see this—EP/kn—at the bottom of a letter, what does it mean?
  ❼ What title should you use for women in business?

2 Multiple-choice

_____ ❶ Which is not an appropriate way of writing an attention line?

(A) Attn: Kim Hunt (B) To the attention of Kim Hunt

(C) Attention Kim Hunt (D) Attention: Kim Hunt

(E) All are acceptable

_____ ❷ Which is not an appropriate salutation for a business letter?

(A) Dear Dr. Jergen (B) Ladies and Gentlemen (C) Hello

_____ ❸ Which is a correct format for the date in a business letter?

(A) 9/21/2023 (B) 21-9-23 (C) September 21, 2023

_____ ❹ Which is correct?

(A) Yours truly, (B) Yours Truly, (C) yours truly,

3 Applying principles

❶ Label the parts of this business letter.

Nobu Design Company
7-2, Marunouchi 4-Chome
Chiyoda-ku, Tokyo 107-8799

❶ _____

November 16, 2023 → ❷ _____

Donald Liu
Research and Development Director
TelTech Group
Shin-An Road 5, #43 → ❸ _____
Taoyuan 330, Taiwan

Dear Dr. Liu: → ❹ _____

❺ _____

Subject: November 2 board meeting summary and minutes

Thank you very much for attending our second board meeting on
November 2 . . .

Best wishes, ← ❻ _____
Eleanor Abe ———————→ ❼ _____
Eleanor Abe, President

❾ _____

_____

Encs ———————→ ❽ _____
cc: Kenneth Takahasi, Mitsubishi; Gordon Day, ACER; Penelope Clarke, Sony;
Cindy Kimura, Nobu
EA/pty → ❿ _____

2 For items 4, 5, 6, and 10 in the previous letter, suggest another phrase for these elements or another way they could have been formatted.

4 _____

5 _____

6 _____

10 _____

3 Look at the following letter. On the numbered lines, write alternative expressions the writer could have used.

Rainbow
34 10th Avenue
New York, NY 12009

September 10, 2023

Sales Manager
Textiles Plus
262 Aardvark Avenue
Olympia, WA 98502

Ref: 1092023 ⟶ **1** _____

⟶ **2** _____

Dear Sir or Madam: ⟶ **3** _____

Regarding your letter of August 28, 2023, we are
pleased to send you our latest catalog. _____

_____

We look forward to welcoming you as our customer. _____

⟶ **4** _____

Yours sincerely, _____

Sylvia Pax _____

⟶ **5** _____

Sylvia Pax, Sales Manager

Enclosure

❹ Write a subject line for this letter.

Fashion Fabrics
20000 Elmwood Circle
Rockville, MD 208888

August 4, 2023

Jonathan Sachs
True Textiles, Inc.
2300 Redwood Lane
Rochester, NY 14604

Our reference: 31623/Your reference: PO38v

Dear Mr. Sachs:

Subject: _____

We are very sorry to inform you of a delay in your shipment of 50 bales of washed blue silk (item number S98). Flooding at our warehouse after last week's massive storm system has damaged some of our inventory. We are committed to providing our customers with the highest-quality textiles, and we cannot ship the damaged goods and still maintain our reputation for quality.

New supplies are on their way now, and we expect them to arrive on Friday, August 7. We will ship your order as soon as possible on that date.

We are very sorry for any inconvenience this may cause. Please know that we are doing our best to make sure all our customers' orders arrive as quickly as possible.

Please feel free to contact me with any further questions or if you need further assistance.

Yours truly,

Samantha Roberts

Samantha Roberts, President
Fashion Fabrics

成功的寫作策略：「以讀者為中心」的寫作方式
How do I focus on the reader in my writing?

① 如何寫出清晰簡潔的商業文件？

每個人都可以寫出**清晰簡潔**的商業文件，這不需要天分，而是需要掌握**技巧**，且這些技巧是可以學會的。只要計劃得好，並遵循幾個基本原則，你就可以用簡單明瞭的方式與對方順利溝通。

② 撰寫商業文件時，應該遵循哪些原則？

首先，撰寫的時候，隨時想到你的讀者，也就是採取「**以讀者為中心**」（reader-focused）的寫作方式，這是商務寫作的特色。在開始動筆之前，也就是開始計劃文件內容的時候，你就應該想到你的讀者了。動筆之前，可透過下列問題考量讀者需求：

1. Who will read your document?	誰會閱讀這份文件？
2. What are the readers' positions in or outside the company?	讀者是什麼職位？是在我的公司還是別的公司？
3. What do they know about the subject?	他們對此主題有多少了解？
4. What do they need to know?	他們需要知道什麼？
5. What will they want to know?	他們會想要知道什麼？
6. Will they be expecting your document?	這些讀者在等著閱讀你這份文件嗎？
7. What will they do with your document (read it, file it, make a decision based on it, use it for evidence, etc.)?	收到這份文件後，他們會怎麼做？（閱讀、歸檔、據此做出某個決定、作為存證……）
8. How can you give them the information they want and need quickly?	如何把他們想要和需要的資訊迅速傳達給他們？

以上這些問題僅提供建議參考。由於**每封商業信件的情境不盡相同**，在設想與讀者有關的問題時，**可能需要更加具體（specific）**。寫信前可以仔細思考：讀者閱讀信件時，會有什麼疑慮？回答這些問題後，你就可以開始動筆了。下頁是一篇寫給主管的報告，主題是辦公室的硬體和軟體更新計畫。

Network Upgrade Team Meeting With Solutions Computer Systems

Executive Summary

❶ We met with Bob Boswell and Marla Bortolin of Solutions Computer Systems (SCS) on June 29. We discussed our current problems and their possible solutions. They have identified a plan to increase our network capabilities and give us the functionality we would like for the future. We have an estimate of the cost.

Meeting Summary

The meeting with Bob and Marla started half an hour late because they had a flat tire. After some coffee, we got started.

❷ Catherine explained the problems we are having. She also talked about the capabilities we would like to have in the future. Bob and Marla had some very good initial ideas about how to solve our current problems, and they even brought up some issues that we hadn't considered yet. They will need more information before they can give us a concrete plan, but they have a direction in mind for us. They have suggested a plan for network solutions that includes hardware and software upgrades. Their plan seems to fit the needs we have discussed in the past.

❸ When we discussed our budget, we were a little surprised at their estimate, but they are quoting based on their solutions for the new issues that came up for the meeting. Even though their estimate was one of the higher ones we have received so far, I think the price is fair and that we will end up with much improved functionality in our network . . .

與 Solutions Computer Systems 討論網路更新問題

行政摘要

我們在 6 月 29 日與 Solutions Computer Systems（SCS）的 Bob Boswell 及 Marla Bortolin 會面，討論了我們目前的問題及他們可能提供的解決方案。目前他們已擬定出一個計畫，以增進我們的網路效能，並給予我們未來需要的網路功能。我們已進行成本預估。

會議摘要

與 Bob 及 Marla 的會議晚了半小時才開始，因為他們的車爆胎了。喝了咖啡後，我們就開始進行討論。

Catherine 跟他們解釋了我們目前的問題，也說明我們未來希望擁有的網路功能。Bob 及 Marla 就如何解決我們的現有問題，提出了幾個非常好的草案，甚至提到幾個我們自己都沒有想到的問題。他們需要更多的資訊，才能給我們具體的計畫，但是他們已經為我們想好方向。他們提出了解決網路問題的計畫，其中包括更新軟硬體。他們的計畫看來很符合我們過去一直在討論的需求。

談到預算的時候，我們對他們的報價有些意外，但是他們的報價是依據會議中提到的新問題處理方式。所以他們的報價雖然是目前為止比較高的，但是我想這個價錢還算合理，他們的解決方案應該會大大增進我們的網路功能……

撰寫這份報告的人有沒有考慮到讀者會提出什麼問題？想想這份報告的讀者究竟想得到什麼資訊。看看下面的分析。

Network Upgrade Team Meeting with Solutions Computer Systems

Executive Summary

We met with Bob Boswell and Marla Bortolin of Solutions Computer Systems (SCS) on June 29. We discussed our current problems and their possible solutions. They have identified a plan to increase our network capabilities and give us the functionality we would like for the future. We have an estimate of the cost.

Meeting summary

The meeting with Bob and Marla started half an hour late because they had a flat tire. After some coffee, we got started.

Catherine explained the problems we are having. She also talked about the capabilities we would like to have in the future. Bob and Marla had some very good initial ideas about how to solve our current problems, and they even brought up some issues that we hadn't considered yet. They will need more information before they can give us a concrete plan, but they have a direction in mind for us. They have suggested a plan for network solutions that includes hardware and software upgrades. Their plan seems to fit the needs we have discussed in the past.

When we discussed our budget, we were a little surprised at their estimate, but they are quoting based on their solutions for the new issues that came up in the meeting. Even though their estimate was one of the higher ones we have received so far, I think the price is fair and that we will end up with much improved functionality in our network . . .

❶ 有什麼地方不對？

這段內容很含糊，沒有給予任何具體的資訊。應寫出具體有用的資訊，比如公司網路具有哪些具體的問題？這些問題要怎麼解決？確實的報價是多少？讀者得花時間把整份報告讀完才能獲得這些問題的答案。寫報告的人當初應該把焦點放在這些問題上面：

◆ 公司想要解決哪些問題？
◆ SCS 提供了哪些解決方案？
◆ 他們的報價是多少？
◆ 寫報告的人有何建議？

❷ 有什麼地方不對？

以上兩段太冗長，包含太多完全沒必要的資訊，像是開會的時間、爆胎的問題，甚至還有誰說明了什麼問題。對於欲據此文件做出決定的忙碌主管，這些資訊一點都不重要。主管想要得到的資訊，如 SCS 提出了什麼新的問題，根本沒有得到詳細的說明。寫報告的人應該要回答這類問題：

◆ 公司想要解決哪些問題？
◆ 會議中提出了哪些新的問題？
◆ SCS 提供什麼具體的解決方案？
◆ 此解決方案如何符合公司的需求？
◆ 寫報告的人有何建議？

❸ 有什麼地方不對？

同樣地，這裡作者只給了含糊籠統的資訊。讀者想要知道確實的報價到底是多少！作者在這裡還提出了一個關鍵的建議（報價雖高，但公司的網路功能將能獲得改善），但是這個建議被埋沒在正文裡，關鍵的資訊應該以醒目的格式突顯出來。

Unit 9 撰寫、檢查和修改
Write, Review, and Revise

在盡量回答完所有的關鍵問題之後，就可以起草（draft）你的文件，此時應注意內容的組織與格式安排。

Dear Dr. Liu:

❶ Subject: November 2 board meeting summary and minutes

Thank you very much for attending our second board meeting of November 2. We were very pleased to host all of the members of our board, and we were very happy with the board's response to our progress and your advice regarding the future of our company.

As agreed, we have attached copies of the meeting minutes. We would like to present the main points of the minutes in this letter.

Goals for the next six months ❷

In the meeting, the board gave us very good advice on how to make our company grow over the next six months. Our key goals are to

1. Reach out to new markets in Canada through our contacts there,
2. Formalize our company policies with an employee handbook, and
3. Continue to seek out government contracts as well as private sector sales.

Lessons learned from the past six months

We have had a great deal of success over the past six months. We have also learned how to approach challenges differently in the future. The main lessons learned were

1. To ensure that company files are accessible and compatible with all employees' computers by installing a company server,
2. To allow ample time for government bids and the awards process, and
3. To have Nobu's financial records vetted for the government contracting process.

Thank you again for your valued input on Nobu Design. Enclosed are the full meeting minutes. Please don't hesitate to contact us with any additional suggestions or questions.

We are looking forward to the next meeting of the Nobu Board. We hope to have more great progress to report to you at that time.

---

❶ 一開始就說明目的

在開頭就清楚說明這份文件的目的與主旨，讀者會想一開始就知道你這份文件的重點。

❷ 加入標題，方便讀者瀏覽

在內容中加上小標題，讓讀者一眼就看出文件的「骨架」。記住，讀者不會細讀，只會瀏覽過去。如果你的文件只是一段接一段、灰茫茫一片，他們就很難找到重要的資訊。用標題把段落組織成一個一個的資訊單元，這樣讀者就可以從標題去判斷內容，迅速找到需要的資訊。

❸ 採用列表，以符號或數字編號列出重點

以符號或數字編號的列表，也有助於讀者立刻看到重要的資訊。如果你有好幾點重要的資訊要傳達，例如會議中做了哪些重要的決定、產品進行了哪些重要的更新、企畫上有哪些問題或解決方案，或是其他的重點，最好把資訊整理成列表，前面加上項目符號。如果這些資訊有固定的順序，就用數字編號。

❹ 檢查和修改

文件寫好後，進行檢查。所有的名字和數字務必要寫對！確定一下內容和格式安排都合理，而且所有重要的資訊都清晰醒目、便於尋找。最後，確定這份完稿適合讀者的身分，並檢查整份文件的拼字和文法。

商業寫作的原則：AIDA 和 8C
Principles of Business Writing: AIDA & The Eight Cs

AIDA 原則

「AIDA」的四個字母分別代表 **Attention**（注意力）、**Interest**（興趣）、**Desire**（欲望）和 **Action**（行動），通常用於銷售和廣告，但也可以應用於書面溝通，如附函（附於包裹或信件中額外提供說明）。

1 Attention 注意力

商業寫作可以語出驚人，引起讀者的注意力，做法可以透過 ❶ **精彩開場白**、❷ **以設問法提出問題**和 ❸ **格式變化等方式**，可參考以下範例：

- Beautiful Women Must Read This
  美麗的女人一定要看這篇
- It has always been my dream to work for your company. 我一直夢想著能在貴公司工作。

❶ 寫出探觸到讀者的問題或需求的開場白，吸引讀者繼續閱讀。

Are you happy with the rates offered by your current paper suppliers?
您對目前紙張供應商提供的價格滿意嗎？

❷ 以「設問法」針對讀者需求做出提問，抓住讀者的注意。

Limited Time Special Offers
限時特別優惠

❸ 改變文字格式，以醒目的粗體和顏色呈現標題，讓讀者眼睛一亮。

2 Interest 興趣

引起讀者的注意後，**應立刻激發他們的興趣**。信中可說明你的產品或服務，而且這一步要盡快，這樣讀者才會一直保持興趣。如果有數項重點要說明，可用項目符號或數字編成列表。其他引起興趣的技巧還有：

❶ **以設問法提問引起興趣**：並請確保提出的問題與己方提供的產品或服務有關。

❶ 以「設問法」讓讀者思考是否有相關需求，有助引發讀者閱讀興趣。

- Do you know how many people are paying too much for their public relations team?
  你知道有多少人花太多錢在公關團隊上？
- Isn't it about time for a modern workstation?
  是時候該引進現代化的辦公座位了吧？
- How often do you get back pain?
  您的背痛多常發作一次？

❷ 提問後，須給出問題的答案：要提供具體事實資訊，但不要給太多，語氣也要輕鬆愉悅，以免導致讀者面對大量枯燥的文字，覺得意興闌珊、不想閱讀。以下為針對前列三點提問的回答範例：

❷ 針對前文向讀者提出的問題，後方要以具體、語氣輕鬆的方式給出問題的答覆。回答時也可給出確切的事實或數據（如研究或調查結果），以增加可信度。

- According to a recent survey by "Corporate Costs Research," 32 percent of large businesses are paying too much for their PR—and most don't even know there's an alternative!
  根據「企業成本研究」最近的調查顯示，32% 的大型企業的公關支出花費過高——而且大多都不知道自己有別的選擇！

- Studies show that employees spend 15% of their days dealing with hardware problems unrelated to their jobs. Do yours?
  研究顯示，公司員工平均把 15% 的時間花在處理跟工作無關的硬體問題上。你的員工也如此嗎？

- Back pain is a common problem, but it can be easily fixed with the right tools.
  背痛是常見的毛病，但只要用對工具，就能輕易治好。

3 Desire 欲望

要激起讀者的慾望，就要**把你的產品或服務跟讀者連結起來**。請提供產品或服務會為讀者帶來的各項好處，這樣讀者就會了解你的產品或服務對他有何效益。激發讀者欲望的其他做法包括：

❶「說故事」：**敘述你的產品或服務曾為其他公司帶來什麼好處，然後解釋怎麼做到**。若為撰寫求職信（cover letter），可以說明過去在其他職位的成功經驗，或是接受過哪些專業訓練。

❶ 說故事給讀者聽，告知提供的服務已對他人有所幫助，而在文中需要提供具體成效。

This system was recently installed at ABC Company, and worker productivity jumped 15%. The system can be installed at your company and requires only minimal funds and resources. It can be in place by the end of the next quarter!
ABC公司最近裝設此系統後，員工生產力大增15%。只需要極少的成本與資源，貴公司便可以裝設此系統。下個季尾就可以裝設完成！

❷ 強調自家產品大受其他消費者好評。

> ❷ 提出其他消費者好評，暗示產品也能對讀者產生效益。

> Nine out of ten hairdressers recommend our shampoo.
> 九成的美髮師都推薦我們的洗髮精。

❸ 避免專業術語（jargon）：簡單明瞭地說明產品或服務會帶來的好處。

> ❸ 使用直白簡單的用語描述自家服務，避免用難懂的專業術語過度包裝。

> Our events help businesses from all around the world connect with each other.
> 我們的活動幫助全球各家企業彼此聯繫。

４ Action 行動

可在寫作中**敦促讀者採取行動（take action）**，這個行動可能是通知你去上班、購買產品或服務、瀏覽網頁等。促使讀者行動的技巧包括：

❶ **告訴讀者你要他做什麼，並給予明確行動指示**：降低行動須付出的門檻，以協助讀者順利完成你希望他採取的行動。

> ❶ 給予明確行動指示，也可告知行動「免費」，讓讀者更願意照做。

> - Visit our website to request a free catalog.
>   請至我們的網站索取免費型錄。
> - Contact me as soon as possible at (123) 456-7899.
>   盡快打 (123) 456-7899 與我聯絡。

❷ **營造迫切感**：強調如果不採取行動會有什麼問題或後果，比如：

> ❷ 營造迫切感，向讀者說明若不盡速行動可能會有何種損失（如危害到生產力、存貨將賣完等）。

> - If your workstation is hurting your productivity, go to www.DEFcompany.com to learn more about our solutions.
>   如果貴公司的辦公座位設計危害到生產力，請到 www.DEFcompany.com 詳細了解我們的解決方案。
> - These models will soon be out of stock—call today!
>   這些型號即將售罄——今天就來電搶購！

8C 原則 The Eight Cs

　　每封商業信函都應務求**有效達成寫信目的（purpose）**，並使字裡行間的**語氣恰當得體**，同時展現**對於讀信者的尊重**。為了達成上述目標，寫信時需掌握商業寫作的**「8C」原則**，分別為以下幾點，請在寫作時格外留意：

8C 原則	
❶ 清晰 Clearness	❺ 體貼 Considerateness
❷ 簡潔 Conciseness	❻ 具體 Concreteness
❸ 正確 Correctness	❼ 完整 Completeness
❹ 禮貌 Courtesy	❽ 和諧 Concinnity

◼ Clearness 清晰

　　「清晰」是商業寫作很重要的原則，寫作者應該讓讀者**一看完每個句子，就了解句子的意義**。要使文件清晰明瞭，可以自問下列這些問題：

❶ 有沒有簡要說明事情相關的**前因後果**（context）？

❷ 有沒有把任何**首字母縮寫詞**（acronym）或**專業術語**解釋清楚？

❸ 有沒有加入**小標題**，方便讀者快速瀏覽（skim）？

❹ 有沒有把重要的資訊用**項目符號**或**數字**編成**清單**？

❺ 句型表達是不是大都**簡短、直接**？

❻ **用字遣詞**是否平易近人（plain）？

> ❶ 提供信件主題相關的前因後果。
>
> ❷ 提及首字母縮寫詞時則需有說明。

❶ The conference will take place in the ❷ Midtown Chamber of Commerce (MCOC) on May 5, at 10 a.m. The hope is to help local businesses thrive.

❸ ❹ **Topics covered will include:**

- How to build a strong local business.
- How to make the most of your business network.
- The Middtown economy.
- What MCOC can do for you.

> ❸ 使用小標題並
> ❹ 使用項目符號清單列出重點。

❺ ❻ We hope you can attend. If so, please let us know using the attached form.

❶ 本次會議將於 5 月 5 日上午 10 時 ❷ 在城中商會（MCOC）舉行，希望藉此幫助本地企業發展成長。

❸ ❹ 會議主題將包括：

- 如何打造堅實的地方企業。
- 如何充分利用人脈網絡。
- 城中地區的經濟
- MCOC 可以提供的幫助

❺ ❻ 誠摯盼望蒞臨賞光。若方便出席，請以附件表格回覆告知。

> ❺ ❻ 用字和句型簡潔、平易近人，每個句子表達簡短直接的重點概念。

2 Conciseness 簡潔

「簡潔」對忙碌的讀者來說非常重要，但必須配合「清晰」的原則，不要為了縮短文件長度而省略重要資訊。正確的做法是**把資訊細分成數小塊**，讓讀者一次掌握一個主題。其他使文件簡潔的技巧還有：

✅ **精簡多餘的字詞，比如：**

- 用 costs（花費）→ 代替 costs the sum of（花費⋯⋯金額）
- 用 complete details（完整的細節）
  → 代替 full and complete details（完整全面的細節）

❌ **避免填充詞（filler）：**

例如 I think（我認為）或 I feel（我覺得）等，因為在大多數的文件中，所呈現的資訊基本上就是寫作者認為或覺得的內容。

要使文件內容簡潔，可以自問下列這些問題：

❶ 是不是**直接切入重點**？
❷ **無關的資訊**都**省略**掉了嗎？
❸ 是否已刪減一再重複資訊的**冗句**？
❹ **多餘字詞**、**片語**和**華麗詞藻**（flowery language）都去掉了嗎？

---

❶ 信件開頭直接切入重點。

❷ 刪減無關內容，只保留重要的相關細節，❸ 也須刪減未提供新資訊的冗句。

❹ 多餘的形容詞、副詞或冗長片語可適時刪去。

Dear Mr. Smith:

❶ I am writing to report a problem with your last shipment of smart TVs (product order 24EX6).

❷ Several of the TVs were damaged and did not turn on when tested. ❸ ~~We tried several times to turn them on but they remained broken.~~ ❹ I ~~really~~ hope we can ~~work together to~~ find a quick ~~and simple~~ solution to this ~~terrible~~ problem.

---

❶ 本次來信意在回報上一批智慧型電視到貨的問題（訂單編號：24EX6）。

❷ 數台電視有損壞狀況，測試時無法啟動。❸ ~~我們屢次嘗試開啟，但機台仍然故障。~~ ❹ 我~~真的~~希望我們能~~攜手合作~~，找出快速~~且簡單~~的解決方案，來處理這個~~嚴重的~~問題。

3 Correctness 正確

務必檢查信裡資訊是否「正確」。提供的資訊若有誤，可能會衍生嚴重後果，而要是信函錯誤屢屢發生，恐使雙方商業關係生變或破裂，損害彼此的業務往來。「正確」的原則關係到許多要素，信件寄出前可檢視下列問題：

① 文件裡所有的**名字**、**日期**、**事實**和**數字**都寫對了嗎？
② 檢查過**拼字和文法**了嗎？
③ 文件的**格式**正確嗎？
④ 有沒有使用**信頭**？
⑤ **信封上的地址**是否謄打正確？信封的格式清晰而專業嗎？
⑥ 文件裡有沒有**明顯的錯誤**？有沒有擦掉或塗改的痕跡？

4 Courtesy 禮貌

「禮貌」原則在商業寫作裡指的不僅是「please」（請）和「thank you」（謝謝）這些用語，而是表示出**願意幫忙的真誠意願**，例如在顧客或商業夥伴有任何疑問時，須立刻以完整正確的資訊加以回覆。你可以用下列方式做到「禮貌」的原則：

① 收到任何來函後**盡快回覆**，讓對方久候相當失禮。
② 對於事件或問題做出**誠實**的回應。
③ 提供對方**需要或要求的資訊**。
④ 使用**正確的頭銜（title）**稱呼對方（如 Dr. 或 Ms.）。
⑤ 使用恰當的**結尾敬辭**。
⑥ 採用恰當的**語氣**。
⑦ 以**問句**表達請求。

✅ 以下為符合禮貌的寫作例句：

誠實回答目前未能滿足對方需求，並交代後續處理方式。

> I'm sorry but I don't have the details you requested at the moment. However, I will let you know as soon as I do.
> 很抱歉，我目前不清楚您所要求的細節資訊。然而，我了解後會盡快向您告知。

❌ 以下為有失禮貌的寫作方式，須避免出現：

寫作者提出不必要的指責並侮辱對方，無益於溝通，寫作中應加以刪除。

> My last order arrived late ~~and it is clearly your fault. You are the worst person I have ever done business with . . .~~
> 我的上一筆訂單貨物延遲抵達，這顯然是你的錯。你是我往來過最糟的人員……

5 Considerateness 體貼

「體貼」這個原則指的是**把注意力放在讀者身上（focus your reader）**，也就是**確實考慮對方的需求**。要做到「體貼」這一點，寫作時可考量下列問題：

❶ 有沒有考量**讀者的身分和角色**？
❷ 有沒有提供所有**讀者想要的資訊**？
❸ 有沒有提供所有**讀者需要知道的資訊**（儘管他們可能並不知道自己需要）？
❹ 是不是**及時**把這些資訊傳達給讀者？
❺ 是不是以讀者**能夠使用與理解的形式**來傳達資訊？

❶ 考量讀信者身分，展現有體諒讀信者職位、工作需求。

❷❸❹ 及時提供對方想要和需要的資訊。

❺ 以讀者能夠使用與理解的形式傳達資訊

❶ I understand that as sales manager you are very busy at this time of year, **so thank you for taking the time out of** your busy schedule **to deal with this.** ❷ ❸ ❹ I have enclosed a list of the orders we have yet to receive, ❺ along with their PO numbers, and the relevant dates . . .

❶ 我理解身為業務經理，您每年這段時間都特別忙碌，所以謝謝您於百忙中抽空處理此事。❷❸❹ 我已附上尚未到貨的訂單列表，❺ 並註明訂單編號與相關日期……

6 Concreteness 具體

「**具體**」的原則指的是給予讀者「具體的資訊」（solid information），不要用比喻（metaphor），也不要用專業術語，而是給讀者具體的事實與分析結果。

用字也盡量具體，避免含糊其辭，比如 situation（情況）這個字若單獨出現而無情境提示，就會太籠統（fuzzy），因為 situation 可以指目前正進行的協商、延遲發貨、勞資糾紛，或是任何其他問題或事件，因此應該**具體指出**你所提及的對象，需留意的重點包括：

❶ 有沒有給予讀者具體的**事實**、**數量**、**日期**等資訊？
❷ 如果沒有，有什麼**合理的理由**嗎？
❸ 有沒有**告訴讀者**，**為什麼**我沒有提供具體的資訊？
❹ 有沒有**告訴讀者**，**什麼時候**可以取得具體的資訊？
❺ 有沒有避免含糊的語詞，而用**具體的**（specific）語句？
❻ 有沒有使用**強而有力**、**明確的**動詞來描述動作？

❶ ❻ 提供確切的數字和時間、日期資訊，並使用直接且明確的動詞（如 order）。

❷ ❸ 對於尚未能告知的資訊（如 shipping costs 運費），提供無法告知的合理理由。

❹ ❺ 以具體明確的語句，說明什麼時候可以告知上述未知資訊。

❻

❶ I ordered two hundred pairs of leather shoes (item # 5646) on March 4. **❷ ❸** I am still waiting for a reply from our delivery partners on the shipping costs for these items. **❹ ❺** I hope to have these details by the end of next week.

❻

❶ 我在 3 月 4 日訂購了 200 雙皮鞋（商品型號：5646）。**❷ ❸** 我目前仍在等候合作的貨運廠商回覆告知商品運費。**❹ ❺** 我希望下周結束前可以掌握這些細節資訊。

7 Completeness 完整

須確定信中訊息內容完整，並務必**包含足夠的資訊**。你必須考慮到對方在閱讀文件時，心裡會提出哪些問題，同時也要考慮到有**哪些是讀者不知道自己需要、但其實相當重要的資訊**。訊息要怎麼樣才算完整，須由寫作者謹慎判斷。

要確保文件內容完整，可檢視下列問題：

❶ 有沒有**回答讀者先前提問**的問題？
❷ 有沒有**回答讀者可能會提出**的問題？
❸ 有沒有給予讀者他們**需要**、而不只是想要的資訊？
❹ 有沒有考慮到讀者會**怎麼處理（do with）**這份文件？

❶ 回答讀者先前的提問（職位相關資訊）。

❷ ❸ 推想讀者可能的問題、或還會需要知道哪些資訊。

❹ 考慮到讀者會怎麼處理該文件，提供後續動作所需的資訊。

Thank you for your interest in the position of office manager. **❶** In answer to your questions: the position will begin on July 4, and the salary range is between NT$30,000 and NT$40,000 based on experience. **❷ ❸** For your reference, I have also enclosed a list of the job's key responsibilities. To apply for the position, **❹** please send us a resume along with two letters of reference.

謝謝您對辦公室經理的職位有興趣，**❶** 以下回覆您的問題：本職位就職日期為 7 月 4 日，薪資範圍落在新台幣 3 萬至 4 萬元，依個人經歷調整。**❷ ❸** 我也附上本職位的主要職務供您參考。若有意應徵，**❹** 請將履歷隨 2 封推薦信寄至本公司。

8 Concinnity 和諧

「和諧」是指文件各部分的連貫性要安排妥當，各個段落**條理分明**、**邏輯清楚**（**clearly and logically**），資訊按明確的順序排列（例如以最重要程度安排），使讀者可以循序漸進從頭讀到尾，而不會有閱讀障礙。在長篇的文件當中，這一點尤其重要。

要做到這一點，可檢視下列問題：

❶ 文件的內容、**起承轉合流暢嗎**？
❷ 文件的**階層安排**合理嗎？
❸ 段落**小標題**的語意清楚嗎？
❹ 標題有沒有用**粗體**或其他**醒目格式**突顯？
❺ 標題與**下方內容相對應**（**match**）嗎？
❻ 讀者能不能在**恰當的地方**找到他們想要的資訊？

❶❷❻ 清楚的開頭、中間段落和結尾。資訊階層的鋪陳具有邏輯性，使讀者能迅速找到所需資訊。

❶❷❻ Thank you for inquiring about our shipping methods and rates.

❸❹❺ **Our shipping methods**
❶❷❻ We use Flymail International Express services for all international orders (delivery time: 5 business days). Customers can choose a priority option (2 business days) for an extra fee.

❸❹❺ **Shipping rates**
Shipping rates depend on the size and weight of each order. Please see the chart enclosed for more details.

❶❷❻ I hope this information has answered your questions. If you have any more questions, please feel free to contact me directly on (908) 978-4567.

❸❹❺ 使用格式醒目的小標題，並且和下方資訊正確對應，有助讀信者快速掌握想要的資訊。

❶❷❻ 感謝詢問本公司送貨方式和收費資訊。

❸❹❺ 送貨方式
❶❷❻ 針對所有境外訂單，本公司使用 Flymail 國際快遞服務（貨運時間：5 個工作天）。顧客可選擇優先送貨服務（2 個工作天到貨），需額外付費。

❸❹❺ 貨運費用
❶❷❻ 運費依各筆訂單大小與重量而定，請參照附件中的表格，以了解詳情。

希望這些資訊有回答您的疑問。若有更多問題，請不吝來電 (908) 978-4567 直接與我聯繫。

<table>
<tr><td>Unit
11</td><td>如何寫出好的開頭與結尾？
How do I write good openings and endings?</td></tr>
</table>

忙碌的商務讀者會**略讀**（skim），只搜尋關鍵的資訊。略讀的過程中，讀者會**先閱讀開頭**，然後**閱讀結尾**，而中間一大部分往往匆匆一瞥。因此要協助你的讀者快速吸收這份文件，就要把重要資訊擺在讀者最有可能找到的地方，也就是**文件的開頭或結尾**，或者用項目符號把重要資訊編成**醒目的列表**。

1 如何寫出好的開頭？

好的文書開頭須根據**讀者身分**和**文件主題**設想，並盡快切入正題，說明文件主題和**寫作目的**，引導（signpost）讀者後續對於文件的處理方式。

如果文件內容較多，包含數個不同的小主題，可在開頭就點出各項主題，協助讀者**了解文件大綱**，例如在討論最新行銷活動的備忘錄裡，可以把內容分成「new print campaign」（最新平面行銷活動）、「new radio campaign」（最新廣播行銷活動）、「new direct mail solicitations」（最新直郵廣告行銷活動）等部分。

綜合來說，商業文書開頭的寫作要點包括：

◆ 考量文件的**讀者**和**主題**。
◆ 清楚說明文件**主題**或**寫作目的**。
◆ 說明目的之外，同時考慮到你望讀者**如何處理這份文件**。
◆ 點出文件的**內容大綱**（outline）。

下面就來看兩種商業報告的開頭，看看哪一個寫得比較好：

❶ The annual Comic Book Sellers Convention was held in San Diego, California, this year. Many comic book vendors attended. There were also many fans. The huge venue held more than 1,500 booths, which were visited by approximately 10,000 people over three days. While there, we had the chance to visit with many colleagues and develop new directions for comics.

漫畫商年度展會今年於加州聖地牙哥舉辦，不少漫畫商都前往參加，此外還有許多漫畫迷。龐大的會場總共有 1,500 多個攤位，三天內有約一萬名來賓參觀。參展期間，我們有機會與許多同行交流，並構想新的漫畫發展方向。

❷ This year's annual Comic Book Sellers Convention proved once again to be a good source of business opportunities. Key developments from this year's convention fall into three categories:

1. New business contacts
2. Possible partners and joint projects
3. New stock to consider.

今年的漫畫商年度展會再次證明為發展商機的好機會。本次展會帶來的三方面新發展為：

1. 新的商業夥伴
2. 潛在的商業夥伴與合作計畫
3. 值得考慮買進的新產品

兩份報告都是漫畫店的員工參加漫畫商展會（convention）後，預計呈交給主管看的內容。看完之後，你認為：

◆ 哪一個版本給了主管想要的資訊？
◆ 主管會想知道展會在何時、何地舉辦的嗎？
◆ 主管是否立刻想了解展會帶來的商業契機？

2 如何寫出好的結尾？

結尾同樣是讀者略讀文件時，會格外注意的部分。好的文書結尾會簡要地**重述文件重點**，並提醒前文的**重要細節**。在結尾處向對方**致謝**也符合商業禮儀，並可向對方表明**願意回答相關問題**，同時確認有留下**聯絡方式**。

綜合來說，商業文書結尾的寫作要點有：

❶ **重點再複述一遍**，也可適時指出相關細節。
❷ 確定**新的資訊**被清楚地標示出來。
❸ 向對方**致謝**。
❹ 表示**願意回答任何問題**，也願意盡量提供更多資訊。
❺ 如果其他地方沒有寫明，就要在結尾處提供你的**聯絡方式**。

Unit 12 如何創造適當的語氣？
How do I set the proper tone?

「語氣」（tone）是寫作當中最難掌握的概念之一。語氣就是文章聽起來的感覺，反映出作者對於讀者的態度（attitude），以及作者跟讀者的關係。視你的寫作主題而定，語氣可以正式、也可以不正式，可以溫馨、也可以冷酷，可以親切、也可以客觀，可以幽默、也可以嚴肅。你在撰寫過程當中所做的每項決定幾乎都會影響到語氣，而創造恰當（proper）語氣的重點有：

❶ **遣詞用字**要清楚直接
❷ 文中**納入的細節**僅保留重點
❸ 依照重要程度**排列資訊**
❹ 正確使用**大小寫**和**標點符號**
❺ **格式**清晰正確、**拼字和文法**無誤

以下將詳細明説會影響文件語氣的因素：

1 遣詞用字（word choice）

下列兩個句子説明了相同的資訊，用字遣詞卻不同。

❶ 使用簡單用字和句型直接說明重點。

❶ Today's activities have been canceled because of the storm.
今日活動因暴風雨而取消。

❷ 用語繞口艱澀，句子長度拖長，使讀者不易掌握重點訊息。

❷ Due to unforeseen weather conditions, the previously scheduled activities are hereby postponed until a later date.
鑒於預料之外的天候狀況，原定活動特此順延至他日舉行。

　　兩個句子的語氣都很正式，但是正式的程度有明顯高低。第一句的用字直截了當，第二句則使用了繞口、艱澀的語詞，其實是矯枉過正了，畢竟句子的目的只是為了提供有用的資訊。寫作商業信函**並不一定**必須使用過於一板一眼的語氣。對讀者來説，太過正經和太過輕浮的語氣，同樣都很不可取。

2 納入的細節（the details included）

　　若是想讓書信維持專業客觀的語氣，就需要**避免透露個人（personal）資訊、觀點、感受**等。若是信裡含括上述內容，會讓信件顯得相對隨興、較不專業。請試著檢視以下的範例備忘錄，看看其中包含的哪些細節影響了整體的語氣：

Memorandum

To: George MacAndrews, CEO

Date: June 5, 2023

Subject: Short-listed candidates for CEO shadowing internship.

We have selected three candidates as our final short list for the CEO shadowing internship. The first candidate is Mira Kumar, a second-year MBA student from Harvard Business School. **Mira is** tall and slightly overweight, with long black hair **and a very pleasant personality.** She must get a lot of attention! **She appears calm and confident. She has a GPA of 3.9 and has been president of her school's Model World Bank for the past year.** Her parents are from Bangladesh.

The second candidate is Barry Enlow of Georgetown University, also a second-year MBA student. **Barry is focusing on international business development and growth. Previously, he interned with USAID, working on projects to facilitate partnerships in Southeast Asia. Barry has a GPA of 3.8.** He comes from Edmonton, Alberta, Canada. Barry is very tall and walks with a slight hunch—in the interview, he mentioned that he has one extra vertebra in his spine, **which causes it to round.** He does not have a girlfriend.

> 在藍色標示的文字中，寫作者正確地將兩名人選就 CEO 實習方案所應具備的條件納入文中，例如是否具備相關商學學歷、成績表現、從事過哪些相關活動或工作等，有助提升文件語氣格調。

> 但在紅色標示的文字中，寫作者將人選與 CEO 實習方案無關的細節納入文中，如外表、無關的身體隱疾、交友狀況等，並且針對第一位人選做出不專業的個人評論，使整體語氣失去專業感。

備忘錄

收件人：喬治・麥安卓斯執行長

日期：2023 年 6 月 5 日

主旨：CEO 實習人選

從 CEO 實習的人選當中，我們已篩選出最後三位。第一位是 Mira Kumar，哈佛商學院 MBA 研二生。Mira 個子高，有些胖，留著黑色長髮，個性開朗樂觀，一定是位引人注目的人！她看起來沉著自信，平均學業成績為 3.9，去年並擔任該校模擬世界銀行主席。她的父母來自孟加拉。

第二位人選是喬治城大學的 Barry Enlow，也是 MBA 研二生，專攻國際商業發展與成長。他之前曾於美國國際開發署實習，實習重點為促進與東南亞合作關係之各項企畫。Barry 的平均成績為 3.8。他來自加拿大亞柏達省艾德蒙頓市。Barry 個子很高，走路時背有點弓。面談時他提到他的脊椎多了一節，所以背會弓起來。他沒有女朋友。

3 資訊的排列順序（information order）

若信件**以最重要的資訊開頭**，會使語氣顯得更為正式、更具有目的性（purposeful）。若是將重要資訊**保留到信尾才出現**，那麼信件就會給人隨便（sloppy）、不甚緊迫的感覺。

❌ ❶ 以讀信者未要求得知的無關資訊開頭，❷ 卻把讀信者提出的問題放到最後才回答，未能分辨事項輕重緩急，使語氣顯得散漫、失去專業感。

❶ 在此通知您，我們即起直到九月底前，對超過 2000 元的訂單提供免運費優惠。若有意利用本次特惠，請再告知我。

❷ 另外，回應您先前的提問：您最近的訂單貨品應將於本月 17 日送達，追蹤編號為 2435 3456 3245。

Dear Mr. Smith:

❶ I would like to inform you that we are currently offering free shipping for any orders over $2,000 up until the end of September. Please let me know if you would like to take advantage of this opportunity.

❷ Also, in answer to your previous question, your recent order should arrive by the 17th of this month. The tracking number is 2435 3456 3245.

✅ ❶ 開門見山切入主旨，迅速回應讀信者先前提出的問題，❷ 之後才轉而提到較不緊急的主題，顯示寫作者具備判斷力，使信件語氣顯得正式、專業。

❶ 回應您先前的提問：您的訂單貨品應將於本月 17 日送達；若希望至貨運公司網站追蹤訂單紀錄，追蹤編號為 2435 3456 3245。

❷ 另外，我們即起直到九月底前，對超過 2000 元的訂單提供免運費優惠。若有意利用本次特惠，請再告知我。

Dear Mr. Smith:

❶ In answer to your question, your order should arrive by the 17th of this month. Should you want to track the order on the shipper's website, the tracking number is 2435 3456 3245.

❷ Also, we are currently offering free shipping for any orders over $2,000 up until the end of September. Please let me know if you would like to take advantage of this opportunity.

4 大小寫和標點符號（capitalization and punctuation）

若使用**全大寫字母（all capital letters）**來書寫（例如：PLEASE FILL OUT THIS FORM〔請填寫表格〕），會讓人覺得是在**對讀信者大聲喝斥**，因此信件語氣會顯得火爆急躁。同理，使用**驚嘆號（!）**的句子，語氣也會顯得激動或不耐煩，一樣不太適用於正式商業書信。

❌ ❶ 使用全大寫行文 ❷ 並使用驚嘆號，使語氣變得像在吼叫且不耐煩。

❷

❶ FILL OUT THIS FORM CORRECTLY ! DO NOT USE COLORED PENS OR PENCILS. DO NOT WRITE OUTSIDE THE INDICATED BOXES. DO NOT TEAR OR REMOVE PAGES FROM THE FORM.

✔ ❶ 大小寫正常，且未使用驚嘆號，語氣較中立和緩。

Fill out this form correctly. Do not use colored pens or pencils. Do not write outside the indicated boxes. Do not tear or remove pages from the form.

5 格式、拼字以及文法（formatting, spelling, & grammar）

上列元素都會影響信件的整體語氣。暫且不論內容，如果信中**格式**、**拼字**或**文法**錯誤連篇，語氣就會顯得馬虎草率、粗心大意。商業書信通常要求專業、嚴謹的語氣，所以盡力避免錯誤就是達到此目標的第一步。

接著讓我們從下一頁的錯誤範例中，學習如何避免使書信的語氣變得草率、不專業。

❶ 流汗先生您好：

主旨：要求折扣

感謝您的來信。❷ 我們致力提供大家最優惠的價格，因此才在過去一年創下破紀錄的成績。

本公司的業務主任 ❸ 人很好，在和他討論過後，我可以提供您下筆訂單享 15% 折扣！！！❹

欲使用折扣，❺ 在此惠請利用特殊訂購表單，如附函。

❻ 另外，需訂購 20 件以上產品方能享有上述折扣。

12-1 | 商業書信寫法：哪裡出了錯？ How NOT to write a business letter

Part

1

商業英文書信

Unit

12

如何創造適當的語氣？

Titan Safety Gear

2600 S Hoover St, Los Angeles, CA 90007, USA

May 12, 2023

Ryan Sweet
Splash! Rafting Tours
23 Dunkeld Rd
Aberfeldy
PH15 2AQ
UK

❶ 收信者的姓氏出現拼字錯誤，且首句有文法錯誤，有損語氣正式感，寫作者必須詳加檢查。

❶ Dear Mr. Sweat:

Re: Discount request

❷ 信件以和讀者無關的資訊開頭。寫作者必須調整，讓第一段內容以讀者為中心。

Thanks you for your letter. ❷ We work hard to give everyone the best prices. As a result, we just had our best year ever.

❸ 寫作者將個人意見寫入信中，未能保持專業口吻，應該避免。

After speaking with our ❸ kind sales director, I can offer you 15% off your next order!!! ❹

❹ 過度使用驚嘆號，讓信件語氣失去正式感。

To claim this, ❺ I invite you to utilize the special order form enclosed.

❺ 此處的語氣太過正式，可改為「. . . please use the special order form enclosed.」（請使用附件的專用訂購單。）

❻ Also, the discount only applies if you order 20 or more items.

Yours truly,

Tina Nowak

❻ 寫作者將此項重點資訊放在最後一段，讓讀者無法快速掌握。應調整到前面的段落。

Tina Nowak, Salesperson

1 Review the concepts

① What is reader-focused writing?

② What are some important questions to ask yourself when you are planning a document?

③ What are some ways to create desire in a reader?

④ Which of the **eight Cs** refers to giving readers definite information (as in "at 4 pm tomorrow") rather than vague information (as in "tomorrow afternoon")?

⑤ Which of the **eight Cs** refers to writing short, clear sentences, not long, wordy ones?

⑥ Which of the **eight Cs** refers to creating harmony and good organization?

⑦ How can you show courtesy in your writing?

⑧ What can affect tone?

⑨ Which of these are part of **AIDA**? (choose all that apply) _____

(A) Attraction   (B) Attention   (C) Investment

(D) Interest   (E) Desire   (F) Drive

⑩ Which is one of the **eight Cs** of good writing? _____

(A) Coaching   (B) Compelling   (C) Courtesy

2 Write headers for this report.

❶ <u>Which laptop is the most suitable? OR The TravelA1 laptop is the most suitable.</u>

The TravelA1 laptop by Big Computers is the most suitable for our needs. After considering the company's most important needs—reliability, portability, affordability, and capacity—we decided that the TravelA1 stands out as the best choice.

❷ _____

_____

Consumers report the second fewest problems with the TravelA1, according to a variety of consumer sources. Although the PlusGo model wins for fewest problems, the TravelA1's excellent customer service program makes it a good choice.

❸ _____

_____

The TravelA1 is the lightest of all the models we compared. According to a poll of our employees, weight is one of the most important factors in purchasing a laptop. Employees identified a weight of 5 pounds or less as the ideal travel size. At 4.5 pounds, the TravelA1 is well within this preferred weight range.

❹ _____

_____

Although the TravelA1 was not the least expensive model we reviewed, it is still a good value at $850 per laptop. Bulk order discounts are also possible.

3 Read the partial memo on the next page and complete the following tasks.

❶ Identify the main problems with the memo. For example, is the tone inappropriate? Is the passage too wordy? Is it clear?

_____

_____

_____

❷ Mark the text that is unclear or too wordy.

Thank you for the time and effort you put into the proposal you placed on my desk last Monday. I have very thoughtfully considered your proposal to split the current and continuing Formatting and Design team into two concurrently functioning teams. I have thought about the positive and negative consequences of making such a split, and I have come to the conclusion that the team should continue to work together as a unit.

Allow me to explain my reasons. First, although formatting and design are certainly very distinct, different, and unique processes, in my opinion the employees function well together as a team. The design of a publication cannot progress or move forward without understanding the limits, boundaries, and barriers of its formatting. Formatting provides the organization, hierarchy, and flow that the design team needs to understand in order to create the clear, non-distracting, but beautiful layouts for which we are famous . . .

❸ Rewrite the marked passages so they are more clear and concise.

Rewrite!

_____
_____
_____
_____
_____
_____
_____
_____
_____
_____
_____
_____
_____
_____
_____

4 Identify the problems with tone in this memo. Then rewrite the memo in a more professional tone.

Memorandum   File no. 2023-18

Date: Monday
To: Everybody
From: Sally
Subject: Professional development training next week!

Dear everybody:

Sry about the late notice, but there are two professional development training sessions next week, and boss wants us to fill them up. On Mon. is "Designing Usable Forms," open to Analysts and Sr. Analysts. Tues. is "Writing for the Reader," open to all. Please register this week with me or Julia. Give us your info, and we'll send the times and schedules to upper management so they'll be informed.

Tnks all!

Sal

Rewrite!

Memorandum   File no. 2023-18

Date: _____

To: _____

From: _____

Subject: _____

_____

_____

_____

_____

_____

_____

_____

5 Look at this problem memo. Choose appropriate details from the list on the right to create a third candidate.

- **The new candidate**
* Name: Brian McArthur
* Age: 24
* Marital status: Married
* Physical attributes: Blond hair, blue eyes
* Education: George Washington University, second-year MA in International Relations, GPA 3.2
* Extracurricular activities: None.
* Interested in international business.

Memorandum

File no. 2023-18

To: George MacAndrews, CEO
Date: June 5, 2023
Subject: <u>Short-listed candidates for CEO shadowing internship.</u>

We have selected three candidates as our final short list for the CEO shadowing internship. The first candidate is Mira Kumar, a second-year MBA student from Harvard Business School. Mira is tall and slightly overweight, with long black hair and a very pleasant personality. She must get a lot of attention! She appears calm and confident. She has a GPA of 3.9 and has been president of her school's Model World Bank for the past year. Her parents are from Bangladesh.

The second candidate is Barry Enlow of Georgetown University, also a second-year MBA student. Barry is focusing on international business development and growth. Previously, he interned with USAID, working on projects to facilitate partnerships in Southeast Asia. Barry has a GPA of 3.8. He comes from Edmonton, Alberta, Canada. Barry is very tall and walks with a slight hunch—in the interview, he mentioned that he has one extra vertebra in his spine, which causes it to round. He does not have a girlfriend.

Now rewrite the whole passage, including information about the new candidate, in an appropriate tone. Use a clear format and include only relevant details. In the last paragraph, recommend one of the candidates.

Memorandum

To: George MacAndrews, CEO

Date: June 5, 2023

Subject:

傳真與電子郵件
Writing Faxes and Emails

Key Terms

attachment 附件
附在電子郵件上、隨電子郵件一起寄出的檔案，收件者可以將此檔案下載到自己的電腦。

cover letter 封面頁
與另一檔案（如履歷、提案、傳真等）一起寄出的短信，簡短說明檔案的內容。

email address 電子郵件地址
電子郵件信箱的名稱。常見的電子郵件地址的格式如下：收件者自選名稱 @ 網域名稱 .com/.net/.org。

emoticon 表情文字
透過可用鍵盤打出的字元組成的文字圖像，用以表示寫作者的心情，如：「:)」、「XD」等，在正式商業文書中應避免。

etiquette 禮儀
社交互動中，對於行為的既定成規或習慣。撰寫商務文書時，亦須注意相關禮儀。

font 字型
文字和字母的字型，如 Arial、Times New Roman 等。

forward 轉寄
把你收到的文件或檔案（通常是電子郵件或備忘錄）再寄給別人。

horizontal table 橫向表格
指表格項目名稱和項目內容採橫向排列的表格；這類表格在傳真封面頁的聯絡資訊欄上常用。

HTML
全稱為「hypertext markup language」（超文本標記語言），是用以在網頁瀏覽器上顯示文件內容的標記語言。大多數的電子信箱客戶端（如 Outlook 等）允許使用 HTML 的子集來提供非純文字的標記。

incoming (fax) 傳進的（傳真）
發給你或你的辦公室的傳真。

medium 媒介
將訊息送達收訊者的方法或途徑，亦稱「媒體」。

outgoing (fax) 發出的（傳真）
你或你的辦公室發給別人的傳真。

signature block 簽名檔
電子郵件最下方的文字區塊，通常包括寄件人的姓名和聯絡方式等資訊，一般可設定為自動附加。

template 樣板
可作為基準的固定模板。撰寫傳真封面頁時，各公司可能備有封面頁寫作樣板供員工套用。

Unit 13

如何撰寫商務傳真？
How do I write a fax?

商務傳真（fax）和商務電子郵件（email）的撰寫原則就跟商務書信一樣，基本上就是要**清晰、簡潔、禮貌、扼要**。傳真或電子郵件裡的資訊，也跟商務書信一樣，要**以讀者為中心**。

由於傳真和電子郵件的傳送速度比信件快，所以可以用來進行快速的往返溝通。任何由傳真機發送的文件都算是「一份傳真」（a fax）。嚴格來說，傳真沒有固定的「原則」或「格式」，比較需要注意的是，你傳真出去的文件應該都要附有一份**封面頁**（cover letter），本單元將來說明撰寫**傳真封面頁的原則與格式**。

撰寫傳真的封面頁時，有三個重點要考慮：

❶ 附上**聯絡方式**（contact information）
❷ 封面頁的**格式**（format）
❸ **正文**（body）的內容

現在很多公司都有自己專用的傳真封面樣板（template），員工要發傳真時，就按照樣板的格式，否則一般就是採用文書處理軟體所附的傳真格式，這些軟體會引導你輸入所有對方需要的資訊。傳真封面頁上的資訊，應該要能夠做到這三件事：**（1）防止傳真遺失；（2）確保傳真被送到正確的收件人手上；（3）讓對方有需要時可以聯絡你**。要做到這三件事，傳真封面頁就應該包含：

❶ 寄件人的姓名
❷ 寄件人的地址、傳真號碼（fax number）、電話號碼
❸ 收件人的姓名
❹ 收件人的傳真號碼
❺ 收件人的公司與部門（如果有需要）
❻ 傳真的頁數（包括封面頁）
❼ 視訊息內容和文件長度，你還可加上參考文號和主旨

傳真有時候會把文件的字縮小，所以封面頁的主文應該用顯眼一點、但仍不失專業的字型，而字級設為 12 級應該就足夠了。傳真封面頁的格式安排，可以仿照商務書信的格式。公司自定的傳真格式通常會加入**信頭**（letterhead），其中便包含了寄件人的聯絡資訊，在信頭下面，你就可以打入**收件人的聯絡資訊**。

如果你不用信頭，那就遵循商務書信的一般原則：在頁面頂端先打入你的聯絡資訊，然後是收件人的聯絡資訊。用一條線或一個空行，跟下面的主要內容隔開，接著你就可以打入稱謂。下面看兩份傳真封面頁的例子，一個有信頭，一個沒有。

Wanderlust, Inc.

124 Fifth Street, Davis, CA 95616
Tel: (530) 755-0985 Fax: (530) 755-0886

❶ 公司的信頭就已包含寄件人所有的聯絡資訊。

FAX

To: Chris O'Riley
Company: Chills 'n Thrills, Inc.
Fax: (907) 456-4857
Subject: IceTech boots bulk order question

From: Laurel Sullivan, Senior Sales Associate
Date: 10/2/2023
Transmitting: 2 pages ❷

❷「Transmitting」這一欄用來表示傳真的頁數。在這個例子裡，傳真有兩頁。

Dear Chris: ❸

Thank you for your order (ref. 92515). After discussing your request, our Sales Director, Cheryl Root, is happy to offer you a 15% discount on any order for 13 or more pairs of IceTech boots. The attached signed authorization will be valid for the next year and should be sent with any bulk orders.

Yours truly,

Laurel ❸

❸ 傳真可以進行正式與非正式的溝通。在這個例子裡，寄件人與收件人已經有很長一段合作關係，因此寄件人在稱謂與簽名的部分都只用名字不用姓。一般最好是使用「頭銜＋姓」的稱呼方式（如右頁的 Dear Mr. O'Riley:）。

Page: 1 of 2

克里斯好：❸

謝謝您的訂單（參考文號：92515）。針對你的要求，經過討論之後，我們的業務主任 Cheryl Root 決定，只要你訂購 13 雙以上的 IceTech 靴子，就給您 85 折折扣。後面附有簽名的授權書，明年一整年都有效，大量訂購時請跟訂單一起寄來。

Wanderlust, Inc.
124 Fifth Street, Davis, CA 95616
Tel: (530) 755-0985 Fax: (530) 755-0886 ❶

❶ 本傳真沒有印上信頭，所以撰文者在頁面頂端打上寄件人的地址、傳真號碼和電話號碼。

To: Chris O'Riley, Marketing Director
Fax: (907) 456-4857
Phone: (907) 456-4850
Re: IceTech boots rental and promotion agreement

From: Andy Francis
Pages: 3
Date: 10/2/2023
Cc: --
❷

❷ 很多傳真範例都採用橫向表格（horizontal table）填入聯絡資訊。

Dear Mr. O'Riley: ❸

Please find enclosed our draft agreement regarding
the rental of our IceTech boots for your Thrills 'n Chills
expeditions. We are pleased to offer you what we believe
will be a mutually beneficial contract. As discussed in our
conference call of September 28, we have addressed the
issues of recycling boots, the placement of our logos, and
how to direct potential sales.

We look forward to receiving your feedback on the contract.

Sincerely,

Andy Francis ❸

Andy Francis, Marketing Manager

❸ 本傳真採用比較正式的稱謂與簽名。

Page: 1 of 3

歐利雷先生您好：❸

隨此傳真附上貴公司 Thrills 'n Chills 考察團租用本公司 IceTech 靴子的合約草案，我們相信此份合約將符合雙方利益。我們也依據 9 月 28 日電話會議的討論結果，在合約裡加上了靴子回收、商標位置、如何引導潛在銷售等相關內容。

希望聽到您對此合約的看法。

傳真主文的撰寫原則就跟其他商務文件相同，傳真封面頁的主文應該寫得跟商務書信一樣，如果你跟收件人**很熟**了，就可以**只稱名不稱姓**，並採用親切的問候。如果你跟對方**不熟**，那就用「**頭銜（title）＋姓（surname）**」的方式稱呼對方。

現在翻到前一頁（p. 67）13-2 的傳真主文，看一下傳真內容：在第一行，寄件人就跟收件人說明傳真文件的內容，隨後立刻點出合約包含的重點；接著他表達出對於互相合作的期盼與提供協助的意願，禮貌地把信結束。

下面則是對前兩頁（p. 66）13-1 的傳真主題提供進一步說明的傳真主文：

Dear Chris:

❶ Thank you for your order (ref. 92515). Regarding your question about bulk ordering IceTech boots: after having discussed your long patronage of our company, our Sales Director, Cheryl Root, would be happy to discuss a discount for a bulk order of boots, as long as the order is for 25 pairs or more. ❷ We have some questions we need you to answer before we can proceed: Exactly how many boots would you like to order? What is your time frame for the order? What sizes will you need? Will you be wanting to make more bulk purchases in the future?

❸ Please reply with more details about this order and we will be happy to accommodate you as best we can.

Yours truly,
Laurel
Laurel

❶ 在這封傳真裡，寄件人確認收到訂單，還回答對方的問題。基於禮貌，她先謝謝顧客傳來的訂單；接著她在第二句就回答對方的問題。

❷ 寄件人提出問題，請對方提供更多資訊，以利公司繼續進行下一步動作。

❸ 在最後一句她再次提醒對方回答傳真中的問題，以利進展。

克里斯好：

❶ 謝謝您的訂單（參考文號：92515）。關於您提到大量訂購 IceTech 靴子的問題：考慮到您長期以來一直是我們的忠實顧客，我們的業務主任 Cheryl Root 決定，只要訂購數量在 25 雙以上，便樂意討論折扣事宜。❷ 不過首先我們有幾個問題：您想訂購的確切數目是多少？您的交貨時間限制是？您需要的鞋碼為？以後您有意進行更多的大量訂購嗎？

❸ 請給我更詳細的資訊，我們將盡力滿足您的需求。

Unit 14　如何撰寫商務電子郵件？
How do I write emails?

　　電子郵件現在可能是商務領域中使用最頻繁、最廣泛的溝通方式了，使用起來很簡單，傳送速度又快，撰寫起來也很容易。要記住的是，不管是用哪一種溝通方式來從事商業活動，商業寫作的原則永遠都適用，也就是：**把焦點放在你的讀者身上**，注意他**有什麼需求**，並**回答他會提出的問題**。

1 如何安排商務電子郵件的格式？

　　電子郵件是個獨一無二的溝通媒體（medium），具有獨特的功能與靈活的格式安排。如何安排電子郵件的格式？商務電子郵件中有幾個部分的內容與格式，必須確認填寫正確，這幾個部分就是：**地址欄**、**主旨欄**和**簽名檔**。

寄件者	From:	此欄位顯示**寄件者**（sender）電子郵件地址。電子郵件帳號應該要正式而專業，**最好顯示全名**（full name），不要用暱稱或具玩笑性質的帳號，如 hellokittyfan@xxx。
收件者	To:	輸入**收件者**（recipient）的電子郵件地址。
副本	Cc:	如果信件要寄給**需要掌握信中所述的事件發展者**，就用副本的方式寄出。
密件副本	Bcc:	Bcc 是 blind carbon copy 或 blind courtesy copy 的縮寫。這欄地址**不會被其他收件人看到**，但 Bcc 收件人可看到其他收件人地址。希望保有隱私、不被其他收件者看到的收件者，應將其電子郵件地址輸入此欄。
主旨	Subject:	信件主旨要**簡潔具體**，涵蓋本次信件溝通的重要主旨，能讓收信者**快速掌握信件的討論重點**，而決定是否要打開信閱讀。主旨句未必是完整句子，不影響文意的單字可刪除，因此寫法很像新聞標題。
附件	Attached:	顯示郵件**所附的檔案**

② 如何寫出簡潔有力的主旨？

　　主旨欄（subject line）在電子郵件中非常關鍵：主旨和寄件人的地址是對方第一個會看到的內容，你必須有效利用主旨欄，這樣對方才會打開郵件，閱讀你的訊息。要寫出簡潔有力的主旨，應遵守下列原則：

❶ **清晰具體**（Be informative and specific.）：**清楚傳達**（convey）郵件的主題，避免籠統（general）或太過模糊（vague）的說法，以便對方判斷（determine）信件內容重要性、及時處理你的郵件。可參照下列不同主旨寫法的對照：

> ❌ 內容籠統，無法判斷郵件性質和急迫性。

> ✅ 內容具體清晰，讀信者可以掌握郵件重要性。

- ❌ Business plan 商務計畫
- ✅ Revisions to business plan from 9/13 board meeting.
  9月13日董事會商務計畫修訂結果

> ❌ 若讀信者未事先得知首爾會議事宜，就可能判斷為無關的信件並加以忽略。

> ✅ 內容具體，讀信者可清楚了解信件目的和自己的關聯性。

- ❌ Conference in Seoul 首爾的會議
- ✅ Invitation: Keynote speaker at Seoul Conference
  邀請：首爾會議主題演講者

❷ **簡短**（Be brief.）：主旨這一行要簡短，否則太長可能會超過（run off）欄位。你不需要把郵件裡所有的資訊都寫進主旨欄，只要**清楚點出主題**即可：

> ❌ 內容過於冗長，讀信者難以掌握信件重點。

> ✅ 內容精簡，讀信者可快速抓到信件目的。

- ❌ Meeting requested for next week to discuss discrepancies in vacation policy, overtime policy, and salary
  要求下週開會討論休假政策、加班政策與薪水的差異
- ✅ Meeting requested for next week to discuss job benefits
  要求下週開會討論工作福利

❸ 寫出期限（Mention deadlines.）：若信件有具體**回覆（respond）期限，應在主旨中標示清楚**。商務人士每天都會收到眾多郵件，因此若信件主旨未表明有回覆期限，對方可能就不會立刻打開郵件，導致時限錯失。

❹ 適用一般標點符號規則，但是句尾不需標點（Follow punctuation rules, except for end punctuation.）：主旨應依照一般的規則，正確使用逗號（comma）、撇號（apostrophe）等標點符號，但是**句尾不加上句號等其他標點符號**。

❺ 寫法類似標題，不需是完整句（Write it like a headline, not a sentence.）：主旨的寫法和新聞標題相似，並不完全遵守一般文法規則。**若不影響文意（meaning），可以把不重要的字去掉**，只須盡量符合文法即可，不一定需寫成具備主詞（subject）、動詞（verb）、受詞（object）的完整句子。

3 電子郵件的簽名檔

簽名檔（signature block）就是可以設定插入每封**電子郵件底端**的圖文檔（.sig 檔），會被放在郵件底端**靠左**的位置，位於在**簽名的下方**，並通常與郵件的主文以虛線或其他形式的線條隔開。簽名檔裡應該包含以下內容：

❶ 寄件者全名
❷ 寄件者職稱、公司名稱
❸ 寄件者電子郵件地址
❹ 寄件者公司地址／電話等聯絡資訊

4 信件內容架構

撰寫商務電子郵件時，**應避免冗長的文字段落**，而在**段落間留白**會讓整體訊息較清楚易讀。此外，須使信中訊息應盡量清楚、簡短，整體架構和其他注意事項如下：

❶ 開場白（opening）： 開場先寫出有禮貌的問候語（可稍微不正式），接著寫出收件者的名字，最後加上逗號。

❷ 正文（body）： 為電郵主要內容，應直接切入重點，並遵守下列原則：

- 段落宜簡潔，各段間保留一行空行。
- 可用編號或分項列表。
- 言簡意賅，避免無關資訊。
- 在信件收尾處，提出明確的要求。

❸ 結尾（closing）： 以有禮貌的告別問候或致謝詞作為結尾，後面接逗號，接著寫上寄件者名字。

❹ 簽名檔（signature block）： 簽名檔上應要附有寄件者的全名和其他聯絡方式，例如公司的電話號碼和網址。

From: Lynne Contra <lynne@bigorchid.com>
To: Andrew Lloyd <a.lloyd@catererspuls.com>
Bcc: Ophelia Price <ophelia@bigorchid.com>
Subject: Flower selection for July 19 event—please respond by July 7
Attachment: bigorchidselections.doc ❺

Dear Mr. Lloyd,

Thank you again for confirming Big Orchid's services for the July 19 Tastebud Gala. I am writing to ask about your flower selection for the event. To ensure that your top choices will be in stock, we must have your flower selections by the end of this week. Below are three of our most popular options:

1. Happy Time (sunflowers, lilies, etc.)
2. Ice and Fire (cornflowers, roses, etc.)
3. Eastern Earl (orchids, peonies, etc.)

❺ Please use the attached Word file to make your selections and email them to us no later than July 7.

We look forward to the Gala!

Thank you,

Lynne Contra

....

Lynne Contra
Manager
Big Orchid Floral Design
Tel: 23547684
www.bigorchid.com
lynne@bigorchid.com

❺ 附件（attachment）： 如果有附件，記得在信件本文提及，並告知收件者要如何處理附件。忘記加上附件的意外也時常發生，因此最好在開始寫信時就先把附件附上。

14-1 | Email requesting a report 請對方交報告的電子郵件

From:	Greg Clarke (clarkeg@biosafe.com)	
To:	Anton Lubbe (lubbea@biosafe.com)	
Bcc:	Oliver Freud (freudo.director@biosafe.com)	
Subject:	Data Analysis report status	

寫信人用密件副本（Bcc）的方式把郵件寄給老闆，也許是想讓老闆看到自己的確已盡力催這份報告，其他的收件人不會看到老闆 Oliver Freud 的名字或電子郵件地址。

Segoe UI ▾ 14 ▾ B *I* U A. ≣ ≣ ≣ ≣ ≣ ≣ ≣ ≣ ≣ ≣

Dear Anton,

I appreciate getting the warning that your report will be late. We have all been very busy lately, and I really appreciate your hard work on the RFO project. However, I do need the report as soon as possible. In our conversation on Tuesday afternoon, you said it could be ready by tomorrow morning. I hope that is still the case. Please let me know as soon as possible when you will be able to get the report to me.

Thank you,

Greg

....

Greg Clarke
Project Manager
BioSafe Testing
www.biosafe.com
clarkeg@biosafe.com

安東好：

謝謝你來信告知報告會晚一點完成。我們最近都很忙，真的很感激你這麼辛苦地做這份 RFO 企畫。不過，我真的需盡快拿到這份報告。星期二下午你跟我說，明天早上你就可以弄完了，希望這句話還成立。請盡快告訴我可以交付報告的時間。

謝謝。

古瑞葛

電子郵件禮儀
Email Etiquette

　　撰寫電子郵件主文的原則，就跟所有商業寫作的原則一樣：**簡短。如果你有很多的資訊要傳送，內容會超過一頁時，那最好把它寫成備忘錄（memo）、報告（report）或其他形式的文件，然後以附件形式寄出。**這時你的電子郵件就可以用來點出重點，擔任文件的封面頁。要寫出簡潔有力的電子郵件，就遵照下列的電子郵件禮儀（etiquette），並在主文裡把你要傳達的資訊寫清楚：

❶ **像寫商務書信一樣撰寫電子郵件，並採用稱呼：**私人電子郵件可以寫得像對話，但是商務電子郵件務必要寫得像正式信件。如果是寫給商業夥伴、客戶、不熟的同事或主管，就**用 Dear 稱呼**，Hello 或 Hi 則用於非正式場合或熟識寄件對象時。如果郵件會寄給很多人，可以只稱呼主要的收件人，或是稱呼整個團體，像是 Dear Design team，但是要記住：不要用 Hello all 這樣的寫法。

❷ **採用結尾敬辭（closing line）：**採用標準的結尾敬辭，並在最後輸入你的名字。

❸ **注意禮貌，全用大寫字母並不禮貌：**因為這樣郵件內容看起來就像是在對著人大吼。留意字型和格式對讀者的感受會有何影響。

❹ **使用文字，不要使用表情符號：**用文字表達你的意思，**不要使用表情文字**（emoticon，例如私人電子郵件、通訊軟體或手機簡訊常用到的笑臉符號）。也避免使用縮寫或字首縮寫，除非是很常見的縮寫（如 ASAP、FYI 等）。

❺ **使用簡單的格式：**一般最好採用純文字（plain text），HTML 碼有時候並不一定能夠轉換過去，而你設定的格式傳到對方電腦後也可能會走樣。

❻ **使用拼字檢查（spell checker）：**拼字錯誤（typo）會使郵件顯得有失專業。

❼ **注意附件的大小：**加入附件時，留意讓附件維持在合理的大小之內。過大的檔案開啟時很可能會出現問題，或是減慢網路速度。如果你必須附加非常大的檔案，先告知對方。

❽ **避免無謂的轉寄（forwarding）：**有必要時才轉寄，並簡短說明為什麼要把這封郵件轉寄給對方。

　　以上禮儀大多適用於**商務電子郵件**，寄給親朋好友的私人郵件並不需要採用這些禮儀；甚至同一間辦公室同事之間的電子郵件，也可以稍微隨興（casual）一點。但是要寫電子郵件給**商業夥伴、客戶、顧客**和**自己公司的高級主管**時，務必遵守這些禮節，並採用嚴肅專業的語氣。

1 Review the concepts

❶ What are three important things to consider when writing a fax cover letter?

_____

_____

❷ Which of the following elements should be included in a fax cover letter?
(A) Your name
(B) Your fax number
(C) Your email address
(D) The recipient's fax number
(E) The recipient's street address
(F) The total number of pages in the fax

❸ What information should be put in the subject line of a fax or email?

_____

❹ What does "Transmitting" mean? What should you write next to the "Transmitting" line of a fax?

_____

_____

❺ How can you make someone's email address "invisible"?

_____

2 True (T) or False (F)

❶ ☐ True ☐ False An outgoing fax is one you are sending to someone.

❷ ☐ True ☐ False A .sig file belongs at the top of your email message.

❸ ☐ True ☐ False Smileys and emoticons may be used in formal business emails.

❹ ☐ True ☐ False Fax and email subject lines should be punctuated like any other sentence.

❺ ☐ True ☐ False Business email messages should start with a salutation.

3 Look at the email below. Answer the following questions about the email.

❶ Who is the main recipient of the email?

_____

❷ Who else can read the email?

_____

❸ Which addresses are not visible to the reader?

_____

❹ What is the attachment?

_____

From:	Jonas Andrussen (jonas.andrussen@global.net)	⌄
📖 To:	Tilak Ravenu (tilak.ravenu@global.org)	
📖 Bcc:	Jens Svenson (jens.svenson@global.org), Ann-Brit Bech-Nielson (a.bech-nielson@usg.edu)	
Subject:	Upcoming performance review	
Attachment:	performancereview.doc	

Segoe UI | 14 | ⌄ | B *I* U A | ☰ ☰ ☰ ☰ | ☰ ☰ ☰ ☰ | — 🔗 🖼

Dear Tilak:

I was very impressed with your enthusiasm during your summer internship with us at Global Nonprofits. However, I have been concerned about your performance recently, particularly with regard to your lateness in completing tasks.

It is almost time for your performance review, and I would like to give you a chance to earn a good review before it is too late. Please look at the attached document and honestly rate your performance in each of the categories. In the next few weeks, if I can see that you are making an effort to rise to our standards, I will be happy to give you a positive review. If not, we may need to have a more serious discussion.

Sincerely,

Jonas
****
J. Andrussen
Founder, Global Nonprofits
www.global.net
jonas.andrussen@global.net

4 According to email etiquette guidelines, what is wrong with the following email? Find the mistakes and rewrite the email in a more professional manner.

From:	Annie (anniespanks@hotmail.com)	⌄
📖 To:	heather.jones@nexttech.com, rolypolyjoely@yahoo.com, clint.brown@nexttech.com, georgieboy@hotmail.com	
📖 Cc:		
Subject:	MEETING	
Attachment:		

Segoe UI · 14 · 𝐄̲ · **B** *I* U̲ A̲ · ☰ ☱ ☲ ☲ · ☰ ☱ ☲ ☰ · — 🔗 🖼

Hi, everybody.

Just writing to let you know that the Expansion Project team meeting tomorrow is CANCELLED. :(We will reschedule for some time next week. I'll get back to you on when. Sorry, should have told you guys earlier. And Heather, can I get those files from you before close of business? thx.

Rewrite!

From:		⌄
📖 To:		
📖 Cc:		
Subject:		
Attachment:		

Segoe UI · 14 · 𝐄̲ · **B** *I* U̲ A̲ · ☰ ☱ ☲ ☲ · ☰ ☱ ☲ ☰ · — 🔗 🖼

Dear _____

_____

_____

_____

_____

_____

_____

_____

_____

5 What information is missing from the following fax cover letter?

Smithson Global
Smithson Forum, DLF CYBERCITI,SECTOR-15A,
GURGAON - 122 002 HARYANA INDIA
Tel:+91 124 2560808/4080808 Fax: +91 124 2565454

FAX

To: Dilip Rathee

Date: 20 July 2023

Subject: Clarifying new product specs

Dear Mr. Rathee:

I have read the questions from your previous fax, and I believe I can answer all of them. Let's start with . . .

---

6 Write a fax to your employer that conveys the following information:

- ✓ You have to take urgent leave beginning tomorrow.
- ✓ You will return no later than 10 days from tomorrow.
- ✓ You hope to work remotely as much as you can.
- ✓ You will be available at this number: (304) 886-4895.
- ✓ You will check your email frequently.
- ✓ People should contact your colleague June Chester with questions about your current projects.

To: John Smith, Branch Director

Fax: (212) 568-0009

Tel: (212) 445-6678

Subject: Taking emergency leave from 2/13-2/23

From: M. Witte

Date: February 12, 2023

Pages: 1

Cc:

Dear _____ :

_____

_____

_____

_____

_____

_____

_____

_____

_____

_____

_____

_____

_____

_____

_____

_____

_____

_____

_____

_____

Key Terms

call to action 行動呼籲
要求或鼓勵溝通對象如何行動的陳述，通常也會在備忘錄的結尾中出現。

chronologically 按照時間順序地
依照事件發生的順序講述的方式，可用於說明備忘錄內容的相關背景時。

context 背景
事件發生的背景狀況。

direct writing 直接的寫作
直接講到要點，不停頓、不拐彎抹角。

heading 標題區
備忘錄的第一部分，列出備忘錄的撰寫人與收件人、日期、主旨等重要資訊。

indirect 間接
不直接講到重點，拐彎抹角。

layout 版面配置
文件中各部分在紙張或版面上的配置方式，各類商務文件的版面配置可能各不相同。

memorandum (memo)
備忘錄
用以提醒的便箋，通常指辦公室之間用來溝通的便箋。

passive voice 被動語態
把動作受詞當作句子主詞的英語語態，如「The contract was signed by the employee.」（合約由員工簽了名。）是被動語態，而「The employee signed the contract.」（員工簽了合約。）則是主動語態。

task 任務
待完成的工作。

Unit 16 撰寫備忘錄有哪些原則？
What are the principles for writing a memo?

什麼是備忘錄（memo）？備忘錄是辦公室、公司或團隊內部用來溝通訊息的文件，通常用來宣布事情、描述問題或說明解決方式，也常用來敦促受文者採取行動，像是報名參加某個訓練課程、閱讀某份報告、改變某個流程等。

撰寫備忘錄有哪些原則？備忘錄主要用來在公司或團隊內進行溝通，所以不必像一般商務文件那麼正式。不過，備忘錄依舊是用來傳達重要資訊的文書，所以一定要清晰、易讀、正確。備忘錄應具備以下特點，就跟其他商務文件一樣：

- ◆ 以讀者為中心
- ◆ 清晰簡潔
- ◆ 包含恰當的訊息
- ◆ 格式清楚

1 如何做到以讀者為中心？

❶ **仔細選擇你的讀者**：備忘錄通常會一次寄給很多人，然後又轉寄給更多人，商務人士每天都會被無數的備忘錄轟炸！所以務必依據主題仔細選擇你的讀者，**只把備忘錄寄給真正需要的人**。

❷ **預想讀者的問題**：就跟其他的商務文件一樣，備忘錄也應該**預想到讀者的問題，並回答這些問題**。請針對讀者設想應回答哪些問題，做法就跟撰寫其他商務文件一樣。

❸ **訊息要完整**：除了要預想讀者會提出哪些問題，還要**考慮他們是否還需要其他的資訊**。

另外，由於備忘錄會把訊息傳達給很多人，所以務必仔細考慮如何安排訊息的**語氣和內容**。想一想你的訊息可能會如何影響讀者的情緒：

❶ **直接寫出正面的訊息**：如果要傳達的訊息是**正面或中性的**，例如公布培訓活動的時間，或介紹團隊的新成員，那就按照一般的原則，**先把重點寫出來**，然後再說明細節。

❷ **婉轉表達負面的訊息**：備忘錄也常用來傳達**壞消息**。要公布壞消息時，一開始就把重點寫出來可能並不是最好的做法，不妨**先把原因或證據列出來**，讓讀者有時間做點心理準備，然後再把負面的資訊清楚呈現出來。

❸ **避免指名道姓**：由於備忘錄會寄給很多人，之後又會層層轉寄出去，所以**盡量避免指名道姓，歸咎於人**。這時不妨**被動句**取代用主動句，或使用**複數主詞**：

✕ 以主動句指名道姓	Monica lost the Big Company contract. 莫妮卡把跟 Big Company 的合約搞砸了。
	Peter made a mistake with the billing. 彼得把帳單打錯了。
✔ 使用被動句	The contract with Big Company was lost. 與 Big Company 的合約沒了。
	Mistakes were made with the billing. 帳單出了錯。
✔ 使用複數主詞	We lost the Big Company contract. 我們失去了與 Big Company 的合約。

這份備忘錄傳達的資訊是中性的，所以可以直接寫出重點。作者在第一句就清楚說明期望讀者採取的行動。

**Alamo Food
Service Industries**

Memo

To:	Store Managers
From:	Senior Management
Date:	Nov. 30, 2023
Subject:	Please use the new display cases arriving this week

Please use the new plastic in-store display centers that should be arriving at your stores in the next week. Each display should arrive with clear instructions and all the equipment needed to assemble it. If you have questions about the display, please call Ben Gravel at 413.189.2374, ext. 25.

These display centers are part of a new sales and marketing concept that takes into account the individual store's design. By using displays that are customizable to individual stores, we hope to provide customers with a unique experience that is tailored to their region's needs.

As you know, Alamo has been growing rapidly the past few years. One of our goals is to be a part of every meal Americans eat. We hope this new marketing concept helps us achieve that goal. Please help us by assembling and implementing the new display cases as soon as possible.

請一律開始採用新的店內塑膠展示櫃，新的展示櫃應可於下週送達各分店，並附有清楚的裝置說明與所需組裝用具。如對展示櫃有任何問題，請打 413-189-2374，分機 25 聯絡班‧葛佛。

這些展示櫃裝置是公司最新的銷售與行銷策略的一環，考量到的是各分店擁有自己的設計。展示櫃外觀可由各店自行調整，以迎合各區顧客的需求，提供獨特的體驗。

如各位所知，Alamo 過去幾年來成長非常迅速。我們的目標之一便是成為美國居民飲食的一部分，而我們希望這個新的行銷策略，能夠帶領我們達到這個目標。請盡快裝設新的展示櫃，助我們一臂之力。

16-2 | A bad news memo 傳達壞消息的備忘錄

▮▮▮▮ STAR FINANCIAL GROUPS

Memo

To: Information Design Team

From: Johan Rutger, Executive Vice President

Cc: Agota Gabor, Chief of Operations

Date: Nov. 11, 2023

❶ Re: Your team-building conference travel request has been reviewed

❶ 本備忘錄用「Re:」（regarding / in reference to 的縮寫）點出主旨。這是很常用的用法，不過有些指導手冊會建議用 **Subject** 比較好。

The senior managers reviewed your request to take your team to the Team Building International conference in Hawaii on December 1. We appreciate your interest in building good working relationships within our office and in our branches worldwide. However, given the current economic situation, our shareholders are unlikely to approve the expense. We are sorry to have to decline your request.

❷ 在這一段裡，作者沒有先就重點寫出「無法批准申請」，而是先肯定同事的努力（第二句），然後說明無法批准的理由（第三句）。如此可以減緩壞消息（最後一句）對讀者帶來的心理衝擊。

Please feel free to resubmit your request for next year's conference, when we may be in a better position to approve travel. We appreciate your commitment to good team building, and will be happy to review requests for other opportunities. ❸

❸ 作者在這裡對同事的努力再次表達肯定，並帶給他們希望，但是這通常只是為了在傳達壞消息之外，說些好聽的話。

主管高層已就貴團隊申請於 12 月 1 日，參加在夏威夷舉辦的「團隊培訓國際會議」進行過審核。我們非常樂見你們致力於在公司內和國外分公司建立起良好的工作氣氛，但是基於目前的經濟狀況，公司股東不太可能批准此項經費，因此很抱歉我們無法批准此項申請。

但是你們仍可以申請參加明年的會議，也許明年我們就有足夠的資金資助出差費用。我們非常感謝諸位同事如此盡心建立良好的工作團隊，也非常樂意審核其他的申請事項。❸

如何撰寫備忘錄？
How do I write a business memo?

1 如何寫出簡潔的備忘錄

❶ 內容簡短（Keep it short.）：備忘錄是商務書面溝通中最簡短的形式之一，讀起來應該要具備**快速又易讀**的特性。寫作重點如下：

　　❶ 切中要點：在第一句或第二句就講到重點，尤其是在你請求對方採取行動時。

　　❷ 段落要簡短：每一段只處理一個小主題就好。

　　❸ 重新考慮格式：如果備忘錄的內容偏多，就要重新考慮一下你要傳達的資訊，想一想是不是把整篇內容改成一篇報告，然後寫個備忘錄當作封面頁比較好。備忘錄應該頂多只有兩頁的長度。

❷ 資訊具體（Be specific.）：備忘錄應該要傳達**具體的資訊**。如果你要用備忘錄告訴同事們有個會議或活動，那就把具體的日期時間告訴他們。記得 8C 的原則——資訊要具體（concrete）。

❸ 內容有組織（Be organized.）：備忘錄的內容要**有清楚的組織**，這樣讀者才能迅速找到需要的資訊。不管你是直接或委婉，內容都要有組織，不要讓對方還得浪費時間思考你是什麼意思。

2 備忘錄的基本格式與內容

　　大多數的公司都有自己的備忘錄格式，就跟傳真封面頁一樣。備忘錄的格式有三個基本元素：

❶ 名稱（title）：備忘錄的名稱就是 memo 或 memorandum。名稱這個部分很重要，應置於最上方，以便讀者一看就知道這是一份備忘錄。

❷ 標題區（heading）：版面安排與內容就跟電子郵件和傳真的標題區很類似。標題區應該包括：

備忘錄的撰寫人 （sender）	寫出發文者的**全名**，寫給同事時也需附上。視備忘錄的正式程度，還可以加上**頭銜**或**職稱**。
備忘錄的收件人 （receiver / distribution list）	在這裡寫出**所有受文者的全名**，有需要時加上**頭銜**或**職稱**。
備忘錄的發送日期 （date）	寫出**完整的日期**，月分可以採用**英文縮寫**，大多數的寫作指導手冊都會建議不要只用數字，例如應寫出「Sept.」而非「09」來表示「九月」。
備忘錄的主旨句 （subject）	主旨句要**簡短**，但是**明確具體**。

❸ 訊息主文（body）：主文部分應該完整傳達你的訊息。如果長度只有一、兩句也沒有關係。如果資訊比較多，可以把主文分成三個部分：

❶ 開頭（opening）
❷ 背景情況、任務、問題（context/task/problem）
❸ 結論（conclusion）

3 撰寫備忘錄的開頭

在備忘錄裡**不需加上稱謂**，直接寫出重點，並用一到兩個句子把主要的訊息寫出來。下面是幾個備忘錄的開頭句範例：

- Use of different memo formats has caused confusion among staff members. Starting on December 13, all memos should be written using the following standard format.
  備忘錄格式不統一，經常在辦公室夥伴之間引起問題。從 12 月 13 日起，所有的備忘錄一律採取下列的標準格式。

- All frontline staff members are required to participate in the upcoming customer service training program.
  所有的第一線員工，都要參加將於近期舉辦的顧客服務訓練課程。

- We are happy to announce the addition of Sabrina Kerr as office manager.
  我們很高興宣布莎賓娜·科爾的加入，擔任辦公室經理。

4 描述背景情況／任務／問題

這個部分應該就重點進行更多的描述。視備忘錄的目的，你可以解釋**為什麼要有這些改變**（背景情況），或是指導同事們該**如何行動**（任務），或詳細說明備忘錄**欲提出的問題**（問題）。細節說明請見下表：

說明背景情況 （context）	根據你要傳達的資訊，安排訊息的順序。通常可以**按照時間順序**（chronologically），說明背景原因。例如，在說明公司活動取消的備忘錄當中，可以說明導致取消的背景因素（經濟狀況、當前傳染病情形等）。
說明任務 （task）	說明任務的備忘錄不一定需要說明背景，但是一定要給予**詳細的指示**。比如說，如何使用最新的語音留言系統。在這種情況下，時間順序就不是那麼重要了，重要的是**一步一步的流程說明**，以及執行上**有問題時該聯絡誰**。
說明問題 （problem）	說明問題的備忘錄應該解釋問題**是什麼**、該問題**如何衝擊到公司**、現在有哪些可能的**解決辦法**，或是哪些辦法已經在執行，以及該問題致使公司制定了**哪些新政策**等。

5 撰寫備忘錄的結論

結論的部分，應該**再提一次本備忘錄最主要的訊息**，並常用來**敦促對方採取行動**。如果備忘錄是用來鼓勵員工參加某個訓練課程，那就在結論的部分提醒他們去報名，並確定你已經給了所有報名所需的資訊。如果備忘錄是用來指出一個問題，那就在結論的部分請大家思考解決辦法，或是重述問題的後果。

6 其他備忘錄寫作注意事項

撰寫成功的備忘錄可以幫助公司或組織內部溝通更有效率，但若備忘錄寫作失當，則可能導致溝通問題或引發內部糾紛。以下為幾點撰寫備忘錄時應注意的其他事項：

❶ 勿包含無關資訊

備忘錄**應遵守簡潔的原則**，勿讓組織同事閱讀無關緊要的細節資訊，而浪費工作時間，因此寫作完成後，可檢查是否已經刪去無損整體內容的句子或段落，除非相關支持性的資訊有助傳達內文要旨。

❷ 避免錯誤或誤導的資訊

雖然備忘錄的正式程度低於一般商務書信，但在發文之前仍應和對外書信一樣，**仔細檢查內文的資訊和文字正確性**。若文中資訊不清或含有錯誤，可能誤導同事相信不正確的資訊，進而引起業務上的問題。

❸ 考量備忘錄是否為最佳溝通方式

公司內部溝通訊息的方式有很多種，除備忘錄之外，尚有電子郵件、即時通訊平台或當面及電話溝通等，因此選擇撰寫備忘錄前，**應考量欲傳達的資訊性質**。若是迫切性高而需要同事立刻得知的資訊，可考慮使用電話、即時訊息等速度更快的溝通方式，以免錯失溝通時機。

MEMO

To:	Gabi Bakos, Liesel Van Der Colff, Jeffrey Blais
Subject:	Train the Trainers is nominated for an award
Date:	29 March, 2023
From:	Heather Kesey, President

Wonderful news! Thanks to your hard work, our terrific Train the Trainers program has been nominated for a Red Pencil Award in the overall Excellent in Training category. Being nominated is a great honor and a tribute to your thoughtful design and implementation of the program.

The awards will be announced next month. We will all be receiving invitations to the honorees banquet, but the date has not been determined. I will let you know as soon as I hear more.

Congratulations again, team! Keep it up.

> 這份備忘錄的語氣親切隨和，這一句的使用在這裡也很恰當，因為這份備忘錄是用來公布好消息的，而且對象是具有密切工作關係的同事。

好消息！感謝大家的努力，我們的 Train the Trainers 計畫，被提名 Red Pencil 最佳培訓獎。這次提名對大家的精心籌劃與執行是莫大的榮譽與肯定。

得獎名單將於下個月揭曉。我們都會受邀參加頒獎盛宴，只是日期還未確定。一旦有進一步消息，我會立刻通知各位。

再次恭賀各位團隊夥伴！大家繼續努力！

FUDIO SYSTEMS

Memo

To	Sharon Soemardjan, Marketing Manager; Lawrence Halim, Marketing Manager
From	Arthur Tran, President, Sales Division
Date	27 April, 2023
Subject	Change in fall personal electronics promotion

New market research and analysis has shown that the proposed advertising media for the new fall personal electronics promotion must be changed. Last month's focus groups and surveys showed that we need to update our advertising efforts in order to appeal to our target audience. The promotion as currently planned was seen as "stale" and "out of date." The full report of the survey and focus group results is attached for your review (see "Summer Market Research Results Report 2023: Survey and Focus Group Findings"). The main points of the report are summarized below.

Please note that a meeting to revise the promotion will be arranged soon.

Drop the characters
The cartoon characters in the current campaign are seen as "childish." They don't attract young users because they aren't considered "hi-tech." Although the characters make the products seem warm and friendly, they don't encourage customers to make a purchase.

Change the color scheme
The current pastel palette of the promotional materials is seen as too soft and inappropriate for the electronics consumer market. The colors send the message of a user-friendly but low-functionality product. Market research shows that current buyers value increased functionality over ease of use. As the market becomes more comfortable with the technology, ease of use becomes less important.

Increase Internet advertising
Our market identified the Internet as the most trustworthy source for electronics information. According to surveys, 72% of our target market uses the Internet for 20 hours or more per week. Shifting efforts from media sources such as radio and magazines to popular Internet sites will more effectively promote our product.

Attachments: Summer Market Research Results Report 2023: Survey and Focus Group Findings

這份備忘錄比較長，在此擔任一份完整報告的封面頁，總結附件之報告的重點。寫作者在第一句就破題點出核心訊息（必須改變宣傳方式），接著說明支持核心訊息的細節，並透過小標題與後續段落進一步說明現有問題。

根據最新的市場調查與分析結果，新的秋季個人電子產品的宣傳媒體需要重新調整。上個月的焦點團體研究與調查顯示，我們需要改變廣告宣傳的方式，以吸引目標消費者。目前計劃中的宣傳方式被指太過「陳舊」、「過時」。完整的調查及焦點團體結果已附上供參（見「2023 夏季市場調查結果報告：調查與焦點團體研究結果」）。下面整理出報告的重點。

另請注意，近期將開會討論改變廣告宣傳的方式。

去掉卡通人物

目前的卡通人物設計被認為很「幼稚」。卡通人物無法吸引年輕消費者，因為看起來不夠「高科技」。雖然卡通人物會使產品看起來更溫馨親切，但是無法鼓勵消費者購買產品。

改變顏色設計

目前宣傳資料採用的柔色系列太過柔和，不符合電子產品的消費者市場。柔和的色彩傳達出易使用、但是功能性低的感覺。市場調查的結果顯示，目前的消費者對高功能的重視遠勝過使用的簡易性。在消費者越來越習慣高科技的狀況下，簡易性便越來越不重要了。

加強網路宣傳

市場消費者認為，網路是取得電子產品相關資訊最可靠的來源。根據調查結果，72% 的目標消費者每週至少使用網路 20 個小時。如果把花在廣播、雜誌等其他媒體上的宣傳資源，轉移到熱門網頁上，將能夠更有效推廣我們的產品。

附件：2023 夏季市場調查結果報告：調查與焦點團體研究結果

1 Review the concepts

① What kind of information is sent in a memo?

② Which of the following details should be included in the heading of a memo?

(A) Who the memo is from
(B) Who the memo is to
(C) The address, phone number, and fax number of the writer's company
(D) The date
(E) The subject

③ What is a good length for a memo?

④ What are the three parts of the body of a longer memo?

⑤ When should you use the passive voice in a memo?

⑥ How should bad news be presented in a memo? How is this different from presenting positive or neutral news?

2 True (T) or False (F)

① □ True □ False A memo should be at least three paragraphs.

② □ True □ False A memo should begin with a salutation.

③ □ True □ False Memos are usually less formal than business letters.

④ □ True □ False Memos are usually sent to internal colleagues.

3 Write a memo for the following situation

Paul Lennard, office manager for Moonrise Stationery, needs to inform all employees that their paychecks will now arrive twice a month instead of once a month (starting February 1). Employee paychecks will arrive on the 1st and 15th of each month. Paul's contact number is 301-258-0145.

Memo
To: _____
From: _____
Date: _____
Subject: _____
_____
_____
_____
_____
_____

4 Write a memo for the situation described below

Your company wants all employees to complete an "Employee Satisfaction Survey." Write a memo that will be sent with the attached survey.

Memorandum

To: _____

From: _____

Date: _____

Subject: _____

_____

_____

_____

_____

5 Write a memo for the following situation

You are the vice president of Radio Radio. You need to tell the president that 500 radios sent to the London Radio Radio store were defective. Write a memo explaining the situation. Imagine what actions you would take to correct it and suggest a time line for completing them.

Radio

Memorandum

To: _____

From: _____

Date: _____

Re: _____

_____

_____

_____

_____

_____

_____

_____

Key Terms

appendix 附錄
置於書籍或報告的主要篇幅之後,用於提供補充資訊的部分。

bibliography / reference list
參考書目／參考文獻列表
彙整書籍或研究報告中,參考或引述的文獻資料所製成的列表。

commission 下令完成
要求從事一項業務,通常為委任寫出和製作一份文件或事物(如藝術品和文書),用法可如:
「to commission a report」,即「下令完成一份報告」之意。

methodology 一套方法
搜尋資訊或完成事情的方式,包括用來收集和分析報告資訊的種種做法、流程和技術,尤其指稱學術人員或調查人員所採用的研究方法、流程和規定。

poll 民意調查
針對特定主題或人物,詢問人們的意見,為數據資料常用的資料蒐集方法。

procedure 流程
執行或促成某事的方式;完成事情的步驟。

qualitative research 質性研究
使用觀察、訪談、意見詢問等方式的研究調查,所蒐集的資料通常為非數據資料。若以統計數據等測量結果為分析對象的研究,一般則稱為「量化研究」(quantitative research)。

raw data 原始資料
蒐集後尚未經過分析討論的最初資料。

scope 內容範圍
一篇報告內容包含的範圍。例如,如果你在寫一篇關於電玩軟體利潤的報告,可能就會把推銷新電玩的資訊放進報告的內容範圍內,至於這些電玩怎麼玩,就不會放進報告裡了。

synopsis, or executive summary 摘要
針對內容的簡短陳述。報告的摘要一般會涵蓋內文各部分的提要說明。

terms of reference 職權範圍
說明一篇報告的背景、目標與目的。通常包括:報告是寫給誰看的、報告主要討論的主題,以及報告須何時繳交,此外也可能包括此份報告是如何作成的。

viability 可行性
業務企畫或商業投資成功的可能性。

Unit 18 什麼是報告？
What is a report?

1 什麼是報告？

簡單説來，**報告（report）**就是**清楚有組織、就一特定主題提供資訊的長篇文件**。更嚴謹的説法是，報告就一特定主題提供詳細資訊，並組織成文章、圖表或表格的形式。報告內容可以涵蓋特定的時段、活動、事件或主題，目的通常是用來提供資訊，但是常常也含有建議或説服的成分。**商務報告**則是專門用來傳達商務決策所需的資訊，一篇商務報告應該做到下列五個基本事項：

❶ **定義報告**：説明報告的作者是誰？標題是什麼？報告是寫給誰看的？什麼時候寫的？

❷ **定義內容**：指出報告所討論的企畫或問題。

❸ **給予背景資訊**：説明該企畫或問題產生的背景。

❹ **給予相關資訊或發現**：呈現你收集到的資訊。

❺ **提出結論與建議**：協助讀者做出商務決策或採取恰當的行動。

2 報告的種類

報告內容可以依不同的主題與情況區分，常見種類與説明如下：

業務企畫 Business plans	用來説明業務策略、管理模型、產品的目的、生產流程與新企畫的可行性等。
財務報告 Financial reports	分析公司的財務狀況，確認公司的獲利能力，建議增進獲利能力的做法，或是討論其他的財務問題。
市場調查報告 Market research reports	可用來分析目標市場的習慣或組成。
行銷報告 Marketing reports	可分析公司目前的行銷策略，或是建議新的行銷策略。
進度報告 Progress reports	説明進行中的專案進展。
技術報告 Technical reports	通常用來説明技術或科學研究的過程、進展或結果，或者是技術或科學研究遇到的問題。
其他	商務報告還可以用來討論員工關係、辦公室資源管理、和其他所有與公司或產業運作有關的主題。

3 撰寫報告有哪些原則？

　　開始動筆寫報告之前，需先擬定大綱，然後把文中資訊依此清楚呈現，並確定內容的組織合乎邏輯。長篇報告的章節分段會比短篇報告更明顯，但是所有的報告都會包含**導言**（introduction）、**討論**（discussion）、**結論**（conclusion）和**建議**（recommendation）等部分，每個部分都應按照下面的寫作原則撰寫：

❶ **專注在報告的主要目的**：一篇報告不應該把所有跟主題相關的資訊都呈現出來，而是應該界定明確的焦點或範圍。確定報告的目的後，你就知道該收集和呈現多少資訊。

❷ **考量讀者需求**：在第一步的時候，你就要先想想你的**讀者是誰**，這樣才能決定報告的目的。他們看完報告後會怎麼反應？報告的目的應該要反映出讀者要採取的行動，然後想想他們對此主題已經有多少了解，對此主題有什麼看法，又還需要知道什麼。

❸ **進行研究**：收集需要的資源與資訊，接著依據報告的目標和目的，分析收集到的資訊，最後根據分析研究的結果，決定要提出什麼樣的結論和建議。

❹ **決定合適的格式**：如果報告內容較多，最好用編號的方式把內容組織起來。如果不是很多，用大標題、小標題的方式應該就可以了。如果報告內容非常多，最好把內容分成幾個大章。

4 報告含有哪些基本元素？

　　報告的結構取決於報告的內容範圍與主題，因此每篇報告含有的元素可能都不同。較短的報告可能就不需要**摘要**（executive summary）、**目錄頁**（contents page）、**附錄**（appendix）和**參考文獻列表**（reference list）。在某些報告中，也許研究流程已經很清楚，因此不需要正式說明，而報告的格式最終還是取決於公司規定和報告主題。以下是報告的五大部分，後續單元將分別說明前四大主要部分。

報告包含哪些基本元素？

❶ **前導部分**

前導部分可包括：封面頁、目錄、摘要、前言與職權範圍。

❷ **討論部分**

報告的討論部分可以包括：
- 研究調查的方法和流程（methodology, or procedures）。
- 詳細的結果說明（findings）。

❺ **參考資料部分**

參考資料部分包括：附錄、參考書目、參考文獻等。

❸ **結論部分**

整理報告的發現，提出從中得到的心得想法。

❹ **建議部分**

根據發現與結論，提出認為應該採取的明確行動建議。

Unit 19 撰寫報告的前導
Writing the introductory section

比起其他形式的商業寫作，報告的內容更長也更正式。撰寫報告時除了同樣要跟撰寫商務書信和備忘錄時一樣，遵循良好寫作的原則，還需要更仔細地**規劃內容和結構**，因為報告的內容往往更龐雜。

報告開頭前導的部分分為以下幾個項目：

❶ 封面頁（Title page）
❷ 目錄（Contents）
❸ 摘要（Synopsis / Executive summary）
❹ 前言與職權範圍（Introduction and terms of reference）

1 封面頁（title page）

報告的封面頁應該列出**撰寫人姓名、日期及報告名稱**，有時還可以寫上報告的收受者。

19-1 | Sample title page 範例封面頁

Feasibility Study: Establishing a Branch Office in Kuala Lumpur

Written by: Mathuram Anbuselvan
Submitted to Business Expansion Committee, May 25, 2023

吉隆坡設置分部可行性研究

撰寫人：Mathuram Anbuselvan
於 2023 年 5 月 25 日提交業務擴展委員會

2 目錄頁（contents）

目錄的部分應標出報告的各章節名稱及對應頁數。

19-2 | Sample contents 目錄頁範例

3 撰寫摘要（synopsis or executive summary）

摘要（summary）濃縮了報告的主要內容，除了應該把重點放在**結論**與**建議**，同時也應該簡短地說明報告的**主題**與**研究方法**。摘要的功能，就是讓沒時間把整份報告看完的忙碌主管，能夠在短時間內掌握最重要的資訊。摘要應該說明：

❶ 問題或主題的主要相關**背景資訊**
（Important background information about the problem or topic）
❷ 重要的**職權範圍**（Important terms of reference）
❸ **研究方法**中重要的部分（Important information about your methodology）
❹ 重要的**研究結果**（All key findings）
❺ 重要的**結論**（All key conclusions）
❻ 重要的**建議**（All key recommendations）

摘要不應該用冗長的篇幅介紹相關背景、流程或方法，也不應該包含不重要的研究結果、結論和附錄等。摘要應該在保留所有重要資訊的前提下，盡量簡短。通常**一到兩頁**是最恰當的長度，但是確切的長度還是取決於你需要呈現的資訊量。有些指導手冊會建議，不要讓摘要超過整篇報告長度的 10%，但是這方面並沒有硬性的規定。

Maritime Satellite Research Report: Executive Summary

For the past sixteen months, the Maritime Satellite (MS) laboratory has been developing a system that will allow companies with large fleets of commercial boats to communicate directly with their captains. Using a satellite link, this communication can take place any time.

We tested the concepts for the first time from August 11 to August 20, using a fleet of Van De Camps fishing boats that were assigned to move throughout a 600-nautical mile area, using the MS5-x satellite.

We transmitted more than 33,000 data and voice messages and had a success rate of 89 percent. Data and voice messages were equally successful (the failure rate was slightly higher for data messages, but the difference is statistically insignificant). The successful transmissions were judged to be audible and clear by all the participating data receivers. When transmission failure occurred, it was a result of human error in operating the machinery, boats moving outside the satellite broadcast area, and obstruction of the line of sight between the boat's receiver and the satellite. The most important factor was human error, affecting 6% of messages sent.

The test clearly demonstrated the possibility of this form of communication and how close MS is to having a marketable product. We recommend that its development continue to be fully funded. To that end, we make the following recommendations.

- Develop a training program to show captains how to use the satellite receiver
- Map the precise boundaries of satellite coverage over the North Atlantic (maps to be extended as the product is developed)
- Continue market research to establish interest in the upcoming product

海事衛星研究報告：摘要

過去 16 個月來，海事衛星（MS）實驗室致力研發一套通訊系統，方便擁有龐大商業船隊的企業與其船長直接進行溝通。採用此衛星連結，雙方可隨時進行直接溝通。

我們於 8 月 11 日至 8 月 20 日期間進行第一次測試：Van De Camps 漁船隊受派在 600 海里的範圍內航行時，我們採用 MS5-x 衛星與之進行通訊。

我們傳輸了 33,000 多份的資料與語音訊息，最後成功率達 89%。資料與語音訊息的傳輸同樣成功（資料訊息的失敗率稍高一些，但是在統計上未具顯著差異性）。如果所有參與的接收器接收到的訊息都可聽取且很清楚，就被視為成功的傳訊。傳訊失敗皆起因於人為操控機器出錯、船隻超出衛星收訊範圍，和船隻接收器與衛星之間視線距離上出現阻礙物，其中以人為因素為最主要原因，影響了 6% 的訊息傳輸。

本測試充分證明了此溝通形式的可行性，以及 MS 可望將於不久的未來推出相關產品。

我們建議繼續全面資助該研發過程，並為此提出下列具體建議：

♦ 開設訓練課程，訓練船長使用此衛星接收器。

♦ 標出衛星在北大西洋的確切傳訊範圍（隨著產品的研發，可擴大地圖範圍）。

♦ 繼續進行市場調查，建立消費者對此未來產品的興趣。

4 撰寫前言與職權範圍（introduction and terms of reference）

前言和職權範圍的部分為讀者說明報告的**主題**、**內容範圍**、**目的**和**結構**。雖然前言位在報告最前面的部分，但是不妨等研究結果、結論和建議的部分都寫完後，再來撰寫前言，這樣寫起來更容易。畢竟前言就像是**整篇報告的總結**。前言應該：

❶ 說明報告的**目的與目標**。

（State the purpose and the objectives of the report.）

❷ 說明重要的**職權範圍**。（Provide important terms of reference.）

❸ 提供重要的**背景資料**，如簡述報告主題相關的發展。

（Provide background details important to the situation, such as a brief overview of developments leading to the report's topic.）

❹ 定義讀者可能不熟的**術語**。

（Define any terms that your readers may not recognize.）

❺ 總結報告中描述的**問題**、**主題**、**研究流程與建議**的解決辦法。

（Summarize the problem or topic, your procedures, and your recommended solutions.）

如果有需要，亦可說明**報告的限制或假設（limitations or assumptions）**。例如，假如你的報告是針對這個季度寫的，但是針對下個季度提出建議，那就要把這一點寫出來。也許你當初對人、對資訊只能進行有限的蒐集研究，或是只有有限的資金，此時若這些因素對你的報告可能有影響，也需提出來。除非你的報告非常長，否則一、兩頁應該就足以呈現這些資訊了。以下是範例：

Janet Davis, Director of Finance, requested this report on the company's financial status over a three-year period. The report was to be submitted to her by July 9, 2023.

Introduction

This report covers the profitability, liquidity, and financial stability of Exploration Duds Ltd during the period of 2021–2023. Ratio analysis was used to collect these data. The report focuses specifically on the credit management, debt management, inventory management, and earning power of Exploration Duds. It highlights key strengths and weaknesses and offers explanations for changes observed over the stated period. (There are limitations to the observations, which will be explained). The report also addresses Exploration Duds' future prospects and recommends strategies for improving the company's performance.

財務部主任簡內特·戴維斯下令完成此份公司近三年的財務表現報告。本報告應於 2023 年 7 月 9 日交給戴維斯主任。

前言

本報告涵蓋 Exploration Duds 有限公司 2021 年至 2023 年之盈利能力、流動資產與財務穩定狀況。研究方法採用比率分析。本報告將焦點放在 Exploration Duds 之信用管理、債務管理、存貨管理及獲利能力，指出公司的主要優勢與弱點，並就本段期間觀察到的改變提供解釋。（本觀察過程有一定的限制，報告中將說明。）此外，本報告還會就 Exploration Duds 的前景提出評論，並就提升公司績效提供策略。

Environmental Impact Report 2023

In Environmental Impact Report 2023, we cover a wide range of issues related to the environmental impact of SunTech's manufacturing and marketing branches as well as its economic performance. In addition to covering issues identified as having the most significant impacts and topics of growing interest, we also address the following questions:

❶ How do SunTech's business activities affect the environment and society?

❷ How do SunTech's operations create wealth, and how does this benefit stakeholders such as employees, suppliers, and local communities?

❸ How is SunTech achieving sustainable packaging and sourcing of its materials?

❹ How is SunTech limiting impacts to climate change and groundwater pollution?

❺ How do we manage sustainability and corporate responsibility to some of our key stakeholders, including consumers, customers, employees, suppliers, local communities, and the government?

❻ How can SunTech introduce proven clean technologies into its manufacturing plants without impeding its economic performance?

The principal audiences for both the online report and the overview are SunTech's employees, consumers, and investors, as well as the government and trendsetters in the fields of business and the environment.

在「2023 環境衝擊報告」中,我們針對 SunTech 公司的製造與行銷部門,以及公司經濟表現對環境的衝擊,探討一系列廣泛的相關議題。除了涵蓋被指出為影響最為顯著的議題、以及逐漸備受關注的主題外,我們也探討了以下問題:

❶ SunTech 公司的商業活動如何影響環境與社會?

❷ SunTech 的營運如何創造財富,此一點又如何為員工、供應商和當地居民等利害相關人帶來福利?

❸ SunTech 如何在包裝與原料取得上達到永續經營的目標?

❹ SunTech 如何限制在全球氣候變遷與地下水汙染上的衝擊?

❺ 我們如何達到永續經營,並對消費者、顧客、員工、供應商、當地居民與政府等重要利害關係人善盡企業責任?

❻ SunTech 如何在製造廠採用已獲驗證的綠色科技,同時又不影響經濟表現?

本線上報告及報告概要的主要目標讀者群為公司員工、顧客、投資人、政府及商業和環保領域之潮流先鋒。

Unit 20 撰寫報告的討論：研究方法
Writing the Discussion Section: Methodology

討論（discussion）的部分可能會包含很多**資訊性的內容**，所以務必要組織得清晰有條理。這個部分應該說明：

❶ 研究的方法或流程（methodology or procedures）

❷ 研究的結果（findings）

說明研究方法或**研究流程**的部分，是要解釋你是**如何收集資料的**。因為你的報告最後會依據這些資料提出建議，所以讀者需要知道這些資料是如何收集而來，並相信這些資料真實無誤。這部分應該做到下列兩件事：

◆ 解釋你執行哪些步驟（Explain what actions you took.）

◆ 解釋你為什麼執行這些步驟（Explain why you took the actions you did.）

最好**一步一步解釋你的流程**。首先，解釋你的研究方法，除非讀者已經熟悉報告的研究方法。如果你進行了某種測試，那就解釋這是什麼樣的測試，為什麼你做了這個測試。如果你之前讀了某些文獻，也說明原因。

接著，一步一步說明你的流程，例如，首先你招募了受試者，然後進行了測試，然後分析了測試的結果。或者是，首先你對員工進行問卷調查（polling），然後依據員工的需求跟電腦供應商聯絡，然後再把供應商能夠供應的電腦跟員工的需求進行比較。

這個部分在特定性質的報告中會比較長，比如市場調查報告，因為市場調查通常會與消費者進行多種不同的測試。如果是彙整多份書面資料製成的報告，研究流程的部分就會比較短。

20-1 | Sample: procedures section for a report on a form design project
流程範例：表格設計專案報告

Methodology

A qualitative research process was ideal for accomplishing our goals. Qualitative research uses small numbers of participants to realistically explore how and why consumers react to a form. For this project, we used focus groups to tell us what consumers see as barriers to their use of the form.

Testing

We tested 67 participants in seven test rounds in various locations based on the form's regional distribution. The testing was conducted over three months.

- Three focus groups with 10 participants in each (St. Louis, MO)
- Three focus groups with 10 participants in each (Portland, OR)
- One focus group with 7 participants (Tucson, AZ)

方法

質性的研究過程最適用於達到我們的目標。質性的研究利用少數受試者，實際探討消費者如何及為何對某一表單設計產生特定反應。就本專案，我們採用了焦點團體法。焦點團體能夠告訴我們，消費者會將哪些因素視為表單使用上的障礙。

測試

我們依表單分區發送的狀況，分成 7 輪在不同的地區對 67 名受試者進行測試。第一次測試與最後一次的測試時間相距三個月。

- 三組焦點團體，每組 10 名受試者（密蘇里州聖路易市）
- 三組焦點團體，每組 10 名受試者（奧勒岡州波特蘭市）
- 一組焦點團體，7 名受試者（亞利桑那州土桑市）

20-2 | Sample: procedures section for a report on job hunting
流程範例：說明蒐集求職報告資料

The data used in this report were gathered through two methods—a questionnaire survey and small group interviews. The baseline data were gathered through the questionnaire given to a large sample of graduates from a Singapore university in February 2023. The questionnaire was divided into three main sections: personal information, job hunting strategies, and views about current employment.

The survey sample consisted of 480 females and 510 males who were drawn proportionally from the areas of Business Studies, History, and Economics. Of the 990 questionnaires sent out, 900 were returned, and 876 were judged complete enough for meaningful analysis. In addition to the survey, interviews were held with small groups of recent graduates in their first year of full-time employment.

本報告採用的資料以兩種方法蒐集而來：問卷調查與小組訪談。基準資料乃透過問卷調查蒐集而來，大宗調查的對象為新加坡的大學畢業生，問卷於 2023 年 2 月發放。問卷內容分為三大部分：個人資料、求職策略、對現職工作的看法。

問卷調查的受訪者包括 480 位女性與 510 位男性，乃從商學系、歷史系和經濟系按照比率抽樣得來。發出去的 990 份問卷收回了 900 份，其中 876 份被判斷為填寫正確完整，足以進行分析。除問卷調查之外，也針對正職工作第一年的近期畢業生執行小型團體訪談。

也可以用表格的方式把資訊呈現出來

Type of test	Sample size	Date and site	Purpose of test	Form version tested
Focus group	Three groups with 10 participants in each	January 4, 2023; St. Louis, MO, and Portland, OR	To gather exploratory information	Paper form V1, Electronic form V1
Focus group	One group with 7 participants	March 15, 2023; Tucson, AZ	To gather exploratory information; to explore issues from first testing round	Paper form V1, Paper form V2, Brochure V1

測試類型	規模大小	日期與地點	測試目的	測試格式
焦點團體	三組焦點團體，每組 10 名受試者	2023 年 1 月 4 日，密蘇里州聖路易市與奧勒岡州波特蘭市	收集探索性資料	紙本 V1，電子形式 V1
焦點團體	一組焦點團體，7 名受試者	2023 年 3 月 15 日，亞利桑那州土桑市	收集探索性資料；探索從第一次測試中發現的問題	紙本 V1、V2，手冊 V1

撰寫報告的討論：結果
Writing the Discussion Section: Findings

結果（findings）的部分應包含哪些資訊？這會是報告中最長的一部分，因為在這裡要把調查過程中得到的事實資訊呈現出來。報告的結果應該要能回答這類的問題：

- ◆ 對報告的主題或問題來說**最重要的結果／因素**為何？
- ◆ 研究的結果**支持任何理論**嗎？
- ◆ 研究有沒有發現**新的資訊或問題**？
- ◆ 研究結果中有**令人意外的地方**嗎？

撰寫這個部分時，記得仔細想想讀者對此已經有多少了解，不要浪費時間報告已經是眾所周知的事情，但另一方面，也不要報告太過複雜、讀者無法理解的內容。這部分的內容要**有組織、有條理**，最好**按照主題**分項呈現結果。比如說，在一份可行性報告中，可以按照「發展費用」、「人力可能性」、「地點可能性」等主題呈現調查的結果；市場調查報告則可以按照年齡層或媒體種類呈現調查的結果。撰寫報告結果時，仔細想想怎麼組織這部分的內容最好。

1 如何在報告上呈現研究結果？

呈現結果的方式主要取決於你的主題和資訊的量。技術（technical）和統計（statistical）資訊，通常整理成表格最易於理解。你可以把表格插入文中，有需要時請讀者回頭參考。如果你做的是質性（qualitative）研究，最好能引述受訪者的話來支持你的結果。

Z1-1 | Short sample: findings section 短篇結果範例

Findings

❶ Employees are generally dissatisfied with the current benefits package.

❷ Three-quarters of employees chose "dental benefits" as their top priority for an additional benefit.

❸ Half of all employees would like more paid sick leave.

❹ Two-thirds of employees would like the option of taking more unpaid leave.

❺ Older employees repeatedly complained of trouble getting prescription medicine through the current HMO.

❻ Employees aged 22-32 cited slow accumulation of vacation time as the biggest flaw in the current package.

❼ Half of all employees would be interested in more stock options.

結果

❶ 公司員工對目前的福利政策普遍感到不滿。

❷ 四分之三的員工最希望優先選擇「牙科醫療福利」加入目前的福利政策。

❸ 一半的員工希望增加帶薪病假的日數。

❹ 三分之二的員工希望有更多的無薪假。

❺ 年紀較長的員工一再抱怨，透過目前的 HMO 健保組織取得處方藥困難重重。

❻ 二十二到三十二歲的員工認為，目前福利政策中最大的缺陷是假期累積速度太慢。

❼ 一半的員工希望有更多的認股權。

21-Z | Longer sample: findings section 長篇結果範例

Target Market Use of Technology

Respondents spend many hours each week doing online activities for school, work, and recreation. The most frequent answer was 7–11 hours per week (28 percent), followed by 12–15 hours per week (17.5 percent). The overall mean is 19.0 hours per week, and the median is 16 hours per week. Some respondents reported spending a major amount of time online—6.0 percent of respondents spend more than 40 hours a week online.

For students in the target market, time spent online varied by major. Engineering students had the highest use, whereas life sciences and education majors had the lowest use (see Appendix C). For working adults in the target market, time spent online seems to be a personal choice, affected somewhat by income but otherwise unrelated to other factors. (Respondents with incomes greater than $50,000 per year spent slightly more time online.)

Table 3. Frequency of Online Activities

	Percentage of respondents engaged	Frequency of use
Accessing email	99.7%	Daily
Shopping online	80%	Monthly
Browsing the Internet	90%	Daily
Researching projects	81%	Several times per week
Playing computer games	69%	Weekly
Sending instant messages	89%	Daily
Blogging	25%	Weekly

目標市場之科技使用現況

受訪者每週花好幾個小時為課業、工作和休閒娛樂等目的使用網路，其中以每週花 7 到 11 個小時在網上的受訪者占最大比例（28% 的受訪者），每週花 12 到 15 個小時在網上的受訪者次之（17.5% 的受訪者）。整個結果的總平均值為每週 19.0 小時，中位數為每週 16 小時。也有受訪者每週花大量的時間在網上：6% 的受訪者每週花 40 個小時以上使用網路。

目標市場中的學生使用網路的時間依主修科目而不同。工程科系學生使用網路時間最長，生命科學系學生與教育系學生使用網路時間最短（參見附錄 C）。對目標市場中的在職成年人來說，使用網路的時間似乎取決於個人的喜好；收入稍微有些影響，但是此外與其他因素都無關。（年收入超過 50,000 美元的受訪者，花在網路上的時間稍多一點。）

表格三　網路活動頻率

	受訪者的使用比率	使用頻率
電子郵件	99.7%	每天
線上購物	80%	每個月
瀏覽網頁	90%	每天
專案研究	81%	每週幾次
電玩	69%	每週
傳送即時訊息	89%	每天
部落格	25%	每週

Unit 22 撰寫報告的結論
Writing the Conclusions Section

　　結論（conclusion）的部分，是你就收集的資訊發表意見的地方。你可以說明你從研究結果中得到什麼想法。（**但是你在結論中還不需要建議該怎麼行動，因為這一點可以在後面的建議部分說明**。）結論是報告中非常重要的一部分：讀者當然想看到你的原始數據（raw data），但是你就這些數據得出的結論才能夠支持你提出的建議，甚至影響讀者的行動。

　　結論應該明確地得自你的**數據資料**，有時候結論部分可以同時呈現研究結果與提出建議，以清楚顯示兩者之間的關係。如果你覺得你的結論跟前面的數據資料沒有明顯的關聯，可以簡短提及結論是從何而來。

22-1 | Sample: conclusions section 1 結論範例 1

Conclusions

Upon investigation, both the Plum Computers ProBook 555 and the Laser 8500 Series laptop computers suit our corporate needs and meet All Purpose Training Company requirements.

The long-term benefit to the company was the foremost consideration in our comparison of available laptop computers. The main factors analyzed were initial purchasing expenses, warranty, speed, size, memory, and software suitability. The computers also had to be easily adaptable to new technology such as email, video conferencing, and presentation aids to meet future company requirements.

Although both companies have the corporate user in mind, the two computers are distinct. Plum Computers appears to offer the exceptional corporate package.

結論

經過調查之後，我們發現 Plum Computers ProBook 555 和 Laser 8500 系列筆記型電腦都符合本公司（All Purpose Training Company）的需求與要求。

對公司的長期利益是比較各款筆記型電腦時的首要考量。主要的分析因素包括初期購買開銷、保固服務、速度、大小、記憶體與軟體適配性。此外電腦應能依公司未來需要，靈活更新技術，如電子郵件、視訊會議和簡報輔助工具等。

雖然兩款電腦都有考量到企業用戶的需求，但兩者仍相當不同。Plum Computers 似乎提供絕佳的企業方案。

Keep it simple

Our research consistently showed that target audiences are bewildered by complex comparisons, disorienting typefaces, too much text, and competing ideas. When given too much complex information, test subjects often don't even bother to read it. Our revised pamphlet minimizes the burden on consumers by simplifying the presentation. We eliminated redundancies and wordiness, used simpler language, clarified concepts, and gave key context information up front.

On the other hand, test subjects have reacted negatively to a lack of information and to oversimplification. A pamphlet that does not present enough information or enough options would be accessible, but terribly uninformative. We value clarity over brevity. The challenge is to find the balance between as few words as possible and enough information so audiences are educated.

越簡單越好

我們的研究一再顯示，複雜的比較、繁複的字體、太多的文字和互相矛盾的內容，常使目標讀者看得一頭霧水。如果資訊太多，受試者甚至根本看都不會看。我們修訂版手冊便以精簡為宗旨，以減少消費者閱讀的負擔。我們刪掉了多餘的文字和語句，採用簡單的語言與清晰的概念，並一開始就點出關鍵的背景資訊。

另一方面，如果資訊不足或過於簡化，受試者也會產生負面的反應。一本資訊不足或選擇不多的手冊雖然容易閱讀，但是無法傳遞資訊。我們重視清晰的原則，勝過簡短的原則，其中的挑戰就在於在下列兩者之間找到平衡：文字越少越好，但給讀者的資訊也要足夠。

Don't believe me? Maybe you'll believe the brainy looking exec pointing at the flow chart.

　　「建議」（recommendation）部分將根據前面的結論，說明你覺得**應該採取什麼行動**。你的建議應該要**具體明確**，並清楚地延伸自前面的結論。「建議」部分的格式，取決於整份報告的長度與整體格式：有些報告會以編號列表的格式，依照重要程度列出建議的行動；有些報告則按照結論部分的大綱，依序提出建議。不管你選擇哪種格式，最重要的就是這些建議要連貫、有條理（coherent），並與前面的數據、資料及結論直接相關。

23-1 | Sample: recommendations section 建議範例

5. Recommendations

To manage the current influx of customer complaints and prevent new complaints in the future, we recommend the following policies.

5.1 To assuage current complaints:

5.1a Compensate customers: When a customer has justifiably complained, we should refund his or her money in whatever form it was originally paid. To maintain goodwill, we also recommend giving these customers a voucher worth 10% of the price of the original goods to encourage repeat visits to our company.

5.1b Dismiss underperforming staff: Any staff member who is the object of more than two justifiable complaints should be summarily dismissed. Returning customers will not want to interact with the same staff members who caused them trouble in the first place. Staff who cannot uphold our company standards should be replaced.

5.2 To prevent future complaints:

5.2a Train staff: To ensure that sales staff members no longer advise customers to purchase the wrong products, we should provide product training before they begin the job. This guideline should be added to our training manuals.

5.2b Monitor new staff: To reduce the possibility of new salespeople making incorrect recommendations to customers, we recommend instituting a "shadowing program." New staff members will shadow experienced sales team members for the first month of their employment. This guideline should also be in our staff manuals and procedures. This new policy will create some extra cost, as more staff will have to work certain shifts, but the added costs will be offset by maintaining our current customer base.

5. 建議

為了解決目前顧客投訴橫生的問題，並預防未來發生再有客訴，我們建議下列的政策。

5.1 安撫目前顧客客訴：

5.1a 補償顧客：如果顧客的投訴合理有根據，我們應該全額依原付款方式退回顧客所付金額。為了維護信譽，我們建議再贈送價值原消費金額 10% 的禮券，以吸引顧客再次向本公司購物。

5.1b 解僱表現欠佳的員工：被顧客合理投訴超過兩次的員工應該立即解僱，因為回訪的顧客不會想再跟這些曾引起困擾的員工有任何接觸。無法達到公司要求的員工應該被取代。

5.2 預防未來再發生客訴：

5.2a 員工訓練：為預防業務人員再就產品選擇方面，給予顧客錯誤的建議，員工應該在開始就職之前，先就產品內容接受訓練。這個準則應該加入公司的訓練手冊。

5.2b 監督新進員工：為預防新進業務人員給予顧客不當建議的可能性，我們建議設立「影子實習」的制度。新進業務人員將於第一個月跟隨資深業務員進行影子實習；此準則也應該加入公司的員工手冊與流程。此新政策會增加一些額外的成本，因為特定時段需上班的員工會增加，但是維持目前的顧客群將能抵銷此成本。

3. Program Management Organization

a. **Finding:** The Project Now (PN) Program Management structure outlined in the Business Case is understaffed.

b. **Description:** Section 5 of the Business Case discusses an action plan for PN, including an organizational structure. In the Business Case, staffing for the various milestones relies on dedicated PME employees, with support from outside contractors and temporary staff from other company offices. However, the staff members dedicated to the PN team are not adequate to fill the task hours involved. Relying on non-dedicated staff for critical tasks increases the risk of mistakes. The planning and design phases for the first period of PN are particularly thinly staffed.

c. **Recommendation:** The Company must consider adding more dedicated staff to PN. Instead of bringing in contractors, allocate dedicated staff hours to focused working groups formed for specific short-term tasks. A high-level senior management board could help oversee these work groups. Work groups themselves can help organize outside contractors and other temporary staff as needed.

4. Hardware/Software Specifications

a. **Finding:** The hardware and software recommended in the Business Case are out-of-date.

b. **Description:** Section F2 of the Business Case discusses the hardware/software specifications. These specifications were developed using technology available at the time. They do not represent current options.

c. **Recommendation:** Given the rapid advances in technology, we must update our equipment needs to reflect the current state of the art. Equipment recommendations should be reviewed for the required level of performance for PN's data storage needs. Input from IT professionals should be collected.

3. 計畫管理小組的組織

   a. **結果**：提案企畫書中提出的 Project Now（PN）計畫管理小組人員不足。

   b. **描述**：企畫書第 5 節討論到 PN 的行動計畫，包括其組織人員結構。企畫書中寫到，各里程碑之參與人員主要為專職的 PME 同事，輔以外包支援人員和自其他部門暫時調來的同事。然而 PN 計畫的專職人力並不足以完成任務所需的時數，而於重要任務中採用非專職員工，又會增加出錯的風險。PN 第一期的籌劃與設計階段人員不足的狀況尤為嚴重。

   c. **建議**：公司必須考慮增加 PN 計畫專職的人數。我們建議不要引入外包人員，並把專職同事的工作時間，用於運作為特定短期任務成立的專門工作小組，可由資深高層主管組成的管理委員會協助監督這些工作小組，而工作小組自己可以依需要，來安排外包人員和期他臨時人力的事宜。

4. 硬體及軟體規格

   a. **結果**：企畫書中建議的硬體及軟體已過時。

   b. **描述**：企畫書 F2 一節討論到硬體及軟體規格。這些規格為當時技術的產品，無法呈現目前的可選方案。

   c. **建議**：鑒於電腦科技日新月異，我們必須更新公司的設備需求，以反映當代潮流。設備建議須以 PN 資料儲存所需的功能級別重新檢討，此外應參考資訊技術專業人員的意見。

DISCUSSION & EXERCISE 7   Units 18–23

1 Review the concepts

   ❶ What are the major parts of a report?

   ❷ In which section or sections of a report can you express your opinions?

   ❸ What kind of information should you include in the methodology section of a report?

   ❹ What does "scope" mean in reference to reports?

2 True (T) or False (F)

   ❶ ☐ True ☐ False   A report is more formal than a memo.

   ❷ ☐ True ☐ False   An executive summary should not contain recommendations.

3 Multiple choice

1 What kind of report tells the status of an ongoing project? _____

(A) A business plan   (B) A progress report   (C) A market research report

2 What kind of report explores the possibilities for a new business? _____

(A) A business plan   (B) A financial report   (C) A market research report

3 What kind of report provides information about the people who are likely to buy a certain product? _____

(A) A progress report   (B) A technical report   (C) A market research report

4 Write a paragraph to explain the findings in this table.

	Read the whole report	Read the executive summary only	Read the introduction, conclusions, and recommendations	Read some other combination of sections	Do not read reports
Front-line staff	1%	2%	2%	5%	90%
Analysts	85%	6%	4%	4%	1%
Senior analysts	72%	13%	12%	0%	3%
Managers	51%	24%	6%	7%	12%
Senior managers	15%	39%	11%	9%	26%
Executives	48%	34%	6%	6%	6%

Table 1: Report reading patterns by position

5 Context: *BigTime* magazine sales have been down for the last two quarters. Its publisher has commissioned a report to find out why. Fill in the Conclusions and Recommendations sections based on the findings in the report.

Findings

Price: The price of *BigTime* and similar magazines has stayed the same for the last three years.

Readership: The majority of *BigTime* readers are aged 18-25; the second largest category is 25-35. Polls of readers found that they tend to subscribe to *BigTime* for no more two years.

Content:
- Readers aged 25-35 say they "like" the content of the magazine (as shown in cover story titles)
- Readers aged 18-25 say they "like" the content of the magazine
- Readers aged 14-18 say they are not interested in the content of the magazine

Design: All readers say they find the covers "dull"

Improvements: When polled, readers over 18 preferred to have more "freebies" in the magazine—for example, sweepstakes and contests. Readers under 18 wanted more quizzes and games. All readers were interested in monthly product samples. Few readers were interested in a new gaming section.

1. Conclusions

_____

_____

_____

_____

_____

_____

_____

_____

_____

_____

2. Recommendations

_____
_____
_____
_____
_____
_____
_____
_____
_____
_____
_____
_____
_____
_____

6 **Which section of a report should this paragraph be in?**

Trial customer dissatisfaction was centered around the new product's limited battery life and its easily scratched surface. There were few, if any, complaints about its function, sound, appearance, or cost. The following changes would bring the product more in line with customer expectations. First of all, we suggest extending the battery life of the product (either by using higher-quality batteries or changing to a different type of battery) or offering customers a lightweight, portable battery charger free with the purchase of the product. Secondly, we suggest selling the product with a clear protective cover to prevent scratching. Finally, we suggest using new materials for the face.

(A) The recommendations section.

(B) The procedures section.

(C) The conclusions section.

(D) The terms of reference.

Ans: _____

請求信與回覆信
Letters of Request and Letters of Response

---

catalog 產品型錄

業者用來列出旗下各項販售商品的書冊。

copyright 版權

獨家生產、出版、販賣或經銷某一產品之內容與形式的法定權力（如文學、音樂、藝術品）。

follow up 追蹤詢問

追蹤或詢問某事的後續發展。寄出請求信後，應耐心等待一段時間再做追蹤詢問。

grant 允許

同意對方的請求。收到請求信後應回覆對方，說明是否允許該請求。

**letter of recommendation
推薦信**

由熟識的人撰寫的信，通常是老師、雇主或具有相當威信之人士，在信中評估、並肯定被推薦人有擔任某一職位的能力。

promotion 升職

在職位或級別上被提升。

raise 加薪

也稱 salary increase，也就是薪水增加。

request 請求

請求對方提供某項事物，或是請求對方提供的事物。

response letter 回覆信

回覆對方來信的信件。為求禮貌，回覆信應在收到來信後盡速寄出。

**stamped, self-addressed envelope
回郵信封（貼好郵票並寫上地址）**

貼好郵票並寫上回郵地址的信封，方便對方直接將所需資料寄回給來信人。

tact 得體

知道如何待人接物最恰當、最周到，不會傷到別人或引起不悅。

Unit 24　如何撰寫請求信？
How do I write a letter of request?

1 什麼是請求信？

「request」的意思就是跟對方提出特定請求，因此**請求信（letter of request）就是向對方做出請求的信**。常見的商務請求包括：

- 請求面試
- 請求會面
- 請求撰寫推薦信（reference）
- 請求加薪或升職（raise or promotion）
- 請求捐款
- 請求准許使用版權內容（copyright permission）
- 請求提供特定資訊或產品

2 如何撰寫請求信

請求信的撰寫原則就跟其他商務書信一樣，應該**清晰有組織**，並有一定的**正式性**。請求信是用來請求對方，所以務必要**禮貌得體（tactful）**。撰寫請求信前需要仔細的計劃，好讓你提出的請求對對方來說**越簡單越好**，這樣對方也更有可能應允你的請求。一般來說，撰寫請求信應遵照下列的原則：

❶ **禮貌**：語氣要禮貌客氣，並顯示你珍視對方的時間與付出。
❷ **直接**：一開始就説明你的要求（除非是會違背禮貌得體的原則），這樣對方就會立刻看到你的請求，以免對方還沒看到請求就把信丟掉。要讓對方知道，你不是在浪費他的時間，而是立刻講到重點。
❸ **簡短**：直接説明你要什麼，不要浪費文字。
❹ **減輕對方的負擔**：清楚告訴對方，你希望他如何滿足你的請求，並盡一切力量讓對方可以簡單地完成你的請求。（例如如果你想請對方為你寫推薦信，那就把你的簡歷或成績一併附上，並附上貼好郵票、寫好收件地址的回郵信封。）
❺ **盡量不要道歉**：不要為你引起的麻煩道歉；相反地，利用這個機會稱讚對方。
❻ **有耐心**：信件寄出後，給對方一些時間，之後才寫信或打電話追蹤詢問。

3 撰寫簡單或常見的請求信

根據你的請求和讀者，自行檢視下列兩個問題：

- 我的請求**合理**嗎？
- 這種請求**常見**嗎？（例如零售商就會常常收到索取產品目錄的請求信；教授或教練可能常常收到學生來信要求推薦信。）

如果兩個問題的答案都是「是」，你的請求信就可以寫得簡明扼要。

4 撰寫複雜的請求信

　　如果你的請求比較複雜，或是會引起對方比較多的麻煩，寫信前就要多思考一下。同樣地，先自問一些關鍵問題，然後依此計劃信的內容。

◆ 我的請求**合理**嗎？（所有的請求都應該要合理。）
◆ 對方**需要做什麼**？（想想對方需要採取哪些步驟，才能滿足你的請求。）
◆ 我**如何協助對方**完成這些步驟？（並在信中盡量提供協助）

　　列出對方需要採取哪些步驟後，看看其中有**哪些步驟是你可以協助他完成的**。如果你需要對方寄東西給你，那你最好就附上貼好郵票、寫好地址的回郵信封。如果你需要對方跟另外一個人聯絡，那就附上這個人的聯絡方法。如果你請求加薪或升職，那就列出你認為自己應該加薪或升職的原因。

Z4-1 | Requesting a catalog 索取產品目錄

Universidade de Brasilia

Campus Universitario Darcy Ribeiro
Predio da Reitoria, 3 andar, 70910-900 Brasilia, DF, Brasil

May 8, 2023

Xiaowei Yang
OneZero Technology Co., Ltd
3F, 222 Jhongshan N Road, Section 2
Taipei, 10450 Taiwan

Dear Ms. Yang:

I am the chairman of the New Technology Acquisition Committee at the University of Brasilia, and I am interested in learning more about your Acronis products. Please send me a current product catalog at your earliest convenience. If you have any other literature on the Acronis brand, I would appreciate receiving that as well.

Thank you for your attention.

Yours truly,

Beatrice Azevedo

Beatrice Azevedo
Professor, Ciência da Computação
Universidade de Brasilia

> 這封信簡短、簡單、扼要。信中的請求對對方來說並不是很麻煩的事，所以寫信人也沒有必要用長篇大論說明為什麼她需要產品目錄，或是怎麼把目錄寄過去。

> 楊女士您好：
>
> 我是巴西利亞大學新科技購進委員會的主席，想多了解貴公司的 Acronis 產品。方便的話，請您盡快寄一份最新的產品目錄過來。如果您還有 Acronis 相關的資料，希望也能一併寄來。
>
> 謝謝費心。

Catherine Davies
15 Qingtong Road, 26-1011
Pudong New District, Shanghai, PRC 201203

November 2, 2023

Nina Lin
Double Design
Room 205, Building 3
Lane 2498, Pudong Avenue
Shanghai, PRC

Dear Ms. Lin:

I am writing to request an interview regarding Double Design's opening for a graphic designer.

I am a recent graduate of the Academy of Art with a degree in graphic design. For the past six months, I have interned with Studio Design in Shanghai, learning to apply the skills I gained in school. A friend and fellow student at my university, Wayne Hu, who is currently working at Double Design, recommended that I contact you about the graphic design position. I would appreciate an opportunity to learn more about the position and to discuss how I can contribute to your company.

I have enclosed my résumé for your reference. Please feel free to contact me for any reason at (021) 5184 3155 or by email at cath.davies@bmail.com. Thank you for your attention. I look forward to hearing from you.

Best regards,

Catherine Davies

Catherine Davies

Enc. (1)

林女士您好：

本次來信意在請求面試貴公司平面設計師一職。

我近期自藝術學院平面設計系畢業，過去六個月在上海的 Studio Design 實習，學習學以致用。我的大學同學兼友人 Wayne Hu 目前也在貴公司任職，他推薦我寫信給您洽詢平面設計師一職事宜。非常希望能有面試的機會，以多了解該職位的工作性質，並探討我能如何為貴公司效勞。

隨信附上個人履歷。我的聯絡方式：(021) 5184 3155 或 cath.davies@bmail.com，歡迎不吝與我聯繫。謝謝您，希望能得到您的回覆。

Daniel Clarke
Flat 2, 17 Jones St
NORTH SYDNEY NSW 2060
Australia

May 8, 2023

回覆信 → P. 129

Professor Beatrice Azevedo
Universidade de Brasilia
Campus Universitario Darcy Ribeiro
Predio da Reitoria, 3 andar
70910-900 Brasilia, DF, Brazil

Dear Professor Azevedo:

I am writing to request a letter of recommendation from you based on my performance in your class and my experience working with you on my thesis. ❶ I appreciate the time and effort you will have to put into writing a letter of recommendation, so please allow me to provide some background information that should be helpful. ❷

I took your class PHP Programming during the Spring 2020 semester. I received an A on my final exam and for my overall course grade. During the Fall 2021 semester, I worked on my final thesis, "Performance Measurement of Program Executions," in which I compared current methods of performance measurement and proposed a new version, which has been successful so far and is, I think, a superior assessment tool. During that time, we met biweekly to discuss my progress. Thanks to your guidance, I earned an A on my thesis. After graduation, I went to work for HH Network Solutions in Sydney, Australia.

I am now applying for a position as a programmer at Top Integrated Performance, a cutting-edge company also located in Sydney. The main responsibility of the position will be programming with C#, C++, and embedded C. The main qualities I believe they are looking for are innovative thinking and a strong work ethic. ❸

I hope the information in this letter is helpful and that you feel comfortable enough with my performance to write this recommendation. ❹ Please find enclosed a self-addressed, stamped envelope that you can use to mail the recommendation. ❺

Thank you again for your time. Please feel free to contact me for any reason at clarkedaniel@gmail.com or + 61-2-97876131.

Yours truly,

Daniel Clarke

Daniel Clarke

Enc. (1)

❶ 這封信比較長，寫信人想確定他提供了足夠的資訊，讓教授能夠想起他，並寫出中肯而正面的推薦信。此處的說法在請求撰寫推薦信的信裡經常用到：其中的 based on 用來指出雙方之間曾有過什麼樣的接觸，例如「**based on our collaboration on the XZY project**」（基於我們在XZY企畫的合作經驗），或是「**based on my performance as your web designer**」（基於我身為您旗下網頁設計師的表現）。

❷ 這句話顯示寫信人知道自己提出的要求比較複雜（I appreciate the time and effort . . . ），因此他主動提供相關的資訊，一方面證明他的在學表現不錯，一方面也減輕對方的負擔（. . . please allow me to provide some background information . . . ）。

❸ 在第二段回顧自己在教授課上的表現後，寫信人簡短解釋了他目前欲申請的職位，並特意提到新職位所需的特質，這樣教授就知道在寫推薦信時應該評論學生這方面的特質。

❹ 請求對方為你寫推薦信時，最好表示你知道對方可能沒有時間寫這封推薦信，或是像在這封信裡，表示你知道對方可能無法寫出只有褒獎的推薦信，暗示你了解對方可能並不會如你自己這麼讚賞自己，是謙遜的表現。

❺ 最後，隨信附上寫好地址、貼好郵票的回郵信封，減輕對方的負擔，因為他就不用自己再買郵票、寫地址，而你也可以確保信封上的地址是對的。

阿茲維多教授尊鑒：

您好，寫這封信是想請您為我寫一封推薦信。我是您過去課上的學生，畢業論文也由您擔任指導教授。❶ 寫一封推薦信必定會占據您不少時間與精力，所以容我在此提供可能會有幫助的相關資訊。❷

我在 2020 年下學期上過您的 PHP 程式設計課，期末考成績和期末總成績皆為 A。2021 年上學期我專心撰寫畢業論文《程式執行效能衡量》，在論文中我比較了現行的程式效能衡量方法，並提出一套新的衡量方法；該方法目前為止運用起來很成功，而且我認為是更佳的衡量工具。那段時間我跟教授每兩週見一次面，討論論文的進展。多虧教授的指導，最後我的畢業論文成績得到 A。畢業後，我開始在澳洲雪梨的 HH Network Solutions 上班。

目前我計劃應徵雪梨頂尖的 Top Integrated Performance 公司程式設計師的職位。該職位的主要職務是以 C#、C++ 和嵌入 C 語言來設計程式。我相信他們要求的主要特質是創新思考和強烈的工作倫理。

希望信中資訊對您有些幫助，也希望我的表現讓教授樂意寫這封推薦信。❹ 隨信附上寫好地址的回郵信封，屆時您可以用該信封把推薦信寄出。❺

再次謝謝教授為此付出的時間。如果有任何問題，我的聯絡方式是：clarkedaniel@gmail.com 或 + 61-2-97876131。

Daniel Clarke
Flat 2, 17 Jones Street
NORTH SYDNEY NSW 2060
Australia

May 8, 2023

Professor Beatrice Azevedo
Universidade de Brasilia
Campus Universitario Darcy Ribeiro
Predio da Reitoria, 3 andar
70910-900 Brasilia, DF, Brasil

Dear Professor Azevedo:

I am writing to request a letter of recommendation from you. I took your PHP Programming class during the Spring 2020 semester. Then, during the Fall 2021 semester, I met with you biweekly to discuss my final thesis.

I hope that you feel comfortable writing a letter of recommendation for me. I appreciate the time and effort that it requires. ———————————

Thank you again for your time. Please feel free to contact me for any reason at clarkedaniel@gmail.com or + 61-2-97876131.

Yours truly,

Daniel Clarke

Daniel Clarke

阿茲維多教授尊鑒：

您好，寫這封信是想請您為我寫一封推薦信。我在 2020 年下學期上過您的 PHP 程式設計課，然後在 2021 年上學期，我跟教授每兩週見一次面討論我的畢業論文。

希望教授樂意為我寫這封推薦信。這一定會花去教授不少時間與精力，我非常感激。

再次謝謝教授為此付出的時間。如果有任何問題，我的聯絡方式是：
clarkedaniel@gmail.com 或 + 61-2-97876131。

這封信在文字上是很有禮貌（I appreciate the time and effort that it requires.），但是因為寫信人幾乎沒有提供任何相關資訊，所以收信人必須自己收集所有相關的資料去寫這封推薦信，因此這樣提出請求很不尊重對方，做法太過草率，完全不顧慮對方寶貴的時間。

The University of Sydney
NSW 2006, Australia
+61 2 9361 3332

August 31, 2023

Susan Waray
Hirshorn Library
The University of Sydney
NSW 2006
Australia

Dear Susan:

❶ 寫信者在第一段先表明感謝和對工作的喜愛，作為請求的伏筆，最後一句才點出請求加薪的重點，避免若是一開頭就要求加薪，會顯得太過唐突。

❶ As you know, I have been employed at the Hirshorn Library for the past two years. As you also know, I am grateful for all the opportunities that have come my way during this time. I enjoy my work very much. As the new semester starts, I have been considering the new responsibilities that I have either been assigned or taken on. I would like to discuss the possibility of a pay raise to reflect these increased responsibilities.

❷ I began working in Access Services and am now serving as "Access Services Chief." As such, my responsibilities include:
- Monitoring the lending cycle of books to ensure stock levels are appropriate and accurately reflected in the computer system.
- Co-managing the Wheaton storage facility.
- Coordinating with building security.
- Maintaining basic library machines.
- Compiling some circulation statistics.
- Assisting with the annual report to the director of the university.

❷ ❸ 寫信者分別以兩個項目符號列表，說明職務內的工作內容以及職務之外的活動，方便讀信者可以評估請求是否合理。

❸ In addition, I have been voluntarily involved in activities or responsibilities outside my job description, including:
- Organizing and hosting the "Know Your Undergraduate Library" program that ran through September, familiarizing students with our facilities and policies.
- Designing a more efficient system for scheduling student staff.
- Designing a more efficient system for tracking library reserves.

❹ I believe that a merit raise is a reasonable request in light of my current contributions and my continued initiative in improving our library services. I would appreciate the opportunity to discuss a pay raise in person. I can be available at your convenience.

Thank you for your attention to my request. I love working at the library and look forward to discussing updated list of my contributions.

Sincerely,

Wanda Kerr

Wanda Kerr

請求信亦可用來請求主管給予加薪或升職，此時信中也要提供詳細的資訊。公司沒有義務平白提供更高的薪水或職位，所以寫信者有責任提出證據和理由支持自身請求。

蘇珊您好：

您知道我在 Hirshorn 圖書館工作已經兩年了，您也知道我非常感激這段時間我遇到的各種機會。我非常喜歡我的工作。隨著新學期的開始，我仔細考慮了一下我被指派或主動擔起的各種新責任。基於工作責任的增加，我想跟您討論一下加薪的可能性。

我就職起初在圖書檢索服務組工作，現在的職稱是「圖書檢索服務組組長」，職務包括：

◆ 監控圖書的借閱週期，確定館內有足夠的存書量，並如實反映在電腦系統上。
◆ 共同管理 Wheaton 存書系統。
◆ 與大樓保安進行協調。
◆ 館內基本機器設備之維護。
◆ 編纂部分的圖書流通統計資料。
◆ 協助完成呈交大學主任之年度報告。

此外，我還主動參與職務範圍之外的活動或責任，包括：

◆ 九月分籌劃和主辦「了解你的大學圖書館」活動，協助學生熟悉圖書館的設備和政策。
◆ 為安排工讀生工作時間設計更有效率的系統。
◆ 為追蹤圖書館藏書設計更有效率的系統。

考慮到我目前的貢獻與持續增進圖書服務的努力，我想要求加薪是一個合理的請求。希望能有機會跟您面對面地討論加薪事宜，討論的時間由您決定，我都可以配合。

謝謝您抽空看完我的請求，我真的很喜歡在這間圖書館工作，期待和您討論我最新的職務列表。

❹ 寫信者再次強調加薪的請求，並表示願意在任何時間和主管就請求事宜進行討論，顯示自己對請求的自信，有利對方更認真考量。

Quality Training, Ltd
1000 Condor Drive, Suite 4
San Bruno, CA 94066
415.734.9857

July 9, 2023

Permissions Department
Harbinger Publishing
309 Ditmas Avenue
Brooklyn, NY 11218+4901

Dear Permissions Editor:

I am writing to ask your permission to reprint the cartoon *Big Bang* (2013) by Norbert Papp in an industry report. The report will be published in *Trade Magazine Quarterly*, Winter 2023 issue.

If you do not control sole copyright for the requested materials, I would appreciate any information you can provide whom I should contact, including current addresses if available.

Thank you for your attention. Please let me know if there is anything I can do to facilitate this process. Feel free to contact me for any reason at 415.734.9857 or by email at cooks@quality.com.

I look forward to hearing from you.

Regards,

Sam Cook

Sam Cook

版權部編輯惠鑑：

本次來信是想請貴出版社准許我們在一份產業報告中，轉載 Norbert Papp 繪製的漫畫《Big Bang》（2013）。該報告將發表於《產業雜誌季刊》2023 年冬季版。

如果貴社並不獨家擁有這份漫畫的版權，懇請告知我應和何人接洽，若方便也請提供最新的聯絡地址。

非常謝謝您的幫忙。如果過程中有什麼我能夠幫上忙的地方，或是有任何的問題或需要，歡迎與我聯絡：415.734.9857 或 cooks@quality.com。

誠心期盼您的回覆。

programmer

graphic design

catalog

Unit 25　回覆請求信：答應對方的請求
Letter of requests: making positive responses

　　如何回覆一封請求信，當然**取決於你是否要答應對方的請求**。

　　答應對方請求的回覆信（response letter）可以盡量**簡短直接**。但是如果是要**拒絕**對方的請求，那最好**婉轉**一點，並説明拒絕的原因。

　　如果是給予肯定的回覆，那就可以盡量**簡單扼要**。為了確認雙方都完全了解請求的內容，最好**再提一次對方的請求信**，並**簡短覆述對方的請求**。

　　下面是就前一單元看過的 24-2、24-5 兩封請求信，給予肯定回覆的回覆信。

DOUBLE DESIGN

Room 205, Building 3
Lane 2498, Pudong Avenue
Shanghai, PRC

November 9, 2023

Catherine Davies
15 Qingtong Road, 26-1011
Pudong New District, Shanghai, PRC 201203

Dear Ms. Davies:

Thank you for your letter inquiring about the graphic design position at Double Design. Unfortunately, we had already filled the position by the time I received your letter.

However, I am impressed with your résumé and the work samples you sent. I expect Double Design to continue to expand, given the number of upcoming projects. I would like to meet with you to discuss a possible internship or temporary work on some projects that could lead to a permanent position here.

If these possibilities interest you, why don't we meet at the Double Design office next Friday, November 17, at 10 a.m.? Please call my secretary, Li-Ping Lin, at (021) 6194-2105 to confirm.

Best,

Nina Lin

Nina Lin
Creative Director
Double Design

> 雖然這封信嚴格來說並沒有答應對方的請求，但是仍然算是肯定的回覆，因為提出請求的人還是得到面試的機會，而且有機會能夠在該公司工作。

戴維斯女士您好：

謝謝您來信洽詢本公司平面設計一職。可惜在我收到您的來信時，本職缺已經找到合適的人選。

不過您寄來的履歷和設計樣本非常出色。我們近期將有不少新的專案，所以我預期 Double Design 會繼續擴展，因此我希望能跟您見個面，討論可否請您可以先實習一段時間，或是暫時加入專案工作，之後就有可能得到全職的職位。

如果您有興趣，也許我們可以下星期五（11 月 17 日）早上 10 點在本公司見個面？請您再來電跟我的祕書林立萍確認：(021) 6194 2105。

下面也是一封簡短、直接、肯定的回覆信。如果當初 Daniel Clarke 寄出的是第二封草率、資訊不全的版本（24-4），你覺得他還會得到這麼肯定的回覆嗎？

25-2 | Responding to a request for a letter of recommendation
回覆 24-3 請求撰寫推薦信

請求信 → P. 120

Universidade de Brasilia

Campus Universitario Darcy Ribeiro
Predio da Reitoria, 3 andar, 70910-900 Brasilia, DF, Brasil

May 25, 2023

Daniel Clarke
Flat 2, 17 Jones Street
NORTH SYDNEY NSW 2060
Australia

Dear Daniel:

I am happy to write your letter of recommendation. Thank you for sending such a detailed account of your college career to help refresh my memory.

Your recommendation is enclosed. Congratulations on being considered for a position at Top Integrated Performance—they are doing very interesting work!

Best of luck,

Beatrice Azevedo

Beatrice Azevedo
Professor of Computer Science

Enc. (1)

丹尼爾您好：

我很樂意為你寫推薦信。謝謝你這麼詳細地敘述你大學的學業表現，幫助我重新喚起記憶。

隨信附上了推薦信。恭喜你有機會加入 Top Integrated Performance，這間公司進行的工作非常有趣！

回覆請求信：婉拒對方的請求
Letter of requests : Negative responses

當然不可能每封請求信的請求都會得到答應。如果你無法答應對方的請求，還是**要迅速給予明確的回覆**。盡快讓對方知道你的回答，是尊重對方的表現，這樣對方就不用浪費時間，可以立刻開始尋找其他的可能性。

否定的回覆比肯定的回覆**需要給予更多的細節**。有時候被你回絕的人是跟你一起共事的人，此時回信務必禮貌和得體，避免得罪對方和傷害感情。**也可以找出可以稱讚的地方**，並且一定要**說明回絕的原因**，不要只寫個「不行」！如果回絕的原因不在你可控制的範圍之內，要跟對方說明這一點；如果回絕的原因出於你自己的考量，也盡量解釋清楚，並保持禮貌的語氣。下面為兩封給予否定回覆的回覆信。

26-1 | Responding to a request for a raise or promotion
回覆 24-5 請求加薪或升職

請求信 → P. 124

The University of Sydney
NSW 2006, Australia
+61 2 9361 3332

September 10, 2023

Wanda Kerr
Hirshorn Library
The University of Sydney
NSW 2006
Australia

Dear Wanda:

❶ 寫信人蘇珊稱讚提出請求者汪達的工作表現。

I appreciate the time you took to craft such a clear description of your work at the library over the past few years. And of course, I appreciate the time and effort you have put into your work here. It does not go unnoticed. Your performance has always been excellent. ❶

❸

Unfortunately, the economy has affected policies at universities across Australia. Like the rest, we are facing rising costs and flat-lining income. I'm afraid that the directors have advised us against anything other than standard cost-of-living increases this year.

❷

I wish that I could grant your request for a merit raise, but at this time it is not possible. I hope you will continue to perform up to your exacting standards at the library, and I hope you will issue this request again in a more hospitable economic climate.

Warm regards,

Susan Waray

Susan Waray

這封信的語氣很親切，但是沒有應允對方的請求。由於寫信人和提出請求者平時一起共事，因此回覆的時候務必體貼周到，以免影響工作氣氛。

汪達您好：

你一定花了不少時間，才能夠這麼清楚地列出過去幾年來你在圖書館擔任的工作。當然我也很感激你為這份工作所付出的時間與精力。你的貢獻大家都有目共睹，你的表現一直非常出色。❶

❷ 只不過最近的經濟狀況對全澳洲的大學都帶來了一定的影響。我們也跟其他大學一樣，面對成本增加、收入平平的問題，因此很抱歉，校方主管已指示我們除了因應例行生活成本增加之外，不可另外加薪。

我很希望能夠幫你加薪，但是目前這段時間是不可能了。我希望你還是會繼續拿出最佳表現，並在經濟狀況好轉之後再次提出加薪的申請。

❷ 她嘗試說明她個人與這個決定沒有直接的關係。

❸ 蘇珊採用親切的口吻，回信也有一定的長度，
避免讓汪達覺得被得罪或被占便宜。

HARBINGER PUBLISHING

309 Ditmas Ave
Brooklyn, NY 11218+4901

July 23, 2023

Quality Training, Ltd
1000 Condor Drive, Suite 4
San Bruno, CA 94066
(415) 734-9857

Dear Mr. Cook:

Thank you for your interest in Norbert Papp's work *Big Bang* (2013). Unfortunately, the author will not allow his work to be reprinted in formats other than a cartoon collection or collections of his work.

Yours sincerely,

Nathan McLeod

Nathan McLeod
Editor
Harbinger Publishing

這封信簡短而直接。由於回絕的決定並不來自寫信人本身，而是由第三者決定的，所以寫信人可以直接把這個決定告訴對方，不需要再嘗試安撫對方。

庫克先生您好：

感謝您有興趣採用 Norbert Papp 繪製的《Big Bang》（2013）漫畫，可惜作者並不願意讓他的作品以漫畫集或個人作品集之外的形式出版。

Unit 27 請求信與回覆信常用說法
Common phrases for request letters and responses

1 Writing request letters: Making request 撰寫請求信：提出請求

❶ I would like to request . . .　　　　　　　我希望請求……

❷ I am interested in receiving more information about . . .
我希望能夠就……得到更多資訊。

❸ Would you please send me . . .　　　　　能否寄來……

❹ Can I trouble you for a . . .　　　　　　能否麻煩您……

2 Writing request letters: Acknowledging the reader's effort
撰寫請求信：感謝對方的付出

❶ Thank you in advance for your time.　　先謝謝您為此付出的時間。

❷ I appreciate your taking this time on my behalf.
很感激您為了我的緣故，付出這些時間。

❸ Thank you for taking the time to . . .　　謝謝您花時間……

❹ I know you are busy, so I really appreciate your time and effort in addressing my request . . .
我知道您很忙碌，所以我非常感激您為回應我的請求所付出的時間與精力

❺ I know you are busy, so I really appreciate your consideration of my request . . .
我知道您很忙碌，所以我非常感激您考慮這項請求。

3 Writing request letters:
Expressing hope, acknowledging a possible negative response
撰寫請求信：表示希望得到肯定的回覆，同時也接受否定的回覆

❶ I hope you have time to review my proposal.　希望您有時間考慮我的提議。

❷ I hope you have time to write a recommendation for me . . .
希望您有時間為我寫一封推薦信……

❸ I hope you have time to send me the supplies I am requesting . . .
希望您有時間寄來我所需的產品……

❹ I hope you are free to . . .　　　　　　　　希望您有時間……

❺ I hope you are confident enough in my performance to . . .
希望您對我的表現感到滿意，能夠為我……

❻ Based on our working history, I hope you feel comfortable writing this recommendation . . .
根據我們過去的共事經驗，我希望您願意撰寫這封推薦信……

❼ I understand that you may not be able to . . . 我了解您可能無法……

4 Responding to request letters: Sending a positive response
回覆請求信：給予肯定的回覆

❶ I am happy to provide the contact information you requested . . .
我很樂意提供您所要求的聯絡資訊……

❷ I am happy to provide an employment reference . . .
我很樂意為您撰寫求職推薦信……

❸ I am happy to provide a review of your report . . .
我很樂意提供我閱讀報告後的評論……

❹ I will gladly provide . . .　　　　　　　　我很樂意為您提供……

❺ I will gladly write . . .　　　　　　　　　我很樂意為您撰寫……

❻ I will gladly send . . .　　　　　　　　　我很樂意為您寄出……

⑦ It is with pleasure that I enclose . . .　　我很樂意為您附上……

⑧ It is with pleasure that I provide . . .　　我很樂意為您提供……

⑨ It is with pleasure that I send . . .　　我很樂意為您寄出……

⑩ We are pleased to give . . .　　我們很高興能夠給予您……

⑪ We are pleased to provide . . .　　我們很高興能夠提供您……

⑫ We are pleased to send . . .　　我們很高興能夠寄給您……

⑬ We are pleased to write . . .　　我們很高興能夠為您撰寫……

5 Responding to request letters: Sending a negative response
回覆請求信：給予否定的回覆

❶ Unfortunately, I am unable to grant your travel request at this point . . .
可惜我目前無法批准此項出差申請……

❷ Unfortunately, I am unable to review your report before the end of the month . . . 可惜我要到月底才能檢閱你的報告……

❸ Unfortunately, I am unable to give you a salary increase at this time . . .
可惜我目前無法為您加薪……

❹ At the moment, I am simply too busy to . . .
這陣子我實在太忙了，無法……

❺ New regulations prevent me from writing a complete letter of recommendation . . .
基於新的規定，我無法為您撰寫一封完整的推薦信……

❻ New regulations prevent me from offering you a merit raise . . .
基於新的規定，我無法為您加薪……

❼ New regulations prevent me from commenting on your petition . . .
基於新的規定，我無法就您的請求表示意見……

❽ I regret to inform you that I am unable to . . .　　很遺憾通知你，我無法……

❾ I am very sorry that I cannot . . .　　非常抱歉，我無法……

1 Review the concepts

❶ What are three key questions to ask yourself before writing a letter containing a complex request?

_____

_____

❷ How can you help your reader grant your request?

_____

_____

_____

❸ What is a letter of recommendation?

_____

_____

❹ What information should you include in a letter requesting a raise?

(A) An outline of your responsibilities

(B) A list of coworker's salaries

(C) Other jobs you are interested in

❺ What is a common request made in business letters?

(A) Requests for a meeting

(B) Requests for references

(C) Requests for donations

(D) Requests for copyright permission

(E) All of the above

❻ What should you include in a letter requesting a job interview?

(A) Your educational history

(B) Your résumé

(C) Your physical description

2 True (T) or False (F)

❶ ☐ True ☐ False   In business writing, a positive response should be short and direct.

❷ ☐ True ☐ False   In business writing, negative responses are often longer than positive responses.

❸ ☐ True ☐ False   In business writing, common requests can be short and direct.

3 List some problems with this letter of request.

Quality Cosmetic, Inc.

302 Beauty Lane, Suite 5
San Bruno, CA 94066
415.748.9852

July 9, 2023

Permissions Department
Harbinger Publishing
309 Ditmas Ave
Brooklyn, NY 11218+4901

Dear Permissions Editor:

I am so sorry to trouble you. I would like to use one of your illustrations in my in-house report titled "Third Quarter Growth in the Cosmetics Industry." The illustration is called "Girl Applying Lipstick."

I apologize for any inconvenience. Please contact me as soon as possible at 415.748.9852.

Regards,

Irina Safarova

Irina Safarova, Analyst
Quality Cosmetics

1 _____

_____

2 _____

_____

3 _____

_____

4 _____

_____

4 Write a letter requesting a meeting.

You want to arrange a meeting with Harriet Thomas, vice president of Marketing at Flower Power. You want to discuss a possible combined marketing campaign using your stuffed teddy bears from Bear America.

Bear America
915 W. 95th St., Leawood, KS 66206
913-301-8911

August 3, 2023

Harriet Thomas
Flower Power
25 W. Town St., Suite 400
Columbus, Ohio 43215

Dear _____ :

_____

_____

_____

_____

_____

_____

_____

_____

_____

_____

_____

_____

---

5 Imagine that you have received this letter. Write one negative response and one positive response to it.

Leah James

22 Qingtong Road, 26-1011
Pudong New District, Shanghai, PRC 201203

November 2, 2023

Rex Hong
FoodSafe Industries
Lane 2498, Pudong Avenue, #39
Shanghai, PRC

Dear Mr. Hong:

I am a trained food testing technician with five years of experience at Intertest, Inc., in Australia. I have recently moved to Shanghai, and I am very interested in continuing my career here.

I would appreciate a chance to meet and talk with you about any openings at FoodSafe and about the food testing industry in China.

I have enclosed my résumé and a letter of reference from the branch director at Intertest.

Please feel free to contact me for any reason at (021) 5189 2835 or by email at leahjames2004@gmail.com. Thank you for your attention. I look forward to hearing from you.

Best,

Leah James

Enc. (2)

❶ Negative response

FoodSafe Industries

Lane 2498, Pudong Avenue, #39, Shanghai, PRC

November 9, 2023

Leah James
22 Qingtong Road, 26-1011
Pudong New District, Shanghai, PRC 201203

Dear _____ :

_____

_____

_____

_____

_____

_____

_____

_____

_____

_____

_____

_____

_____

❷ Positive response

FoodSafe Industries

Lane 2498, Pudong Avenue, #39, Shanghai, PRC

November 9, 2023

Leah James
22 Qingtong Road, 26-1011
Pudong New District, Shanghai, PRC 201203

Dear _____ :

_____

_____

_____

_____

_____

_____

_____

_____

_____

_____

_____

_____

_____

感謝信
Business Thank-You Letters

Key Terms

advisory board 諮詢委員會

對企業或組織提供策略建議的委員會，所提供的建言不具強制性（non-binding），因此和**董事會**（**board of directors**）有所差異，後者有權表決公司決策。

automatic 自動的

設定由機械或電腦系統等裝置自行完成，而非透過人力直接操作執行的作業方式。不少業者會設定在客戶下單或交易後，寄出自動的感謝訊息。

form letter 制式信函

針對常見特定場合或用途撰寫的簡易信件，可寄給相似情境下的不特定收件人。

general praise 籠統的讚美

可適用於大多數不特定情況的讚美，如 good（好的）、great（很棒的）。在感謝信中，應盡量使用較為具體的讚美，避免籠統用詞。

hiring manager 招聘經理

企業內負責招聘人力的主管。求職者在面試結束或錄取後，建議可向招聘經理寄送感謝信。

milestone 里程碑

個人或組織達成的重要成就。若公司達成一項里程碑，可寄發感謝信給過程中提供協助的人們。

office manager 辦公室經理

在職場中負責協調辦公室運作和一般行政工作的人員。

press release 新聞稿

由企業等團體組織發給媒體，供媒體對外發布給公眾的文稿。

reference/recommendation 推薦信

由推薦人所寫，幫助被推薦人應徵就業或申請入學的信件，內容常為對被推薦人的能力介紹與讚揚。

<table>
<tr><td></td><td>撰寫給具特定對象的感謝信</td></tr>
</table>

Unit 28	撰寫給具特定對象的感謝信 **Thank-You Letters With a Specific Audience**

1 感謝信是什麼？

「感謝信」是為了表達**感謝之意（gratitude）**的信函，寄信的對象可以是私下寄給特定的企業、團體或個人，也可以公開供不特定的公眾、社區居民、顧客群等閱覽。本單元將先介紹具特定發信對象的感謝信，並於下一單元（Unit 29）介紹如何寫感謝信給不特定對象。

有時寫信者是**作為個人**寄感謝信，有時則可能需**代表所屬企業或團體**感謝對方。兩者立場的不同，可以透過信中的第一人稱主詞來區別：若使用的主詞是「**we**」（我們）而不是「**I**」（我），就表示這封感謝信是以整個企業／團體的名義而寫，而非從個人出發。

在商界或學術界生涯中，需要寄送感謝信的原因很多，例如可能是要答謝對方贈送的**禮物（gift）**、**提供的服務（service）**，或者對方帶給你值得感謝的**體驗（experience）**。以下舉例幾種適合寄送感謝信的時機：

代表……	感謝緣由	說明
Individual 個人	**求職面試 job interview**	求職**面試結束後**，可寫封感謝信給**面試官（interviewer）**。
	職缺機會 job offer	接到工作的錄取通知後，可寫封感謝信給**招聘經理（hiring manager）**。
	推薦信 reference / recommendation	對於幫你寫商務推薦信的人，應寫封感謝信。
	獎學金 scholarship	可寫封感謝信給提供獎學金給你的機構。
Corporation/ Organization 企業／組織	**新任委員會成員 new board member**	應寫感謝信給同意成為商務**諮詢委員會（advisory board）**成員的人士。在他們擔任諮詢成員期間，也建議可以定期寫感謝信向他們致謝。
	新合約 new contract	在與別家公司簽完新的合約後，理應寫封感謝信給對方。
	處境艱難時的協助 help in a tough situation	如果有人在公司陷入緊急情況（emergency）時給予協助，公司可能會以私人感謝函向對方致謝。

	個人出力幫忙 personal favor	如果有人對公司**提供協助**，像是同意免費提供諮詢等，禮貌上要寄送感謝信給對方。
個人或企業／組織	優質服務 excellent service	當一家企業為你提供了**非常優質的服務或產品**，你可能會想要寫封感謝信，例如可以寫封感謝信給去過的餐廳，讚美（commend/compliment/praise）當天的侍者服務周到，或是也可以寫信感謝曾替你緊急維修物品的維修業者，甚至也可以寫給曾經特別為你創作作品的藝術家。
	捐贈 donation	若特定人士或企業對於你的公司行號**給予餽贈**，或是捐款給你支持的組織機構，可寫封感謝信致謝。

個人或企業需要寫感謝信的原因尚有各式各樣，並不侷限於以上列舉的例子。

2 感謝信要怎麼寫？

感謝信的語氣應該**親切**、**友好**而**專業**，而信中內容應該**具體明確**，信件應**及時傳達**，且行文需**直截了當**：

❶ 具體明確（specific）：

感謝信的主題應著重於**明確的餽贈**、**特定的服務**或**具體的經歷**上，並在信中解釋這項餽贈、服務或經歷的重要性（importance），以及對自己的影響為何。感謝信的內容不應含糊不清，對讀信者的讚美也**不宜流於空泛**（general）或**逢迎誇大**（flattering）。

❷ 及時傳達（timely）：

信件寄出的時間點（timing）也很重要，應該在**想要致謝的事件發生後不久**，就寄出感謝信給對方，最佳時機為**事件發生後的幾天內**，或者**最多數週內**。

❸ 直截了當（direct）：

感謝信**不宜長篇鋪陳**，而是要在開頭的**第一或第二句話就立即（immediately）向對方致謝**，接著詳加說明為何來信感謝，並於結尾時換另一種說法（expression）重申感謝之情。

感謝信有不同的寄送方式。許多人常會在求職面試完，或在收到推薦信後，透過**電子郵件**寄發感謝信給對方。不過，有些情況則非常適合寄送**紙本（paper）感謝信**或**卡片**，例如獲得捐贈後、歡迎董事會新成員加入時，或是感謝新客戶時。

28-1 | Thanking a job interviewer 感謝面試官

Dear Ms. Kwan:

Subject: Thank you for meeting with me

Thank you for meeting with me today to discuss the office manager position. I appreciated the chance to learn more about the job and the company. It was also very useful to speak with the other members of the office team and hear about their daily tasks. Now, I'm even more excited to bring the skills from my recent training program to the office manager role.

Please contact me if you need any more information. Thanks again for meeting with me. I look forward to hearing from you.

Sincerely,

Darla Watts

Darla Watts

寫信者透過主旨句直接表明感謝的意思和感謝原因,並在主文中詳述讀信者對他的幫助,最後不忘呼籲讀信者可採取行動。

關女士您好:

主旨:感謝您與我會面

謝謝您今天與我見面,和我討論辦公室經理的職缺。我很感激能藉此機會進一步了解這份工作的內容,以及貴公司的概況。能夠與辦公室其他員工交談,聽他們談論自己的日常工作內容,也令我深感受用。現在,我更加期待能將近期培訓課程中學到的技能,應用在辦公室經理的職位上。

若您需要更多的資訊,請您與我聯繫。再次感謝您與我見面,在此滿心期待您的通知。

Global Scholars Projects

1624 East 73rd Street
New York, NY 10021

June 1, 2023

Albert Grouse
Grouse Designs
100 Winding Creek
Dobson NC 27017-8589

> 寫信者在第一段就點出感謝的主題,後續
> 段落則以具體事實和故事說明讀信者的幫
> 助有何貢獻,並在信末重申感謝之意。

Dear Mr. Grouse:

Thank you so much for your $1,500 donation to the Global Scholars Project. Generous gifts like yours help us enormously in advancing our important mission.

Your donation will help us buy school books and backpacks for 100 students in Central Asia next year. It will also help us build 10 new school buildings and five health clinics. Your contribution will impact hundreds of families!

One of these families is the Akhbetov family of Tajikistan. Because of your donation, eight-year-old Timur Akhbetov will get a backpack, paper, pencils, and books for the coming school year. His family could not afford these supplies. Now they can!

Thank you once again for this donation and for your continued support. Your gift will help students' dreams come true.

Many thanks,

Susanna Charles

Susanna Charles

古魯斯先生您好:

非常感謝您為我們的「全球學員計畫」捐助了 1,500 美元。您這樣的慷慨解囊,大力幫助到我們推展重要使命。

您的捐款將幫助我們明年為 100 名中亞地區的學生,購買學校用書跟書包,還能幫助我們興建 10 座新校舍、5 間健康中心。您的貢獻將造福數百個家庭!

其中一個受惠的家庭是位於塔吉克的阿赫貝托夫一家人。因為有您的捐款,八歲大的鐵木爾·阿赫貝托夫,將於新的學年得到書包、用紙、鉛筆和書本。他的家庭原本無力負擔這些學用品,但如今他們負擔得起了!

再次感謝您的捐款以及持續支持,您的餽贈將幫助學生實現夢想。

Flora Event Planning

3115 Park Road NW
Washington, DC 20010

August 31, 2023

Stellar Plumbing
2616 V Street
Arlington, VA 20301
Attention: Client Services Manager

寫信者同樣在開頭處就點出感謝的主旨，並具體描述感謝的緣由，另外也寫出特定致謝對象，以及未來可以為對方提供什麼回饋（向其他人推薦其服務）。

Dear Sir or Madam:

I am writing to say thank you for the actions of the Stellar Plumbing team last week. Your workers helped save an important event for my business. A pipe burst in our ballroom during one of our most important events of the year. Thanks to the quick work of the Stellar Plumbing team, the problem was solved and our event was able to continue. I want to thank manager David Crane in particular. He was very kind and helpful during our crisis.

I want to commend the work of the team and to thank them once again for arriving so quickly. I will definitely call you for any future plumbing needs and I will recommend Stellar Plumbing's services!

Thanks again for saving our event.

Sincerely,

Iris Root

Iris Root
Principal, Flora Event Planning

收件人：客服經理

尊敬的先生或女士：

我寫這封信是為了感謝「杰星水電」工程團隊上週的活躍表現。貴公司的員工幫本公司挽救了一場重要的活動。當時，我們正在舉辦年度的重要活動，但宴會廳有條水管卻突然爆裂，幸好杰星水電的團隊動作迅速，問題得到解決，而活動也得以繼續進行。我想特別感謝經理大衛・克蘭，他在我們陷入危機時，非常親切地提供許多幫助。

我在此肯定貴公司團隊的工作表現，並再次感謝他們這麼快就趕到現場。今後若有任何水電方面的需求，我一定會打電話給貴公司，也會向大家推薦杰星水電的服務！

再次感謝你們挽救本公司的活動。

Photo Journeys
4223 16th Street NW
Washington, DC 20010

September 5, 2023

Milton Daniels
88 Chevy Chase Boulevard
Bethesda, MD 20817

Dear Milt:

Thank you so much for agreeing to be part of the Photo Journeys board.
As you know, this is a new challenge for me. I need all the advice I can get.
I know you have a busy schedule, so I really appreciate you making time to
advise me on this project. I truly hope, with your advice and the input of the
rest of the board, to build a business we can all be proud of.

Thank you for your investment in me.

Sincerely,

Matt Peterson

Matt Peterson
President, Photo Journeys

本篇為寫給特定個人的**不公開**感謝信，作者在開頭表明感謝之意後，在後續文字中肯定讀
信者的費心，並表示期待未來和讀信者展開良善合作，最後則又表達一次感謝之情。

親愛的米爾特：

非常感謝您同意加入「攝影旅程公司」的董事會。如您所知，在我眼前的是嶄新的挑戰，
我需要聽取各方先進的意見。我知道您的行程繁忙，所以非常感謝您能撥冗就此專案提供
建議。我衷心希望，有了您的建議、以及其餘董事的協助下，能夠建立我們都能引以為傲
的企業。

感謝您對我的費心。

企業撰寫給未具特定對象的感謝信及公開謝函
Corporate Thank-You Letters With an Unspecified Audience and Public Thank-You Messages

1 感謝不特定的對象

　　企業常也需要撰寫感謝信來向**不特定的個人或群體**致謝，這種信件除了可以**大宗（mass）、制式信函（form letter）**的方式，以**不公開**的媒介（電子郵件、紙本書信等）寄給大量收件人，也常發布在**社群媒體（social media）**，或是以**新聞稿（press release）**形式刊載在報章媒體上，作為**公開謝函**，對公眾、顧客群或其他不特定對象統一表示謝意。以下為幾種企業可能撰寫感謝信給非特定對象的時機：

感謝緣由	說明
達到特定的里程碑 hitting a milestone	公司在達到重要的目標後，可能會公開感謝顧客對他們的支持。
選擇特定類型企業 choosing a certain type of Business	小型企業可能會為了感謝顧客選擇自家公司，而非中大型企業，而公開向顧客致謝。
度過艱困期 after a difficult time	公司有時會經歷艱辛的（tough）低潮時期。對於在艱困期間依然不離不棄的顧客，公司理應公開向他們致謝。
感謝社區民眾 thanking a community	有時社區民眾會受邀對當地企業進行評比，其中一例便是地方報紙每年彙整的「最佳」業者名單（"best-of" list）。頂尖排名的企業，可能會想要公開感謝顧客的忠實支持。
大筆捐款 large donation	公司若獲贈不具名的大筆捐款，可能希望公開感謝捐贈者。
參與活動 participation in an event	繁忙的活動過後，公司可能會想公開感謝參與者（participant）的蒞臨。
感謝顧客下單 placing an order	公司可能在顧客下單後，設定由系統自動（automatically）寄出感謝函給顧客。這類感謝信通常都很簡短，而且寄給所有顧客的內容完全相同，寄出方式可能是跟著顧客的訂單一併寄出，或以電子郵件發送。

2 如何寫作給不特定對象的感謝信／訊息

　　具／不具特定對象的感謝信，在寫作上有幾項重要差異，但也有許多共同處。主要差異例如：寫給不特定對象的**大宗**、**制式感謝函**，內容可能非常簡短，或許只有一、兩句話，並且只針對某項**特定行動**表示感謝，例如顧客下單購物後，常會收到制式的感謝訊息。

　　其他具／不具特定對象的感謝信的異同處有以下幾點：

❶ 所有的感謝函都應**內容具體**（specific）、**及時寄出**（timely）且行文**直截了當**（direct）。

❷ 首先，寫信者應清楚說明**致謝的原因**，然後描述對方的善舉**對己方有何正面影響**（impact）。通常公司在公開發布的感謝函中，會敘述公司與讀信者之間的關係，或者表達希望將來如何和讀信者往來互動，而寫給特定個人或團體的感謝函就不一定需要。

❸ 無論是否寫給特定對象，感謝信的語氣都應該**親切**、**友善**且**專業**。一般來說，大宗感謝信和公開謝函是**以企業的名義**寄出，因此信中自稱應該使用「**we**」（我們／本公司），而不用「**I**」（我）。

29-1 | Publicly posted thank-you letter to a community in a local newspaper 地方報紙上致當地居民的公開感謝函

THANK YOU, BROWNSVILLE

We at Fast Times Car Repair want to thank the people of Brownsville for making us your number one choice for auto repairs! We know you have many options when it comes to auto repair. So we are proud to have earned your trust. Fast Times Car Repair has served this community for 15 years. With your continued support, we hope to keep this town's automobiles running smoothly for many years to come.

We are grateful for your business, this year and every year!

本篇為公開發布的感謝信，對象為當地社區居民，除了明確表示感謝之意和原因，也提及未來希望和讀信者保持何種互動關係。

感謝布朗斯威爾全體居民

「迅時代汽修廠」感謝布朗斯威爾的居民，將本廠視為您汽車維修的首選！我們深知您們在汽車維修上，尚有眾多選擇，所以本廠非常自豪能獲得各位的信任。迅時代汽修廠已經在地深耕 15 年。有了大家持續支持，我們希望在未來繼續為本市居民長久服務，確保各位的愛車行車順暢。

今年及未來的每一年，我們都感謝您的惠顧！

July 3, 2023

Press release

From: Big Baskets Bike Shop CEO Shireen Wheeler

Thank you to all 2023 Big Baskets 10 km participants

Big Baskets Bike Shop wants to express our thanks to all who took part in our 10 km bike race this year! In 2023, we welcomed almost twice as many people as last year. We were happy to see everyone who joined for a second time. And we were honored to meet all the new cyclists racing for the first time. We hope to see even more friendly faces next year!

We didn't do this alone, of course. Thank you to local businesses Sweetie Donuts and the Soda Shack for providing food and drink. And thank you to Squeaky's Bike Repair for helping everyone ride safely. Once again, thank you to the community of Jackson Falls! This is not only a bike race but also a chance to become better neighbors. Thank you for taking part.

See you next year!

本篇為採新聞稿形式的公開感謝訊息，感謝對象包括活動的參與者和協力商家，並表明期待未來和讀信者保持良好的關係。

新聞稿

發文者：大籃自行車行 執行長 席琳・惠勒

感謝所有參加 2023 年大籃盃 10 公里自行車賽的車手

「大籃自行車行」欲向參加今年我們 10 公里自行車賽的全體車手致謝！參加 2023 年的自行車賽選手人數，幾乎是去年的兩倍。我們很高興看到每位再度參賽的車手，也很榮幸見到所有初次參賽的新車手。希望明年，我們能看到更多朋友前來共襄盛舉！

當然，本次活動非僅由敝店之力所能完成。在此感謝本地企業「甜心甜甜圈」以及「蘇打小屋」提供的餐點與飲料，還要感謝「史奎奇單車維修站」，協助確保每位車手的行車安全。最後再次感謝傑克森瀑布市的居民！這不僅是場自行車賽，更是敦親睦鄰的好機會，感謝各位的參與。

我們明年見！

29-3 | Mass/form private thank-you letter thanking customers for their orders 感謝客戶下單的不公開大宗／制式感謝函

Dear Valued Customer:

Thank you for choosing Taylor's Cosmetics for your beauty needs. Enclosed are your goods as ordered. We hope they meet your satisfaction.

At Taylor's we always want to provide the best goods and services for our customers. If you have time, please visit our website and fill out a customer opinion form.

Thank you once again for your order.

Sincerely,

The Taylor's Cosmetics Team

本篇為制式的大宗感謝信，每個消費者向該店家下單後，收到的信函內容可能都相同。由於感謝事由並不特殊或具太大重要性，信件有禮貌而簡短，僅簡單表示感謝並說明必要資訊。

尊貴的客戶您好：

感謝您選擇「泰勒化妝品」來滿足您對美容的需求。隨函附上您所訂購的商品，希望您能滿意。

本公司一向希望能為顧客提供品質最佳的商品與服務。若您有時間，請撥冗到本公司官網，填寫顧客意見調查表。

再次感謝您訂購本公司商品。

感謝信常用說法
Common phrases for thank-you letters

1 Expressing thanks 表達感謝之意的用語

❶ Thanks for meeting with me today.　　謝謝您今天和我見面。

❷ Thanks to the quick work of the team, we were able to continue.
由於團隊的動作迅速，我們才得以繼續進行。

❸ Thank you so much for your advice.　　非常感謝您的建議。

❹ We at Eckington Steel want to thank you for your business.
我們埃金頓鋼鐵廠衷心感謝您的惠顧。

❺ I'd like to express my thanks for your donation.
我想就您的捐款一事表示感謝。

❻ We are very grateful for your feedback.　　我們非常感謝您的意見回饋。

❼ I want to share my gratitude for your trust.　　我想感謝您對我的信任。

2 Describing the impact of a service or experience
描述服務或經歷的影響的用語

❶ It was very useful to learn more about the job and the company.
能夠更了解這份工作的內容與公司概況，對我受用匪淺。

❷ Our meeting helped me understand my new responsibilities.
這次見面讓我明白了自己的新職責。

❸ Your donation will help us build a new clinic.
您的捐款將幫助我們興建一間新診所。

❹ Your contribution will impact hundreds of families!
您的貢獻將造福數百個家庭！

⑤ Because of your quick response, we were able to continue with our event.

由於您們反應迅速，我們的活動才得以繼續進行。

⑥ Your letter of reference helped me get my dream job.

您的推薦信幫我找到了我夢寐以求的工作。

⑦ The flowers you provided for our party created an elegant atmosphere.

您為我們的宴會準備的鮮花，營造出高雅迷人的氛圍。

⑧ Without your advice, our business would not be as productive.

若非有您的建議，本公司無法達成如此成效。

3 Writing publicly posted thank-you letters 撰寫公開張貼的感謝信

❶ Thank you to the community of Jackson Falls.

感謝傑克森瀑布市的居民。

❷ We know you have many choices, and we thank you for choosing us.

我們知道您的選擇眾多，所以很感謝您選擇了本公司。

❸ Thanks for helping us get here.

感謝您幫助本公司達到如今的成就。

❹ Thank you for making us your top choice.

感謝您優先選擇本公司。

❺ We appreciate your support during this difficult year.

我們很感激您在這艱難的一年裡，對本公司的支持。

❻ Thank you all so much for your participation.

非常感謝各位的參與。

❼ We want to express our gratitude for your support.

我們想對您的支持，表達由衷感謝。

4 Describing the relationship between writer and reader
描述寫信者與閱信者之間的關係

❶ We are proud to do business in this town.

我們很榮幸能在本鎮提供服務。

❷ Fast Times has served this community for 15 years.

「迅時代」已經在地深耕 15 年。

❸ We hope to keep this town's automobiles running for years to come.

我們希望將來繼續在本鎮確保各位的愛車行車順暢。

❹ Thanks for helping us each become better neighbors.

感謝您讓我們彼此成為更好的鄰居。

❺ We couldn't have done it without you.

沒有您的支持，我們就沒有今天的成就。

❻ We will work hard to be your number one choice every year.

我們會努力成為您每年的首選。

❼ Your support keeps us in business.

您的支持讓本公司得以持續經營。

1 Choose three of the sentences in the box below to complete the thank-you letter.

- I have worked at my current job for five years.
- I will be sure to use your services for any future events we throw.
- The event was a big success.
- I have some ideas about how things could have run more smoothly.
- Please also pass along my special thanks to Martin Douglas.

Shelter for All
88 Mayflower Road
Washington, DC 20395

January 31, 2023

Tina Gray
Flora Event Planning
3115 Park Road NW
Washington, DC 20010

Dear Ms. Gray:

I am writing to thank you for all your hard work on our fundraising event last week. Thanks to you and your staff, everything ran smoothly. **❶** _____

_____

❷ _____

He did an excellent job hosting the charity auction. Because of him, we raised a lot of money for our cause.

I am very glad we chose Flora to run this event. **❸** _____

_____

Thank you again for your great work.

Sincerely,

Rhonda Tan

Rhonda Tan
Director, Shelter for All

---

2 Copy the following paragraphs into the body of the mass thank-you letter in the correct order.

> Please visit our website for more details about our sale. Thank you once again for your order.

> For your information, our 2023 summer sale begins on 1 May. Many of our goods will have a discount of 20% or more.

> Thank you for choosing Chef's Kiss Cookware for your purchase. Your goods are enclosed. We hope they meet your satisfaction.

Chef's Kiss Cookware
88 Grange Road
Exeter
EX22 2KN

1 April 2023

935 Highfield Road
Watford
WD33 3QU

Dear Valued Customer:

1 _____

_____

2 _____

_____

3 _____

_____

Sincerely,

Chef's Kiss Cookware

3 Here is a publicly posted thank-you letter from Chef Mike's Fine Food to everyone who supported them in their first year of business. Follow the instructions in the box to complete the letter.

- Identify your company and the purpose of your letter.
- Thank three other local businesses (Millie's Bakery, Bart's Interior Design, and Kitchen Planet) for their help in your business's success.
- Promise to continue providing your popular dishes at affordable prices.
- Thank everyone again for their support.

❶ _____

_____ . Starting a new business is always difficult, and new businesses cannot survive without the support of the local community. We knew our first year would be a challenge, but with your support, it has also been a great success. ❷ _____

_____

_____ .

With your continued support, we hope that our second year will be even better than our first. ❸ _____

_____ .

We will also be introducing some new and exciting items to our menu, which we are very excited for you all to try.

❹ _____ .

Yours sincerely,

The Chef Mike's Fine Food Team

Now, work with a partner to compose a public thank-you letter of your own. Here is the scenario:

You are the owner of a bookshop. You just had a successful event where several authors read aloud from their work, answered questions from fans, and signed copies of their books. You want to write a thank you letter to everyone who supported the event.

Key Terms

assume 承擔

承擔起特定的義務或任務，或為特定事項承擔責任，用法例如：「to assume costs and risk」（承擔成本與風險）。

commission
回扣（或稱佣金）

經紀人或代理商為辦理一項業務所收取的費用。

inquiry 詢問

詢問、打聽或調查事情經過或處理原則；有系統的調查。

offer 報價（或稱報盤）

一般指賣方願意出售貨物的價格，也可以指進行交易時所提出的報價。報價者除了提出明確的條件，在對方接受報價時也必須履行交易的義務。

prospective customers
潛在客戶

指雖然目前尚未成為顧客，但在未來有機會向其銷售產品的對象。若對方向自家公司寄送詢價表單或信件，一般可將其視為潛在客戶。

purchase in bulk 大量訂購

相對於少量零售，大量訂購訂單會要求多於平常的商品數量，通常可獲得供應商給予單價折扣。

quotation 報價

個人或公司為提供特定產品或服務，願意接受的價格。

solicit 請求

請求個人或公司提供某物。

sales representative 業務員

代表公司對外銷售產品或服務的人員，其他說法尚有「salesperson」、「salesman/saleswoman」等。

specification 規格

商品、設計或服務所必須滿足的一套既定規範。

ZIP / postal code 郵遞區號

ZIP 在此為美國「Zone Improvement Plan」（地區改進計畫）的縮寫，美國郵政使用的郵遞區號稱為（ZIP Code）；其他國家的郵遞區號一般可稱為「postal code」。

Unit 31 如何撰寫詢問信？
How do I write a letter of inquiry?

1 什麼是詢問信？

詢問信（letter of inquiry）功能為**索取資訊**：inquiry 是「詢問；調查」的意思，所以詢問信就是向對方詢問事情的信。在商務領域中，inquiry 特別指潛在顧客看到廣告宣傳或促銷活動（promotional campaign）後的初步反應，此時詢問信目的是用來**詢問報價或價格**，因此中文也稱**「詢價信」**。（就非營利組織來說，詢問信通常用來募捐，但是本課不討論這類的詢問信。）

2 如何寫詢問／價信？

通常各公司都有自己的**詢價表格（inquiry form）**，可以從網路上或公司的出版物中取得。在這些表格中，詢價者要就自己的公司、產業、需求等回答一些問題，然後對方可以依據這些資訊提供報價。如果你沒有找到詢價表格，就必須自己寫一封詢價信，此時要先考慮下面幾個問題：

- ◆ 我應該寫給誰？
- ◆ 我需要得到什麼資訊？
- ◆ 對方需要從我這裡得到哪些資訊？

3 詢問／價信應該寫給誰？

詢價信應該**寄給出售該產品的人**。如果出售產品的是個人，而非公司，那就直接寫信給這個人。寫信時最好都能**寫出明確的收件人**，但是因為詢價信很常用到，也很容易回覆，所以寄給公司時，就**不一定**非要寫出特定收件人，而是可以把詢價信寄給該公司的業務或行銷（sales or marketing）部門。

4 信中需要詢問那些資訊？

這個問題的答案會視實際的狀況而不同。詢價信通常用來**詢問每單位（per unit）產品的價格**，但是依狀況不同，有時候可能還須提出其他的問題。比如說，如果你想大量訂購某一產品，你可能還會想問有沒有**打折的可能性**。

下表為一些你可能會想在詢價信中提出的問題：

有關產品價格	**您的產品價格是？** → 如果大量訂購（purchase in bulk），價格是？ → 有沒有可能得到折扣（discount）？折扣後價格是？
有關產品運送	**訂購手續完成後，我什麼時候可以拿到產品？** → 產品的運送方式（delivery method）是？ → 產品可以直接送到我的所在地嗎？
其他產品資訊	**有沒有其他的產品可能更符合我的需求？**
有關服務報價	**該服務如何收費（charge）？** → 按小時計費（charge by the hour）嗎？ → 若透過此項服務購買產品，對方會從中收取回扣（commission）嗎？

5 對方需要得到哪些資訊？

你在詢價信或詢價表格中提供的資訊，有助於對方（賣方，seller）更確切地了解和滿足你的需求。因此在詢價信中，務必說明你想要**什麼**產品或服務、需要的**數量**（amount）及你的**地點**（location）。在詢價表格中，你可能需要回答更多問題，因為收集顧客的資訊有助於廠商改善行銷策略。

詢價表格會就產品、運送方式、你的所屬產業和需求提出問題。**下面彙整了詢價表格中常見的問題**，不過很少詢價表格會包含所有下列問題：

關於你	◆ 你的聯絡方式（contact information）？ ◆ 你的職稱（job title）？ ◆ 你在採購過程中擔負的責任（responsibility）？ ◆ 你所屬的產業（industry）類別為何？	關於運送	◆ 你的公司地點是？ ◆ 產品要送到哪裡？ ◆ 你希望運費包含在報價（quote）裡嗎？ ◆ 你希望採用特定的運送方式（delivery method）嗎？ ◆ 產品的運送期限（delivery time）為何？
關於產品	◆ 你需要哪項產品？ ◆ 你需要的產品數量？ ◆ 你需要的產品規格（product specifications）？	關於你的需求	◆ 你希望報價採用的貨幣（currency）是？ ◆ 您購買產品的目的是？ ◆ 您目前有使用本公司其他的產品嗎？ ◆ 您如何知道本公司訊息？

自行撰寫詢價信的時候，不需要把這些資訊全寫進去，但是不妨就其中幾個問題提供相關資訊，這樣對方也更容易配合你的需求。下面就來看幾個詢價表格和詢價信的範例。

31-1 | Inquiry form (1) 詢價表格

Big Ten Home Cleaning Supplies Inquiry Form（Big Ten 家用清潔用品詢價表格）

Name:	Email:
Company name:	Address:
City:	State:
Zip:	Country:
Phone:	Fax:
Message:	How did you find us? 您如何得知本公司？
Use:	

✲ **Which product(s) are you interested in?** 您有興趣的產品是？

FiberSave	Big Ten Carrier Tool
Original Tile Tool	ProTex Tile tool
Brush-Cleaning Tool	Other

✲ **Would you like to be contacted by a sales representative?**
您希望我們的業務人員跟您聯絡嗎？

✲ **Would you like leasing information?** 您想得到租用產品的相關訊息嗎？

✲ **Would you like the name of your nearest Big Ten supplier?**
您想知道離您最近的 Big Ten 經銷商店名嗎？

這份表格就顧客本身、顧客所在的地點和需求提出了各種問題。

If you would like to talk to a 123 sales representative about products, pricing, or other ways in which we can serve you, please Call 1 (800) 600-6770 in the USA or Canada, Go to http://www.123.com for more contact information, or Complete the form below.

如果您希望親自與 123 的業務人員洽詢產品、價格或任何其他服務項目,請打美國或加拿大電話:1 (800) 600-6770,也可以上我們的網站 http://www.123.com 查詢其他聯絡方式,或是填寫下面的表格。

First name	Last name
Company	Email
Industry	Job title
Address 1	
Address 2	City
Country	State/Province
Zip/Postal code	Phone number

✿ **Best time to contact you** 最方便聯絡的時段

✿ **I would like information about** 我希望得到下列資訊

☐ Products 產品	☐ Services 服務
☐ Software solutions 軟體解決方案	☐ Other 其他
☐ Pricing 價格	

✿ **Are you interested in a specific 123 product or** product family?
您是否對 123 的特定產品或產品系列有興趣?

✿ **Other questions or comments** 其他問題或批評指教

Product family(產品系列)指被歸為同一類別的產品,這些產品一般會採用相同的機器、原理,或是具有相似或互補的功能。

31-3 | Letter of inquiry (1) 詢問產品報價的詢價信

報價信 → P. 170

Part

7

詢價與報價

Unit

31

如何撰寫詢問信？

MOOD MUSIC

Elm Corner, Upper Cam Lane
Addlestone, Surrey KT15
United Kingdom

16 February 2023

Big Sound
95 Cross Road
BUSHEY
Hertfordshire WD 194 DQ
England

Attention: Sales Director

Dear Sir or Madam:

Subject: Request for quotation

I am the purchasing manager for Mood Music, London. I would like to request a quotation for the following products:

- **One 24-track hard disk recorder**
- **One 8-channel MIDI fader**
- **One 8-channel control surface extender**

Thank you for your attention to my inquiry. Please feel free to contact me with any questions at 1488 68 9485 or via email at <u>t.brookes.wolgar@moodmuse.co.uk</u>.

Regards,

Thomas Brookes-Wolgar

Thomas Brookes-Wolgar, Manager
Mood Music

這是一封沒有使用詢價表格的詢價信，作者在信中列出他想購買的產品，但是沒有指明廠牌。

經辦人：業務主任

敬啟者：

主旨：詢價

您好，我是倫敦 Mood Music 公司的採購經理，想就下列產品詢問報價：

- 一個二十四軌硬碟記錄器
- 一個八頻道樂器數位界面推桿
- 一個八頻道操縱面板擴充器

謝謝您閱讀我的詢價，若有任何問題，請與我聯絡：1488 68 9485 或 t.brookes.wolgar@moodmuse.co.uk。

ARTHUR CONSULTING

Metro South, 135 Auburn Ave. NE
Atlanta, GA 30303
404-521-2739

August 3, 2023

Hannah Hossein
Kilroy Interiors
1122 Peachtree Street
Savannah, GA 31406

Dear Ms. Hossein:

The purpose of this letter is to solicit quotes, work specifications ❶, and other relevant information from your company with respect to ❷ the following services:

(1) Painting 3 interior rooms.
(2) Redecoration advice and assistance.
(3) Office furniture: desks, bookshelves, conference tables, display shelves.

If there are any special offers or opportunities to obtain these items at reduced prices, please be sure to include this information with your response. Please feel free to contact me at 404-521-2739 if you need additional information.

Thank you for your assistance.

Yours truly,

Sue Hanks

Sue Hanks, Office Manager
Arthur Consulting

---

❶ to solicit quotes, work specifications . . .（詢問價格、工作細節）：solicit 在這裡是「請求」、「詢問」的意思，而 quotes 在這裡指「報價」。Specifications 是商品、材料或服務的基本和技術要求，包括公司用來確保達到特定標準的流程；就商品和材料來說，可能還包括就保存、包裝、標示等所設定的標準。

❷ with respect to . . .（就……；關於……）：這是比較正式的說法，在此也可以用 with regard to、in relation to，或是也可以簡單用 about。

這封信的用詞較前一封更專業、正式。寫作者在首段立刻點出詢問報價的目的，接著利用編號列表依序列出需要報價的服務和產品，並在倒數第二段詢問折扣的可能性，也留下聯絡方式供對方聯繫以確認其他資訊。

海珊女士您好：

本信意在 ❷ 就下列服務 ❶ 詢問貴公司的**價格、工作細節**及其他相關資訊：

(1) 粉刷三間室內房間。
(2) 裝修建議與協助。
(3) 辦公家具：辦公桌、書櫃、會議桌、展示櫃。

如果有任何的促銷活動或上列產品的折扣機會，請務必在回信中告知。如果還需要額外資訊，歡迎來電與我聯絡：404-521-2739。

謝謝您的協助。

Lee Chef Supply

65 Chien Hsing Road, San Min District
Kaohsiung City, Taiwan

March 25, 2023

Blumenschein, Inc.
Adickesallee 3
94855
Frankfurt am Main
Germany

Dear Sirs:

We have noted your advertisement in *Appetite* magazine and are interested in your assortment of utensils, particularly knives.

We would appreciate a quote for the entire Blumenschein Large Knife Collection, the Braun Standard Kitchen Line, and the Modern Quality Chef's Set. Please indicate prices ❶ C.I.F. Kaohsiung, Taiwan. Please indicate your earliest delivery date, terms of payment, and discounts for regular purchases. We would also appreciate receiving your catalog.

Respectfully,

Lee Wen

Lee Wen
Lee Chef Supply

貴公司諸君您好：

我們看到貴公司於《Appetite》雜誌上登的廣告，對於貴公司的各項器具非常有興趣，尤其是刀具。

想請您就 Blumenschein 大型刀具全系列、Braun 標準廚具系列和現代高品質主廚組合提供報價，並以台灣 ❶ 高雄港 CIF 價為準。此外也請您告知最早能交貨的日期、付款方式和就定期採購可提供的折扣，並也附上貴公司的產品目錄。

❶ CIF 是「cosls, insurance, and freight」（成本、保險、運費）的縮寫，在國際貿易中用來表示所報的價格包含所有產品的保險費與運費，此時由賣方安排和支付所有將產品運送到目的地所需的費用；在本篇範例裡，目的地就是台灣高雄港。

其他的運送方式還有：

• CFR：為「cost and freight」（成本與運費）的縮寫，表示所報的價格包含將產品運至目的港口所花的運費，但是產品在出發港口上了船後，遭受的損失或損害得由買方承擔。由於 CFR 價不包含保險，所以通常是進口國政府想讓本國保險公司提供保險時，才採用 CFR 價。

• C&F：為 CFR 的舊式的寫法。

• FOB：為「free on board」（船上交貨）的縮寫。採用此送貨方式時，買方與賣方會先指定特定 FOB 點（即交貨地點），此地點可能是買方公司所在地，或其他指定地點。賣方會承擔將產品包裝、運送到 FOB 點的費用，而買方則會承擔貨品離開 FOB 點後的成本，包括貨品在出口國內陸的運輸費用與保險費，以及其他運費（例如將貨物裝載到船上的支出）。

如果合約上寫 FOB vessel，指的是賣方會承擔貨物運至買方指定商船的費用，以及將貨物裝載上船的費用，類似說法有 FOR（free on rail 火車上交貨）和 FOT（free on truck 卡車上交貨）等。

Unit 32 什麼是報價信？
What is a letter of quotation?

1 什麼是報價信？

報價信（letter of quotation）就是**對詢價信進行的回覆**。在商務領域中，「報價」就是告知對方產品或服務的價格。報價信可以用來進行「**穩固報價**」（或稱 offers with engagement「**實盤**」），也可以進行「**非穩固報價**」（或稱 offers without engagement「**虛盤**」）。

2 什麼是穩固報價？

穩固報價（firm offer）表示承諾以特定**固定價格**出售特定產品，而且該報價通常會設有一定的**期限**。對方一旦接受此穩固報價，就不能撤回（withdraw）。提出穩固報價的報價信應包含下列元素：

❶ 提及對方之前寄來的詢價信或詢價表格。
❷ 產品的名稱。
❸ 必要的工作細節描述。
❹ 每單位的價格。
❺ 願意提供的折扣。
❻ 下訂單的期限。
❼ 下訂單的方式，包括付費方式。
❽ 交貨方式，包括包裝方式、運送方式和運送時間。

3 什麼是非穩固報價？

非穩固報價（non-firm offer）可依情況進行調整，意思就是**報價的內容還可以改變**。提出非穩固報價的報價信通常不會包含上述所有的資訊，尤其是交貨方式和工作細節，且信中通常也會表明，報價的相關條件是可以改變的，此時可用「this quotation is subject to our final consideration」（此報價會依我們最後的考量進行調整）這樣的句型。下面就來看幾封報價信。

BIG SOUND

95 Cross Road
BUSHEY, Hertfordshire WD 194 DQ
England

16 February 2023

Thomas Brookes-Wolgar
Mood Music
Elm Corner, Upper Cam Lane
Addlestone, Surrey KT15
United Kingdom

Ref: Q230216

Dear Mr. Wolgar:

Thank you for your inquiry of 16 February. I am pleased to provide you with the enclosed product and price list for our 24-track hard disk recorders, 8-channel MIDI faders, and 8-channel surface extenders. The prices quoted here are valid for the next 30 days and include all shipping costs. We are also happy to offer you a 3% cash discount on payments made within 10 days of delivery.

We require cash in advance for first-time orders. We accept bank transfers, money orders, and credit card payments over the phone. For shipping within England, we use Monarch Mail or GlobeShip.

To place an order, please contact me at 01 472 441335 or send another letter listing:

- The products you would like.
- The quantities of each product.
- The shipping address.
- Any shipping preferences. (If no preferences are listed we use the Monarch Mail Parcel Tracking service.)
- Your preferred method of payment.
- A telephone number and a time to contact you to arrange payment in advance.

Please don't hesitate to contact me if you need further information.

Yours faithfully,

Miranda Snow

Miranda Snow
Sales Manager, Big Sound

Enclosure (1)

Enclosure 附件

BIG SOUND

95 Cross Road
BUSHEY, Hertfordshire WD 194 DQ
England

Q230216

Product type	Brand	Price
24-track hard disk recorder	Compass 24-track recorder	£735.00
	A-track recorder	£870.00
	Beringer 24-track recorder	£990.00
8-channel MIDI fader	Compass MIDI fader	£999.00
8-channel control surface extender	Wacky surface extender	£489.95
	A-track extender	£525.00

華格先生您好：

謝謝您於 2 月 16 日來函詢價，在此欣然附上本公司二十四軌硬碟記錄器、八頻道樂器數位界面推桿，及八頻道操縱面板擴充器之價目表。此價格之有效期限為 30 天，包含運費。若您在交貨 10 天之內付款，還可享有 3% 的現金折扣。

第一次訂購我們的商品時，須在交貨前付款。我們接受銀行轉帳、匯票和透過電話以信用卡付款。就英國境內訂單，本公司委託 Monarch Mail 或 GlobeShip 運送。

若欲下訂單，請打 01 472 441335 與我聯絡，或是來信列出：

- 您欲購買的產品
- 各項產品訂購數量
- 送貨地址
- 偏好的送貨方式（若無特別指定的送貨方式，我們將透過 Monarch Mail 寄送包裹）
- 偏好的付款方式
- 電話號碼及聯絡時間，以安排預先付款事宜。

如果還需要任何資訊，歡迎隨時與我聯絡。

Q230216		
產品	品牌	價格
二十四軌硬碟記錄器	Compass 二十四軌記錄器	735.00 英鎊
	A-track 記錄器	870.00 英鎊
	Beringer 二十四軌記錄器	990.00 英鎊
八頻道樂器數位界面推桿	Compass 樂器數位界面推桿	999.00 英鎊
八頻道操縱面板擴充器	Wacky 操縱面板擴充器	489.95 英鎊
	A-track 擴充器	525.00 英鎊

詢價信 → P. 167

BLUMENSCHEIN, INC.

Adickesallee 3, 94855
Frankfurt am Main, Germany

April 4, 2023

Attention: Lee Wen
Lee Chef Supply
65 Chien Hsing Road, San Min District
Kaohsiung City, Taiwan

Dear Mr. Lee:

Thank you for your inquiry of March 25. The prices you requested (quoted in US dollars) are as follows:

- Blumenschein Large Knife Collection $240.00
- Braun Standard Kitchen Line $275.00
- Modern Quality Chef's Set $300.00

Expedited shipping plus insurance to Kaohsiung, Taiwan, is estimated at $230.00, bringing the total to an estimated $1,045.00. Please understand that this offer is subject to the final quote from our shipping partner and does not constitute a firm offer.

Orders are filled and shipped the day after they are received. Using Globe Ship expedited service, we can deliver an order to Taiwan within 3 days of the order's placement. For first-time customers, we require payment in advance through either an international wire bank transfer or a credit card payment over the telephone. We offer a 2% cash discount, a 7% discount on orders over $600, and a 10% discount on orders over $1,000. Orders over $1,200 are subject to negotiation. We offer discounts for large orders on a case-by-case basis. To discuss a large order, please call me at +49 69 674561 or fax a completed order form from the enclosed catalog to +49 69 670002.

Sincerely,

Karl Blumenschein

Karl Blumenschein
Sales Director
Blumenschein Inc.

Enclosure: catalog

李先生您好：

謝謝您於 3 月 25 日來函詢價。您詢問的產品價格（以美元計價）如下：

- Blumenschein 刀具系列 $240.00
- Braun 標準廚具系列 $275.00
- 現代高品質主廚組合 $300.00

到台灣高雄港的快捷運費加保費估計為 230 美元，加上產品後總價為 1,045 美元。但是此報價會依運輸公司之最後報價進行調整，因此為非穩固報價。

所訂購之產品將於收到訂單次日發貨。我們採用 Globe Ship 快捷運輸服務，貨品將可於下單三日內送達台灣。首次向本公司訂購產品之顧客須事先付款，可以透過國際電匯，或透過電話以信用卡付款。我們提供 2% 的現金折扣，600 美金以上的訂單可享有 7% 的折扣，1,000 美元以上的訂單可享有 10% 的折扣。1,200 美元以上的訂單折扣可再議價。對於大宗訂單，我們視個別情況給予折扣。若您有意就大宗訂單進行討論，請打 +49 69 674561 與我聯絡，或是將附件的產品目錄內的訂單填寫完整，傳真至 +49 69 670002。

KILROY INTERIORS
1122 Peachtree Street, Savannah, GA 31406
912-534-9986

August 14, 2023

Arthur Consulting
Metro South
135 Auburn Ave NE
Atlanta, GA 30303

Ref: AG08c

Dear Ms. Hanks:

Thank you for your inquiry of August 3. I'm afraid I will need more specifications about the work you require before I can give you a firm offer for this project.

Regarding (1) *Painting 3 interior rooms.* The cost for this service depends on the paint selected and the size of the room. Typical rates for painters are $16 to $23 per hour.

Regarding (2) *Redecoration advice and assistance.* Our corporate design consulting rate is $85 per hour.

Regarding (3) *Office furniture: desks, bookshelves, conference tables, display shelves.* Our usual policy is to have a consultation about styles and tastes and then bring you samples and quotes from three or four sources before we purchase the furniture. We charge an 8% commission on the price of the furniture.

It is also possible to create a flat rate for your redesign; however, we would require more information about your needs and your time frame.

We offer a free consultation for first-time clients. If you are interested in pursuing this redesign, I would like to set up a meeting to discuss how we can move forward. Please contact me at your earliest convenience at 912-534-9986. Thank you again for your interest in Kilroy Interiors.

Best wishes,

Hannah Hossein

Hannah Hossein
Designer
Kilroy Interiors

漢克斯女士您好：

謝謝您於 8 月 3 日來函詢價。不好意思，在此需要請您提供更詳細的資訊，我們才能夠就此案提供穩固報價。

關於 (1) 粉刷三間房間。此服務之價格取決於選用的粉刷材料與房間大小。一般粉刷服務的工錢為每小時 16 到 23 美元。

關於 (2) 裝修建議與協助。本公司的企業設計諮詢費用為每小時 85 美元。

關於 (3) 辦公家具：辦公桌、書櫃、會議桌、展示櫃。我們通常的做法是購買家具前，先與顧客就風格與品味進行諮詢，然後提供三到四間家具商之樣品與報價。我們會從購買家具的價格中，索取 8% 的佣金。

如果您可以更詳細説明您的需求與時限，也有可能提供您裝修的固定費率。

對於新顧客，我們提供一次免費的諮詢服務。若您有意與本公司進行此裝修計畫，我們可以安排一次會面討論後續事宜。請您方便時盡快撥打 912-534-9986 與我聯絡。再次謝謝您有意選擇 Kilroy 室內設計。

1 Making inquiries 詢問：詢問資訊或報價

① I am interested in your _____ [name of product] and would like more information about it, including a quotation.

我對貴公司的〔產品名稱〕非常有興趣，希望能得到更多的相關資訊，包括報價。

② I would like to receive pricing information about your . . .

我希望就貴公司的……得到價格相關資訊。

③ Please tell me the current price of your . . .　請告知貴公司……目前的價格。

④ Please send me more information about . . .　想請您就……寄來更多資訊。

⑤ Please send me a quotation for the work specified below.

請就下列工作內容提供報價。

⑥ Please explain how you would charge for the work detailed in this letter . . .

請說明貴公司就信中工作內容如何收費。

2 Responding to inquiries: Providing information
回覆詢價：提供資訊

① We are pleased to provide you with the information you requested in your letter of . . .

我們非常樂意提供您……的來信內要求的相關資訊。

② We are happy to send you information about . . .

我們非常樂意為您就……提供資訊。

③ I hope the information in this letter answers your questions . . .

希望這些這封信上的資訊能夠回覆您的問題……

④ I hope the information enclosed answers your questions . . .
希望附上的資訊能夠回覆您的問題……

3 Responding to inquiries: Making a quotation 回覆詢價：提供報價

① Please find a quotation enclosed for . . .　　　請看隨信附上的……報價。

② Please find a quotation below for . . .　　　請看下面列出的……報價。

③ We are pleased to offer you pricing information on _____ [product name] . . .
我們很樂意為您就……〔產品名稱〕提供價格相關資訊。

④ Our current rate for _____ [type of work] is _____ [amount per hour, amount per day . . .]
我們目前〔服務內容〕的價格為〔每小時 / 每天〕……

4 Responding to inquiries: Making a firm offer
回覆詢問：進行穩固報價

① This offer is good for _____ [amount of time].
此報價於……〔時間〕內有效。

② The information in this offer is valid for _____ [amount of time].
此報價中的資訊於……〔時間〕內有效。

③ This offer will not be valid after _____ [date].
〔日期〕之後，此報價便無效。

④ This letter constitutes a firm offer.　　　本信之報價為穩固報價。

⑤ Please consider this letter an offer with engagement.
此信為穩固報價。

5 Responding to inquiries: Asking for information
回覆詢價：詢問資訊

❶ In order to give you an accurate quote, we need the following information . . .

為了提供您正確的報價，我們還需要下列資訊……

❷ Please send us the following information to help us prepare a correct quotation . . .

請寄來下列資訊，方便我們提供您正確的報價……

❸ I am sorry, but I cannot offer you a quote without the following information . . .

很抱歉，但我們還需要下列的資訊，才能夠提供您正確的報價……

❹ If you will answer these questions, I will be happy to send you a quotation as soon as possible . . .

若您能回答這些問題，我很樂意盡快給您報價。

6 Responding to inquiries: Indicating a non-firm offer
回覆詢價：表明為非穩固報價

❶ This offer is subject to our final consideration.

此報價還有可能依我們最後的考量進行調整。

❷ The prices quoted here are subject to change.

這裡的報價還有可能調整。

❸ This quote is subject to consideration and does not represent a final offer.

此報價還有可能再考量調整，並非最終報價。

1 Review the concepts

❶ What is a letter of inquiry?

❷ What information should be included in a letter of inquiry?

❸ Which of these questions would likely appear on a sales inquiry form? _____

(A) How long have you been in your current position?

(B) What is your title?

(C) What is your role in purchasing?

(D) What is your opinion about our products?

(E) How many products are you interested in purchasing?

❹ Which questions might you ask when writing a letter of inquiry about a service? _____

(A) How much does your service cost per hour?

(B) How do you bill for your service?

(C) Who else provides similar services?

(D) What is your commission for the service?

❺ To which department or person should a letter of inquiry be sent? _____

(A) The sales or marketing department

(B) The human resources department

(C) The CEO

❻ What is a letter of quotation? _____

(A) A letter describing work specifications

(B) A letter describing prices for goods or services

(C) A letter requesting prices for goods or services

❼ A firm offer _____

(A) can change.

(B) cannot change.

(C) cannot change within a certain time frame.

❽ An offer without engagement _____

(A) can change.

(B) cannot change within a certain time frame.

(C) is a firm offer.

2 Fill in the sales inquiry form appropriately.

Imagine that you want to order a new server for your office. You also want a technician to look at your current server situation and suggest necessary upgrades or changes. Fill in the sales inquiry form appropriately.

If you would like to talk to a 123 sales representative about products, pricing, or another way in which we can serve you, please:

- Call 1 (800) 600-6770 in the USA or Canada.
- Go to http://www.123.com for more contact information.
- Complete the form below.

First name	Last name
Company	Email
Industry	Job title
Address 1	
Address 2	City
Country	State/Province
Zip/Postal code	Phone number

❋ **Best time to contact you**

❋ **I would like information about**

    ☐ Products   ☐ Services

    ☐ Software solutions   ☐ Other

    ☐ Pricing

❋ **Are you interested in a specific 123 product or product family?**

❋ **Other questions or comments**

3 Write a letter of inquiry.

Imagine that your company is interested in training courses from Tops Professional Training. Write a letter of inquiry asking for all the necessary information about two courses: Writing for Success and Spectacular Sales Writing. You do not have a contact at the company.

November 30, 2023

Tops Professional Training
Montgomery Village Center
20038 Watkins Mill Road
Gaithersburg, MD 20879

Dear _____ :

_____

_____

_____

_____

_____

_____

_____

_____

_____

_____

_____

_____

_____

_____

_____

_____

_____

_____

_____

_____

_____

4 Send a response.

Imagine that you work for Blumenschein, Inc. You received the letter of inquiry on page 167 (31-5). Send a response, this time making a firm offer. The total cost of the Blumenschein Large Knife Collection is $398; the Braun Standard Kitchen Line is $214; and the Modern Quality Chef's Set is $200.

Shipping and insurance for the whole order is $150. With expedited shipping, the order will arrive within three days of order placement. You offer a 7% discount on orders over $700 (not including shipping costs). Payment must be made in advance either through a bank transfer or credit card payment. Your offer is valid until April 31.

BLUMENSCHEIN, INC.
Adickesallee 3, 94855
Frankfurt am Main, Germany

March 30, 2023

Lee Wen
Lee Chef Supply
65 Chien Hsing Road, San Min District
Kaohsiung City, Taiwan

Dear _____ :

_____

_____

_____

_____

_____

_____

_____

_____

_____

_____

_____

_____

_____

Key Terms

catalog number / item number / model number
產品號碼、產品編號、商品型號

公司就產品給予的編號，方便識別該產品。

COD 貨到付款

Cash on delivery 的縮寫，訂購商品時可選擇的付款方式之一，意思是貨到之後，買主就付款。

consignment 未付貨品

在訂貨業務中，指買方尚未付清的訂貨。

execute 執行

用於 to execute an order 時，指處理訂單的內容，進行發貨事宜。

expedited 快捷

這個字有「更快速的」之意，指發貨和送貨都更快速。

invoice 帳單、發貨單

列出對方購買之商品或服務、並索取付費的清單。要請買方付費時，賣方就會寄出帳單。

merchandise 商品

被買賣的產品。

net 淨得的

扣去所有該扣去的項目後，所得到的數目。
如要算出公司的淨獲利（net profit），便須從毛（總）獲利（gross/whole profits）中扣掉所有的支出。

place 下 (訂單)

用在 to place an order，表示下訂單訂購商品。

purchase order (PO) 訂購單

買主寄給賣主的文件，上面列出訂購的商品種類、數量，及雙方談成的價格，此外通常也包含送貨方式、付款方式等資訊。

take 接 (訂單)

用在 to take an order 時，表示接受顧客訂購商品的訂單。賣主接（take）訂單，顧客或買主下（place）訂單。

terms 條款

一間公司的商品價格、送貨政策，及其他有關如何處理訂單的細節規定。

Unit 34 訂單和訂貨信／回覆信
What are orders and order letters?

1 什麼是訂單？

在許多商務領域中，你需要第一線負起為顧客提供商品或服務的責任。在這一章，我們就來看看訂單、訂貨信，以及如何回覆訂貨信。**訂單（order）** 就是顧客用來跟你訂購商品或服務的文件，訂單有很多種形式。在本單元，我們會討論有／無附上訂單的訂貨信。

2 我會如何收到訂單？

每間公司的訂貨程序可能各不相同，本單元把重點放在如何立刻掌握你需要的資訊，並跟顧客索取他們沒有提供的資訊。通常如果顧客同意你的**訂貨條件（terms）**，他們就會跟你下訂單，也就是填好一份正式的**訂單表格（order form）**，附上封面頁（cover letter）寄給你。訂單應該要能給你下列的資訊：

- 顧客的姓名與地址
- 供應商的姓名與地址
- 訂單參考文號
- 訂貨日期
- 訂貨內容，包括數量、大小、顏色、型號（model number）等
- 送貨方式、付款方式及其他相關細節

如果顧客沒使用訂單表格，就要透過雙方的通信得到這些資訊。

3 如何回覆訂單？

收到訂單後，務必**迅速給予明確的回覆**。首先要仔細閱讀訂單，確定你都看懂了，然後跟顧客確認所有的細節。如果顧客沒有給你所有你需要的資訊，要立刻詢問顧客。尤其是口頭（verbally）下的訂單，一定要立刻跟顧客確認所有的細節，避免誤會發生。

你的公司可能會以不同的方式回覆訂單，比如說公司可能會要求對所有的訂單都回覆書面的**確認信（confirmation letter）**，就算訂單是以電子郵件的形式寄來也一樣。有些公司可能會依收到訂單的形式進行回覆：以電子郵件寄來的訂單，便以電子郵件回覆，以傳真寄來的訂單便以傳真回覆等。因此回覆訂單的時候，需確實按照公司規定的流程。

4 什麼是訂貨信？

訂貨信（order letter）就是跟收件的公司訂購商品或服務的信。許多公司都有自己專用的訂貨信格式，該格式應該能夠給你所有你需要的資訊。但是訂貨信有時候也會以電子郵件、電話、傳真等其他形式送來，這時候你就要注意對方是否提供了所有你需要的資訊，如果沒有，就要立刻詢問顧客。

訂貨信常常會跟**訂單表格或訂購單（purchase order, PO）**一起送來，但有時候訂貨信本身就充當訂單，說明顧客想要訂購的內容。無論如何，收到訂貨信後，要立刻讓顧客知道你們已收到訂單，準備開始送貨事宜。以下分別是附有訂單、以及未附訂單的訂貨信範例。

Trading Group Ltd
33 Wilderness Road
Toronto, Ontario M5R 1X8
(416) 987-2290

March 12, 2023

Large Machines Co.
86 Hsin Li Road
Hsinchu 300, Taiwan
(886) 03-5626733

Reference: Our purchase order number 458/23

Attention: Mr. John Jameson

Thank you for your letter and catalog of February 15. We agree to your terms of payment and shipment. Please find enclosed our purchase order number 458/23.

Please note that we have requested expedited shipping because we need these items urgently. Please inform us as soon as possible if expedited shipping is not an option, as we cannot use the items if they arrive later than March 30, 2023.

Sincerely,

John Kingsley

John Kingsley
Chief Process Officer
Trading Group Ltd

Enc. (1)

經辦人約翰・詹姆生先生：

謝謝您於 2 月 15 日的來信與目錄。我們同意貴公司提出的付款方式與送貨方式。隨信附上訂單（訂單號碼 458/23）。

請注意我們要求的是快捷遞送，因為我們急需這些商品。如果無法以快捷遞送，請盡快通知我們，因為如果貨品於 2023 年 3 月 30 日之後才送達，我們就無法利用了。

34-1- ② | Purchase Order 訂單

正式訂單號碼：方便買賣雙方追蹤訂單

Official Purchase Order number 458/23

Trading Group Ltd
33 Wilderness Road
Toronto, Ontario M5R 1X8
(416) 987-2290

March 12, 2023

Large Machines Co.
86 Hsin Li Road
Hsinchu 300, Taiwan
(886) 03-5626733

Attention: Mr. John Jameson

Please supply the following items:

Quantity	Description	Item number	Unit price	Total price per item(s)
8	Window cutting machine	LJZB2B	$2,020.00	$16,160.00
1	Bench lathe	CQ6230A-1	$750.00	$750.00
				Total: $16,910.00

Payment terms shall be standard 2%-10/NET 30. ❶ —— 付款方式：說明如何付款

Please ship the items as soon as possible using UPS expedited shipping. ❷

Please deliver all items no later than March 30, 2023.

送貨方式：說明運送方式和運送地點

Ship all items to : Receiving Office
Trading Company Ltd
33 Wilderness Road
Toronto, Ontario M5R 1X8
(416) 987-2290

❶ 說明付款方式：「2%-10/NET 30」的意思是，如果顧客在 10 天之內付款，就可以得到 2% 的折扣，如果沒有，就須在 30 天內付清全額。從公司或個人寄來的訂貨信都有可能看到這個用法。有時候折扣會多於 2%，也可能少於 2%；付款期限通常是 30 天，但是也有可能更多或更少。

❷ 送貨方式：說明貨品如何及何時寄出。你可以寫「using UPS」、「via UPS」或「by UPS」。UPS（United Parcel Service）是一間美國的包裹遞送公司。

訂購產品如下：

數量	產品	型號	單位價格	單品加總價格
8	窗戶切割機	LJZB2B	$2,020.00	$16,160.00
1	檯式車床	CQ6230A-1	$750.00	$750.00
				總計：$16,910.00

採標準付款條件：10 天內付款，享 2% 折扣／ 30 天內付款，須付全額。❶

請盡快以 UPS 快遞 ❷ 寄出貨品。
請在 2023 年 3 月 30 日前寄到所有貨品。

34-1- ③ | Responding to the letter and purchase order 回覆訂貨信和訂單

Large Machines Co.
86 Hsin Li Road
Hsinchu 300, Taiwan
(886) 03-5626733

25 March 2023

John Kingsley
Trading Group Ltd
33 Wilderness Road
Toronto, ON 12302

Ref: Order No. 458/23 ❶ ——

❶「Ref」是「referring to」（關於……）的縮寫，用來快速告訴對方，這封信是就哪份訂單或訂貨信而回的，這樣也方便對方找到該訂單或訂貨信。

Dear Mr. Kingsley:

We thank you for your reply of 12 March. Our company is very happy to fill your order no. 458/23 for eight window cutting machines, model LJZB2B CNC-500x5000, and one bench lathe, model CQ6230A-1.

Special attention will be given to the execution of your order. We will notify you as soon as the consignment is ready for transport.

We hope this first order will lead to future business. ❷

❷「We hope this first order…」是用來結束確認信非常友善的說法。這間公司希望給對方留下親切友善的印象，但在訂貨信裡就不需要加上這個句子。如果你跟對方已經有過合作關係，也不應該在信裡加上這一句。

Yours sincerely,

John Jameson

John Jameson, Sales Manager
Large Machines Company

purchase order

這封信簡短地確認了訂貨信的重要細節，包括商品的數量、名稱和訂單號碼。對方是第一次跟這間公司訂貨，因此這封回信內容詳細、口氣親切，而這間公司當然希望以後能跟這個顧客繼續進行買賣，因此在最後一段表明未來合作意願。

參考文號：訂單編號 458/23 ❶

謝謝您於 3 月 12 日的回覆。我們非常高興收到您的訂單（訂單號碼 458/23），您與本公司訂購八個窗戶切割機（型號 LJZB2B CNC-500x5000）及一個檯式車床（型號 CQ6230A-1）。

我們會特別注意送貨事宜。一旦貨品準備好寄出，我們會立刻通知您。

敬盼貴公司繼首筆訂單後，能繼續關照本公司業務。❷

Industrial Upkeep, Inc.
293 Maintenance Drive
Toronto, Ontario
M5G 1E6

September 15, 2023

Sales and Orders Department
Universal Chemical Supply Company
Hong Kong Science Parks
Shatin, New Territories, Hong Kong

Dear Orders Officer:

This is an order for the merchandise listed herein. ❶

❶「Listed herein」可以代替「the products mentioned in this letter」（本信列出的產品）和「the following products」（以下產品）等說法。

10 EA. AMMONIUM HYDROXIDE 55 GAL. @212.50=2125.00 ❷
3 EA. CHAMBERS INDUST. SOLVENT HI-CONCENTRATE 55 GAL.
@122.00=366.00

Please ship as soon as possible. Payment terms shall be standard 2%-10/NET 30. Method of shipment: APEX.

Any questions regarding this order should be directed to Mike Chambers at 416-521-1668 EXT. 243 in the Toronto office.

Thank you for your prompt and expeditious handling of this order.

Sincerely,

Mike Chambers

Mike Chambers, Director
Toronto Division
Industrial Upkeep, Inc.

訂單負責主管敬啟：

在此就下列 ❶ 商品下訂單：

10 桶 55 加侖裝氫氧化銨 x 212.50 美元／桶 = 2125.00 美元 ❷
3 桶 55 加侖裝 Chambers 高濃縮工業溶劑 x 122.00 美元／桶 = 366.00 美元

請盡速送貨。採標準付款方式：10 天之內付款，享 2% 折扣／ 30 天內付款，須付全額。
送貨方式：APEX。

若有任何訂單問題，請聯絡多倫多辦公室的麥可‧錢伯斯：416-521-1668 分機 243。

謝謝您迅速處理此訂單。

---

❷ 這個句子以縮寫列出了顧客欲訂購的商品數量、大小和價格：

• 「10 EA.」是「ten each」（每樣 10 個）的意思，即本項產品要訂 10 份。

• 「AMMONIUM HYDROXIDE 55 GAL.」表示他要訂的產品是 55 加侖（GAL.= gallon）
裝的氫氧化銨。

• 「@212.50」的部分說明了產品的單價為 212.5 美元。

• 「=2125.00」表示每桶的價格（$212.50）乘以訂購數量 10 桶，合計為 2125.00 美元。

Sales and Orders Department
Universal Chemical Supply Company
Hong Kong Science Park
Shatin, New Territories, Hong Kong

September 23, 2023

Mike Chambers
Industrial Upkeep, Inc.
293 Maintenance Drive
Toronto, Ontario
M5G 1E6

Dear Mr. Chambers:

Thank you for your order of September 15, 2023. We are very pleased ❶ to confirm your order of ten units of ammonium hydroxide/55 gallons (item number 453) and three units of Chambers Industrial Solvent/55 gallons (item number 485x), for a cost of $2,491.00.

Please use the enclosed catalog to confirm the item numbers of your order.

Enclosed are our standard payment forms, should you wish to pay in advance. Please complete the relevant form and send it back to us at your earliest convenience ❷ or contact us for other payment options. Otherwise, we will present our invoice at the time of delivery. We will ship the items via APEX as soon as the order is ready.

Thank you for your order. We look forward to serving you.

Yours truly,

Ken Won

Ken Won, Sales Associate
Universal Chemical Supply Company

Enclosures (2)

錢伯斯先生您好：

謝謝您 2023 年 9 月 15 日的訂單。很高興 ❶ 能夠在此跟您確認訂購產品：10 桶 10 加侖裝氫氧化銨（產品型號 453）及 3 桶 55 加侖裝 Chambers 高濃縮工業溶劑（產品型號 485x），共計 2,491.00 美元。

請從所附產品目錄確認訂單產品型號。

隨信附上標準付款表格。若您欲事先付款，請填寫相關表格，並盡速於方便時 ❷ 寄回，或者與我們聯絡，以其他方式付款。不然我們將隨貨附上發貨單。一旦貨品準備好，將交由 APEX 寄送。

謝謝您的訂購。誠心期盼能為您服務。

在這封信裡，供應商跟對方確認訂單內容，並且同時附上產品目錄，方便顧客確定信中的產品型號的確是他要訂購的產品，此外他還附上了對方可能需要的付款表格。

❶ 「We are very pleased . . .」創造出親切友善的語氣。如果要讓語氣正式一點，你可以寫「We confirm your order」（在此確認您的訂單）或是「Please accept this letter as confirmation of your order」（本信確認您的訂單）。

❷ 「At your earliest convenience」是請對方盡快採取行動非常禮貌的說法。這暗示寫信人希望對方趕快完成某個行動，但是聽起來又沒有 as soon as possible（盡快）、immediately（立刻）那麼急。

The Edge Technologies
#18, Yoido-dong
Youngdeungpo-gu
Seoul, South Korea
150-790

November 2, 2023

TelNEXT
Lishin Fifth Street, #89
Hsinchu 300
Taiwan

Attention Sales Department:

Thank you for your catalog of October 1, 2023. Please confirm our order of ten Topline LCD screens. Please fill our order as soon as possible.

Sincerely,

Joanne Kim

Joanne Kim, Office Manager
The Edge Technologies

這樣的訂貨信給予的資訊非常少：顧客列出了她想訂購的產品廠牌與數量，但是此外就沒有其他資訊了。這時你還需要跟她索取哪些資訊？以下就看看可以怎麼回覆。

經辦人：業務部門

謝謝您於 2023 年 10 月 1 日寄來的產品目錄。在此向您訂購 10 個 Topline 液晶螢幕，請與我們確認訂單，並盡快處理此訂單。

TelNEXT
Lishin Fifth Street, #89
Hsinchu 300
Taiwan

November 16, 2023

The Edge Technologies
#18, Yoido-dong
Youngdeungpo-gu
Seoul, South Korea
150-790

寫信人就訂單進行了回覆，但是沒有進行確認。她跟顧客索取確認訂單所需的資訊：液晶螢幕的尺寸、型號、付款方式和送貨方式。

Dear Ms. Kim:

Thank you for your order of November 2, 2023. Before we fill your order, please provide the following information:

1. What size Topline LCD screens do you want to order?
2. What is the model number of the screens? (You can find the model numbers in the enclosed catalog.)
3. How would you like to pay? Enclosed are instructions for payment by bank transfer or credit card.
4. Which shipping option would you like to use? You can find our shipping options in the enclosed catalog.

Thank you for your attention. Please respond with the information requested above, and we will be happy to confirm and ship your order. Please understand that we cannot confirm your order until we receive your answers to the questions above.

Best,

Susan Lin

Susan Lin
Sales Manager/Hsinchu
TelNEXT

Enc. (2)

金女士您好：

謝謝您於 2023 年 11 月 2 日寄來的訂單。在處理此訂單前，我們還需要下列的資訊：

1. 您希望訂購多大尺寸的 Topline 液晶螢幕？

2. 該液晶螢幕的產品型號是？（您可以在所附產品目錄中找到產品型號。）

3. 您希望如何付款？隨信附上銀行轉帳或信用卡付款說明。

4. 您希望的送貨方式是？您可以在所附產品目錄中找到可選擇的送貨方式。

感謝您閱讀以上內容。請您就上述問題進行回覆，之後我們將非常樂意確認並處理您的訂單。請了解我們必須先就上述問題得到答案，才能確認此訂單。

TelNEXT
Lishin Fifth Street, #89
Hsinchu 300
Taiwan

November 16, 2023

The Edge Technologies
#18, Yoido-dong
Youngdeungpo-gu
Seoul, South Korea
150-790

在這封信裡，供應商表示無法接下對方的訂
單，因為顧客指定的產品已經停產且賣光
了，於是寫信人跟顧客推薦另外兩個廠牌，
並表示願意提供相關的協助。

Dear Ms. Kim:

We are very sorry that we are unable to fill your order for 10 Topline LCD screens.
Topline has recently ceased production of all small-sized LCD screens, and our
previous stock has been depleted. We are very sorry for the inconvenience.

Topline is not expected to produce home- or business-sized screens again in the
near future.

We recommend Starbyte and Ace screens, which are similar in function and price
to the Topline products.

Please find enclosed another copy of our current catalog. Again, we regret that we
are unable to provide you with the Topline screens. Please feel free to contact me
with any questions. I will be happy to recommend other products for your specific
needs.

金女士您好：

非常抱歉，我們無法處理您訂購 10 個 Topline 液晶螢幕的訂
單。Topline 不久前停止生產所有小尺寸的液晶螢幕，我們的
存貨也已售光，非常抱歉造成您的不便。

預計 Topline 近期內也不會再生產家用或商用尺寸的液晶螢幕。

我們推薦您考慮 Starbyte 和 Ace 的螢幕，這兩個廠牌的液晶
螢幕與 Topline 的產品功能相似，價格也相仿。

隨信附上我們最新的產品目錄。再次跟您說聲抱歉，我們無法
提供您 Topline 液晶螢幕。如果有任何問題，歡迎與我聯絡，
我會非常樂意針對您的特定需求，為您推薦其他產品。

Best,

Susan Lin

Susan Lin
Sales Manager/Hsinchu
TelNEXT

Enc. (1)

Unit 35 訂貨信常用說法
Common phrases in order letters

1 Placing orders 下訂單

❶ We herewith order the following items . . .

在此訂購下列產品……

❷ Enclosed please find our order.

隨信附上訂單／訂單已隨信附上。

❸ Our order is enclosed.

隨信附上訂單／訂單已隨信附上。

❹ We agree to your payment and shipping terms: Payment will be provided in full within X days of delivery, and shipment will be made via APEX's international priority service.

我方同意您的付款方式與送貨方式：款項於交貨後 X 天內付清，
貨品以 APEX 國際優先快遞寄送。

❺ We reserve the right to cancel the order if . . .

在……狀況下，我們保留取消訂單的權利。

❻ Would you please place our order for the following items . . . ?

是否能請您為我們訂購下列產品……？

❼ We are pleased to give you an order for . . .　　我們非常高興跟您訂購……

❽ We acknowledge receipt of your offer and enclose our order No. for . . .

在此確認收到您的報價，並隨信附上……的訂單號碼。

2 Requesting quick deliveries 請對方盡速出貨

❶ We have an urgent need for the goods.　我們急需這些商品。

❷ We would appreciate it if you could deliver the order as soon as possible.

若能盡速出貨,我們將非常感激。

❸ Please expedite our delivery.

請盡快寄送我們訂購的商品。

3 Confirming orders 確認訂單

❶ This letter confirms your verbal order of _____ [date] . . .

本信確認您於……〔日期〕口頭下的訂單。

❷ Thank you for your order, which we acknowledge as follows . . .

謝謝您的訂單,在此進行確認……

❸ We are pleased to receive your order . . .　非常高興收到您的訂單……

❹ We assure you that your order will receive our full/immediate attention . . .

我們保證將妥善/盡速處理您的訂單……

4 Thanking suppliers 謝謝供應商

❶ Thank you for your prompt and expeditious handling of this order.

謝謝您迅速處理此訂單。

5 About payment 關於付款方式

❶ Payment terms shall be standard 1%-10 days, Net 30 days from date of invoice.

採標準付款方式：10 天之內付款，享 1% 的折扣／ 30 天內付款，須付全額。

❷ Payment shall be rendered upon delivery.

貨到付款。

❸ COD is not accepted.

我們不接受貨到付款。

6 About shipment 關於送貨方式

❶ Partial shipment not permitted—This means the customer wants all of the ordered items to arrive together, not at different times or in different shipments. (However, large orders may be shipped in more than one box or container as long as all containers arrive at one time.)

不接受分批送貨——這表示顧客希望所有訂購的商品一起送達，不要在不同的時間送達，也不要用不同的方式運送（大批的訂貨當然有可能裝在不同的箱子或貨櫃裡運送，只要同時送達就可以了）。

❷ Insurance will be covered by us.　　　　保險費由我方承擔。

❸ Packing should be strong enough to ensure sufficient protection.

包裝方式應能（為產品）提供足夠的保護。

❹ Goods of inferior quality will be returned at the supplier's risk and expense.

品質不佳的產品將退回，由供應商承擔風險與費用。

1 Review the concepts

❶ "Expedited shipping" means _____
(A) standard shipping.   (B) insured shipping.   (C) fast shipping.

❷ "This letter is an order for the _____ described below."
(A) goods   (B) merchandise   (C) items
(D) products   (E) All of the above

❸ Which word does not mean similarly as "ship" in the context of an order?
(A) confirm   (B) deliver   (C) mail

❹ An invoice is sent to _____
(A) request payment.
(B) request a service.

❺ **Choose the correct preposition:** Thank you for your order _____ May 2.
(A) with   (B) to   (C) of

❻ What is a model number or catalog number? How is it useful?

_____

_____

❼ What does this mean? Please explain the phrase in English.

> 3 EA. CHAMBERS INDUST. SOLVENT HI-CONCENTRATE
> 55 GAL. @122.00=366.00

_____

_____

❽ What information is typically found in a purchase order?
(A) Company histories   (B) Product names
(C) Prices per unit   (D) Shipping terms
(E) Product recommendations

❾ When a customer orders a product or service from you, is the customer placing an order or taking an order? What is the difference?

_____

_____

❿ Think about your company or about the information presented in Part 8. List all the information you need from a customer to fill an order.

_____

_____

2 Write the purchase order.

You want to order five laptop computers (item number 332, price $800 each), three desktop computers (item number 431a, price $500 each), and one scanner (item number 555, price $350 each). Complete this purchase order for the merchandise. Your contact at the company is Charlie Watts. You would like him to use DHL expedited service for shipping, and you would like the shipment to arrive no later than December 10. You would like to receive the invoice and pay at delivery. Use the sender's address as the shipping address.

PO 120212

XYZ Incorporated
1650 Mount Pleasant Street NW
Washington, DC 20010 USA

December 2, 2023

Computer Supplies Inc.
No. 420, Section 1
Keelung Road, Sin-yi District
Taipei 11051, Taiwan

Attention: _____

Please supply the following items:

Quantity	Description	Item number	Unit price	Total price
_____	_____	_____	_____	_____
_____	_____	_____	_____	_____
_____	_____	_____	_____	_____

Total: _____

Payment terms shall be standard 2%-10/NET 30. Payment will be made at delivery.

Please ship all items using _____.

Please deliver all items by _____.

Shipping address: _____

_____

_____

3 Write a response to the order.

Imagine you have just received the following letter from a customer. Write a response to her confirming her order, her payment, the expected delivery date, and any other information she might want.

February 15, 2023

Subject: Furniture and equipment order

Please ship the following items from your sales catalog dated January 29, 2023.

ITEM	CATALOG #	COLOR	QTY	PRICE
Conference Desk	HN-33080-WB	Sandalwood	2	$378.60 ea.
Credenza	HN-36887-WK	Sandalwood	2	$231.40 ea.
Executive Chair	HP-56563-SE	Toasted Tan	4	$222.00 ea.
File Cabinet	HN-5344C-K	Beige	2	$75.90 ea.

The items ordered above should be shipped C.O.D. to this address:

> Worthington Marketing
> 16 Stanhope Road
> Harlow
> Essex
> CM19 6EA
> Great Britain

The costs above reflect a discount of 3%/10, with net due in 30 days after the invoice date. The merchandise is to be shipped by your company's own truck line at a rate of 7% of the total net cost.

Sincerely,

Susan Montag

Susan Montag, Supervisor
Clerical Services

February 16, 2023

Worthington Marketing
16 Stanhope Road
Harlow, Essex
CM19 6EA
Great Britain

Re: _____

Dear Ms. Montag:

_____
_____
_____
_____
_____
_____
_____
_____
_____
_____
_____
_____
_____
_____
_____
_____
_____
_____
_____

付款相關書信
Payment

Key Terms

bill of lading 提（貨）單

運送人承認收到貨物以供運送的文件，用以確保出貨商可取得付款、收貨者可拿到貨品。在「跟單託收」的付款方式中，提單和「發貨單」、「保險證明」是三項最重要的文件。

credit 信貸、信用

credit 有很多個意思。在本章節裡，credit 用來指借來的款項，或是個人或公司借款的能力。

credit file 信貸檔案

信貸檔案會詳細記錄你借款、賒購（以賒帳方式訂購）、是否及時付清款項及債務的歷史。一間公司可能會為其顧客建立信貸檔案。

credit reference 信用擔保人

保證信貸申請人能夠及時付清款項之個人或公司。銀行有可能擔任某公司的信用擔保人，就信貸申請人之開戶時間、透支或逾期付款等歷史提供基本資料，此外還可能提供信貸或貸款歷史，以證明該申請人的信用度。

credit score 信用評分

用來表示個人財務信用程度的分數。

credit worthy 有信用的

有信用的顧客就是有資格借款的顧客，該顧客通常有良好的信貸歷史、財務報表或信用擔保人。

certified financial statement 審定財務報表

由合格會計師審查證明過的資產負債表、損益表，及其他財務檔案。

delinquent (account) 呆帳

沒有付清的款項。

draft 匯票

賣方發出給買方銀行的文件，要求將款項在當下或特定時間支付。

history of repayment 還款紀錄

償還借用款項的紀錄。若還款紀錄不佳，一般會影響到該個人或單位的信用評分。

insurance certificate 保險證明

由保險公司所開立的正式文件，用來證明保險政策存在，並說明該保險方案提供何種財務保障。

invoice 發貨單

由賣方向買方寄發的文件，其中會向買方列舉出售的產品或服務的名稱、數量以及協議價格等資訊。

outstanding 未付的

未付清的，用法如 an outstanding account（未付的款項）或 an outstanding invoice（未付的貨單）。

payment in installments 分期付款

將一筆款項分到不同時間點逐次支付的付款方式。

remit 匯款

應要求、帳目或匯票匯出款項。

settle 付款

（用在帳戶）支付；結算。

Unit 36 信用調查信
Credit inquiry letters

1 什麼是信用調查信（credit inquiry letter）？

信用調查信用來收集**顧客的信貸資料**，就個人或公司的**資金、付款模式、債務利息**（interest rate）或**其他財務狀況**蒐集資訊，以協助公司了解該顧客是否有能力償付帳單。

初次交易的新顧客跟你或你的公司下訂單後，你通常會想先收集他的信貸資料，以建立**信貸檔案（credit file）**。要為新顧客建立一個貿易帳戶（記帳帳戶）前，你必須先了解他是否有信用，而通常的做法就是寄信用調查信給**顧客**及**其信用擔保人**（credit reference），同時要求對方提供信貸歷史或信用評分的副本。

信用調查信基本上有兩種：一種寫給顧客所提供的**信用擔保人**，一種寫給**顧客**，下面將介紹這兩種不同的信用調查信。

2 寫信用調查信給信用擔保人

要向顧客的信用擔保人寄出信用調查信前，顧客會提供其信用擔保人的姓名與地址，接著就可依此寫信給信用擔保人，就顧客的還款紀錄（history of repayment）收集資訊。寫這一類信用調查信的原則，就跟寫一般的詢問信一樣：

- 直接、切中重點。
- 清楚說明你需要什麼資訊。
- 給對方所有需要的資訊，方便回答你的問題。
- 跟對方保證，你會尊重他的隱私。
- 有可能的話，提供回郵信封。

3 寫信用調查信給顧客

寄給顧客的信用調查信就要比較有技巧了，**尤其要得體周到**，你應該要讓顧客覺得受到重視，而不是受到質疑。寫信用調查信給顧客有幾個訣竅：

- 謝謝顧客的訂購與惠顧。
- 說明信用調查是公司的例行步驟，而非代表不信任對方。
- 簡短說明你們例行的（routine）信用政策程序。
- 強調如果顧客提供完整的信貸資訊，有助於你迅速處理他們的訂單。
- 讓顧客知道，盡速提供相關資訊是對顧客本身有益，藉此鼓勵顧客盡快回覆。

EduTech
323 Bannock Street
Denver, CO 80204

4 August 2023

Leslie Broome
Administrative Director
Educational Media Group
2620 Wasach Avenue
Olympia, WA 98501

Dear Ms. Broome:

A purchase order from Kids International Village in Busan, South Korea, for $850 worth of merchandise has listed you as a credit reference.

We would appreciate any information you can provide about Kids International Village's credit history with your company. ❶ Key information includes how long the owner, Soon Yi Choe, has had an account with you and whether she has any outstanding debts. Be assured, we will keep any information you send us confidential. ❷

Thank you for your assistance in this matter. Enclosed please find an addressed, postage-paid envelope for your convenience. ❸

Sincerely,

Arthur Teveli

Arthur Teveli, Sales Director
EduTech

Enc. (1)

❶ 這封信很快就說明目的。這封信是寄給擔保人的，不是寄給顧客的，所以可以直接表明要求。

❸ 附上貼好郵票的回郵信封可以節省對方的時間與精力，也有助於你更快得到資訊。

❷ 跟信用擔保人詢問信貸資訊時，務必要讓對方知道你會將得到的資訊嚴格保密，這樣也有助於你得到真實的資訊。畢竟，如果顧客發現他的信用擔保人提供給你負面的資訊，很可能會危害信用擔保人與該顧客的關係。

布魯姆女士您好：

南韓釜山 Kids International Village 公司向我們下了價值 850 美元商品的訂單，訂單中將您列為信用擔保人。

想請您提供 Kids International Village 與貴公司交易之信貸歷史 ❶，包括該公司負責人 Soon Yi Choe 在貴公司擁有貿易帳戶已有多長時間、是否有未付清債務等。您提供的資訊我們將嚴格保密，敬請放心。❷

感謝您的協助。隨信附上寫好地址的回郵信封，以便回覆。❸

36-2-① | A credit inquiry letter sent to a new customer
給新顧客的信用調查信

EduTech
323 Bannock Street
Denver, CO 80204

20 July 2023

Soon Yi Choe
Kids International Village
830-62 Peomil 2-Dong
Tong-Gu Busan
South Korea

Dear Ms. Choe:

Thank you for your interest in EduTech. We have received your order and are eager to expedite the shipment as soon as possible. We never forget that new customers like you are responsible for our continued growth. ❶

❶ 這封信就不像上一封信那麼直接了，在第一段先謝謝顧客的訂購，到了下一段才進入主題。

With first-time customers, our policy is to request the usual certified financial statements and references, as well as the name of your bank, in order to open your account. Our regular terms of 2%-10 days/net 30 will begin immediately for you when we receive and accept this information. All the information you provide to us will, of course, be kept confidential. ❷

❷ 寫信人說明，跟新顧客索取信貸資料是公司的例行步驟。

We look forward to receiving your information as soon as possible so that we can process your order and provide you with the quality service we pride ourselves on. ❸ We will do everything we can to ensure that this is a long and mutually profitable relationship. Please don't hesitate to tell us how we can be of service to you.

Sincerely,

Arthur Teveli

Arthur Teveli, Sales Director
EduTech

❸ 最後一段暗示收到信貸資料與對方收到貨物之間的因果關係，這樣可以促使對方盡快提供完整的信貸資料。

崔女士您好：

謝謝您屬意本公司產品。我們已收到您的訂單，並希望能盡快把貨品寄出。我們會隨時提醒自己，正是您這樣的新顧客讓我們持續成長。

對於新顧客，我們的例行步驟是要請顧客提供審定財務報表、信用擔保人及銀行名稱，便於我們為您在本公司開設貿易帳戶。一旦您的資料送達並通過審核，10 天之內付款享 2% 的折扣／30 天內付清全額的標準交易條款便開始生效。當然，您提供的所有資料，我們都會嚴格保密。

希望盡快收到您的資料，便於我們可以處理您的訂單，並為您提供我們引以為傲的高品質服務。❸ 我們將盡全力使這次的交易成為長期的互惠合作關係。有任何我們可以提供協助的地方，請儘管告訴我們。

Kids International Village

830-62 Peomil 2-Dong, Tong-Gu Busan
South Korea

3 August 2023

Arthur Teveli
Sales Director
EduTech
323 Bannock Street
Denver, CO 80204

Dear Mr. Teveli:

Enclosed please find the information you requested in your correspondence of 20 July: the name and address of our bank, our latest bank statement, and two business credit references.

I hope this information suffices to open our account and begin a mutually beneficial relationship. Please let me know if you require additional information.

Sincerely,

Soon Yi Choe

Soon Yi Choe, Procurement Manager

Enc.

秦韋利先生您好：

隨信附上您 7 月 20 日來信索取的資訊：我們的銀行名稱及地址、最新的財務報表、兩間作為信用擔保人的公司。

希望這些資訊足以為我們在貴公司開設貿易帳戶，並展開互惠合作關係。如果還需要額外資訊，請不吝告知。

如果老顧客的訂貨量突然增加，或是基於其他的因素，你需要老顧客最新的信貸資訊，那麼可以參照以下信件撰寫內容：

36-3 | A credit inquiry letter sent to an existing customer 給老顧客的信用調查信

BLUMENSCHEIN, INC.
Adickesallee 3, 94855
Frankfurt am Main, Germany

26 February 2023

Lee Chef Supply
65 Chien Hsing Road, San Min District
Kaohsiung City, Taiwan

❶ 這封信跟 36-2-① 一樣，是寄給顧客的，所以信中先謝謝並稱讚顧客，之後才跟對方索取信貸資料。

Dear Mr. Lee:

Thank you for your new order of January 22. It was processed and shipped immediately, as usual. Your business seems to be growing quickly. We are very happy for your success, and we appreciate your continued interest in our knives and kitchen supplies. ❶

Because of the increased volume of your recent order, we ask that you send us a current balance sheet or operating statement. The latest one we have is dated 10 October 2021. This is a routine credit procedure for our company when a customer places a noticeably larger order. ❷

You have always been most cooperative in providing the financial information we need in order to promptly meet your requirements. Therefore, we are comfortable asking you for the updated information.

We want to emphasize that any financial information you provide is, as always, confidential and will be used only for our mutual benefit.

Thank you for your attention to this matter.

❷ 跟顧客索取信貸資料在這裡也被描寫為公司的例行步驟。

Warm regards,

Karl Blumenschein

Karl Blumenschein, Operations Manager
Blumenschein, Inc.

李先生您好：

謝謝您於 1 月 22 日寄來的訂單。我們跟以往一樣，已立刻開始處理訂單及安排發貨事宜。貴公司的業務似乎正迅速成長。我們誠心恭賀你們的成功，並感謝您繼續購買本公司的刀具及廚具。❶

基於貴公司此次訂貨量增加，請您寄來一份最新的資產負債表或營運報表，我們這裡最近一份是 2021 年 10 月 10 日的資料。這是顧客訂貨量突然大增時，本公司例行的信用保證程序。❷

貴公司一向樂於提供相關的財務資訊，便於我們盡快滿足您的需求，因此這次也不避冒昧，向您要求更新的資訊。

僅此重申，您提供的所有財務資訊我們將照例嚴格保密，只用於促進雙方的利益。

謝謝費心。

Unit 37 一般的付款方式
Common payment terms

1 一般的付款方式有哪些？

payment terms 就是**付款方式**。如果是國內的交易，有很多種簡單的付款方式，如**信用卡**、**支票**或**現金**。如果是國際交易，主要有四種付款方式：

❶ 貿易帳戶，或稱記帳（open account; open credit）
❷ 跟單託收（documentary collections）
❸ 跟單信用狀（documentary letters of credit）
❹ 事先付款（cash in advance）

2 貿易帳戶（記帳）

以**貿易帳戶（open account）**付款的方式對賣方來說風險最大，對買方來說風險最小。採用這種付款方式時，通常是雙方已經有穩定的合作關係，或是賣方信任買方付款的意願與能力，這時**買方的帳會先記在帳戶上，等收到貨物後才付款**。

3 跟單託收

跟單託收（documentary collections）的付款方式普遍用於國際貿易。首先買方和賣方就價格、保險和訂單其他內容簽訂合約。接著，賣方把**發貨單（invoice）**、**保險證明（insurance certificate）**、**提貨單（bill of lading）**等文件收齊，而後把貨物交給運輸公司，此時運輸公司會在提貨單上簽名。然後，賣方把上述所有文件（包括運輸公司簽了名的提貨單）交給他的銀行。

賣方的銀行接著會把這些文件，和賣方開出的**匯票（draft）**轉給買方的銀行。這時視雙方談成的交易方式，買方可能會在看到這些文件時付款給他的銀行（稱為 **documents against payment「付款交單」**），或者簽署匯票，同意在一定期限內付款（稱為 **documents against acceptance「承兌交單」**）。一旦銀行把這些文件交給買方，買方就成為貨物的擁有人。此時銀行同時保護雙方的利益，而雙方都有風險，因為買方可能拒絕付款，而賣方可能發出品質不佳的貨品。

4 跟單信用狀

跟單信用狀（documentary letters of credit）是這四種付款方式中**最常用**的一種，是很常見的國際付款方式，因為此方法能夠**為買方和賣方都提供高度的保障**。

開立跟單信用狀是買方的責任，為此項服務他還要付銀行一筆手續費。買方請銀行開立跟單信用狀，信用狀的內容基本上就是保證**買方在賣方開出發貨的證明文件後，一定會付款**。接著買方的銀行把信用狀寄給賣方的銀行（或是通知賣方的銀行信用狀已開出），信用狀裡列出發貨期限、送貨方式及其他交易資訊。賣方的銀行收到信用狀後，賣方就開始發貨。

信用狀有「可撤銷的」（revocable）與「不可撤銷的」（irrevocable）兩種。可撤銷信用狀可在發貨前由銀行撤銷，不可撤銷信用狀顧名思義就是不能撤銷的。此外，信用狀還有許多不同的種類，主要的區別是要求付款的時間：有些信用狀要求買方立刻付款，有些則會給買方好幾年的時間。

5 事先付款

事先付款（cash in advance）對賣方的風險最小，對買方的風險最大；此時買方在發貨前就付款。通常是雙方**第一次交易**、或是**小額交易**時才採用這種付款方式。由於**買方必須事先付款**，因此他必須信任賣方有意願與能力送出自己所訂購的商品。

6 如何撰寫付款方式說明信？

付款方式說明信（a letter of payment terms）的目的就在於向顧客說明你的公司**接受哪些付款方式**，這類的信屬於功能性文件，因此撰寫時要先想想對方可能會提出什麼問題，然後在信中給予回答。下面看幾個例子。

崔女士您好：

謝謝您申請於本公司開立貿易帳戶。我們已收到您所有的文件，明年一整年您都能夠透過此貿易帳戶付款。

未來您的訂單我們都會立刻處理及發貨。發貨單及其他必須文件會與貨品一起送達。（有關常用海關文件，請見隨信附上的資料〈EduTech 產品相關海關規定〉）。根據您的偏好，發貨單也可以於發貨時傳真給您。

如您所知，發貨單須於 30 天內付清，如果於 10 天內付清，可享有 2% 的折扣。請注意，發貨單上所列商品如被任何國家政府課徵任何稅款，皆須由您承擔。帳戶內逾期未繳的款項每月將計以 2% 的利息，但是只要沒有超過 30 天未付清的發貨單，就不收取這項利息。換句話說，帳戶內超過 30 天未付清的款項，我們必須收取 2% 的利息；如果沒有拖欠的款項，就無須繳付利息。詳情請參見隨信附上的資料〈EduTech 付款須知〉。

貿易帳戶的相關規定，包括退貨辦法，請見隨信附上的資料〈貿易帳戶須知〉。

感謝您與 EduTech 展開業務關係。我們誠心盼望滿足您對教育與科技用品的需求。如有任何問題，歡迎隨時與我聯絡。

EduTech
323 Bannock Street
Denver, CO 80204

10 August 2023

Soon Yi Choe
Kids International Village
830-62 Peomil 2-Dong
Tong-Gu Busan
South Korea

Dear Ms. Choe:

Thank you for your application to open an account with EduTech. We have received all of your documents and are pleased to offer you open credit terms for the next year.

Your future orders will be processed and shipped immediately. Invoices will be presented at the time of delivery, along with all other required documentation. (For more information about frequently used customs documents, please see the enclosed information sheet **Customs Regulations Governing EduTech Products**.) According to your preference, we will also fax invoices to you at the time of shipment.

As you know, our invoices are payable within 30 days of receipt, and we offer a 2% discount if payment is remitted within 10 days of receipt. Please bear in mind that any taxes imposed by any government authority on merchandise covered by any invoice shall be your responsibility. Your account will be subject to a finance charge of 2% per month on the entire outstanding balance, but we will waive this finance charge each month that there is no unpaid invoice outstanding more than 30 days from the date of invoice. In other words, if payment is late, we must charge 2% per month on the unpaid balance in your account. If your payments are not late, you will never be subject to the finance charge. Please see the enclosed information sheet **EduTech Payment Policies** for more information.

Guidelines regarding this open credit account, including terms governing returned merchandise, are found in the enclosed information sheet **Open Credit Account Policies**.

Thank you again for beginning a relationship with EduTech. We look forward to meeting your educational and technological needs. As always, feel free to contact me with questions at any time.

Sincerely,

Arthur Teveli

Arthur Teveli
Sales Director, EduTech

Enclosures (3)

BLUMENSCHEIN, INC.

Adickesallee 3, 94855
Frankfurt am Main, Germany

15 April 2023

Lee Chef Supply
65 Chien Hsing Road, San Min District
Kaohsiung City, Taiwan

Dear Mr. Lee:

Thank you for your correspondence of 1 April, in which you provided us with your updated financial information. We have noted your interest in changing your payment plan. After amending our records, we are pleased to offer you documentary collection terms for future orders rather than payment in advance. This method is explained briefly in this letter and in more detail in the accompanying enclosures.

An overview of our documentary collections process

Our documentary collections process binds you to making payment to your bank within 20 days of receiving a shipment. Under these terms, the Deutsch Bank, Frankfurt am Main, will send the necessary documents and instructions to the bank of your choice. To receive a shipment, you accept a time draft sent by us for payment at your bank within 20 days of your receipt of said shipment. Your bank will contact you to make the payment. Payment will be sent to Deutsch Bank and then to us.

Steps in the documentary collections process

1. We ready your shipment and gather the necessary signatures from our shipping partners. Your goods are shipped.

2. We present the signed shipping documents with instructions on collecting payment to Deutsch Bank.

3. Deutsch Bank sends the documents to a bank you have selected.

4. Your bank releases the documents on acceptance of our draft requiring payment within 20 days.

5. You then present the documents to our shipping partner in exchange for the goods.

6. After your bank receives your payment, it forwards the amount to Deutsch Bank, which credits our account.

More detailed information is found in the enclosed information sheet **Blumenschein Documentary Collections Terms.** We have also enclosed all the necessary documents needed to establish a relationship between your chosen bank and Deutsch Bank (**Bank Application Form**). If you are interested in these new payment terms, please fill out the enclosed forms and give them to your chosen bank. Your bank will contact Deutsch Bank to establish a connection.

Thank you for your valuable patronage to Blumenschein, Inc. Please let me know if I can be of additional service.

Sincerely,

Karl Blumenschein

Karl Blumenschein, Operations Manager
Blumenschein, Inc.

Enclosures (2)

李先生您好：

謝謝您於 4 月 1 日的來函，為我們提供貴公司最新的財務資訊，我們也注意到您希望改變付款方式。我們已更改您的資料，未來也樂於向貴公司提供跟單託收的付款方式，無須事先付款。以下簡短說明此付款方式，更多細節請見隨信所附須知說明。

本公司跟單託收付款流程

本公司的跟單託收流程會要求您於收到貨品 20 天內，向您的銀行付款。位於法蘭克福的德意志銀行，會將相關文件與指示寄給您指定的銀行。欲收貨前，您必須在您的銀行接受由我方寄出的定期匯票，同意在收到所訂貨物的 20 天內付款。付款事宜將由您的銀行跟您聯繫。所付款項將轉至德意志銀行，然後再轉至本公司。

跟單託收付款步驟

1. 本公司準備好發貨，並請運輸公司簽署相關文件、發貨。
2. 本公司將簽署好的運輸文件連同收款指示交給德意志銀行。
3. 德意志銀行將文件寄給貴公司指定之銀行。
4. 貴公司簽署匯票，同意於交貨 20 天內付款後，銀行將文件交予貴公司。
5. 貴公司將文件出示給運輸公司，索取貨品。
6. 貴公司之銀行收到您的付款後，會將款項轉給德意志銀行本公司之帳戶。

更多詳細資訊請見所附〈Blumenschein 公司跟單託收付款須知〉。隨信並附上所有貴公司指定銀行與德意志銀行建立聯繫所需文件（〈銀行申請書〉）。如果您同意這個新的付款方式，請填寫隨信附上之表格，並交給貴公司之銀行，您的銀行會與德意志銀行聯絡相關事宜。

感謝您對 Blumenschein 公司的惠顧。如需要其他協助，歡迎與我聯絡。

Lucky Electronics
33 Eunos Road 8
Singapore 408600
Tel: 65 68 482334 Fax: 65 68 482335

January 29, 2023

Attn: Mr. Arnold Chow
Sales Manager
Changi Entertainment Devices
72 Nathan Road
Tsim Sha Tsui, Kowloon
Hong Kong

Dear Mr. Chow:

Thank you for your interest in Lucky Electronics. We look forward to creating a partnership that is beneficial to both of us.

It is our policy to arrange payment with customers outside of Singapore using an irrevocable letter of credit (LC) ❶. In this process, after we have agreed ⎯⎯⎯ on terms, you must arrange for your bank to open an LC in favor of Lucky Electronics. Your bank will transmit the LC to our bank, the Bank of Singapore, which in turn will forward it to us. When we have received the LC, we will ship your goods to a freight forwarder, who will dispatch the goods and submit the relevant documents to the Bank of Singapore. When the documents have been collected, the Bank of Singapore will check them for compliance with the LC, pay Lucky Electronics, and debit your account at your bank. Your bank will then release the documents to you, allowing you to claim the goods from the freight carrier.

We believe this process offers the greatest security for both of us. Please see the enclosed documents for more details about the LC process and a list of banks in Hong Kong with relationships with the Bank of Singapore.

Please don't hesitate to contact me if you have any questions or concerns. I can be reached at +65 68 482334, extension 48. We look forward to providing you with the quality goods and service that have kept Lucky Electronics growing for the past ten years.

Sincerely,

Indira Rajendran

Indira Rajendran, Purchasing Manager
Lucky Electronics

Enc. (3)

喬先生您好：

謝謝您惠顧本公司，我們誠心期待與貴公司建立起互惠合作關係。

對於新加坡境外的顧客，本公司的政策是以「不可撤銷信用狀 ❶」進行付款。雙方就訂單內容達成協議後，您必須請貴公司的銀行開立信用狀（收款人為本公司 Lucky Electronics）。信用狀會由您的銀行交給本公司的銀行（新加坡銀行），再提交給本公司。本公司收到信用狀後便發貨給貨物承攬商，貨運承攬商會進行後續送貨事宜，並將相關文件收集後交予新加坡銀行。在確認這些文件與信用狀之內容相符後，新加坡銀行會付款給本公司，並將款項自您的銀行帳目中扣除。之後您的銀行會將相關文件交給貴公司，貴公司便可持文件與貨運承攬商索取貨物。

相信這樣的流程能夠為雙方都帶來最大的保障。隨信附上此付款方式之詳細說明，以及與新加坡銀行有合作關係之香港銀行列表。

如果有任何問題或疑慮，歡迎與我聯絡：+65 68 482334，分機號碼 48。誠心期盼能提供您十年來推動 Lucky Electronics 不斷成長的高品質產品與服務。

❶ Documentary letters of credit（跟單信用狀，常簡寫為 LC）又稱：

- letters of credit（信用狀）
- commercial letters of credit（商業信用狀）
- documentary credits（跟單信用狀）

Exotic Textiles, Inc.

16, Talkatora Road, New Delhi 110001
Ph: 24787040 Fax: 24787042

20 May 2023

Duds
P.O. Box 748,
Bangkok 10501, Thailand

Attention: Aroon Pradabtanakij

Dear Mr. Pradabtanakij:

Pradabtanakij 先生您好：

謝謝您對本公司之興趣。我們非常樂於從此與貴公司展開互惠合作關係。

對於新顧客，本公司的政策是：一半的款項須事先付清，並最好能以電匯付款。（我們也接受透過電話或傳真以信用卡付款。）剩下一半的款項於交貨 10 天內付清。

隨信附上電匯所需帳戶資料。期盼收到您的首批訂單。

Thank you for your interest in Exotic Textiles. We are very pleased to begin our mutually profitable partnership.

Our policy with new customers is to require a 50% payment in advance for all shipments, preferably via wire transfer. (We can also accept credit card payments by phone or fax.) The remaining 50% is due within 10 days of delivery.

Enclosed you will find all the account details you will need for a wire transfer. We look forward to receiving your first order.

Yours faithfully,

Malika Karmarkar

Malika Karmarkar, Sales Manager
Exotic Textiles, New Delhi

Enc. (1)

Exotic Textiles, Inc.

16, Talkatora Road, New Delhi 110001
Ph: 24787040 Fax: 24787042

Payment information

Bank name（銀行名）	Export Import Bank of India, New Delhi
Bank address（銀行地址）	Statesman House, Connaught Place, New Delhi, Delhi 110001, India
SWIFT number ❶（SWIFT 碼）	EXININBB028
Account name（戶名）	Exotic Textiles c/o Malika Karmarkar
Account number（帳號）	089 28 09384739

Unit 38 撰寫催款信
Writing letters pressing for payment

1 如何撰寫催款信？

很不幸地，有時候會出現顧客拖欠款項的狀況，這也許是顧客的問題，也許是基於其他因素。如果出現這種狀況，你就需要通知顧客，此時溝通中需**維持一貫的禮貌**，但是**態度要堅決**。如果第一次通知（reminder）後對方依然沒付款，後續信件的態度就要慢慢**越來越強硬**（forceful）。催促繳款的信應該遵守下列原則：

❶ **寫給個人**：把信寄給**特定的人**，不要寄給一整個部門。請對方與你這邊負責相關事宜的人聯絡，並留下這個負責人的姓名與聯絡方式。這個負責人也許就是你自己（寫信人），也許是你的同事。

❷ **清晰明確**：為了避免出錯，把所有的**款項、發貨單**或**訂單號碼**都寫出來，方便對方找到相應的紀錄。提醒對方你們的付款條件，以及你希望他如何付款。

❸ **不要責怪顧客**：顧客可能出於各種原因而拖延付款。**保持平時的服務態度**，並務必說明你知道這個狀況可能在顧客的控制範圍之外：顧客可能不知道有拖欠款項的狀況，或是你的紀錄裡可能出了錯。

❹ **除了請對方付款，也請對方回覆**：請顧客跟你**說明拖欠款項的原因**，或是提供相關回覆，讓顧客有機會解釋，這個舉動顯示你關心顧客。此外，如果你在信中跟顧客表示，願意在付款方式或日期上更有彈性（flexible），可能也更容易收到款項。

❺ **謝謝顧客**：即使款項晚了，還是要**謝謝顧客**。

2 如何寫第一封催款信？

撰寫催款信的挑戰就在於在催款的同時，依舊要保持顧客至上的服務態度。**禮貌得體（tact）非常重要**，畢竟你不知道為什麼顧客沒付款，也不知道到底是不是顧客本身的錯。語氣依舊要有禮貌，不要責怪（blame）顧客，把這個狀況視為意外出錯或疏忽（oversight），而這種差錯在付款過程中任何一環都有可能出現。下面就來看一封第一次寄出的催款信。

❶ **SWIFT code**（也稱為 BIC 代碼）是一種國際銀行識別代碼，用於識別全球特定的銀行和銀行分支機構。 SWIFT 代碼通常用於國際匯款，以確保資金被正確轉移到目標銀行。 SWIFT 代碼由 8 或 11 位元字母組成，分別如右：

- 銀行代碼（4 個字母）
- 國家代碼（2 個字母）
- 位置代碼（2 個字母或數字，指該銀行的總部所在）
- 分行代碼（3 個數字）

BLUMENSCHEIN, INC.

Adickesallee 3, 94855
Frankfurt am Main, Germany

4 March 2023

Lee Chef Supply
65 Chien Hsing Road, San Min District
Kaohsiung City, Taiwan

Ref: OD4316

Dear Mr. Lee:

Subject: Your order number 012223

❶「According to our records」這樣的說法暗示也有可能是紀錄出錯，而非顧客沒付款，這樣可以提起未付清的款項，同時又不失禮。「Yet」也暗示顧客可能已經付款了，只是款項還沒到。本信第一段寫得很客氣，但是也很直接。

According to our records, we have not yet received payment for your order number 012223, placed on January 22, 2023. ❶ Below are the details of the order:

❷ 信中務必詳細列出相關資訊，方便顧客找到檔案。

Order Number: 012223
Placed: January 22
Shipped: January 27
Items: One (1) Modern Quality Chef Set (item number S3(A); three (3)
　　　　Blumenschein Large Knife Collections (item number K1(A)
Our invoice number: JI15
Amount due: $700.23 ❷

As you know, our terms are 2%-10/Net 30.
We understand that our invoice may not have
reached you, so we would like to take this opportunity
to send a second copy of the invoice, along with a copy
of your original purchase order. Please process the invoice
and submit payment through your usual account at your
earliest convenience.

❸ 寫信人再次暗示款項未付清可能並不是顧客的錯。

❹ If you have settled the account before this letter reaches you, please ignore this reminder and accept our apologies for troubling you. Thank you for your payment and your business.

As always, please contact me if you have any questions or concerns.

Yours truly,

Karl Blumenschein

Karl Blumenschein, Operations Manager
Blumenschein, Inc.

❹ 寫信人請顧客付款，然後又表示也許款項已在處理中，並為這次打擾道歉。

Enclosures (2)

李先生您好：

主旨：你的 012223 號訂單

根據本公司的紀錄，我們還未收到貴公司於 2023 年 1 月 22 日所下訂單（訂單號碼 012223）之款項。❶ 以下為訂單詳細內容：

訂單號碼 012223
下單日期：1 月 22 日
發貨日期：1 月 27 日
訂購商品：一套現代高品質主廚套組（商品號碼 S3(A)）
　　　　　三套 Blumenschein 大型刀具組（商品號碼 K1(A)）

發貨單號碼：JI15
應繳金額：$700.23

如您所知，我們的付款方式為 2%-10/Net-30（10 天內付款，享 2% 折扣；30 天內付款，須付全額）。我們理解貴公司可能還沒有收到發貨單，所以在此再附上一份發貨單副本，以及原本訂單之副本。請您於方便時盡快處理發貨單，並將款項匯入您平時的貿易帳戶。

❹ 如果您在接到本信前已付清款項，請忽略本信，並容我們為此次打擾致歉。謝謝您的付款與惠顧。

如有任何問題和疑慮，照常歡迎隨時與我聯絡。

3 如何寫後續催款信？

　　如果顧客對第一封催款信沒有任何回應，你的態度應該要**越來越強硬**，客氣的成分也要越來越少。對於處理未付款項，你的公司可能已經有固定的政策。有時候，恰當的做法是**提供顧客新的付款條件**，比如說在某個期限內付款可以享有折扣、分期付款（in installments）、或是延後付款期限，至於實際上該採取哪種做法，**取決於公司的政策**，以及**公司與顧客的關係**。

BLUMENSCHEIN, INC.

Adickesallee 3, 94855
Frankfurt am Main, Germany

28 March 2023

Lee Chef Supply
65 Chien Hsing Road, San Min District
Kaohsiung City, Taiwan

Ref: OD4316a

Dear Mr. Lee:

Subject: 2nd payment reminder for order number 012223

❶ On March 4, we wrote to notify you that we had not received payment
for your order number 012223, placed on January 22. Because we have
not heard from you, we don't know what is causing the delay in payment.
We value our customers and want to provide the best service we can under
all circumstances. If you would like to discuss other payment options,
we would be happy to oblige. ❷

Please contact us at your earliest convenience to discuss making payment
or pay in full through your usual account as soon as possible. If you have
settled the account before this notice reaches you, please accept our
apologies for troubling you.

The details of your order are provided below for your reference.

Order Number: 012223
Placed: January 22
Shipped: January 27
Items: One (1) Modern Quality Chef Set (item number S3(A); three (3)
       Blumenschein Large Knife Collections (item number K1(A)
Our invoice number: JI15
Amount due: $700.23

Thank you for your prompt attention to this matter.

Sincerely,

Karl Blumenschein

Karl Blumenschein, Operations Manager
Blumenschein, Inc.

cc: Christian Blumenschein

❶ 寫信人一開始就告訴對方，這是第二封催款信。告訴顧客你之前已經寄過幾封催款信，有助於顧客預期信件後續內容。

❷ 在這個例子裡，這間公司願意與顧客討論其他的付款條件，並在信中清楚說明了這一點，但不是所有的公司都會願意。

李先生您好：

主旨：訂單號碼 012223 的第二次催款信

❶ 我們已於 3 月 4 日寫信通知您，本公司還未收到貴公司於 1 月 22 日所下訂單（訂單號碼 012223）之款項。我們一直沒有得到您的回覆，因此無法判斷是什麼原因造成款項延遲。我們重視我們的顧客，也希望能夠在各種狀況下為顧客提供最好的服務。如果您希望商量其他的付款選項，我們將盡力配合。❷

請您盡快於方便時與我們聯絡，討論付款事宜，或是盡速將完整款項匯入您平時的貿易帳戶。如果您在接到本信前已付清款項，請接受我們為造成打擾致歉。

以下為訂單內容，供您參閱：

訂單號碼 012223
下單日期：1 月 22 日
發貨日期：1 月 27 日
訂購商品：一套現代高品質主廚套組（商品號碼 S3(A)）
　　　　　三套 Blumenschein 大型刀具組（商品號碼 K1(A)）
發貨單號碼：JI15
應繳金額：$700.23

謝謝您迅速處理此事宜。

BLUMENSCHEIN, INC.

Adickesallee 3, 94855
Frankfurt am Main, Germany

11 April 2024

Lee Chef Supply
65 Chien Hsing Road, San Min District
Kaohsiung City, Taiwan

Ref: OD4316b

Dear Mr. Lee:

Subject: 3rd payment reminder for order number 012223

Your balance of $700.23 for order number 012223 is now more than 60 days overdue. We wrote to you on March 4 and again on March 28, requesting payment or an explanation of your nonpayment; however, I am afraid we still have not heard from you. ❶

We trust that the merchandise we shipped to you was satisfactory and that our records are in order. ❷ If there is some problem with the shipment or the invoice or if you have some question about either, please contact us immediately. If not, we must ask you to pay your account in full as soon as possible, as it has now been outstanding for some time. Without a prompt response from you, we will have to turn the account over to our lawyers. ❸

Enclosed please find copies of the original invoice as well as the two previous reminders. As always, feel free to contact us with comments or questions.

Thank you for your prompt attention to this matter.

Sincerely,

Karl Blumenschein

Karl Blumenschein, Operations Manager
Blumenschein, Inc.

Enclosures (3)

cc: Christian Blumenschein

❶ 這是三封催款信中最直白的一封，寫信人一開始就寫出未付清的款項，以及繳款逾期的時間，接著他提到前兩封通知信，並說明至今一直沒有得到回覆。

❷ 寫信人依舊接受顧客對於貨物可能有疑問或問題的狀況，但是他也很清楚地要求對方立即給予回覆。

❸ 最後，寫信人警告顧客若置之不理，此事不久就會交給公司的律師處理：寫信人在這個句子裡用「have to」這個片語動詞，表示公司並不想因為顧客引起法律問題，但是他們別無選擇。

李先生您好：

主旨：訂單號碼 012223 的第三次催款信

您的 012223 號訂單款項 700.23 美元已逾期 60 多天未付清。我們已於 3 月 4 日及 3 月 28 日去函請您付清款項，或說明未付原因，但是我們至今一直沒有得到您的回覆。❶

我們相信發出的貨物令您滿意，而本公司的紀錄也沒有錯誤。❷ 如果貨物或發貨單方面有問題，或是您對貨物或發貨單有疑問，請立刻與我們聯絡。如果沒有疑問，我們必須請您盡速付清款項，因為這筆款項已經未付一段時間了。如果沒有收到您及時的回覆，我們便必須把此事移交律師處理了。❸

隨信附上原始發貨單副本及前兩封先前通知信副本。若有任何指教或疑問，歡迎與我們聯絡。

謝謝您迅速處理此事宜。

付款相關書信常用說法
Common phrases for letters about payment

1 Credit inquiry letters: Asking for information from customers
信用調查信：跟顧客索取資訊

❶ It is our policy to request the following information from new customers . . .

對於新顧客，依本公司的政策需要索取下列資訊……

❷ In adherence with our policy, we ask you to provide the following information . . .

為遵照本公司的政策，我們要請您提供下列資訊……

❸ It is routine to ask for the following information when a customer places a large order . . .

顧客下大額訂單時，本公司的例行做法是須請顧客提供下列資訊……

❹ Providing the following information will help us create your account . . .

提供下列資訊有助本公司為您開立貿易帳戶……

2 Credit inquiry letters: Asking for information from credit references
信用調查信：跟信用擔保人索取資訊

❶ You were listed as a credit reference for _____ [business name].

〔公司名〕將您／貴公司列為信用擔保人。

❷ As a credit reference for _____ [business name], would you please provide us with information about . . . ?

您身為〔公司名〕的信用擔保人，能否請您就……提供資訊？

3 Credit inquiry letters: Assuring confidentiality
信用調查信：表示得到的資訊將嚴格保密

❶ We respect your privacy and will never share any information you provide to us.
我們尊重貴公司的隱私，絕不會將您提供的資訊外流。

❷ Financial information is always kept confidential.
財務資訊將一貫嚴格保密。

4 Responding to credit inquiry letters: Providing information
回覆信用調查信：提供資訊

❶ Please find enclosed the financial information you requested.
隨信附上您索取的財務資訊。

❷ Below is the information you requested about _____ [business name].
以下是您就〔公司名〕索取的資訊。

❸ In our experience, _____ [business or individual] has always paid on time / has occasionally make late payments . . .
根據我們的經驗，〔公司或個人〕總是準時付款／偶爾會延遲付款……

❹ We have never had a payment or credit issue with _____ [business name].
我們與〔公司名〕從未有過付款或信用問題。

❺ We do not use open credit terms with _____ [business or individual] because of payment issues in the past.
基於過去付款上的問題，我們與〔公司或個人〕並不採用貿易帳戶的付款方式。

5 Letters of payment terms: Offering payment terms
說明付款方式：提供付款方式

❶ Our payment terms are . . .　　　　　　　我們的付款方式有……

❷ For new customers, our payment terms are . . .
對於新顧客，我們的付款方式有……

❸ We are pleased to offer you _____ [payment terms].
我們樂於提供您……〔付款方式〕。

6 Letters of payment terms: Explaining payment terms
解釋付款方式

❶ Here are the steps to follow when making payment . . .
需遵照的付款步驟如下……

❷ In order to make payment, please take the following steps . . .
請按照下列步驟完成付款程序……

❸ Making payment requires one phone call . . .
欲完成付款程序，您必須來電……

❹ Making payment requires you to present the following documents . . .
欲完成付款程序，您必須出示下列文件……

❺ Making payment requires the following steps . . .
欲完成付款程序，您必須完成下列步驟……

7 Letters pressing for payment: Requesting payment
催款信：請求付款

❶ We are still awaiting your payment for order number . . .
我們仍在等候……號訂單的付款。

❷ We are still waiting to process your payment for order number . . .
我們仍在等候處理……號訂單的付款。

③ According to our records, you have not yet paid for order number . . .
根據本公司的紀錄，貴公司還未付清⋯⋯號訂單的款項。

④ It appears that the payment for order number . . . is overdue.
⋯⋯號訂單的付款似乎逾期了。

8 Letters pressing for payment: Avoiding blame
催款信：避免責怪顧客

❶ We understand that delays can occur for a variety of reasons.
我們理解延遲付款可能出於各種原因。

❷ We know that correspondence can sometimes slip through the cracks.
我們知道聯繫過程有時會有遺漏。

❸ We can sympathize with situations that might lead to a late payment.
我們能夠體諒某些狀況可能導致付款延遲。

9 Letters pressing for payment: Referencing legal action
催款信：說明必須採取法律行動

❶ We regret that we will have to inform our lawyers if payment is not made immediately.
如果沒有立刻收到款項，我們就恐怕必須通知我們的律師了。

❷ Without a prompt response from you, we will have to turn the account over to our lawyers.
若未獲得您的迅速回覆，我方就必須將此事交由律師處理。

10 Letters pressing for payment: Thanking customers for payment
催款信：謝謝顧客付款

❶ We thank you in advance if your payment is already in process.
如果付款事宜已在處理中，在此預先謝謝您。

❷ As always, we thank you for your business.
謝謝您一向的惠顧。

1 Review the concepts

1 What is credit?

_____

2 What is a credit reference?

_____

3 What are credit inquiry letters?

_____

_____

4 Why is it important to be clear in a letter pressing for payment?

_____

_____

5 What should you ask for in addition to payment in a letter pressing for payment?

_____

6 To whom would you not send a credit inquiry letter?

(A) Your CEO
(B) A credit reference supplied by a customer
(C) A new customer

7 What are "payment terms"?

(A) Methods or ways a company will accept payment
(B) Open accounts
(C) Details about a customer's credit history

8 What is the most common payment option in international trade?

(A) Open credit
(B) Documentary letters of credit
(C) Cash in advance

9 ☐True ☐False An outstanding invoice is unpaid.

2 Send the customer a routine credit inquiry letter. (I)

You work for Big Sound, Inc. A new customer, Thomas Brookes-Wolgar of Mood Music, would like to place a large order with your company. Send that customer a routine credit inquiry letter.

BIG SOUND
95 Cross Road
BUSHEY, Hertfordshire WD 194 DQ
England

7 December 2023

Mood Music
Elm Corner, Upper Cam Lane
Addlestone, Surrey KT15
United Kingdom

Dear _____ :

_____

_____

_____

_____

_____

_____

_____

_____

_____

_____

_____

_____

_____

_____

_____

_____

3 **Send a reference a routine credit inquiry letter. (II)**

You work for Big Sound, Inc. A new customer, Thomas Brookes-Wolgar of Mood Music, has provided Mia Sandusky of Sounds of the Times as a credit reference. Send her a routine credit inquiry letter.

BIG SOUND
95 Cross Road
BUSHEY, Hertfordshire WD 194 DQ
England

7 December 2023

Mia Sandusky
Sounds of the Times
89 Renfield St.
Glasgow G2 3PR
United Kingdom

Dear _____ :

_____

_____

_____

_____

_____

_____

_____

_____

_____

_____

_____

_____

_____

_____

_____

_____

_____

---

4 Write a first notice of late payment.

Imagine that you work for EduTech. Kid's International Village has not yet paid for its last order and is now two weeks overdue. Write a first notice of late payment. The order was placed on August 3 and was shipped on August 5. The order was for 50 copies of *Kids and Technology*. The invoice number is 080315. The cost of the order was $1000. The order number is AG0308. Your contact is Soon Yi Choe.

EduTech
323 Bannock Street
Denver, CO 80204

19 August 2023

Soon Yi Choe
Kids International Village
830-62 Peomil 2-Dong
Tong-Gu Busan
South Korea

Ref: _____

Dear _____ :

Subject: _____

_____

_____

_____

_____

_____

_____

_____

_____

_____

_____

_____

_____

_____

送貨相關書信
Correspondence About Shipping

Key Terms

billing address 帳單地址
指和買方的付款方式連結的地址。帳單地址和「送貨地址」（shipping address）不同，後者指的是購買的貨品預計送達的地址。

customs agency 海關
負責執行相關法律，以保護國家進出口稅收的政府機關。

customs broker
報關行、報關公司、報關經紀人
（有必要時）由財政部授權之個人或公司，負責為客戶（進口商）處理商品報關事宜。

customs clearance 通關、報關
指將貨物運出或運入某一國家的正式許可過程，通常需要經過一連串官方檢查程序。

duty 關稅
對於進口商品課徵的稅款。

deductible 自付額（英國稱 excess）
保險中必須自行負擔的限額。例如，假如你為貨運保了 20,000 美元的險，條款中明訂自付額為 1,000 美元，那麼 1,000 美元以下的損害，須由你自己承擔，如果損害超過 1,000 美元，保險公司才會開始進行賠償。

freight 貨物
被運送的貨物，也可指運送貨物的費用（運費）。

freight forwarder 貨運承攬商、貨運代理人
貨運公司的經紀人，安排貨物的運送事宜。

insurance 保險
雙方簽訂的合約，明訂貨物在某些特定狀況下遭受丟失或損害時，由一方賠償另一方。

liability 法律義務
法律上負有的義務和責任。

premium 保險費
為某一期限內之特定保險等級所付的費用；依照保險合約所付的費用。

time frame 時間框架
專案或行動預定發生、完成的時間範圍與規畫。在說明送貨方式時，可提及送貨流程是否有固定時間框架。

total loss / all-risk insurance 全損險／全險
為不同的保險分類，全損險（total loss）保障被保險貨品完全損毀的情況，全險（all-risk insurance）的保障範圍，擴及保險契約明定非保障項目以外的各類風險。

Unit

40

說明送貨方式的信件
letters of shipment terms

送貨相關書信（correspondence about shipping），包括**說明送貨方式**（letters of shipment terms）的信件及**裝運通知信**（letters of shipping advice）。信中需要跟顧客說明貨物的運送方式或條件，也需清楚說明相關資訊，並注意顧客可能會有哪些問題。

40-1 | A letter explaining shipping terms 說明送貨方式的信件

PRECISION LASERS, INC.
1840 Poinsettia Boulevard, Elizabeth, NJ 07201
Telephone: (908) 517-4938   Fax: (908) 517-4937

June 24, 2023

Elizabeth Choi
Jupiter Systems
6 Temasek Boulevard
#8-00 Suntec Tower Four
Singapore 038986

Dear Ms. Choi:

Subject: Our international shipping policies

Thank you for your correspondence of June 2, in which you asked about our international shipping policies. I hope the following information answers your questions.

International Shipping Methods:
We use TopShip International Express (by air) services for all international orders. There are two primary express shipping methods to choose from, "TopShip International Economy" and "TopShip International Priority." We believe these are the best international shipping options.

Payment Methods for International Customers:
International customers are invited to pay through PayPoint or through wire transfers (by request). At this time, we can directly accept only U.S. credit cards. However, with PayPoint, you may use funds from an international credit card, debit card, or bank account. To set up a wire transfer or discuss an alternative payment method, please contact us at international@preciselaser.com.

Page 1 of 3

International Shipping Time Frames:

TopShip International Economy service takes 2-5 business days, whereas TopShip International Priority service takes 1-3 business days. It is important to note that the delivery date can be delayed by the customs clearance process of some countries. Please understand that once a package leaves the United States, we cannot influence the time of its delivery. Precision Lasers does not guarantee shipping time frames for international orders.

Customs will usually contact you once your package has arrived so that you can pay the customs fees and clear your package. The shipping time frames mentioned above are for reference only and are estimates provided by TopShip. It is important to be available for contact, as your actions can affect the date you actually receive your shipment.

About Customs Fees & Clearance:

Please be aware that when using international shipping services, you may be charged customs fees for clearance. These fees are a normal part of international shipping. Some of these fees may include but are not limited to the following: import taxes, duties, clearance fees, and/or brokerage fees. Customers are responsible for paying these fees to the shipping carrier or customs department of their given country.

We will provide the shipping carrier with your contact information exactly as you have provided it to us. The customs department of your country will use this information to get in touch with you when your package arrives at customs. When using TopShip International Shipping services, you do not need your own customs broker. TopShip will automatically assign a customs broker to you. That broker will contact you when your shipment arrives. Remember, you must be available for contact by customs in order for your package to properly clear.

International Shipping Rates:

International shipping rates are calculated according to the size, weight, and value of each order. Because of the volume of our orders, we have an agreement with TopShip to provide our customers with discounted rates. The exact discount depends on the dimensions of your order and its destination.

International Shipping Availability:

There are some countries that are not available for International Shipping. This is a decision made by TopShip, not by Precision Laser. Please contact us at international@preciselaser.com with any questions about countries we can ship to.

Limit of Liability on International Orders:
Unfortunately, Precision Laser cannot guarantee shipping time frames or rates for international orders. We are also not responsible for any customs/clearance fees.

Please be aware that while every package we ship is protected by TopShip's insurance policy, Precision Laser will not be liable for any damaged product(s), lost product(s), or shipping delays that result from the international shipping process, the shipping carrier, or the customs department of a given country.

Return Policy for International Orders:
We pride ourselves on our customer service, and we will do everything in our power to ensure that you receive quality goods and service. However, we do not guarantee replacement, reshipment, repair, or return on international shipments. We will do everything we can to help our international customers with problems that may arise during shipment. We ask that you understand that influence is limited once a shipment has left the United States.

Questions About International Shipping:
We understand that international shipping can be confusing and difficult, especially to first-time international customers. Our International Shipping Department is available to answer all of your questions at international@preciselaser.com.

I hope this information has answered your questions. If you have additional questions or concerns, please feel free to email our International Shipping Department. You can also contact me directly at (908) 517-4938 or over email at walshj@preciselaser.com.

Yours truly,

Jade Walsh

Jade Walsh, Export Manager
Precision Lasers

Part

10

送貨相關書信

Unit
40
說明送貨方式的信件

崔女士您好：

主旨：本公司國際送貨政策

謝謝您於 6 月 2 日來函詢問我們的國際送貨方式，希望下面的資訊能夠回答您的問題。

國際送貨方式：

對於所有的國際訂單，我們都採用 TopShip 國際快捷（空運）。TopShip 的國際快捷分為兩種：「TopShip 經濟國際快遞」和「TopShip 優先國際快遞」。我們相信這是最好的兩種國際遞送方式。

國外顧客付款方式：

國外顧客建議透過 PayPoint 或電匯（須事先與我們聯絡）付款。目前我們只能接受美國信用卡，不過若您透過 PayPoint 付款，就能夠以國外的信用卡、簽帳卡或銀行戶頭付款。若需電匯或討論其他的付款方式，請與我們聯絡：international@preciselaser.com。

國際送貨所需時間：

採用 TopShip 經濟國際快遞，貨物可於 2-5 個工作天送達；採用 TopShip 優先國際快遞，貨物可於 1-3 個工作天送達。請注意在某些國家，貨物送達時間可能會因報關程序而延遲。請理解貨物一旦離開美國，我們就無法控制貨物送達的時間。對於國際訂單，本公司無法保證送貨期限。

貨物送抵貴國後，貴國海關通常會通知您繳交報關手續費並領取貨物。上述的送貨所需時間是 TopShip 提供的估計，僅供參考。屆時務必讓海關聯絡得到您，因為您的行動會影響到實際收到貨物的時間。

報關手續費與報關：

請注意，在採用國際遞送服務時，您可能需要付一筆報關手續費，這筆費用是國際遞送的通常程序。報關手續費中可能包含：進口稅、關稅、報關費和／或報關行手續費等。顧客須將此費用交予運輸公司或該國海關。

我們會將您交給我們的聯絡資訊交予運輸公司。貨物抵達貴國海關時，海關將透過此聯絡資訊與您聯絡。採用 TopShip 國際遞送服務時，您不需要自己找報關行，TopShip 會自動為您指定報關行。貨物抵達時，報關行便會與您聯絡。請務必讓海關能夠聯絡得到您，才能順利將貨物報關。

國際送貨費用：

國際送貨費用取決於個別訂單貨物之大小、重量和價值。本公司與 TopShip 合作訂單量大，因此 TopShip 特別為我們的顧客提供折扣費率。實際的折扣取決於訂單貨物尺寸與運送目的地。

國際送貨範圍：

有些國家目前仍不在我們的國際送貨範圍內，這個限制係由 TopShip 決定，與 Precision Laser 無關。若對我們的送貨範圍有任何問題，請來信 international@preciselaser.com。

國際訂單責任限制：

很抱歉，Precision Laser 無法保證國際訂單的到貨期限或運費，也不承擔任何關稅／報關手續費。

請留意：雖然本公司運送的每件包裹都受到 TopShip 保險政策的保護，但國際運送過程、運輸公司或貴國海關所導致的貨物損害、丟失或延誤，Precision Laser 概不負責。

國際訂貨退貨政策：

本公司以完善的顧客服務為榮，並致力於提供您優質的產品與服務。然而對於國際訂貨，我們無法保證換貨、重新送貨、修理或退貨。對於送貨過程中可能出現的問題，我們將盡全力協助我們的外國顧客，但是請您理解，一旦貨物離開美國，我們的影響力就有限。

國際送貨相關問題：

我們了解國際送貨程序可能相當複雜，尤其是對第一次訂貨的國外顧客。我們的國際送貨部將樂於回答您所有的問題，請來信：international@preciselaser.com。

希望這些資訊回答了您的問題。如果您還有其他問題或疑慮，歡迎寫電子郵件給我們的國際送貨部，也可以直接與我聯絡：(908) 517-4938 或 walshj@preciselaser.com。

Unit 41 裝運通知信
Letters of Shipping Advice

裝運通知信（letters of shipping advice）用來通知顧客所訂貨物已經寄出，在現代的社會裡，很多裝運通知都以電子郵件的形式寄給顧客。信中應該清楚寫出：

- 顧客的姓名與地址 The customer's name and address
- 訂單號碼 The order number
- 訂購的貨物 A description of the merchandise shipped
- 運送方式 The shipping method
- 貨物追蹤號碼（如果有的話）Any tracking number (if applicable)
- 估計貨物抵達時間 The date the shipment should arrive

CHANGI ENTERTAINMENT DEVICES

72 Nathan Road, Tsim Sha Tsui, Kowloon
Hong Kong
Tel: 852-36821820 Fax: 852-36821820

October 26, 2023

Gregory McMannis
Bleeps and Beeps
17 Talavera Road
Macquarie Park
NSW 2113

Dear Mr. McMannis:

Subject: Order 10222023

> 謹以此信通知您 10222023 號訂單貨物已於 10 月 26 日星期一發貨。送貨方式為 TopShip 國際遞送。包裹追蹤號碼為 FS1002938466i。（包裹資訊更新最長可能需要 18 個小時。）貨物應會於五個工作天內送達。

This message is to advise you that the items in your order number 10222023 shipped on Monday, October 26. The method of shipment was TopShip International. Your shipment's tracking number is FS1002938466i. (Please allow up to 18 hours for tracking information to be updated.) Your shipment should arrive within five business days.

We thank you for your business and hope you will choose Changi Entertainment Devices again!

> 感謝您的惠顧，並期盼您再次惠顧 Changi Entertainment Devices！

Order number: 10222023 — 訂單號碼
Date ordered: October 22, 2023 — 訂貨日期
Date shipped: October 26, 2023 — 發貨日期

Billing address	Shipping address
Gregory McMannis Bleeps and Beeps 17 Talavera Road 帳單地址 Macquarie Park NSW 2113	Gregory McMannis Bleeps and Beeps 17 Talavera Road 送貨地址 Macquarie Park NSW 2113

Items included in this shipment: — 本批貨物所含品項如下： 數量 總價

Our item number	Description	Price	Quantity	Total
203y	Lucy bookshelf speaker	$75.00	3	$225.00
67y	Dallas bookshelf speaker	$125.00	3	$375.00
1308p	Funbox game system	$350.00	4	$1400.00
			Order total:	$2000.00

商品編號　品名　價格　訂單總額

Best regards,

Customer Service Team
Changi Entertainment Devices

國際送貨是複雜而難以預測的過程，因此買方和賣方通常都會將貨物投保，以降低財務風險。很多供應商可能並不提供保險，有些供應商則開放顧客要求購買保險。不過大多數的貨物都可以跟獨立的保險公司投保，很多貨運承攬商也提供保險。下面來看一封描述投保方式的信。

42-1 | A letter describing discount insurance options 描述投保方式的信

AFFORDABLE SHIPPING INSURANCE AGENCY

187 Davis Blvd. • Suite 4 • Davis, CA 95616
Tel 1-866-892-7533 • Fax 818-892-8758

June 19, 2023

Lee Chef Supply
65 Chien Hsing Road, San Min District
Kaohsiung City, Taiwan

Dear Mr. Lee:

Thank you for your inquiry about insurance for shipments from the United States to Taiwan. I am happy to describe our service options for you.

Our service options
We offer all-risk insurance and total loss insurance for air and sea. The chart below outlines the differences between the two types of insurance.

Total loss insurance protects you from	All-risk insurance protects you from all instances of total loss, as well as
• Sinking	• Stranding
• Fire	• Water or weather damage
• Collision	• Condensation
• Explosion	• Improper handling
• Management error	• Theft
• Flooding from machinery	• Nondelivery
• Preexisting hull damage	• Leaking or breaking

We strongly recommend all-risk insurance for most shipments.

Page 1 of 3

Outline of our policy

We have enclosed the entire *Affordable Shipping Policy* booklet, which we encourage you to read completely. For your perusal, here is a list of the most important parts of our policy.

1 **Insurable interest:** You must be the owner, seller, buyer, shipper, or receiver of the goods you would like to insure. You must complete the insurance process before the goods are shipped.

2 **Place of coverage:** Cargo is insured while at the dock, pier, wharf, or on land before it is loaded onto the transport vessel.

3 **Partial loss:** Unless total loss is reported, we will replace the value of the damaged portion of the goods (beyond the amount of your deductible and not the whole shipment.

4 **Nondelivery or theft:** Goods that are unaccounted for or overdue for more than 35 days will be considered lost. The Insured can recover the value of the goods under an all-risk policy. Claims of theft must be supported by documentary evidence.

5 **Poor packing:** Loss or damage caused by unsuitable packing or preparation carried out by a third party will not be used as a defense against claims.

6 **Loss notification:** You must report any loss or damage that may become a claim as soon as possible after it becomes known. Your claims may be invalidated if you fail to report loss or damage promptly. Please see the Cargo Insurance Claims section of the enclosed *Affordable Shipping Policy* booklet for more information about required documents and procedures.

7 **Returned or refused shipments:** We cover the return trip of cargo that is refused by the Insured.

8 **Major exclusions:** We do not insure shipments containing accounts, bills, currency, evidence of debt, checks, money orders, securities, tickets, deeds, notes, neon items, hazardous material, perishable cargo, ceramic slabs, marble slabs, granite slabs, slate slabs, flowers, plants, seeds, guns, or tobacco.

Our rates

Our insurance rates depend on the value of your shipment and your shipment's destination. Rates run between $0.81 and $5.00 per $100.00 of the declared value of a shipment. For help calculating the value of your shipment, please see our Value Calculator in the enclosed *Affordable Shipping Policy* booklet. Feel free to contact us for a personalized quote at (866) 892-7533 or over email at quotes@affordableshipinsurance.com.

Our global coverage

We currently insure shipments between North America and the Far East. We cover shipments originating in the following places: Australia, Canada, Hong Kong, Japan, Malaysia, Singapore, South Korea, Taiwan, and the United States. We insure shipments from the listed places to all listed places, as well as to Cambodia, China, Indonesia, Mexico, the Philippines, Thailand, and Vietnam. Please refer to the enclosed booklet for special options for places not mentioned here.

Ready to insure?

The enclosed *Affordable Shipping Policy* booklet contains all the documents and instructions needed to apply for insurance for your shipment. Mail in the forms included there, or go to www.affordableshipinsurance/order-shipment-insurance.html to submit your order.

I hope this information is helpful to you. We are always on hand to answer your questions at (866) 892-7533.

Best regards,

Larry Rhykus

Larry Rhykus, Claims Specialist

李先生您好：

謝謝您來函詢問從美國送貨至台灣之保險事宜，我非常樂意為您說明我們的保險服務選項。

我們的保險服務選項

我們為空運及海運貨物提供全險與全損險，下表列出兩種保險的差異。

全損險涵蓋的範圍包括	全險除了涵蓋全損險的範圍，還包括
• 沉船 • 失火 • 撞船 • 爆炸 • 管理疏失 • 機械淹水 • 已經存在的船身損害	• 擱淺 • 水或氣候造成的損害 • 凝結 • 不當處置 • 盜竊 • 未送達 • 滲漏或破裂

我們強烈建議您為運送貨物投保全險。

頁 1/3

- -

頁 2/3

我們的保險條款概要

我們已隨信付上本公司完整的保險手冊《Affordable Shipping Policy》供您詳細閱讀，
以下列出條款重點。

1 **保險利益**：您必須是投保貨物的擁有者、賣家、買家、運輸商或收件人。您必須在
貨物送交運輸前完成投保程序。

2 **保險涵蓋地點**：貨物在碼頭上或陸上、還未裝載至船上之前，仍在受保狀態。

3 **部分損失**：未達到全損失的狀況時，我們將只賠償受損部分的價值（超過自付額的
部分），並不賠償整批貨物的價值。

4 **未送達或盜竊**：貨物超過 35 天未送達並不知去向者，便被視為遺失。投保全險時，
投保人此時可獲賠償貨物之全部價值。申報盜竊須有相關文件證明。

5 **包裝不善**：因第三方執行的包裝或備貨不善，導致丟失或損害者，本公司不會援以
駁回索賠要求。

6 **遺失申報**：貨物若有遺失或損害，請於得知後立刻申報。若無及時申報，便可能無
法索賠。所需文件與程序請見《Affordable Shipping Policy》手冊〈貨物保險索賠〉
一節。

7 **退貨：**投保人拒收貨物之返回運費，由本公司承擔。

8 **主要不承保內容：**本公司不承保含有下列內容之貨物：帳目、帳單、貨幣、債務證明、支票、匯票、證券、票、契約、紙幣、含氪製品、危害性物質、易腐敗貨物、瓷磚、大理石磚、花崗石磚、石板瓦、花、植物、種子、槍械、菸草。

頁 2/3

頁 3/3

我們的保費

保費取決於貨物價值和貨物運送地點。一般保費費率在 $.0.81 至 $5.00 ／每 $100.00 貨物申報價值之間。至於如何計算貨物價值，請見《Affordable Shipping Policy》手冊〈價值計算方式〉一節，也歡迎您來電或來信利用我們的個別估價服務：(866) 892-7533 或 quotes@affordableshipinsurance.com。

我們的全球保險範圍

目前我們的保險範圍涵蓋北美與遠東之間的貨物運輸。我們承保由下列地點送出的貨物：澳洲、加拿大、香港、日本、馬來西亞、新加坡、南韓、台灣、美國。我們承保所有前列地點之間的貨物運輸，以及從這些地點運送至柬埔寨、中國大陸、印尼、墨西哥、菲律賓、泰國、越南的貨物。我們也為某些沒有在此列出的地點，提供特別的貨運保險服務，詳情請見保險手冊。

準備好要投保了嗎？

隨信附上的《Affordable Shipping Policy》手冊，列出了所有投保所需的文件和說明。請將手冊所附的表格填寫完整後寄來，或是上 www.affordableshipinsurance/order-shipment-insurance.html 進行投保程序。

希望這些資訊對您有所幫助。若有任何問題，歡迎隨時來電 (866) 892-7533。

Unit 43 送貨相關書信常見說法
Common phrases for correspondence about shipping

1 Phrases about shipping: Advising about shipment 發貨通知

❶ We are writing to inform you that your order _____ [order number] was sent on _____ [date].

在此通知您，您的〔訂單號碼〕號訂單貨物已於〔日期〕發出。

❷ Please accept this letter as notice that your order _____ [order number] shipped on this date _____ [date] . . .

本信通知您，您的〔訂單號碼〕號訂單貨物已於〔日期〕發出。

2 Phrases about shipping: Describing shipping carriers
貨運公司說明

❶ We ship via UPS . . . 　　　　　　　　我們透過 UPS 送貨……

❷ We ship via the United States Postal Service . . .

我們透過美國郵局送貨。

❸ _____ [Shipping service] handles our domestic shipments . . .

〔遞送公司〕負責我們的國內送貨……

❹ _____ [Shipping service] handles our international shipments . . .

〔遞送公司〕負責我們的國際送貨……

❺ We recommend _____ [shipping service] for its fast, reliable service . . .

我們建議採用〔遞送公司〕迅速可靠的服務……

❻ Your shipping service options are: _____ [list options].

可選擇的送貨方式有：〔列出選項〕

3 Phrases about shipping: Describing shipping time frames
說明送貨期限

1 _____ [Shipping option] usually takes between 3 to 5 business days . . .

〔送貨方式〕通常可於 3 到 5 個工作天將貨物送達……

2 Packages typically arrive within _____ [number of days] of shipment.

包裹通常可於出貨後〔日數〕內送達。

3 Please allow _____ [number of days] for shipping.

商品運送需時〔日數〕。

4 Please be advised that we cannot guarantee international shipping arrival dates.

請留意，我們無法保證國際送貨抵達所需的時間。

5 Please note that these times are estimates, and we do not guarantee any particular arrival date.

這些都是估計的時間，本公司並不保證貨物送達的日期。

4 Phrases about insurance: Describing coverage　保險：說明保險範圍

1 Our coverage includes . . .　　　　　　　　我們的保險範圍涵蓋……

2 With us, you are covered in case of theft, pilferage, fire and water damage, nondelivery, piracy, etc. . . .

與本公司投保，遇到失竊、火災、泡水、未送達、海盜……等事故時可獲理賠。

3 Our coverage insures you against . . .　　　　我們的保險範圍涵蓋……

4 We provide coverage for all commodities including perishable foods . . .

我們為所有的商品提供保險，包括易腐敗食物。

5 We provide coverage for all commodities excluding live animals . . .

我們為所有的商品提供保險，活體動物……等除外。

⑥ Our basic coverage protects you from loss or damage resulting from the perils of the sea . . .

我們的基本險涵蓋海上風險所導致的遺失或損壞⋯⋯

⑦ Our all-risk coverage protects you from extraneous perils, including theft, pilferage . . .

我們的全險涵蓋各種外來的風險，包含盜竊⋯⋯

⑧ Our coverage is for transit damage or loss only and does not include reimbursement for repairs of any preexisting wear or damage . . .

我們的保險只涵蓋運送過程中導致的損害或遺失，不理賠既有的耗損或損壞所產生之修理費用⋯⋯

5 Phrases about insurance: Describing rates, payment, and claims 說明保費費率、付款和索賠方式

❶ Our rates are calculated according to . . .   我們的保費取決於⋯⋯

❷ Insurable items are categorized according to the risk level associated with those items. High-risk categories have higher insurance rates and different deductibles.

受保物品依其風險等級分類。高風險類物品保費較高，自付額也不同。

❸ Your claim amount is tied to the declared value of your goods . . .

理賠金額取決於商品申報的價值⋯⋯

❹ Any visible damage must be noted on the delivery receipt . . .

任何肉眼可見的損害，務必註明於取貨收據上⋯⋯

❺ Required claims documentation includes the supplier's invoice, packing list . . .

申請理賠所需文件包括供應商發貨單、裝箱單⋯⋯

1 Review the concepts

① List four topics that may be addressed in explanations of shipping terms.

② List three topics that may be addressed in letters about insurance terms.

2 Send a shipping notice.

Imagine that you work for Acme Art Supply. You have just shipped an order to John Doe of Kid Art! in Canada. Using the following information, send him a shipping notice.

- **Order number:** 23-511a
- **Customer's billing address:** 18 Chestnut Street, Toronto, ON M5G 1R3, Canada
- **Customer's shipping address:** 10 Bloor Street East, 5th Floor, Toronto, ON M4W 1A8, Canada
- **Date ordered:** May 9, 2023
- **Date shipped:** May 11, 2023
- **Items, item numbers, and prices:** 50 medium paintbrushes (item number pbm13), 10 NT each; 50 large paintbrushes (item number pbl27), 17 NT each; 10 pinewood easels (item number e44), 450 NT each; 100 36"x48" inch canvases (item number cm34), 250 NT each; 50 24"x36" inch canvases (item number cs12), 180 NT each; and 100 beginner watercolor sets (item number wc30), 150 NT each.
- **Shipping method:** FastShip International Parcel Priority (arrival in four business days)
- **Tracking number:** IPP0029384112
- **Expected arrival date:** May 16, 2023

Acme Art Supply

5-7 225 Taichunggang Street, Sec. 3
Taichung 407, Taiwan
886-4-23548849

_____

John Doe

_____

_____

_____

Dear _____ :

Subject: _____

_____

_____

_____

_____

_____

_____

_____

_____

_____

_____

_____

_____

_____

_____

_____

_____

_____

_____

_____

_____

_____

_____

_____

_____

_____

_____

_____

投訴、建言與回覆
Complaints, Suggestions, and Responses

Key Terms

complaints policies 客訴規章
公司為處理客訴的所採取的一系列方法和方針。

compensation 補償
公司為彌補過失所提供的回饋方式。回覆投訴時，可向對方告知公司可提供何種補償措施。

chain of command 指揮鏈；指揮系統
由一系列行政階層或軍事階級組成的行政指揮系統，每一級直接對自己的上級負責。

complaint 抱怨；投訴
表達痛苦、不滿或憎恨。也指引起抱怨的原因；不滿、委屈。本章專門討論的是「customer complaint」（客訴），即顧客對於商品、服務等不滿意所提出的投訴。

documentation 文件證據
用以當作證明的正式書面資料。

discount 折扣
降低商品價格。

feedback 回饋意見
針對產品或服務等提供的意見回饋。

follow up 跟進；跟催
繼續進行已經展開的行動，如 a follow-up letter（跟催信）。

justified 正常合理的
被證明是正確或合理的。

replacement 換貨
顧客在購買商品後，因為不滿意等原因，向賣方要求更換貨品。

refund 退款
顧客對於貨品或服務不滿意，店家退還顧客當初所支付的全部或部分金額。

legitimate 合情合理的
合乎情理；並非立基於錯誤的根據的。

valid 正當的
有正當理由的；有實際意義的。

Unit 44　如何撰寫投訴和建言信？
How do I write complaint and suggestion letters?

1 什麼是投訴信？

投訴信（a letter of complaint）是為了用來陳述公司或個人提供之**商品、服務或其他商務運作具有的問題**。有時候投訴信的目的是就此問題尋求協助；有時候投訴信也會寄給與此問題無關的同事或主管，這時候投訴信就如同該問題的紀錄檔案。

2 如何寫投訴信？

投訴信必須在「**態度堅決**」（being firm）與「**維持理性**」（being reasonable）之間找到**平衡**。你要清楚表達你的不滿，但是不需要把對方當成敵人看待，因此撰寫投訴信的時候，要遵守下列原則：

❶ **確認事實**：確定你已掌握整體事實狀況，而且你的投訴是有根據的。

❷ **確定有無投訴程序**：很多公司設有一定的投訴程序。按照對方的程序去投訴，可以節省你的時間。

❸ **寄給恰當的收件人**：最好把信寄給特定的人。如果你不太確定該寄給誰，那就多寄給幾個人。

❹ **精確具體**：簡明扼要地說明你的問題，以及你採取了（或是嘗試採取了）什麼行動以解決這個問題。把重要的事實資訊呈現出來，包括相關人員姓名、日期、訂單號碼等，但是不要讓解釋變得過於冗長。

❺ **維持禮貌**：威脅（threat）或譏諷（sarcasm）都不會帶來任何好處，因此應保持專業與禮貌的語氣。

❻ **附上文件證據（documentation）的副本**：如果有相關文件可以證明你陳述的問題，把副本一併寄上，但不要把正本寄給對方。

❼ **提出明確的要求**：清楚描述你的要求，例如要求對方在一段合理的時間內回覆，像是二至三星期內。

❽ **跟催（follow up）**：如果對方沒有回信，那就再寄一封語氣更強烈的投訴信，或是把信寄給對方公司更高層的人。

3 建言信是什麼？

在與一家公司往來時，顧客可能會發現該公司在特定方面，服務上有應該加強的地方。

這種情況下，顧客不妨寫封建言信（suggestion letter）給對方公司。在這類信函中，寫信的顧客會針對該公司**應如何改進**，提出**意見（opinion）與忠告**（advice），以期將來顧客可以享有更佳的服務體驗。

4 建言信該怎麼寫？

為使建言信得到重視，寫信時應做到以下幾點：

❶ **語氣要保持專業、客氣友善（professional and friendly）**：這將有助確保該公司會以開放的心胸（with an open mind）接納建言。若以命令的口氣頤指氣使，結果未必能夠如願以償。

❷ **感謝收信者給予提供建言（make suggestions）的機會**：並不是每家公司都樂於聽取他人建言，所以感謝對方願意花時間閱讀建言信，是建言信的重點之一。

❸ **再三斟酌提出的建言（Think about the suggestions carefully.）**：請確定信中建言切實可行。不妨站在該公司的立場思考看看：你的建議是否可能輕易地付諸實行（put into practice）？

❹ **敘述要明確（Be clear.）**：務必具體說明可以**改進的部分**、以及需要**改進的原因**，並將你的想法用簡單明瞭的語言詳盡說明。

❺ **著重未來效益（benefits）**：信中需具體說明這些建言會如何為公司帶來正面影響。若有其他公司也採取了和建言相同的做法，也可以提出來，有助提高說服力。

44-1 | A complaint about an order 投訴訂單

回覆投訴 → P. 263

From:	rajendranl@luckyelectronic.com.sg
To:	chowarnold@changi.com.hk
Cc:	ceooffice@luckyelectronic.com.sg
Subject:	Complaint Regarding PO 030123
Attachment:	PO_030123.pdf; Invoice_030123.pdf

Segoe UI   14   B *I* U A | ≡ ≡ ≡ ≡ | ≡ ≡ ≡ ≡ | — 🔗 🖼

Dear Mr. Chow,

I am writing to inform you that our order of March 1, number 030123, was filled incorrectly. ❶

❶ 寫信人在第一句就把問題清楚陳述出來。

Our order was for 200 Changi Bluetooth speakers (item number CP08) and 20 gaming consoles (item number G01). The shipment arrived yesterday, but instead, we received 20 Bluetooth speakers and 20 gaming consoles. ❷

❷ 第二段則詳細說明出錯的地方，包括交貨日期和問題到底出在哪裡。

The demand for Bluetooth speakers is great, and this error has put us in a difficult position, as we have had to resort to other suppliers to fill our customers' needs. I would like you to please make up the shortfall of Bluetooth speakers immediately and ensure that there are no more mistakes with our shipments. ❸ ❹

❸ 寫信人在這一段描述了該疏失所引起的問題，以及他期望對方採取什麼行動。

I have attached our purchase order and the paid invoice for your reference. Please confirm receipt of this letter.

❹ 這個句子是很正式的說法，但同時也表達出寫信人對該狀況的沮喪感，它暗示如果繼續發生這種疏失，Lucky 公司可能會另找供應商。

Sincerely,
Indira Rajendran
Purchasing Manager

Lucky Electronics

33 Eunos Road 8, Singapore 408600
Tel: 65 68 482334
Fax: 65 68 482335

喬先生您好：

您好。在此必須通知您，本公司於 3 月 1 日所下訂單（訂單號碼 030123）在送貨上有錯誤的地方。❶

我們訂購的是 200 個 Changi 藍牙喇叭（商品編號 CP08）和 20 個電玩主機（商品編號 G01）。貨品於昨天送達，但是我們只收到 20 個藍牙喇叭和 20 個電玩主機。

市場上對於藍牙喇叭的需求量極大，這個疏失使我們一時手足無措，我們不得不跟其他供應商訂貨，以滿足顧客的需求。請貴公司立刻將缺漏的藍牙喇叭寄出，並確保本公司的訂單不再發生類似的狀況。❹

附檔為訂單副本及發貨單（已付清）副本，並請與我們確認收到本信。

44-Z | A complaint about treatment 就招待不佳進行投訴　回覆投訴 → P. 264

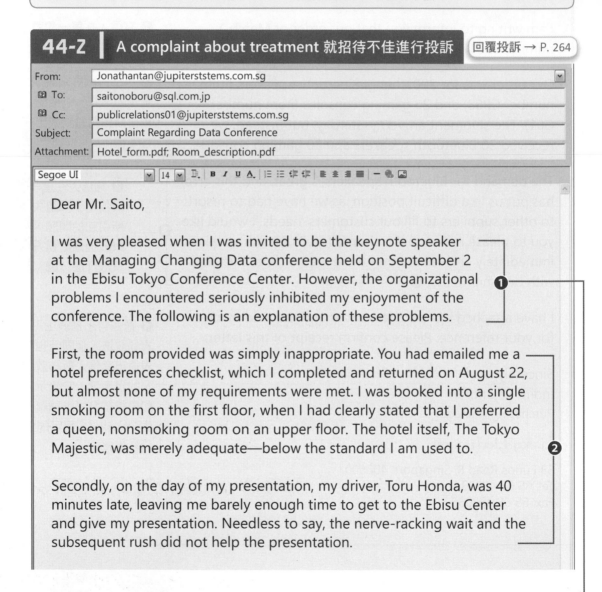

From:	Jonathantan@jupiterststems.com.sg
To:	saitonoboru@sql.com.jp
Cc:	publicrelations01@jupiterststems.com.sg
Subject:	Complaint Regarding Data Conference
Attachment:	Hotel_form.pdf; Room_description.pdf

Segoe UI　　14

Dear Mr. Saito,

I was very pleased when I was invited to be the keynote speaker at the Managing Changing Data conference held on September 2 in the Ebisu Tokyo Conference Center. However, the organizational problems I encountered seriously inhibited my enjoyment of the conference. The following is an explanation of these problems. ❶

First, the room provided was simply inappropriate. You had emailed me a hotel preferences checklist, which I completed and returned on August 22, but almost none of my requirements were met. I was booked into a single smoking room on the first floor, when I had clearly stated that I preferred a queen, nonsmoking room on an upper floor. The hotel itself, The Tokyo Majestic, was merely adequate—below the standard I am used to. ❷

Secondly, on the day of my presentation, my driver, Toru Honda, was 40 minutes late, leaving me barely enough time to get to the Ebisu Center and give my presentation. Needless to say, the nerve-racking wait and the subsequent rush did not help the presentation.

❶ 同樣地，寫信人在第一段就把問題寫出來。在這封信裡，寫信人先禮後兵，先說明自己很高興能受邀演講，這樣可以顯示他一開始還對整個情況充滿期待，並非一心想找麻煩。如此可以使下面提出來的抱怨顯得更正當合理。

❷ 寫信人詳細說明他當時對整個狀況的反應，並提供具體的相關資訊（飯店名、相關人名等）。

Third, the conference schedule was not clear. Attendees did not seem aware of what presentations were being given or when, and few people had access to that information. The schedule had apparently been sent as an email attachment to the invitation, but it would have been wise to provide it in paper form at the venue as well. Presenters were disappointed with small audiences, and attendees were disappointed after missing key presentations. This could easily have been prevented with some forethought.

Finally, on a more personal note, it was disappointing not to be offered some assistance or guidance when exploring Tokyo. Because I was giving a presentation in an unfamiliar city, my expectation was that I would be provided with information on interesting places to go or sights to see. There was no personal assistance—drivers merely dropped me off and picked me up. The hotel had minimal information, and my liaison, Kumiko Yamamoto, and the other SQL Source representatives I spoke to seemed surprised at my questions and were unable to give me any detailed information.

In conclusion, the conference was a very negative experience, although with a little more effort it could have been very positive. As it is, I feel poorly treated by your company and disinclined to participate in future conferences or meetings. I would appreciate a response to this email in the coming weeks, with an explanation of your decisions at the time and your plans for improving future conferences.

Attached are my completed hotel preference checklist and a description of the room in The Tokyo Majestic for your reference.

Sincerely,
Jonathan Tan
CEO

Jupiter Systems

6 Temasek Boulevard,
#8-00 Suntec Tower Four, Singapore 038986
Tel: +65 65299123
Fax: +65 67399124

❸ 結尾段落的語氣仍然很專業，但卻是很重的批評。寫信人要求對方就信中問題進行回覆。

齋藤先生您好：

我非常高興受邀到 9 月 2 日在東京惠比壽會議中心舉辦的「變動資料管理」研討會發表主題演講。然而，幾個組織安排上的問題令我敗興而歸。下面依序說明我遇到的問題。

首先，大會安排的旅館房間非常不理想。您之前曾用電郵寄來一份旅館房間偏好詢問表，我填寫好後於 8 月 22 日傳回，但是最後安排給我的房間幾乎沒有一點符合我的要求。我被安排到一間一樓的吸菸單人房，但是我之前已清楚表明，希望有一間較高樓層的非吸菸加大雙人房。而 Tokyo Majestic 這間旅館本身也差強人意，完全在我習慣的標準之下。

第二，演講當天，我的司機本田徹遲到了 40 分鐘，讓我差一點就來不及趕到惠比壽會議中心發表演講。焦急的等待和隨後慌張匆忙的趕路，對我的演講當然也沒帶來任何好處。

第三，研討會的議程沒有清楚公布。參加研討會的人似乎都不知道什麼時候有什麼演講，也沒有多少人能夠取得這方面的資訊。大會之前顯然曾以電子郵件附件的方式把議程寄給大家，但是應該再於研討會會場以紙本形式提供議程表。最後很多講者因為聽眾太少而感到失望，聽眾則因為錯過重要的演講而感到失望。如果事先考慮到這一點，就很容易避免這種狀況。

最後，就我個人來說，我非常失望在遊覽東京時沒有得到什麼協助或指引。受邀去陌生的城市演講時，我一般都預期大會會提供一些資訊，讓我知道可以去哪些有趣地方或景點遊覽參觀，但是這次我完全沒有得到這些個人的協助。司機只負責接送，旅館也沒有多少資料，我的接待人山本久美子和其他我洽詢的 SQL Source 公司代表，則似乎對我的問題感到很驚訝，而且也無法提供我任何詳細的資訊。

總之，這次的研討會是個非常不愉快的經驗，但是當初大會只要再多花一點心力，整個經歷就會完全不同。我覺得大會的招待與安排非常不理想，以後恐怕也沒有意願參加貴公司舉辦的研討會了。希望能在未來幾星期內收到您的回覆，聽您解釋大會當初為什麼會有這些決定，以及貴公司計劃未來如何改善未來會議安排。

隨信附上我填過的旅館房間偏好詢問表，以及 Tokyo Majestic 旅館房間之描述。

44-3 | A complaint about damage 就損害進行投訴

回覆投訴 → P. 268

Part
11
投訴、建言與回覆

Unit
44
如何撰寫投訴和建言信？

Duds

P.O. Box 748, Bangkok 10501, Thailand
Ph: 66-2-8475934 Fax: 66-2-8470394

May 3, 2023

Attention: Malika Karmarkar
Exotic Textiles, Inc.
16, Talkatora Road
New Delhi 110001

Reference: PO 13m12

Dear Ms. Karmarkar:

「It is with regret . . .」是用來提出客訴時，相當禮貌的說法。寫信人藉此暗示他並不希望對該公司提出抱怨，他並沒有因為這個問題對該公司心存怨恨。

It is with regret that I inform you of some serious problems with your delivery of two boxes of leather sandals, PO number 13m12, received June 26, 2023.

When I opened the consignment today, the sandals appeared to be moldy. Further inspection confirmed this, and though my staff and I tried to clean them, the sandals could not be restored to a salable condition. I can only assume that the low quality of the leather caused the mold growth. I have always been happy with the quality of your goods, but I am afraid I will have to ask for a refund or replacement for this order.

Please contact me at your earliest convenience at 66-2-8475934, extension 2.

Best wishes,

Aroon Pradabtanakij

Aroon Pradabtanakij, Manager
Duds Clothing

Karmarkar 女士您好：

我們很遺憾必須通知您，貴公司於 2023 年 6 月 26 日送達的兩箱皮製涼鞋（訂單號碼 13m12）出現嚴重的問題。

今天我打開這兩箱貨品時，箱子裡的涼鞋看起來都發霉了。經過進一步檢視，我們發現鞋子確實發霉。我和同事努力想把霉斑清掉，但還是無法把鞋子恢復到可以出售的狀況。我只能假定是皮革品質不好，才導致霉菌滋生。我們對貴公司的產品品質一向滿意，但是對這次訂單，我們恐怕只能要求退款或換貨。

請您於方便時盡快與我聯絡：66-2-8475934，分機 2。

Saturn Systems

1176 N. Ventura Avenue, Oak View, CA 93022, USA
Tel: +1 719 392-9068 Fax: +1 719 392-9069

September 15, 2023

Yoichi Fujita
Tech PCO
18-20 Nihonbashi Koami-cho
Chuo-ku
Tokyo 103-0016
Japan

❶ 寫信者並未在一開頭就提供建議，而是先稱讚對方安排妥適，意在減低建議對於讀信者可能的負面觀感。

❷ 寫信者在建議時，不忘肯定讀者已經付出的努力，並提到其他活動的經驗，有助增加說服力。

Dear Mr. Fujita:

❶ Thank you for inviting me to be a speaker at the recent data systems conference. The hotel you arranged for me was great. And the driver who drove me to and from the conference center was polite and on time. If you don't mind, however, I do have a small suggestion for you.

❷ I noticed that many of the talks had small audiences. This was because many guests did not know the event schedule. As a result, they missed key talks. I know the schedule had been sent out to guests in an email. But may I suggest that in the future you also provide the schedule in paper form at the center itself? You could also post it on the event's website so people can access it easily on their phones. This is how things have been done at other events I have been to. Doing so helps everyone avoid being disappointed.

Thank you once again for the chance to present at the event and to provide you with this feedback.

Kind regards,

Kevin Miller

Kevin Miller, CEO
Saturn Systems

如何回覆投訴信和建言信？
How do I respond to complaint and suggestion letters?

1 如何回覆投訴信？

　　如何回覆投訴信，有幾個一般的原則，但是實際上怎麼回覆，還是取決於該投訴是否合理（legitimate），也就是對方是否有正當的理由提出這樣的投訴。收到投訴信時，第一件事就是要**確認信中所陳述的事實**。確定了是否真有對方所說的疏失，以及該投訴是否正當合理（justified）後，你就可以開始傳撰寫回覆信。

2 就合理的投訴進行回覆

　　如果你確定顧客的投訴是合理的，第一步就是要了解公司對於這樣的投訴有何既定政策。畢竟你要能夠明確地告訴顧客，你現在針對投訴的處理方式是什麼、之後會有何作為，以及你可以提供什麼措施。

　　一旦確定了你能夠做什麼，就可以開始撰寫回覆信了。依情況不同，也許你已經能夠告訴顧客，公司已經採取哪些步驟以解決問題；也可能你需要告訴顧客，公司可以採取哪些不同的做法，並能由顧客決定採取哪一種做法。就合理的投訴進行回覆時，需遵照下列的原則：

❶ **快速**：盡快回覆，不要讓已經心有不滿的顧客再為了等待而更加不悅。

❷ **謝謝顧客**：謝謝顧客來信指出商品或服務的問題。

❸ **讓顧客看到你的行動**：告訴顧客你已經具體做了什麼，或是你能夠具體做些什麼。顧客會希望看到你採取行動，因此務必讓他們看到你願意為此採取什麼措施。

❹ **問顧客想要什麼**：如果有幾種不同的做法可以解決問題，需在信中詢問顧客希望採取哪一種做法。讓顧客看到，你關心他們的需求，也願意盡力滿足他們的需求。

❺ **道歉**：在第一段就為該問題道歉，並在信的結尾再道歉一次。道歉可以安撫顧客的情緒。

藤田先生您好：

感謝您邀請我於近期舉行的數據系統會議上做演說。您為我安排的飯店非常好，開車載我往返會議中心的司機很有禮貌也很準時。不過若您不介意，我想提供您小小的建議。

我注意到許多講座的聽眾不多，這是因為很多與會嘉賓都不清楚活動議程表，因此錯過了重要的演講。我知道日程表已用電子郵件寄給與會者了，但是我能建議您日後，也在會議中心現場提供紙本議程表嗎？您也可以發布在活動網站上，這麼一來大家就可以輕易用手機查找議程表。我之前參加過的活動也是採用這種做法，如此便可避免大家失望而歸。

再次感謝給我於此次活動演説，並向您提供回饋意見的機會。

---

3 回覆建言信

收到建言信後，需要鄭重加以回覆。回覆信**不必太長**，但內容中要**感謝對方的回饋意見（feedback）**，並告知公司為此採取的**後續行動**，展現出公司樂於聽取並斟酌顧客的想法。當顧客覺得自身意見獲得傾聽時，就會對這家公司產生更深厚的感情。

為了確保妥善回覆顧客建言，請遵守以下原則：

❶ 簡短（brief）：信件務求簡短並兼顧禮貌即可。

❷ 表達謝意（Say thank you.）：在**信件開頭**與**結尾處**向顧客致謝，感謝他們願意花費時間和心思。即使他們的建言未獲採納，也要讓對方知道，公司很感謝這些好意協助。

❸ 告知後續行動（Share any action.）：告知顧客針對他們提出的建言，**公司有何後續動作**，例如可能已轉交給相關部門處理，或者已付諸實行。就算目前無法以具體動作回應，也要告知已將他們的**意見記錄下來**，留作未來參考。

❹ 告知正面結果（positive results）：讓顧客知道他們的建言提供了哪些幫助，可以簡短說明建議所帶來的**正面效益（benefit）**，這會讓顧客對自己的貢獻（contribution）感到與有榮焉。

Rajendran 女士您好：

謝謝您來信說明 3 月 1 日 030123 號訂單的問題。就跟昨天下午我在電話上跟您說的一樣，我非常抱歉這個疏失為貴公司引起這麼大的麻煩。

調閱所有的相關文件後，我們確定您訂購的商品當初確實已經點清，但是不知為何裝錯了箱子。我保證這是非常罕見的狀況，因為本公司負責收發貨物的員工一向都精確迅速。我已經跟貨運部經理談過，他今天會跟部門員工開會，避免以後再發生這種混亂。

依照您昨天在電話上的要求，我們在今天早上把缺漏的 180 個藍牙喇叭交由 Super Express Shipping 寄出了，包裹應該會在 3 月 25 日下午之前送達。為了表示我們服務顧客的誠意，下一次訂貨您將可以享有 10% 的折扣。

再次請您接受我為此遺憾的錯誤致上最誠摯的歉意。我們重視您的惠顧，希望以後能夠再次以本公司一貫的高品質為您服務。

45-1 | Response to the complaint about an order
回覆 44-1 的訂單投訴

投訴信 → P. 255

Part
11

投訴、建言與回覆

Unit
45
如何回覆投訴信和建言信？

CHANGI ENTERTAINMENT DEVICES

72 Nathan Road, Tsim Sha Tsui, Kowloon
Hong Kong
Tel: 852-36821820 Fax: 852-36821820

March 24, 2023

Indira Rajendran
Lucky Electronics
33 Eunos Road 8
Singapore 408600

Ref: PO 030123

Dear Ms. Rajendran:

Thank you for your email regarding the mistake with your order of March 1, PO 030123. As I said in our telephone conversation yesterday afternoon, I am so sorry you were subjected to such inconvenience through this error. ❶

After collecting all the relevant documents, it is clear that your order was assembled correctly but somehow was put into the wrong box. I assure you that this is an anomaly, as our shipping and receiving staff is usually accurate, consistent, and quick. I have spoken to the shipping manager, and he will meet with his employees today to ensure that mix-ups like this do not happen again. ❷

This morning we shipped the shortfall of 180 Changi Bluetooth speakers via Super Express Shipping, as you requested in our conversation. They should arrive no later than the afternoon of March 25. I would also like to offer you a 10% discount on your next order as a sign of our commitment to customer satisfaction. ❸

Again, please accept my sincerest apologies for this unfortunate mistake. We value your business, and we look forward to providing you with our usual quality service in the future. ❹

Sincerely,
Arnold Chow
Arnold Chow, Sales Manager
Changi Entertainment Devices

❶ 寫信人在第一段就提起訂單號碼、送貨疏失和前一天的電話會談，可推知他在收到投訴信之後就打電話給顧客，以盡快解決問題。

❷ 寫信人詳細描述公司會採取什麼行動，以避免未來發生類似的狀況，並向對方保證公司員工的整體素質，如此可以顯示公司服務顧客的誠意。寫信人強調該疏失是罕見的狀況，言下之意就是該疏失絕非出於草率馬虎，或是因為公司不在乎顧客。

❸ 第三段仔細說明公司已經採取什麼行動以解決問題，也就是把剩下的貨物寄出。寫信人還為對方下一次的訂購提供折扣，這是處理顧客投訴時經常採取的做法。

❹ 最後，寫信人又道歉一次，並表達維持合作關係的誠意。寫信人希望藉此拉攏顧客的心，讓顧客以後還願意跟他們訂購商品。

SQL SOURCE

Hamano IS Building, Shibuya-ku
Tokyo 150-0015 Japan
Tel: 03 3661 9088   Fax: 03 3661 9089

September 15, 2023

Jupiter Systems
6 Temasek Boulevard
#8-00 Suntec Tower Four
Singapore 038986

Attention: Jonathan Tan

Dear Mr. Tan:

Thank you for taking the time to tell us about your problems during the Managing Changing Data conference here in Tokyo. I am extremely sorry to hear about the unpleasantness you encountered. After looking into each of your complaints, I would like to provide you with the following information.

1. **The quality of the room and the hotel.** We sent you the hotel preferences checklist specifically to ensure that you were happy with your room. Unfortunately, rooms of your description were fully booked at The Tokyo Majestic when your booking was made. Instead of seeking another hotel, the new staff member responsible for the reservations simply booked you into one of the remaining available rooms. She has been rebuked and understands in the future to honor our guests' needs over our hotel choices. As for the quality of the hotel, when I stayed there myself years ago, I found it to be charming and equipped with all the desired facilities. It seems that in the intervening years, it has slipped. That was my oversight, and I take responsibility for it. Please accept my apologies. We are undertaking a review of the hotel now, and we will use the results to provide constructive criticism to the management and to determine whether we will use the hotel in the future.

2. **The lateness of your driver.** Mr. Honda came to us highly recommended by a respected client. However, yours was not the only complaint we received about him during the conference. He was told that he fell far short of our expectations and was let go. We are sorry for his performance.

❶ 寫信人就每一項投訴都詳細解釋，並說明已經採取或正在採取的行動。如此能夠顯示出對顧客的尊重，並確保不會遺漏任何一點。

3. **Conference schedules.** As you note, we did indeed email a schedule to all participants. Also, printed brochures containing the schedule were available in the dining hall as well as the lounge area. We spoke to many attendees who found and used the schedules, but it seems that others were unable to locate them. We will reconsider their placement at future conferences. ❶

4. **Finally, your lack of guidance regarding Tokyo.** We are truly sorry that more guidance was not provided, for we would have been happy to showcase Tokyo, our headquarters and my hometown. We thought it best not to impose on busy attendees, but it seems that in doing so, we missed an opportunity to provide a truly special service to our guests.

Again, I am sorry to hear about your negative experience at our conference. We hope that we will have a chance to prove that this is not the norm with our functions and to restore your good opinion of us. To that end, we would like to give you a free pass to our spring conference, Data Management for the Future. Please accept our offer to show you again what SQL Source stands for. ❷

Please feel free to contact me for any reason at 03 3661 9088, extension 235.

Yours truly,

Noboru Saito

Noboru Saito, Executive Vice President
SQL Source

❷ 顧客雖然沒有要求賠償，但是寫信人還是主動提供補償方案，以挽救公司的形象，並顯示他們能夠體會顧客的心情。

Part
11

投訴、建言與回覆

Unit
45

如何回覆投訴信和建言信？

譚先生您好：

謝謝您抽空說明您在東京「變動資料管理」研討會期間遭遇到的問題。聽到您遭遇到這麼多的不愉快，我真的極為抱歉。在調查過您所陳述的各項問題後，以下是我們的說明。

1. **旅館和旅館房間的品質。**我們寄給您旅館房間偏好詢問表，目的就是希望您對旅館房間感到滿意。很不幸，在為您訂房的時候，Tokyo Majestic 飯店裡您希望的房間類型都已訂滿。負責訂房的新進員工沒有洽詢別的飯店，直接就為您在 Tokyo Majestic 飯店訂了另外一間空房間。我們已經訓斥過她，她以後會懂得把顧客的需求放在旅館選擇之上。至於飯店的品質，我自己幾年前住在這間飯店時，還覺得飯店很漂亮，該有的設備也一應俱全。看來這幾年間該飯店品質已經下滑，這是我的疏忽，我要負起責任，請接受我的道歉。我們現在正對該飯店展開檢核，並會以調查結果向飯店經營者提出建設性的批評，同時考慮未來是否還要繼續與該飯店合作。

2. **司機遲到。**本田先生是一位極受重視的客戶大力推薦的。然而，您不是唯一在研討會期間對他提出抱怨的貴賓。我們已經讓他知道，他遠遠達不到我們的要求，並將他解僱了。我們為他的表現深感抱歉。

強納森・譚先生／ 2023 年 9 月 15 日

3. **研討會的議程表。**如您所說，我們的確把研討會的議程以電子郵件的形式寄給所有與會者，此外在研討會期間，餐廳和貴賓休息室也都放有印好議程的小手冊。我們發現有很多參會者找到了這些小手冊，但是顯然也有不少人未能找到。在未來的研討會，我們會重新考慮議程小手冊的擺放地點。

4. **最後，沒有人為您導覽東京。**真的很抱歉我們沒有提供更多的參觀導覽服務，畢竟我們會非常樂意帶您參觀東京市，這裡是我們的總部所在，也是我的家鄉。我們當初的想法是，最好不要打擾忙碌的貴賓們，但是看來這反而使我們失去了提供顧客特別服務的機會。

再次為您在研討會期間遭遇到的不愉快經驗表示歉意，希望我們以後還有機會跟您證明，這並不是我們一貫的服務品質，並恢復您對本公司的信心。為了表示我們的誠意，我們將招待您免費參加於春季舉辦的「迎向未來的資料管理」研討會。請接受我們的招待，讓我們有機會讓您體驗到 SQL Source 真正的口碑品質。

如有任何問題，歡迎與我聯絡：03 3661 9088，分機 235。

45-3 Response to a suggestion about organization
針對 44-4 組織建議的回覆信

建言信 → P. 260

Part
11

投訴、建言與回覆

Unit
45

如何回覆投訴信和建言信
？

TECH PCO

18-20 Nihonbashi Koami-cho, Chuo-ku
Tokyo 103-0016, Japan
Tel: +81 3 3661 9087 Fax: +81 3 3661 9088

September 21, 2023

Kevin Miller
Saturn Systems
1176 N. Ventura Avenue
Oak View, CA 93022
USA

寫信者開頭立刻感謝對方費心提供建議，並在後續段落中描述己方對於建議有何具體回應、以及該建議對公司的幫助何在，最後一段再次表達謝意。

Dear Mr. Miller:

Thank you for taking the time to write to me with your feedback about the recent data systems event in Tokyo. I am glad the hotel was to your liking. I hope you had some time to explore the city while you were here.

Your ideas about schedules are well received. I passed them along to our staff in a meeting this morning. They will make sure that in the future, there will be plenty of paper schedules available at all our events. Our web team will also post the information online. I am sure this will create a better event experience for both guests and speakers.

Thank you once again for sharing your thoughts with us. I hope we can have the pleasure of working together again soon.

Yours truly,

Yoichi Fujita

Yoichi Fujita, Executive Vice President
Tech PCO, Tokyo

米勒先生您好：

感謝您抽空來信，就近期在東京舉行的資料系統活動提出回饋意見。我很高興您喜歡這家旅館，也希望您在活動期間有時間探訪這座城市。

您對議程表的建議，我們欣然接受。我今天早上已將這些建議轉達給我們的員工，未來我們會確保本公司所有活動，都提供足夠紙本議程表。我們的網路團隊也會將資訊透過網路公布，相信這會為來賓和講者創造更好的活動體驗。

再次感謝您跟我們分享想法，期待有榮幸很快與您再次合作。

對不合理的投訴進行回覆
Responding to unjustified complaints

很不幸地，有時候顧客還是會提出不合理的投訴，但是這時你還是要**體諒**（sympathize）並**尊重**（respect）顧客的處境。在撰寫回覆信時，依舊遵守上個單元說明過的原則，不過這時候你就不用說明你會採取什麼行動以解決問題，而是要解釋**為什麼你無法依顧客要求的方式進行補償**。在這類的回覆信中，謹慎周到非常重要，因為你不應讓顧客覺得受到羞辱。

顧客的投訴不合理，並不代表你就不應該提供任何協助。畢竟，投訴的顧客還是你的顧客，提供他完善的服務最終還是對你有益。下面就是 Unit 44 第三封投訴信所進行的回覆。

46-1 | Response to a complaint about damage
回覆 44-3 商品損害的投訴

投訴信 → P. 259

Exotic Textiles, Inc.
16, Talkatora Road, New Delhi 110001
Ph: 24787040 Fax: 24787042

20 May 2023

Duds
P.O. Box 748,
Bangkok 10501, Thailand

Attention: Aroon Pradabtanakij

Dear Mr. Pradabtanakij:

Subject: Your order number 13m12

Thank you for your letter explaining the problem with your order 13m12, which arrived on June 26 of last year. We are very sorry that you are unable to use the shipment of sandals, and we understand how frustrating it is to receive damaged goods.

❶ 寫信人謝謝顧客的來信，並表示能夠體會對方的處境。

However, in light of the fact that the boxes have been in your possession for the past 10 months and were only opened on May 3 of this year, I am afraid we are reluctant to take responsibility for their current condition. Our quality guarantee covers our products while they are in our or our shipper's control. Unfortunately, we have no way of knowing the condition of the sandals when they arrived. Because we have had no other complaints about the quality of these particular sandals, we must entertain the possibility that your storage conditions contributed to the mold.

❷ 在這裡，寫信人清楚解釋公司無法退款的原因：因為現在已無法判斷這些損害是何時和如何產生的。注意寫信人並沒有堅持說鞋子一開始的狀況良好，而是說現在已經無法確切知道到底發生了什麼事。

We do appreciate the problems that unsalable merchandise poses, however. Although we are unable to offer you a refund on your order, we would be happy to take a 10% discount off your next order with us.

As always, we value your business. Please let me know if there is any other way I can be of assistance. Please don't hesitate to call me at 24787040 with any comments or questions.

Yours faithfully,

Malika Karmarkar

Malika Karmarkar, Sales Manager
Exotic Textiles, New Delhi

❸ 寫信人再次表示能夠體諒顧客的處境。雖然寫信人不會為顧客退款，但是為了表示服務顧客的誠意，她還是給顧客折扣優惠，如此有助於維持雙方的合作關係。如果她對顧客的處境顯得漠不關心，顧客可能就不會再光顧了。

Pradabtanakij 先生您好：

主旨：您的 13m12 號訂單

謝謝您來信說明於去年 6 月 26 日送達之 13m12 號訂單商品的問題。對於您無法出售這些涼鞋，我們感到非常抱歉，我們也了解收到損壞的商品有多惱人。

然而，由於兩箱涼鞋過去 10 個月來一直在貴公司手上，一直到今年 5 月 3 日才開箱，因此本公司恐怕無法為其目前的狀況負起責任。我們的品質保證只在產品還在本公司或本公司運輸公司持有時才有效。很遺憾地，我們無法知道這批涼鞋送達時的狀況。由於針對這款涼鞋，我們未接獲其他品質相關的投訴，我們不得不推想，有可能是貴公司的庫存環境導致涼鞋發霉。

不過我們能夠理解涼鞋無法出售為貴公司帶來的問題。我們雖然無法為您辦理退款，但是下一次的訂貨我們願意提供您 10% 的折扣。

我們一向非常重視與貴公司的合作關係。如果還有任何其他我可以提供協助的地方，或有任何指教或問題，請隨時與我聯絡：24787040。

撰寫與回覆投訴和建言信的常用說法
Common phrases for writing and responding to complaints and suggestions

1 Writing complaint letters: Making the complaint
撰寫投訴信：提出投訴

❶ I am sorry to say that the service at your restaurant was shoddy and unprofessional.

很遺憾我必須說，貴餐廳的服務既差勁又不專業。

❷ It pains me to report that the shoes I purchased from you on Tuesday have already developed holes.

很遺憾我必須通知您，我星期二在貴店買的鞋現在已經出現破洞了。

❸ Unfortunately, I could not use the defective product you sent.

很不幸地，我無法使用您寄來的瑕疵品。

❹ I regret to inform you that . . .　　　　很遺憾我必須通知您……

2 Writing complaint letters: Asking for restitution or a replacement
撰寫投訴信：要求賠償或換貨

❶ Please send a new product as soon as possible.

請盡快寄來全新產品。

❷ I would appreciate it if another technician could come to fix the printer.

希望貴公司能夠再派一名維修員來修理印表機，謝謝。

❸ I am looking forward to receiving the replacement . . .

我希望能夠收到換貨……

❹ I hope you can provide me with a new . . .　希望貴公司能夠寄來新的……

3 Writing suggestion letters 撰寫建言信：提供建議

① I have a small suggestion about the music played at your store.

關於貴店播放的音樂，我有個小小的建議。

② May I offer some feedback about your new app?

關於你們的新應用程式，我能提供一點回饋意見嗎？

③ A possible solution to this issue would be putting up a sign.

此問題可能的解決辦法是設置告示。

④ Doing things a different way might produce better results.

改變做法，也許會得到更好的結果。

4 Writing response letters: Apologizing for complaints
回覆投訴信：就投訴表示道歉

① We are so sorry to hear that you experienced poor service in our restaurant.

聽到您在本餐廳經歷不佳的服務，我們感到非常抱歉。

② We deeply regret the problems you have had with our Sophia shoes.

我們非常遺憾我們的 Sohpia 鞋款為您造成問題。

③ We are surprised and very sorry to hear that . . .

我們非常驚訝、也非常遺憾聽到……

④ We apologize for the defective goods.

我們為這些有缺陷的產品道歉。

5 Writing response letters: Offering restitution or a replacement
回覆投訴信：提供賠償或換貨的服務

❶ We will send a replacement _____ [product name] right away.
我們會立刻寄出新的……〔產品名稱〕以便換貨。

❷ We will be happy to send a new technician to repair your computer.
我們很樂意派另外一名維修員去修理您的電腦。

❸ We would like to offer you a _____ [discount, etc.].
我們將提供您……〔折扣優惠等〕。

❹ We will ship your replacement immediately.
我會立刻寄出新的換貨商品。

6 Replying to a suggestion 回覆對方建議

❶ Thank you for taking the time to offer your feedback.
感謝您撥冗提供意見。

❷ Thank you for your excellent ideas regarding how to make the process more efficient.
謝謝您就如何讓流程更有效率，提出的良好意見。

❸ Your suggestions about schedules are well received / received with gratitude.
您對日程表事宜的建議我們充分接受／我們滿心感激地接受您就日程表事宜的建議。

❹ Thank you for sharing your thoughts with us.
謝謝您跟我們分享您的想法。

7 Writing response letters: Denying invalid complaints
回覆投訴信：回拒不合理的投訴

❶ Because we cannot take responsibility for the problem . . .

由於我們無法為此問題負起責任……

❷ I am sorry, but according to our policy, we cannot offer you a
replacement. 很抱歉，但根據本公司政策，我們無法為您換貨。

❸ Because the problem occurred somewhere outside our area of
responsibility, we are not able to . . .

由於這個問題是在我們的負責範圍外產生的，因此我們無法……

1 Review the concepts

❶ What is a letter of complaint?

_____

_____

❷ Why is it important to write back quickly when responding to complaints?

_____

_____

❸ Which is not a guideline to follow when responding to a complaint? _____

(A) Always offer the customer a discount or coupon.

(B) Ask what action the customer would like to see taken.

(C) Apologize.

❹ Which expressions show sympathy in a complaint response? _____

(A) "We understand the problems this must have caused you."

(B) "We cannot see the reason for your complaint."

(C) "I can understand how frustrating this problem has been."

❺ Which expressions are similar to "it is with regret . . . ?" _____

(A) "I am sorry [to say . . .]"

(B) "It pains me [to report . . .]"

(C) "I was very angry . . ."

2 True (T) or False (F)

❶ ☐ True ☐ False You should not thank a customer for sending a letter of complaint.

❷ ☐ True ☐ False You should send original documents to verify your complaint.

3 Apply the principles

Imagine that you work for Duds. You ordered 50 pairs of blue sandals, but you were sent 50 pairs of red sandals. Write a letter informing Exotic Textiles of the error.

Duds
P.O. Box 748, Bangkok 10501, Thailand
Ph: 66-2-8475934 Fax: 66-2-8470394

May 3, 2023

Attention: Malika Karmarkar
Exotic Textiles, Inc.
16, Talkatora Road,
New Delhi 110001

Reference: PO 13m12

Dear _____ :

_____

_____

_____

_____

_____

_____

_____

_____

_____

_____

_____

4 **Write a letter of complaint.**

You work in an office and you recently had your fax machine repaired. The technician who came to repair the machine was very rude—he spoke to you disrespectfully, he tracked mud all over your carpet, he took twice as long to fix the machine as he should have, and now, two days later, your fax machine is broken again. Write a strongly worded letter to the company complaining of his behavior.

PROFESSIONAL PR
12 Eunos Road 6
Singapore 408600
Tel: 65 68 394058   Fax: 65 68 8574965

March 15, 2023

Universal Office Services
6 Temasek Boulevard,
Singapore 038986

Dear _____ :

_____

_____

_____

_____

_____

_____

_____

_____

_____

_____

_____

_____

_____

5 Respond to your customer's unjustified complaint.

You work for EduTech. You have just received a complaint about a shipment—your customer says she ordered 50 copies of a book, but you sent 100. When you go back to check the order, however, you see that it clearly requests 100. Respond to your customer's unjustified complaint.

EduTech
323 Bannock Street
Denver, CO 80204

19 August 2023

Soon Yi Choe
Kids International Village
830-62 Peomil 2-Dong
Tong-Gu Busan
South Korea

Dear _____ :

_____

_____

_____

_____

_____

_____

_____

_____

_____

_____

_____

_____

_____

_____

6 Write a letter of apology.

Imagine that you work for Lucky Electronics. A customer has just informed you that her shipment of five Wi-Fi routers contains two defective machines. Write back to apologize for the situation and let her know that you will send her replacement Wi-Fi routers immediately.

Lucky Electronics
33 Eunos Road 8
Singapore 408600
Tel: 65 68 482334 Fax: 65 68 482335

April 13, 2023

Tracy Wooster
112 Admiralty Road
Tsim Sha Tsui, Kowloon
Hong Kong

Dear _____ :

_____

_____

_____

_____

_____

_____

_____

_____

_____

_____

_____

_____

_____

7 Copy the following paragraphs (Ⓐ~Ⓓ) into the body of this suggestion letter in the correct order.

Green Cloud Technology
66 Ceres Street
San Francisco, CA 94124
USA
Tel: +1 415 822-4712

March 12, 2023

Yoichi Fujita
Tech PCO
18-20 Nihonbashi Koami-cho
Chuo-ku
Tokyo 103-0016
Japan

Dear Mr. Fujita:

Ⓐ While my hotel was comfortable, I would have liked a larger room and one on a higher floor.

Ⓑ Thank you once again for the chance to be one of your guest speakers and for your openness to feedback.

Ⓒ May I suggest that in the future you send out a preferences checklist to your speakers beforehand? I believe this would greatly improve their experience.

Ⓓ Thank you for inviting me to be a speaker at the conference in Tokyo last week. I enjoyed the experience, but I do have a small suggestion about hotel arrangements for your speakers.

❶ _____

_____

❷ _____

_____

❸ _____

_____

❹ _____

_____

Kind regards,

Sandra Lee

Sandra Lee
Chief Operating Officer, Green Cloud Technology

Key Terms

establish 建立、成立；找到
在商務溝通中，指「促使……產生」，或是「找到……」。

market share 市場占有率
企業的產品或特定品牌的商品，在整體市場中所占據的銷售百分比例。

mutual 雙方共同的
雙方共享的。

partnership 夥伴關係
企業之間成為合作夥伴，互助執行業務的關係。

product line 產品線
同一家公司所銷售的一系列相似產品或服務，但彼此有不同的商品特色或價格區間。

promotional 促銷的
有助促進業績成長或發展的，尤其指透過廣告、宣傳或折扣促進商品銷售。

testimonial 表揚、感謝
用以說明或表達從產品或服務中所得到的好處；如在廣告或促銷信中所引用的顧客好評。

sales 銷售量
產品對外銷售出去的數量。「sales」另可用來指稱公司內的業務部門，如「sales manager」即為業務部經理。

snob appeal 崇尚虛榮
指某件商品（如奢侈品等）因為會使購買者滿足其虛榮心態，因而具備的吸引力。

<table>
<tr><td>Unit
48</td><td>什麼是商務關係？
What are business relations?</td></tr>
</table>

1 什麼是商務關係？

商務關係（business relations）就是公司之間的關係，而建立（establish）商務關係的意思就是與另一間公司展開夥伴關係（partnership）或買賣關係。

2 如何寫信與其他公司建立商務關係

要跟另外一間公司建立起商務關係時，通常會寄信（有時候也寄傳真或電子郵件）給對方，在信中跟對方介紹（introduce）你的公司，說明你們的產品或服務對他們有何益處。寫這種信時有幾個原則要遵守：

❶ **了解你的讀者**：如果你想要吸引新顧客，很重要的就是要知道他們的需求。你越知道他們有什麼需求，就越容易成功，因為如此一來，你就可以特別指出對他們來說最有吸引力的產品或服務。

❷ **了解你的公司**：你的讀者會想從信中了解你的公司的具體資訊，像是：
  ◆ 你們的銷售量（sales）
  ◆ 你們的市場占有率（market share）
  ◆ 你們最暢銷或最特別的產品
  ◆ 新產品或比較特別的產品
  ◆ 產品的特色、功能等

❸ **說明「為什麼現在寫信？」**：你會在這個時間點寄信給對方，而不是半年前或一年後，一定是有原因的。如果你是透過雙方共同的供應商或顧客得知對方的訊息，要把相關資訊告訴對方。如果你是在商務雜誌或研討會上聽到對方的公司，也說明這一點，藉此跟對方拉近距離，這有助於順利達到建立關係的目的。

CHANGI ENTERTAINMENT DEVICES

72 Nathan Road, Tsim Sha Tsui, Kowloon
Hong Kong
Tel: 852-36821820 Fax: 852-36821820

December 24, 2023

Gregory McMannis
Bleeps and Beeps
17 Talavera Road
Macquarie Park
NSW 2113

Dear Mr. McMannis:

We were given your information by our mutual colleague, Cheryl Hwang, of HK Computer Accessories. I would like to take this opportunity to introduce Changi Entertainment Devices in the hope that we can work together in the future. ❶

Changi Entertainment Devices was established in 1987 and has grown to be the primary supplier of personal stereo and gaming equipment for Hong Kong, Korea, and Taiwan. Our TUYO Bluetooth speaker is currently the most popular speaker in Hong Kong and Taiwan. We maintain two factories and rigorously monitor the quality of our products. Last year, we were given an AAA business credit rating by the East Asian Trade Board, its highest category of reliability. ❷

We are currently looking to expand our foreign market, and we believe that we are a good match for Bleeps and Beeps. I have enclosed information about our product line and company history for your reference. ❸

Thank you for your attention. I hope to hear from you soon.

Best regards,

Julian Zhang

Julian Zhang, Vice President of Marketing
Changi Entertainment Devices

Enc. (2)

麥曼尼斯先生您好：

我從我們共同的同事，HK Computer Accessories 的雪莉・黃那得知貴公司。我想利用這個機會跟您介紹 Changi Entertainment Devices，以期將來我們可以互相合作。

Changi Entertainment Devices 成立於 1987 年，至今已成長為香港、韓國、台灣主要的個人立體音響與電玩設備供應商。本公司的 TUYO 藍牙喇叭目前是香港和台灣市場上最暢銷的機型。我們有兩間工廠，並嚴格監控產品的品質。去年本公司獲東亞貿易協會給予 AAA 級商務信用評分，這是該協會的最高等級的信賴度評分。

目前我們正努力擴展國際市場，相信本公司會是 Bleeps and Beeps 理想的合作夥伴。隨信附上我們的產品線與公司歷史資訊，供您參考。

謝謝您抽空閱讀本信，希望能盡快收到您的回音。

❶ 寫信人在第一段先提到兩間公司共同的同事雪莉・黃，在雙方之間建立起關聯性，然後點明本信的目的：與對方建立商務關係。

❷ 第二段是 Changi Entertainment Devices「推銷自己」的賣點，也就是就公司提供正面的資訊，以吸引對方跟自己合作。

❸ 最後一段又說明 Changi 寫信給對方的另一個原因：Changi 想擴展國際市場，並附上公司詳細資訊供對方考量。

Exotic Textiles, Inc.

16, Talkatora Road, New Delhi 110001
Ph: 24787040 Fax: 24787042

25 January 2023

Annette Adahl
City Styles
3111 M Street, N.W.
Washington, DC 20007-3705

Dear Ms. Adahl:

I noticed City Styles' advertisement on www.trendwatch.com, where my other
clients, Cool Clothes, Inc., and Sally's, advertise, and I believe Exotic Textiles
would be a good business match for you. Please allow me to introduce myself
and my business.   ❶

Exotic Textiles was founded in 1996 and has been supplying quality clothing
to shops in India and around the world ever since. We pride ourselves on the
quality and uniqueness of our products, which include all-season women's and   ❷
men's clothing as well as several lines of sandals. Our sandals and some of our
clothing are handmade in New Delhi by families who have been making clothes
for generations.

Also, unlike some export companies, we believe in fair wages. We have been
given top marks by the Working Conditions Oversight Board of India for the past
five years, and we received a rating of 5, the highest standard, by the World Fair
Textile Trade Association. We believe that our customers care about the workers
they indirectly employ, and we have always found that buyers will support ethical
companies.

In addition to our ethics, we have a commitment to the highest standards of
quality and a fair price for our goods. I believe you will find that our products
are a perfect match for a trendy, urban audience and a good value for your   ❸
investment. I have enclosed information on all of our product lines for your
reference.

Yours faithfully,

Malika Karmarkar

Malika Karmarkar, Sales Manager
Exotic Textiles, New Delhi

Enc. (1)

阿達爾女士您好：

我在 www.trendwatch.com 上看到貴公司 City Styles 的廣告，我們的客戶 Cool Clothes Inc. 和 Sally's 也在這個網站上登有廣告。我相信 Exotic Textiles 將會是貴公司理想的商務夥伴，請容我在此跟您介紹我本人與本公司。

Exotic Textiles 成立於 1996 年，自此為印度及世界各地服飾店提供高品質的服裝，我們尤其以產品的品質與獨特風格感到自豪，其中包括全季男女服飾及多款涼鞋。我們的涼鞋及部分服飾乃由新德里世代傳承的製衣家庭手工製成。

此外，與某些出口商不同的是，我們堅持提供合理工資。本公司過去五年連續榮獲印度工作條件監督委員會之最高等評分，並得到世界公平紡織貿易協會之最高評分 5 分。我們相信顧客關心這些他們間接僱用的工人，我們也一再發現顧客願意支持具有道德良心的公司。

除了道德良心，我們也致力於提供品質優良、價格公道的產品。相信您會發現我們的產品完美契合時尚、都會消費者的品味，值得您惠予投資。隨信已附上我們所有的產品線資訊，供您參考。

本信件和前一封信結構雷同，在第一段先說明得知對方企業的契機，表明建立商務關係的目的。

後續段落說明自家公司有何過人之處，吸引對方願意和己方合作。

最後提出新的理由，強調雙方合作將貢獻的效益，最後附上自家公司或產品的詳細資訊。

其他推銷信
Other sales letters

1 什麼是推銷信？

「推銷信」是用來**推銷**公司、新服務、新產品線（product line）或**宣傳促銷**活動的信。推銷信比一般的廣告更加客製化，因為推銷信是寄給特定的個人，而非放在公開的地方供大眾瀏覽。推銷信的目的是**讓對方對你的公司和產品產生興趣**，比一般的促銷信（promotional letter）更進一步，因為信中還會嘗試促使讀者採取具體的行動，比如瀏覽你們的網站，或是訂購特定的產品。

2 如何寫推銷信？

在動手寫推銷信前，先自問下列這些問題：

◆ 這封信的**目的**是什麼？（What is the purpose of the letter?）
◆ **讀信者**是哪些人？（To whom am I writing?）
◆ **為什麼**對方會**想要我的產品**，或**使用本公司服務**？
（Why might people want my product or use my business?）
◆ 使用本公司服務**有什麼好處**？
（What are the benefits of using my business?）
◆ 我可以在信中附上**哪些輔助資料**？
（What supporting material can I include in my letter?）

❶ 這封信的目的是什麼？

推銷信不外具備下列三種不同的基本目的：**引起對方對產品的興趣、直接銷售產品、吸引讀者造訪商店或商品展場**。

推銷信的目的	推銷信要提供的資訊
引起對方對產品的興趣	提供**足以使對方產生好奇的資訊**，但是不要提供過多資訊，以免對方當下就斷定不需要你的產品。信中**不需要**詳細說明訂貨程序或如何下訂單，只要留下聯絡資訊，讓顧客能夠跟業務代表聯絡即可。
透過信件直接銷售產品	此時銷售信等於是完整的銷售活動，因此**需要**就產品提供詳細完整的資訊，以及向對方說明**怎麼下訂單**。
吸引讀者造訪商店、網站、商品展場等	寫出**所有吸引人的產品資訊**，用詞要有說服力，不過**不需要**提供訂貨或業務員聯絡資訊。

❷ 讀信者是那些人？

　　基本上，推銷信就跟其他的商務書信一樣，如果**一開始就考慮到讀者可能會提出的問題**，效果會最大。最有效率的推銷信是針對個人或特定機構量身打造，並緊扣住對方的需求，但是在忙碌的現代，不太可能有時間這樣撰寫推銷信，因此在撰寫推銷信的時候，內容必須要能夠吸引多數讀者的興趣，不能只是針對特定少數顧客而寫。按照下列幾個原則，你就能夠寫出可以同時吸引更多讀者的推銷信：

❶ 從讀者的角度看這封信：想想你要寫給**哪幾類不同的讀者**，然後列出**他們可能會提出的問題**。

❷ 檢視這些問題，想想哪些**最重要**、**最普遍（universal）**，並回答這些問題。

❸ 把最不重要的問題刪去，因為太多資訊會使讀者厭煩。

❹ 確定你也考慮到**讀者**對此產品**會有興趣**知道的地方，而非只顧慮到產品本身的特色。

❺ 仔細規劃信件內容。你可以在信中包含很多資訊，但要把內容組織成**簡短清晰的段落**，並有明確醒目的**標題**。

❻ 記得在**稱呼中**和**信封上**都寫出**對方的名字**（即使同樣的內容會寄給上千個不同的人）。

❼ 最後，說明你希望讀者**採取的行動（call to action）**，內容要具體明確。

❸ 為什麼對方會想要我的產品，或使用本公司服務？

❹ 使用本公司服務有什麼好處？

　　以上兩個問題的概念相似：寫信時要從各個不同的角度檢視你的產品或公司，研究你的產品或服務，然後仔細想想有什麼特點能夠吸引顧客。寫信時可設想：

❶ 顧客會從你的產品或公司得到什麼**好處**？

❷ 你的產品或服務有什麼**吸引人的地方**？

❸ 有什麼特點能夠促使讀者**採取行動**？

❹ 如何在信中**特別標出**這些資訊？

❺ 我可以在信中附上哪些輔助資料？

　　附上相關資料可以增加推銷信的可信度（credibility），因為讀者可以驗證你提供的資訊，可提供的資料比如：

❶ 呈現事實的**報告**或**摘要**，比你的口說無憑更有力。

❷ 附有圖片的資料，像是**宣傳冊**和**目錄**，有助於讀者更進一步了解你的產品或服務。因為無論你怎麼描述，人們還是希望能夠看到產品實際的樣子。

❸ 如果你隨信附上了相關資料，**務必在信中說明**，可使用以下句型：

> In the enclosed brochure you will find . . .
> 隨信附上的宣傳冊中可以找到……

3 記得 AIDA 的原則

我們在 Unit 10（Part 1）討論過寫作的基本原則，包括增進說服力的 **AIDA 的原則**：Attention（注意力）、Interest（興趣）、Desire（欲望）和 Action（行動），這個原則很適合用來創造有效的推銷書信，因此撰寫推銷信時可以盡量把握這個原則。你可以按照下列的順序在推銷信中應用 AIDA 的原則：

AIDA 要素	段落安排	說明
Attention 注意力	第一段	一開頭就要讓讀者注意到你的產品，常見技巧包括： ◆ 透過**技術細節**讓對方注意到產品。 ◆ **主旨一行**點出信的內容。 ◆ 用**問句**或其他容易**引起注意力的句子**，抓住讀者的注意力。
Interest 興趣	第二、 第三段	說明為什麼讀者需要你的產品或服務，例如信中可以： ◆ 說明該產品能夠**解決什麼問題**，然後就產品或服務本身進行描述。 ◆ 想想你的讀者**可能會有哪些不同的購買動機**，從這些動機著手：也許你的讀者想省錢，或需要具有最新功能的產品。 ◆ 從人們的**虛榮心理（snob appeal）**下手：強調有哪些名人用過你的產品或服務，或者是你的產品或服務有什麼特殊的威望或地位。
Desire 欲望	第四、 第五段	可以用多種不同的方式激起讀者的欲望： ◆ **引用其他顧客的好評**，顯示你的產品或服務有多成功。 ◆ 給予顧客**退貨的權利**，這樣顧客就不怕白花錢。 ◆ 不妨寄一份免費試用品。
Action 行動	最後一段	一定要**清楚寫明**讀者可如何**採取行動**：是應該上你的網站？打開你的產品目錄？還是撥打特定電話號碼？ ◆ 隨信**附上訂購表格或回覆表格**，方便讀者立刻行動。 ◆ 如果有**特別的條件或優惠**，也要特別強調出來。

以上架構只是原則，不是規則，不是每封推銷信都要包含六個段落。也許你在第一段就可以同時抓住讀者的注意力和引起讀者的興趣，又也許你想多花幾行說明你的產品或優惠活動，以激起讀者的欲望。最重要的原則就是從讀者的角度考量，想想什麼做法對他們最有效。

總結來說，促銷信是寄給**潛在客戶（potential customer）**的信件，其功能是促進銷量和激起對方對商品的興趣。下面就來看幾封推銷信。

GATHERERS
3001 Sinclair Street, Winnipeg, MB R2V 3K2 Canada
Tel: 204-339-8737 Fax: 204-586-0487

May 2, 2023

這封信大致上是按照 AIDA 的原則寫成。第一句宣布新店開張，藉此抓住讀者的注意力，儘管它並沒有採用我們在 AIDA 一節中提到的技巧。第二段和第三段描述店內提供的商品，以引起讀者的興趣。產品列表和訂貨服務用來激起讀者的欲望。最後一句則客氣地敦促讀者採取行動。

382 Hartford Avenue
Winnipeg, MB R2V-3K2

Dear Mr. Lee:

I am pleased to inform you that *GATHERERS* is now open for business at 3001 Sinclair Street, Winnipeg, MB.

We pride ourselves on our complete and diverse line of camping and mountaineering equipment. We specialize in products designed for the North American climate, but we are also able to supply you with quality gear from desert boots to ventilated summer tents, which will serve you across the globe.

Because we do not represent individual manufacturers, we are impartial in our assessments of products. Our sales staff is trained and eager to help you find just what you need for your next excursion. Enclosed for your review is a partial list of our current stock. We invite feedback from customers—if there is something you would like us to carry, please inform us, and we will do our best to order it.

We hope that you will visit *GATHERERS* soon!

Warm regards,

Holly Gillan

Holly Gillan
Manager, GATHERERS

Enclosure (1)

李先生您好：

我非常高興能夠通知您，「GATHERERS」已於曼尼托巴省溫尼伯市 Sinclair 街 3001 號開張了！

我們自豪擁有齊全的露營與登山設備，除了專精於提供為北美氣候所設計的產品，另外從品質保證的沙漠用靴到夏用通風帳棚等設備也一應俱全，供您暢遊世界各地。

我們並不代理特定廠商，因此我們能夠公正客觀地評估產品。我們的銷售人員都訓練有素，也樂於協助您為下一次的遠行找到最合適的設備。隨信附上我們目前部分的產品列表。我們期待得到顧客的回饋，如果您希望我們提供任何特定的產品，請告知我們，我們將盡全力購買。

希望不久就能看到您來店造訪！

ARTHUR CONSULTING

Metro South, 135 Auburn Ave. NE
Atlanta, GA 30303
404-521-2739

June 17, 2023

Joseph Jeannet
Freelancers United
384 Macombe Street
Savannah, GA 31406

Dear Mr. Jeannet:

Re: Introducing Arthur Consulting

We met at the Small Business Task Force meeting at the Atlanta Marriott
in May. I am writing now to introduce you to my business. Arthur Consulting
has been in operation for six years, providing specialized communications
training to the public and private sectors.

At the Small Business Task Force meeting, we chatted briefly about the
challenges small businesses face. Now, I ask you to consider the
organizations that you interact with. How many of them communicate
clearly with you? How many of their documents leave you frustrated,
with more questions than answers? Do you find yourself wishing they
would just get to the point? I think we all do. That is my mission at Arthur
Consulting—to provide the training that will help frustrated writers connect
with frustrated readers. Clear information is everyone's right.

My academic study of organizational communication breakdowns was
what originally piqued my interest in this field nearly 12 years ago. I began
building my experience and expertise at Transparency, Ltd., and later in my
own work at Arthur Consulting. So far, we have received three annual
Excellence in Training Awards and have recently been awarded a multiyear
contract to help reorganize the document center at the Georgia State
Assembly. My website, www.arthurconsult.com, provides more details
about my approach to training and my educational and employment
background. My résumé is available at www.arthurconsult.com/resume.htm.

❶ 這封信同樣採用 AIDA 的原則。第一句
先提到作者與讀者的關係,抓住讀者的注意
力。第二段再次提到他們見面的經過,然後
提出各種問題,並說明 Arthur Consulting
能夠協助解決這些問題,藉此引起興趣。

❷ 第三段敘述作者長期的經歷與公司獲得的獎項,使作者
和公司顯得具有一定的威望,以激起讀者的欲望。

❸ 在第四段，寫信人提供免費
諮詢，再次激起收件人的欲望。

For my friends and yours, I am pleased to offer a no charge consultation to discuss their concerns and needs. If there is a desire to move on after our meeting, I can prepare an initial needs analysis to begin isolating their problems. We can discuss the possibilities and consulting fees later, after a conversation about their needs and our solutions.

❸

Thank you for your time. Please feel free to contact me with any questions at 404-521-2739. Please also spare a moment to look at my website, www.arthurconsult.com, to learn more about what I have done for others and what I can do for you.

❹

❹ 最後一段提供了聯絡資訊，
並客氣地呼籲讀者採取行動。

Sincerely,

Simon Arthur

Simon Arthur
President, Arthur Consulting

珍內特先生您好：

主旨：介紹 Arthur Consulting

我們五月分在亞特蘭大 Marriott 飯店舉辦的「小型企業專案小組」研討會上見過面，現在寫信給您是想跟您介紹我們的業務。Arthur Consulting 已經成立 6 年，為公部門和私營企業提供專門的溝通技巧訓練。

我們在「小型企業專案小組」研討會上，簡短聊過小型企業所面對的挑戰。現在，我想請您想一想跟您往過來的機構。有多少機構能夠跟您清楚溝通？有多少文件讓您看了一頭霧水，問題反而比答案還多？您是不是常常希望對方能夠切中要點？我想我們都有這種經驗。而這就是我在 Arthur Consulting 的理念：提供溝通方面的訓練，讓原本雞同鴨講的寫信人能跟收信人順利溝通。得到清楚的資訊，是每個人的權利。

約 12 年前，我從事了組織溝通瓶頸的學術研究，激起了我對這個領域的興趣。其後我在 Transparency, Ltd. 累積工作經驗與專業技能，之後成立 Arthur Consulting 精益求精。至今我們已榮獲三個年度最佳訓練獎項，最近更與喬治亞州議會簽署長期合約，協助重新組織其檔案中心。我的網站 www.arthurconsult.com 就我的訓練方式、教育背景與工作經歷提供了更詳細的資訊，我的簡歷也可以在 www.arthurconsult.com/resume.htm 找到。

對於我們的朋友，我很樂意提供一次免費諮詢，討論他們在溝通上的擔憂與需求。如果諮詢之後還有繼續進一步的意願，我可以安排初步的需求分析，開始細分各個問題。我們可以在談過他們的需求與本公司的解決方案之後，再討論可行方式和諮詢費用等。

謝謝您抽空閱讀本信。如果有任何問題，歡迎來電與我聯絡：404-521-2739。請您也不妨抽空參觀我的網站：www.arthurconsult.com，看看我們為其他客戶的服務經歷，以及我們能如何為您效勞。

Karma Furniture

984 NE Blaine Avenue, Salem, OR 97302
(503) 639-2227

November 10, 2023

Mr. Hugh Frizzell
543 SE Blossom Lane
Grants Pass, OR 97526

I want to help you profit from your used office furniture.
I have real buyers who are looking for high-quality used office furniture.

Dear Mr. Frizzell:

I would like to present you with an opportunity you've probably never thought of: profiting from your office furniture. Have you been thinking of investing in new office furniture? Would you like the funds to do so? If so, we should talk. You've probably never considered selling your used office furniture—but don't let that stop you. This is a real opportunity.

Karma Furniture has made its name by providing top-quality, pre-owned office furniture. We have established a base of customers who are always on the lookout for high-quality, lightly used desks, conference tables, bookshelves, and other common office pieces. We are currently among the few people with access to this market. If you want to sell your old furniture or are looking for a way to fund new furniture, now is the perfect time to act.

Few people know about the untapped market for pre-owned office furniture. Since I started advertising used office furniture, walk-through of our showroom has increased 20%. Credenzas are now our top-selling item. Customers have also created waiting lists for:

- ■ **Wooden desks.**
- ■ **Corporate bookshelves and display shelves.**
- ■ **Large-scale art.**
- ■ **Conference and drafting tables.**
- ■ **Almost any kind of office furnishing you can imagine.**

If you own any of these furniture pieces, please call me today to set up an appraisal appointment. This appraisal is purely intended to provide you with information about the value of your furniture. It puts you under no obligation. However, once you see the prices you can get for your used furniture, I believe you'll find that now is the right time to part with it.

Here's what some of Karma's customers have to say:
"*I had no idea my office furniture was so valuable! With the money we earned from selling it, we were able to upgrade our entire office network.*"
Hannah Brown, Brown's Accountants

"*Karma Furniture buys and sells only top-quality furniture. I was so happy with the prices they got for my office furniture, I bought my new living room set there.*" Julian Shulman, KP Productions

Let me and my team help you sell your used office furniture or buy new furnishings. To access this market for pre-owned furniture, please call today at (503)-639-2227 for a free, no-obligation appraisal. Then take a peek at our virtual showroom at www.kmfurniture.com. I know you will be very impressed with what you see.

Yours very truly,

David Bennet

David Bennett, President
Karma Furniture

我想協助您從您的舊辦公家具賺回一筆
我知道有人想買品質優良的二手辦公家具

費傑先生您好：

在這裡要告訴您一個您可能從來都沒想過的好商機：從您的辦公家具賺回一筆。您是否在考慮購買新的辦公家具？您希望有採購所需的資金嗎？如果是的話，我們應該談一談。也許您從來沒想過要把您的舊辦公家具賣掉，但是不要為此卻步，因為機會就在眼前。

Karma 家具以供應品質優良的二手辦公家具知名。我們已經有一批固定的客源，這些顧客隨時都在尋找使用不久、上等品質的二手辦公桌、會議桌、書櫃等常用辦公家具。目前只有少數業者掌握這個市場的門路，我們便是其中之一。如果您想把舊辦公家具賣掉，或是想籌措資金購買新辦公家具，現在就是最恰當的時機。

鮮少人知道這個未開發的二手辦公家具市場。自從我開始為我們的二手辦公家具展開廣告宣傳以來，我們商品展場的參觀率增加了 20%。櫥櫃是我們目前最暢銷的品項，此外顧客們的願望清單也包含以下家具項目：

- 木製辦公桌
- 公司用書櫃和展示櫃
- 大型藝術品
- 會議桌和製圖桌
- 各式各樣您能想到的辦公家具。

如果您有這類的辦公家具，請今天就來電約定估價時間。估價的目的僅是讓您知道您的辦公家具擁有多少價值，您絕無出售的義務。不過，一旦您看到二手家具估價的結果，我相信您一定會覺得告別這些家具的時候到了。

以下為部分 Karma 的顧客好評：
「我從來不知道我的辦公家具這麼值錢！賣掉辦公家具的錢，足以讓我們升級整間辦公室的網路。」（漢娜‧布朗，布朗會計事務所）

「Karma 家具只買賣品質優良的家具。我很滿意他們為我的辦公家具提供的價格，所以我在它們那裡買了整套的客廳家具。」（朱蘭‧休曼，KP 製造）

讓我和我的團隊為您的舊辦公家具除舊布新。想一探這個二手家具市場，今天就來電(503)-639-2227，預約免費估價的時間。也可上 www.kmfurniture.com 看看我們的線上虛擬商品展場，您一定會印象深刻。

Air Freight Inc.
No. 98 Xuan Thuy Road, Cau Giay District, Hanoi, Vietnam
Phone: +84 4 3 3849574   Fax: +84 4 3 9485475

February 8, 2023

Phuong Lo
Jolie Boutique
65 Hang Bac Street
Hanoi, Vietnam

Dear Ms. Lo:

We appreciate your use of Air Freight Inc. for your past shipments.

We thought you might be interested in our new, expedited international service, International Express. With International Express, most of our international deliveries can now be made overnight! Costs for this service vary by destination; however, as always, we believe you will find our costs to be highly competitive.

We have also broadened our delivery area to include most countries of the world.

We look forward to serving you again. We hope you will take the next opportunity to try International Express and explore the new possibilities for international shipping.

Best wishes,

Dac Kien Phan

Dac Kien Phan, Manager
Air Freight Inc.

羅女士您好：

感謝您先前選擇 Air Freight Inc. 寄送貨物。

也許您會對我們新的國際快捷服務 International Express 有興趣？若採用這項服務，大多數的國際包裹隔天便可送達目的地！International Express 的費用依目的地而不同，但是相信您會發現我們的費用一如往昔經濟實惠。

此外，我們也擴展了遞送區域，現在世界上大多數國家都在我們的遞送範圍內。

期盼能再次為您服務。希望您願意利用下一次的機會試試 International Express，體驗我們新的國際遞送方式。

Jupiter Systems

6 Temasek Boulevard, #8-00 Suntec Tower Four, Singapore 038986
Tel: +65 65299123   Fax: +65 67399124

July 10, 2023

Yvonne Chin
Blue Water Financial
International Plaza
10 Anson Road #10-03
Singapore 079903

Dear Ms. Chin:

Will your server help you win clients this year? It can. Will your office software make your employees more efficient? It should. Will your network help you make sales? It could.

How is your office hurting you?

I am often called in—too late—to organizations whose computer systems have failed them. I fight to help organizations whose technology is costing them time, money, and clients. Isn't it time to make our systems work for us in the way they are intended? We have to stop this constant struggle against obsolescence, damage, misinformation, and misuse.

Did you know that 40% of offices are underutilizing their current systems? And another 60% could double the impact of their current systems with an inexpensive upgrade? I bet those 40% and 60% don't know either, so I've made it my mission to inform them. ❶

What can the Neptune Office do for you?

It can grow with you!
The new Neptune Office Package is designed to fit your needs and grow as those needs change. Far from being a complicated system that needs constant tech support, Neptune Office is user-friendly and easy to modify by referencing a simple user pamphlet. ❷

It can speak to you!
It has a unique, cutting-edge function that detects when storage limits are being reached and alerts a central administrator, who can then access more storage before an employee's unit slows down and begins to cost him or her time, as well as his or her good attitude.

Page 1 of 2

296

秦女士您好：

您的伺服器能夠幫助您在今年贏得更多客戶嗎？本該可以。您的辦公軟體能夠使您的員工工作更有效率嗎？理應如此。您的網路能夠幫助您提高銷售量嗎？按理要能。

您的辦公室如何危害您？

經常有公司組織請我去修理故障的電腦系統，但是通常都為時已晚。我努力協助這些機構，修理這些浪費時間、浪費金錢、還趕走客戶的電腦科技。我們的電腦系統不就應該為我們工作嗎？我們必須一勞永逸地解決科技過時、故障、資訊和使用方式錯誤的問題。

您知道有 40% 的辦公室沒有充分利用現有的電腦系統嗎？您還知道另外的 60% 只需花少許的經費，就可以更新現有設備，使現有功能加倍嗎？我打賭在這 40% 和這 60% 的辦公室員工自己也不知道，所以我立志要喚醒大家。

Neptune Office 可以為您做什麼？

可以跟您一起成長！

最新的 Neptune Office 套裝方案設計宗旨為符合你的需求，並隨著需求的變化一起成長。這套系統並不複雜，不需要隨時仰賴技術支援，只需參考一本簡單的使用手冊，使用者就可以自己進行調整更新。

會跟您溝通！

Neptune Office 套裝方案具有獨特的先進功能，也就是在儲存量快接近極限時，會通知中央管理員，而中央管理員就能在員工電腦速度減慢、開始浪費員工時間、考驗員工脾氣之前，設定更大的儲存量。

頁 1/2

❶ 這封信按照 AIDA 的原則寫成。一開頭幾句以具挑釁性質的問題抓住讀者的注意力，下面一段則請讀者思考一下自己的狀況。信中的粗體標題用來維持讀者的注意力，並讓讀者知道相關的細節就在標題之後。

❷ 中間幾段描述 Neptune Office 的功能，用來激起讀者對該套產品的興趣。這裡還悄悄利用虛榮的心理，把產品描述為「unique」、「cutting-edge」，還說「Your employees are specialists in their field.」。

It can save you time!

Your employees are specialists in their field. They shouldn't need to be computer experts as well. Neptune Office communicates with a central administrator. He or she is the one who is alerted to problems before they happen, allowing your employees to spend their time using their strengths, not yelling at screens.

②

It can connect your entire office!

Neptune Office can be configured to include most new model fax machines, scanners, and printers. This way, it eliminates surprises not only from computers but also from most of your office equipment. Neptune can store and access locking passwords and remotely power on or off. You can manage your whole office with one keyboard!

It can improve morale!

Listen to the voices of current users of Neptune Office:

"*Neptune Office is the best business purchase I have made so far. My first attempt at an office server was a disaster—I didn't know how to manage it, and data kept getting lost. I was afraid of losing employees because I was looking so incompetent. Neptune Office makes me look like a genius!*"

③

"*My office manager begged me to install Neptune Office, but I resisted. I worked from home, and I had no problems. Then I spent a day at our headquarters, watching hardworking colleagues struggle just to keep their units functioning. I ordered Neptune Office the next day, and now my employees are regularly beating deadlines, not missing them.*"

How can I learn more about Neptune Office?

The business world is tough enough without grappling with technology as well as the competition! I hope this letter has shown you how Neptune Office can give you an edge.

Contact our sales team!

To learn more about how Neptune Office can help you, please visit our website at www.jupitersystems.com/newproducts/neptune.htm. Salespeople are waiting to answer all of your questions at 65 65299123.

Take advantage of this offer!

④

For some valued clients, including you, we are pleased to offer a special discount on the Neptune Office package.

Keep this letter and tell your salesperson you would like to use discount code **NEP0708** to purchase your own office package.

Thank you for your time and attention. I truly hope that you will try Neptune Office today and give your business a better chance to thrive.

Yours truly,

Richard Lee

Richard Lee, Marketing Director
Jupiter Systems

❺ 最後的附筆使整封信顯得更親切。提供退貨服務，讀者購買產品的欲望會更強烈：如果知道可以退貨，讀者就更樂意試用產品了。

PS: Don't worry about commitment—you don't have to!
We're sure you'll want to stick with Neptune Office once you've tried it, but if you
don't, never fear. We will be happy to refund your money if you are unsatisfied
with Neptune Office and return it within two weeks.

Enclosure: brochure

❸ 這部分引用顧客的好評，可以激起對方購買產品的欲望，例如：「Neptune Office makes me look like a genius!」

❹ 寫信人希望讀者採取什麼行動，在這裡寫得很清楚：跟銷售小組聯絡，把握優惠折扣。寫信人把優惠碼以粗體形式表現，使其更醒目。

頁 2/2

能夠節省您的時間！
你手下的員工在他們各自的領域都是專家，但是他們不需要是電腦專家。Neptune 系統會與一名中央管理員溝通，此中央管理員負責在問題出現之前解決問題，如此你的員工就能夠把時間花在他們擅長的工作上，不用對著電腦螢幕大吼大叫。

能夠連結整間辦公室！
Neptune Office 可連結大部分新型的傳真機、掃描機、印表機等，如此一來可以減少電腦以及多數辦公室設備的意外狀況。Neptune 可以儲存和存取密碼，並且遠端進行開關機。只需要一組鍵盤，你就可以管理整間辦公室！

可以提升工作士氣！
聽聽目前的 Neptune Office 使用者怎麼説：

「Neptune Office 是我至今做過最好的投資。我買的第一款辦公室伺服器是個慘痛的經驗：我不知道怎麼管理，結果資料一直流失，當時我真怕員工看到我這麼無能，都要走人了。現在 Neptune Office 讓我看起來像個天才！」

「我辦公室的經理求我安裝 Neptune Office，但是一開始我沒答應。我自己在家上班，所以沒有類似的問題。但是有一天我在我們公司總部，看到認真工作的同事們掙扎著讓電腦正常運作，隔天我就訂了 Neptune Office。現在我的員工大多都能如期完成任務，沒有來不及的現象了。」

如何得到 Neptune Office 更多的資訊？
就算不需要跟科技掙扎，不需要跟競爭對手對抗，商務世界就已經夠累人了！希望這封信已經讓您了解，Neptune Office 能夠為您帶來更多優勢。

跟我們的業務小組聯絡！

欲詳細了解 Neptune Office 能夠如何幫助您，請瀏覽我們的網站：

www.jupitersystems.com/newproducts/neptune.htm。

我們的業務人員也樂意回答您所有的問題，請洽：65 65299123。

把握優惠折扣！

對於我們特別重視的顧客，包括您，我們很樂意就 Neptune Office 套裝方案提供特別的優惠折扣。

請保存好這封信，並告訴我們的業務人員，您想用折扣碼 **NEP0708**，以優惠價格購買 Neptune Office 套裝方案。

謝謝您抽空閱讀本信。希望您今天就開始嘗試 Neptune Office，讓您的企業更有優勢。

……

PS 不需要擔心後悔的問題，您可以退貨！

我們相信，一旦您試用過 Neptune Office，就會想持續使用；如果不是，也不用害怕。如果您對 Neptune Office 不滿意，只要在兩週內退回，我們將全額退回款項。

附件：產品手冊

Unit 50 跟催信
Follow-up letters to customers

跟催信（follow-up letter）可表示你對顧客的重視。逢下列情況時，可寄跟催信給新的顧客：

- ◆ 造訪過你的商店後
- ◆ 對促銷活動進行回應後
- ◆ 第一次訂購商品後

對於老顧客，也可以在有下列狀況時寄跟催信給他們：

- ◆ 訂購大量商品或進行特別的訂購後
- ◆ 一段時間沒有光顧後

跟催信可展現公司提供良好的顧客服務，如以下兩封信就感謝顧客前來參觀商品展場，以示對顧客的重視。

50-1 | A follow-up letter (1) 跟催信 (1)

推銷信 → P. 292

Karma Furniture
984 NE Blaine Avenue, Salem, OR 97302
(503) 639-2227

November 25, 2023

Mr. Hugh Frizzell
543 SE Blossom Lane
Grants Pass, OR 97526

Dear Mr. Frizzell:

Thank you for visiting us in our showroom in downtown Salem. I hope you were impressed by our high-quality furniture! I also hope you have had a chance to look over our price list regarding your used office furniture. If you believe you have furniture that meets our needs, I would love the chance to meet with you again. As always, please feel free to contact me at (503) 639-2227.

Thank you once again for your visit.

Yours truly,

David Bennet

David Bennet, President
Karma Furniture

費傑先生您好：

非常感謝您前來參觀我們在 Salem 市中心的商品展場，希望我們的家具品質讓您印象深刻！也希望您已看過我們的二手辦公家具買進價格表。如果您覺得有合適的家具可以賣給我們，我很樂意再次與您見面，請不吝照常與我聯絡：(503)-639-2227。

再次謝謝您的光臨。

BIG SMOKE
401 Park Avenue, New York, NY
212-891-0808

March 2, 2023

Isabella Rothkopf
42 W. 33rd Street
New York, NY 10001

Dear Ms. Rothkopf:

Thank you for visiting our cigar shop and signing our guest register. We hope you found something to your liking in our assortment of cigars and cigar accessories.

We pride ourselves on our constantly changing stock. We are always bringing in unique items, so we encourage you to come by and browse often to find merchandise that you cannot find anywhere else.

We hope you enjoy the enclosed catalog, and we look forward to seeing you again soon.

Yours sincerely,

Sylvia Willis

Sylvia Willis, General Manager
Big Smoke

Enc. (1)

羅斯寇夫女士您好：

非常感謝您光臨我們的雪茄店，並留下您的來訪資料。希望您在本店的各式雪茄和相關配件中，找到了中意的產品。

我們以店內不斷更新存貨為榮。我們不時買進獨特的商品，因此在此邀您常來造訪本店，以尋覓別處買不到的精品。

隨信附上產品目錄，盼您喜歡，也希望很快能夠再見到您。

Unit 51 推銷信常用說法
Common phrases in sales letters

1 Announcing sales and discounts 宣布優惠折扣活動

① We would like to announce our annual winter sale.
我們的年度冬季特賣活動即將展開。

② We are pleased to offer you our new customer discount . . .
我們樂於提供您新客折扣優惠……

③ It's time again for our annual winter sale.
我們的年度冬季特賣又要開始了。

④ It's time again for our spring sales event.
我們的春季特賣會又要開始了。

⑤ It's time again for our prized customer coupon distribution.
我們對重要顧客的優惠券大放送活動又要開始了。

⑥ We would like to make you a limited-time offer . . .
在此提供您限時折扣優惠……

⑦ This offer is available for only 10 days . . . 此優惠只限 10 天有效……

⑧ A rare opportunity has come up, and we would like to tell you about it . . . 機會難得，想通知您敬請把握……

⑨ Please use the enclosed coupon code the next time you order from us . . . 下一次跟我們訂購商品時，別忘了使用隨信附上的優惠碼……

2 Introducing yourself or your business 介紹你或你的公司

① Please allow me to tell you more about our services . . .
在此容我跟您進一步介紹我們的服務……

② Please allow me to tell you more about product X . . .
在此容我跟您進一步介紹產品 X……

❸ Please allow me to tell you more about what we can do for you . . .
在此容我跟您進一步介紹我們能夠為您效勞之處……

❹ I would like to take this opportunity to give you more information about . . . 在此藉機想為您詳細說明……

❺ I'd like to tell you more about my business . . .
在此想跟您詳細介紹本公司……

❻ _____ [business name] is famous in its field because . . .
〔公司名〕在同業中以……知名

❼ If you haven't heard of _____ [business name], you're probably missing out on a great opportunity . . .
如果您還沒有聽過〔公司名〕，恐怕要錯過一個大好機會

❽ If you haven't heard of _____ [business name], you're probably missing out on the lowest prices for product X . . .
如果您還沒有聽過〔公司名〕，恐怕要錯過產品 X 的最低價

❾ At _____ [business name], we believe . . . [explain philosophy, mission, etc.].〔公司名〕堅信……〔說明其理念、使命等〕。

❸ Explaining your purpose 說明你的目的

❶ We would like to discuss working together in the future.
想與您討論未來合作的機會。

❷ We would like to discuss possibilities for a future work relationship.
想與您討論未來業務關係的可能性。

❸ I believe we can create a mutually beneficial partnership.
相信我們能夠建立互惠合作關係。

❹ Our companies could work together and increase profits for both of us by . . . 本公司與貴公司可以透過……的方式合作，提高雙方的利潤。

❺ It seems that a business relationship would profit us both.
建立商務合作關係應對我們雙方都有利。

4 Following up 跟催

❶ It was so nice to see you in our shop on_____ [date] . . .

很高興在〔日期〕在本店見到您……

❷ We appreciated your visit on_____ [date] . . .

感謝您〔日期〕的光臨……

❸ We hope you are happy with your order of _____ [name of product].
Please let us know how we can serve you again!

希望您對訂購的〔產品名〕感到滿意，有任何我們能夠再次為您服務的
地方，請不吝告知！

❹ We haven't heard from you in a while, and we wanted to let you know
about . . . [great new products, a promotion, etc.]

我們有一段時間未獲您的關照了，在此想告訴您……〔優良新貨、促銷活動等〕

5 Grabbing attention 抓住讀者的注意力

❶ Did you know that most telephone systems fail 15% of the time?

您知道大部分電話系統有 15% 的時間是在故障狀態嗎？

❷ Why is it that business owners are always complaining about how
hard it is to find qualified staff?

為什麼公司老闆總在抱怨很難找到可以勝任的員工？

❸ _____ [name of product] comes with a unique . . . [feature]

〔產品名〕具有獨一無二的……〔特色描述〕。

❹ The new _____ [name of product] is [faster] than ever thanks to the
cutting-edge. . . [feature]

基於其先進的……〔特色描述〕，此新〔產品名〕速度比以前都要快
〔或可以套用其他形容詞〕……

6 Stimulating interest 引起讀者的興趣

❶ With the _____ [name of product], you can . . .

有了〔產品名〕，您就可以……〔行動描述〕

② If you have this problem, you need . . . [name of product]

如果你有此問題，就表示您需要〔產品名〕……

---

③ The _____ [name of product] will change your life by . . .

〔產品名〕將會透過……改變您的生活。

---

7 Creating desire 激起讀者的欲望

① The _____ [name of product] has been used with great success for more than _____ [length of time] . . .

〔產品名〕過去〔一段時間〕來不斷受到顧客好評……

---

② Hear what other satisfied customers have to say about [name of product]: . . . 聽聽其他顧客對〔產品名〕的滿意好評：……

---

③ We think you'll love _____ [name of product]—but we understand that you might not. That's why we offer a complete refund if you aren't happy with the _____ [name of product].

我們相信您一定會愛上〔產品名〕，但是我們也了解許您未必滿意，因此如果你對〔產品名〕不滿意，我們將全額退回款項。

---

④ The 10-year warranty is our guarantee that _____ [name of product] will always work for you . . .

十年保固的服務保證〔產品名〕一定會為您順利運行……

---

8 Calls to action 敦促讀者採取行動

① Why wait? Call our offices now! 還等什麼？現在就打電話來！

---

② Why wait? Visit our website now! 還等什麼？現在就上我們的網站！

---

③ Why wait? Visit our showroom now!

還等什麼？現在就來參觀我們的展場！

---

④ Hurry, before this offer expires. Contact one of our salespeople to use your limited-time [coupon/discount] . . .

機會難得，欲購從速。立刻與我們的業務員聯絡，把握這次的限時〔折扣券／優惠〕……

1 Review the concepts

❶ What is the main purpose of a promotional letter? _____

(A) To create interest in a business.

(B) To announce a merger.

(C) To distribute a coupon.

❷ What does it mean to establish business relations with another company?

❸ Which information is not usually included in letters establishing business relations? _____

(A) Information about the letter writer's market share.

(B) Information about the letter writer's management team.

(C) Information about the letter writer's products.

❹ Which is not a valid reason for using headers in a sales letter? _____

(A) They help readers skim and find information.

(B) They help make your letter longer.

(C) They help break up long passages of text.

❺ What are other ways to say "We would like to tell you . . ."? _____

(A) We want you to know that . . .

(B) We are happy to inform you that . . .

(C) We told you . . .

❻ What is one thing you can do in a sales letter to create interest in your product?

❼ What is the call to action in a sales letter? Where should it be placed?

❽ Under what circumstances should you send a follow-up letter?

2 True (T) or False (F)

❶ ☐ True ☐ False   A testimonial is a statement from a satisfied customer.

❷ ☐ True ☐ False   Statements from satisfied customers can stimulate desire.

3 Write a letter to establish business relations.

Imagine that you work for Air Freight Inc. You would like to establish business relations with Jolie Boutique. Use the following information in your letter:

❶ You saw the company's name and address on a Vietnam Exporters website.

❷ You think you can give the company a competitive price for its shipments.

❸ You have been in business for more than eight years.

❹ You have a reputation for reliability and speed.

❺ You have never lost a package.

❻ You have unique business relationships with other shippers that allow you to combine shipments to get lower rates.

Air Freight Inc.

No. 98 Xuan Thuy Road, Cau Giay District, Hanoi, Vietnam
Phone: +84 4 3 3849574   Fax: +84 4 3 9485475

February 19, 2023

Phuong Lo
Jolie Boutique
65 Hang Bac Street
Hanoi, Vietnam

Dear Ms. Lo:

_____

_____

_____

_____

_____

_____

_____

_____

_____

_____

_____

_____

_____

_____

_____

_____

4 Send a promotional letter. (I)

You work for Professional PR. Send a promotional letter to Wallace Attorneys. Use the following information, but feel free to add your own ideas.

> ❶ You represent several of the largest companies in Singapore, including Jupiter Systems, Alliance Office Solutions, and the Bank of Singapore.
>
> ❷ You can act as a strategic business partner to establish and promote the right image for companies.
>
> ❸ You can provide proactive media relations, strategic counsel, branding and positioning, crisis communications, website launches, and special events planning.
>
> ❹ You are part of the Public Relations Global Network, which means you can handle international as well as national projects—with more than 35 affiliate offices worldwide.
>
> ❺ Your customer service is superior. You promise results.

PROFESSIONAL PR
12 Eunos Road 6
Singapore 408600
Tel: 65 68 394058   Fax: 65 68 8574965

March 15, 2023

Wallace Attorneys
6 Temasek Boulevard
Singapore 038986

Dear _____ :

_____

_____

_____

_____

_____

_____

_____

_____

5 Send a promotional letter. (II)

You work for Big Smoke. Send a letter advertising your new stock of handmade Dominican cigars called Dominica Vivas. The purpose of your letter is to get customers to come into your shop for a free sample of these new cigars. Use the following information:

> Some rate these cigars as the best in the world. Their taste is described as "chocolaty" and "fresh." They are wrapped in a special traditional leaf and are made using an ancient cigar-rolling tradition. No other shop in America is able to stock these cigars, and quantities are limited. One customer said, "This cigar is like none I've ever smoked. I never thought I would have a chance to try a Dominica Viva. I am so thrilled to be able to experience this so close to my home." And also, "Big Smoke has the correct quiet ambience for savoring such a special cigar. I almost wish I could keep it a secret."

BIG SMOKE
401 Park Avenue, New York, NY
212-891-0808

March 2, 2023

Isabella Rothkopf
42 W. 33rd Street
New York, NY 10001

**"Big Smoke has the correct quiet ambience for savoring such a special cigar.
I almost wish I could keep it a secret."**

Dear _____ :

_____

_____

_____

_____

_____

_____

_____

_____

_____

_____

_____

_____

_____

6 You work for GATHERERS.

You have just shipped a special order of ice picks and glacier boots for a new customer. Send a follow-up letter to check that the order was satisfactory and to thank the customer for his business.

GATHERERS
3001 Sinclair Street, Winnipeg, MB R2V 3K2 Canada
Tel: 204-339-8737 Fax: 204-586-0487

May 12, 2023

Joshua Dillon
382 Hartford Avenue
Winnipeg, MB R2V-3K2

Dear Mr. Dillon:

_____

_____

_____

_____

_____

_____

_____

_____

_____

_____

_____

投標與出價
Tenders and Bids

Key Terms

award (of bid) 決標

評估各家投標者提出的標案之後,將決定將相關合約給予特定得標者。通常招標者會在招標書(request for proposal)中寫出評估和決標方式。

bid 出價、投標

出價;提議的價錢。例句:「We lost the contract because our bid was too high.」(我們出價太高,所以沒有得標。)

code of conduct(公司的)行為準則

公司或組織的一套內部規範,寫明其成員或特定職位者從事業務或活動時,應遵照的行為規則。

criteria 衡量標準(單數形為 criterion)

指用以衡量事物優劣的一套標準。通常在招標時,招標者會寫明對於投標書的衡量標準,以利投標者準備。

demographics 人口統計資訊

針對人類群體所做的人口相關統計資料,如性別、年齡、財務水準等,特指在商業行銷上可用的資料,來引導廣告或產品推銷策略。

initiative 新措施;新計畫

為了達成特定目的或解決問題,所提出的一系列新的做法或方案。當組織或公司推出一套新措施時,可能會對外招標,尋找能夠幫助實踐計畫的承包商。

leeway 餘地

可供斡旋協議的空間。在撰寫招標書時,一般建議在實際操作方法上,為承包商留下一點可彈性調整的餘地,或許更有利未來順利達成任務。

public sector 公部門

指公共所有的機關、單位等,通常意指政府機關和其他公營單位。相對於「公部門」的組織則為「私部門」(private sector),指非屬政府管轄範圍的私人企業、公司組織等。

penalty 處罰(如罰款等懲罰措施)

對於不當行為給予的懲罰。在招標書中,招標者可以寫明若得標者未來無法達成合約內容、或成效不佳時,將會給予何種處罰措施,例如拒絕付款、中止合約等。

performance 績效;表現

用在商務情境時,常用以指稱員工或承包人員辦理業務的成果。招標者撰寫招標書時,可在內容載明希望得標者達成的績效標準,並提醒對方若表現不善可能需承擔的後果。

supply contract 供給合約

指買賣雙方簽訂的長期貨物或服務買賣合約,通常會規定在合約期間內有固定的購買價格,合約內常也會先約定付款方式、貨物送達方式、如何處理相關爭議等必要條款。

tender 投標書

表示願以特定價格提供商品或服務的正式文件。

Unit

52

投標與出價相關書信
Correspondence regarding tenders and bids

1 「tender」與「bid」是什麼意思？

本章將介紹何謂**「投標」**（tender）與**「出價」**（bid）、投標過程如何進行、如何撰寫「招標書」，以及幾種典型的相關書信。「投標」和「出價」都是指就產品或服務提議一個價格，尤其常是跟公家機關（public sector）出價。投標和出價是為了爭取長期的供應合約（supply contact）或其他大型工作項目，而非針對個別的產品出價。

「tender」當名詞時也可指**「投標書」**，是表示願以特定價格提供商品或服務的正式文件。投標亦可用**「bid」**來表示：在商務用語中，bid 即代表**出價的提案**，表示投標者（bidder）願以特定的價格，在特定的時間內完成特定工作。投標書備妥後會交給招標單位，與其他投標者的出價競爭。tender 和 bid 有時也可稱為「proposal」。

2 投標過程如何進行？

通常當合約的價格超過特定數目時，以及當此企畫需要高度專業的產品或服務時，發出此合約的機構（通常是政府機關）常會以協商的方式徵詢供應商。這表示他們會邀請各家供應商提出計畫書，即「投標」，然後從中選出價格與技術程序最佳者與之簽約，這種邀請對方投標的文件就稱為**「招標書」**，其英文名稱有以下幾種：

- ◆ Requests for Proposal (RFPs)
- ◆ Request for Tender (RFTs)
- ◆ Request for Quotation (RFQs)

3 投標過程中會撰寫哪些文件？

在投標過程中，招、投標雙方可能會撰寫下列幾種不同的書信：

❶ 招標書（**Requests for Tender**）：用來公開邀請所有的供應商，就特定需求遞交正式的計畫書（也稱 RFP 或 RFQ）。

❷ 招標信（**Invitation to Tender**）：用來寄給特定一間公司，邀請其就完成特定企畫遞交計畫書。

❸ 意向書（**Letters of Intent**）：由投標公司呈交的聲明，告知對方其有意就特定企畫遞交投標書，並請對方通知任何企畫上的改變。

❹ 投標書（**Tender Letters or Proposals**）：投標的供應商用以說明其計劃如何完成該特定企畫的文件。

❺ 得標通知書（**Letters of Award**）：招標單位用以正式通知某一公司其被選中完成該特定企畫的文書。

本單元把重點放在如何撰寫招標書（RFP），並提供其他種投標書信的範例。

4 撰寫招標書

　　撰寫招標書時，應**將焦點放在你們想看到的結果**，不要把焦點放在方法上。畢竟，你是在請別人來完成這個工作，所以細節的部分不妨交給他們的專家處理。**清楚說明你想看到的結果**，但是留些餘地（leeway）讓對方建議完成的方式。清楚的招標書應該包含下列資訊，你可以把它們分節，或是組織成大段落：

❶ 說明目的（Statement of purpose）：描述你的公司在尋找**什麼樣的產品或服務**，以及此企畫的**整體目標**為何。

❷ 背景資訊（Background information）：**簡短介紹**你們的公司、業務、優點和弱點。附上相關的文件，例如統計資料、顧客組成（demographics）等。

❸ 工作範圍（Scope of work）：列出你們**希望對方完成的具體任務**，以及你們想看到的成果，並清楚說明誰該負責哪些部分。

❹ 成果與表現標準（Outcome and performance standards）：說明你們希望達到的成果，及**能夠接受的最低表現標準**。清楚說明你們會如何監督表現，及必要時會如何進行改正。

❺ 分期成果（Deliverables）：Deliverables 意指對方在企畫進行期間的**不同階段，須交給你們的文件、產品或服務**。這可能是計畫、報告、產品或完成的服務，需就此提供一完整列表。

❻ 合約期限（Term of contract）：清楚說明企畫的**開始與結束日期**，也列出在哪些狀況下，合約可能可以更改或延期。

❼ 付款與扣款（Payments and penalties）：說明你們會**如何付款**，以及對方表現未達標準時**如何扣款**。

❽ 簽約條件（Contract terms and conditions）：附上所有與得標公司簽約所需的表格、證明、擔保。

❾ 投標說明（Requirements for the proposal）：說明**投標書的架構**，並列出所有**你們需要的文件**。提供投標書的架構格式可以使你們自己的評估過程更簡單，也便於對方撰寫投標書。

❿ 評估與決定過程（Evaluation and award process）：說明你們會**如何進行評估**，及**如何宣布你們的決定**。

⓫ 投標過程時間表（Process schedule）：列出整個**投標過程**（一直到最後決定誰得標）**的時間表**，包括遞交相關文件的期限。

⓬ 聯絡人員（Points of contact for future correspondence）：列出相關的**聯絡人員**，包括其姓名、職稱、職務和**聯絡方式**。

Request for Proposal
New York State Department of Taxation
Page 1 of 3

Section I – General Information

(A) Background

The New York State Department of Taxation collects tax revenues and provides associated services in support of government services in New York State. As a result of our Strategic Plan for the next five years, we are committed to improving our customer service across the board.

In 2022, New York State instituted a Plain Language Initiative (PLI), calling for a review of all state documents, testing of all documents, rewriting and redesigning forms and documents, and implementing staff training to support new writing guidelines and customer service practices. In order to comply with the PLI, we are reviewing and redesigning all of our state tax forms and related documents.

(B) Statement of Purpose

The objective of the PLI is to ensure that all documents issued by the state are usable by our constituents and compliant with plain language principles. As part of ensuring this objective, it is key that staff involved in creating documents learn to apply these principles consistently. We hope to achieve a holistic solution in which experts undertake the review and testing of existing documents, provide sample redesigns, and then train our staff members to be able to undertake subsequent redesigns on their own. To this end, we expect that we will require contractor assistance with the following processes:

1. A review of existing documents.
2. A review of the document process, including writing and editing, designing, and production.
3. Testing of documents to ensure usability, including all reports and documentation resulting from the process.
4. Customized training for staff on plain language writing and design.
5. Customized training for frontline staff on using the new documents.

Our ultimate goal is the conversion of our entire writing process and our documents to comply with both the spirit and the letter of the PLI.

Section 2 – Project Details

(C) Scope of Work

Contractors will be expected to provide:

1. A complete review of all documents intended for public use, with analysis of each document.
2. A complete review of the writing and reviewing process for public documents, with analysis of document "blockages" and recommendations for streamlining.
3. Testing of all publicly used documents with representative populations.
4. Testing of reports and recommendations for changes.
5. Customized training for non-managers on writing in plain language.
6. Customized training for managers on writing in plain language and reviewing constructively.
7. Training for frontline staff on plain language principles and using the new documents.

(D) Outcomes and Performance Standards

Desired outcomes are:

1. Complete testing and analysis of all public forms.
2. Reports and recommendations for the redesign of all public forms.
3. Complete redesigns of two model forms.
4. Analysis, report, and recommendations for the writing process at the New York Department of Taxation.
5. Design and implementation of a customized curriculum to teach plain language writing skills to staff.
6. Design and implementation of a customized curriculum to teach plain language writing and constructive review skills to managers.
7. Design and implementation of a customized curriculum to ensure frontline staff members are familiar with plain language principles and all redesigned forms.
8. Design and implementation of a customized curriculum to train management how to train other staff on plain language principles, basic plain language writing principles, and the use of redesigned forms.

Performance will be judged on usability and relevance of reports on tested documents, documentation of increased usability of redesigned forms, course evaluations completed by staff in training, and testing done on staff-redesigned documents.

(E) Deliverables

1. Work plan for each segment of the project, i.e., "testing," "designing," "training."
2. Proposed testing plan for documents.
3. Report of results of testing, including recommendations.
4. Two redesigned documents.
5. Report on writing processes at the New York Department of Taxation.
6. Training plan and materials for three separate training modules.

Section 3 – Contract Information

(F) Terms of Contract

This contract shall be awarded no later than March 15, 2023. Work on the contract will begin no later than March 30 and continue according to the first contract terms until September 30, 2023. The contract may be renewed by both parties. Proposals with time lines longer than one year will be considered. Failure to complete the entire work plan within one year will not be considered inadequate performance if both parties have agreed to a longer time line.

(G) Payments and Penalties

The time line and deadlines for each of the deliverables will be decided on by the successful candidate and the New York State Department of Taxation on the basis of discussions with the candidate and proposal provided. Payment of invoices will be aligned with the milestones and will be written into the contract.

Inadequate performance will be discussed in a meeting with the project principles, then written into a document distributed to the Better Business Bureau of New York State. Deliverables that are judged unsatisfactory will not be paid for. Two consecutive unsatisfactory deliverables will result in the cancellation of the contract.

(H) Proposal Requirements

Proposals should be no longer than 15 pages and should include the following information:

1. An overview of the candidate's proposed work plan for the development of the project.
2. A cost breakdown with comparison options that will outline what level of development would be included at each level.
3. A proposed time line.
4. A recounting of relevant experience, including contacts for three references.
5. Any other details or information that the candidate feels is relevant.

(I) Evaluation and Awards Process

Proposals will be evaluated by the PLI compliance committee of the New York State Department of Taxation and key staff people on March 1.

Proposals will be evaluated based on the following criteria (in no particular order):

1. Cost efficiency and work value.
2. Clarity of work plan and time line.
3. Reference check.
4. Overall impression.

We thank you in advance for your consideration.

(J) Evaluation and Awards Schedule

RFP issued:	January 5
Proposals due:	February 25
Contract awarded:	March 15
Anticipated start date:	March 30
Contract conclusion:	September 30 (can be negotiated)

(K) Key Contacts

For questions about the New York State Plain Language Initiative, please contact

· Katrina Bailey, Special Assistant to the Governor, at 518-455-5199 or bailey.ks@ny.gov

For questions about this proposal, please contact

· Miriam Blessing, Compliance Director, at 518-333-9389 or blessing.md@ny.gov
· Christopher Marley, Professional Development Manager, at 518-333-9384 or marley.cp@ny.gov

招標書
紐約州稅務局
頁 1/3

第一節：一般資訊

(A) 背景

紐約州稅務局的業務為徵稅，並提供相關服務項目，以協助辦理紐約州政府的服務。基於往後五年的策略計畫，我們致力於全面改善顧客服務。

紐約州政府於 2022 年發起「簡化公務語言計畫」（Plain Language Initiative，簡稱 PLI），要求檢討和評測所有的政府機關文件、重新撰寫與設計各種表格與文件，並進行員工訓練以配合新的書寫原則與服務方式。基於此一計畫，我們目前正在檢討並重新設計州內所有的稅務表格與相關文件。

(B) 目的

PLI 的目的，是讓所有的州政府文件都更便於選民使用，使文件語言符合「簡單明瞭」的原則。其中關鍵的一環，便是要讓寫作這些文件的人員學會隨時都遵照這些原則。我們希望聘請專家檢討並評量現行的文件、提供新的設計樣本，並在之後訓練我們的職員獨立進行後續的改善，使目前的狀況達到全面的解決。欲達到這個目的，我們需要承包商協助進行下列的過程：

1. 檢討現行公務文件。
2. 檢討文件製作過程，包括撰寫、編輯、設計和產出。
3. 檢測文件之使用便利性，包括所有在流程中產生的報告與文件。
4. 提供專屬訓練，讓職員在撰寫與設計上採用簡單明瞭的語言。
5. 為第一線服務人員提供專屬訓練，教導使用新的文件。

我們的最終目標，是改變整個公文撰寫過程與文件設計，名符其實地達到 PLI 的目的。

第二節：企畫細節

(C) 工作範圍

承包者須：

1. 全面檢討所有供公眾使用之公務文件，並進行個別分析。
2. 全面檢討公務文件之撰寫與審閱過程，分析文件的不妥之處，建議簡化方式。
3. 透過具代表性之受試民眾，測試所有供公眾使用之公務文件。
4. 測試結果與改善建議。
5. 訓練非主管級職員以簡單明瞭的語言撰寫公文。
6. 訓練主管級職員以簡單明瞭的語言撰寫公文、並進行建設性的審閱。
7. 訓練第一線服務人員熟悉簡單明瞭的語言原則，以及使用新的文件。

(D) 成果與表現標準

期望的成果：

1. 全面測試與分析所有的公務表格。
2. 針對如何重新設計所有的公務表格，提供報告和建議。
3. 重新設計兩份樣本表格。
4. 紐約州稅務局公文撰寫過程之分析、報告與建議。
5. 設計並實施量身訂做的訓練課程，訓練職員以簡單明瞭的語言撰寫公文。
6. 設計並實施量身訂做的訓練課程，訓練主管級職員以簡單明瞭的語言撰寫公文，並進行建設性的審閱。
7. 設計並實施量身訂做的訓練課程，訓練第一線服務人員熟悉簡單語言的原則和所有重新設計的表格。
8. 設計並實施量身訂做的訓練課程，教導管理人員訓練其他職員熟悉此簡單語言的原則、採用簡單的語言撰寫公文，和使用重新設計的表格。

成果評估將依據：文件測試結果報告的實用性和適切性、重新設計之表格的方便性、職員對訓練課程進行的評估結果、職員自行重新設計之文件的測試結果。

(E) 分期成果

1. 每一階段的工作計畫，如「測試」、「重新設計」、「訓練」。
2. 文件測試計畫。
3. 測試結果報告，包括改善建議。
4. 兩份重新設計的文件。
5. 紐約州稅務局公文撰寫過程報告。
6. 三種訓練課程之計畫與教材。

第三節：合約資訊

(F) 合約期限

此合約將於 2023 年 3 月 15 日前簽訂。實際工作最晚須於 3 月 30 日開始進行，並根據合約條款進行至 2023 年 9 月 30 日。合約可經雙方同意後展期。工作時程表超過一年者也在考慮之列。如果雙方就延長工作期限達成協議，未在一年內完成所有工作者不會被視為表現欠佳。

(G) 付款與扣款

每份分期成果之繳交時程及期限，由得標者與紐約州稅務局依據共同討論結果與招標書內容決定。帳單之付款將配合各期進度，並納入合約內容。

成效欠佳狀況將依計畫準則開會討論，並行文交予紐約州商業改善局。品質未達標準的分期成果將不付款。連續兩次分期成果品質未達標準，合約將解除。

(H) 投標需知

投標書請勿超過 15 頁，並應包含下列內容：

1. 分期工作計畫表。
2. 費用細項說明，並附可供比較之選項，描述每個進程項目可達到的成效等級。
3. 估計工作時程。
4. 相關工作經歷，包含三位推薦人之聯絡資訊。
5. 其他相關細節或資訊。

(I) 評估與決標過程

紐約州稅務局 PLI 執行委員會與重要職員將於 3 月 1 日評估各投標書。

各投標書將依據下列標準進行評估（順序不拘）：

1. 成本效率與工作價值。
2. 工作計畫表與工作期限清晰度。
3. 推薦人調查結果。
4. 整體印象。

在此先謝謝您考慮投標。

(J) 評估與決標時間表

發招標書：	1 月 5 日
投標期限：	2 月 25 日
合約決標：	3 月 15 日
預計工作展開日期：	3 月 30 日
合約期限：	9 月 30 日（可協商）

(K) 聯絡資訊

對於紐約州「簡化公務語言計畫」若有任何問題，請聯絡：

· 州長特別助理卡崔納‧貝里：518-455-5199 或 bailey.ks@ny.gov

對此招標若有任何問題，請聯絡：

· 米麗安‧布萊辛（法令遵循主管）：518-333-9389 或 blessing.md@ny.gov
· 克里斯多福‧馬力（專業發展經理）：518-333-9384 或 marley.cp@ny.gov

Jupiter Systems

6 Temasek Boulevard, #8-00 Suntec Tower Four, Singapore 038986
Tel: +65 65299123   Fax: +65 67399124

September 11, 2023

Berkley Building Services
120 Cecil Street
Singapore 069543

Re: Request for Tender - Maintenance Project - RFT 15911

Dear Sirs:

You are invited to submit a tender for the maintenance works for our building at 6 Temasek Boulevard, #8-00 Suntec Tower Four, Singapore 038986.

The details of the work requirements are as shown in the enclosed Form of Tender. If your company is interested in bidding for these maintenance works, please submit the completed Form of Tender and Schedule of Rates in a sealed envelope to the Tender Box in the lobby of 6 Temasek Boulevard, #8-00 Suntec Tower Four, Singapore 038986, on or before October 30, 2023. Late submissions will not be accepted.

Your tender should also include a photocopy of your company code of conduct, Business Registration Certificate, certificate(s) of Registered General Maintenance Contractor/Registered Pipes Service Installation Contractor/Licensed Plumber. Please also submit the details of similar projects you have undertaken, including contact details of referees.

For instructions regarding site visits, please contact Juliette Zhang at 65299123, extension 12. For any queries, please contact Leo Arnold at 65299123, extension 5.

Yours sincerely,

George Wong

George Wong, Chairman, Building Works Committee
Jupiter Systems

Encl. Form of Tender and Schedule of Works

主旨：維護工程招標書 15911

貴公司諸君您好：

在此邀請貴公司就新加坡 038986 Temasek 大道 6 號 #8-00 Suntec 4 號塔維護工程進行投標。

工程需求的細節請見所附投標表格。如果貴公司有意投標此維護工程，請將投標表格填寫完整，連同價格表以密封信封於 2023 年 10 月 30 日前或當日，投至新加坡 038986 Temasek 大道 6 號 #8-00 Suntec 4 號塔大廳投標信箱。逾期之投標書將不予考慮。

投標書中請附上貴公司之工作行為準則副本、營利事業登記證副本、一般維護工程承包商登記證副本／管道裝置承包商登記證副本／水管承裝商登記證副本。此外也請附上貴公司曾完成之類似工程的細節，包括推薦人之聯絡資訊。

有關參觀工程現址的說明，請聯絡茱麗葉‧詹：65299123 分機 12。若有任何其他疑問，請聯絡里奧‧安諾：65299123 分機 5。

附件：投標表格和工程時間表

Berkley Building Services

120 Cecil Street, Singapore 069543

Tel: +65 65889124　　Fax: +65 65889123

September 21, 2023

George Wong
Jupiter Systems
6 Temasek Boulevard
#8-00 Suntec Tower Four
Singapore 038986

Re: RFT 15911, Maintenance Project

Dear Mr. Wong:

I would like to indicate our interest in the request for tender noted above and ask to be notified of any updates and amendments to the RFT.

Sincerely,

Lee Ho

Lee Ho, Executive Vice President
Berkley Building Services

主旨：維護工程招標書 15911

翁先生您好：

在此跟您表示本公司投標上述維護工程之意向，此招標活動若有任何更新或修改，請不吝通知本公司。

Jupiter Systems

6 Temasek Boulevard, #8-00 Suntec Tower Four, Singapore 038986
Tel: +65 65299123   Fax: +65 67399124

November 16, 2023

Lee Ho
Executive Vice President
Berkley Building Services
120 Cecil Street
Singapore 069543

Re: Maintenance Project RFT/Contract No. 15911

Letter of Award

Jupiter Systems accepts your tender dated October 15 for Building Works RFT Contract No. 15911.

The Fee shall be a combination of lump sum and hours worked multiplied by the hourly rates up to a maximum amount of $500,000.

The project manager must provide evidence of insurance for Worker's Compensation and Public Liability before undertaking the maintenance works of the Agreement.

Sincerely,

George Wong

George Wong
Chairman, Building Works Committee

主旨：維護工程招標書／合約 15911

得標通知書

Jupiter Systems 接受貴公司於 10 月 15 日就維護工程招標書 15911 進行之投標。

工程費用包含工程總額及工作時薪，最高可達 50 萬美元。

進行合約所述維護工程前，專案經理任須提交勞工賠償險和公共責任險證明。

Unit 53 投標與出價書信常用說法
Common phrases for letters about tenders and bids

1 Writing requests for tender: General information and project details 撰寫招標書：一般資訊和專案細節

❶ The objective of _____ [project name] is to ensure that . . .

〔專案名稱〕的目的在於確保……

❷ As part of ensuring this objective, it is key that . . .

為了協助確保此目標，……相當重要

❸ Our ultimate goal is . . .　　　　　　　　我們的最終目標是……

❹ Contractors will be expected to provide:　承包商應提供以下事項：

❺ Desired outcomes are:　　　　　　　　　我們希望的成果有：

❻ Performance will be judged on . . .　　　　成效判斷的標準為……

2 Writing request for tender: Contract information
招標書：合約資訊

❶ This contract shall be awarded no later than _____ [date].

合約將於〔日期〕以前決標。

❷ Proposals should be no longer than . . . pages and should include the following information:

投標文書勿超過……頁，並應包含以下資訊：

❸ Proposals will be evaluated by . . .　　　　投標案將由……進行評選。

❹ Proposals will be evaluated based on the following criteria:

投標案評選的標準如下：

❺ We thank you in advance for your consideration.

在此預先感謝您考慮（投標）。

3 Writing invitations to tender 撰寫招標信

1 You are invited to submit a tender for _____ [project name].

在此邀請您／貴公司針對〔專案名稱〕提出投標。

2 The details of the work requirements are as shown in the enclosed . . .

工作需求的細節說明如附件的……所示。

3 Your tender should also include . . .

您的投標文書也須包含……

4 Please also submit the details of similar projects you have undertaken, including . . .

請也繳交您所從事過類似專案的細節，包括……

4 Writing letters of intent/award 撰寫意向書／得標通知書

1 I would like to indicate our interest in the request for tender noted above.

我想就前述專案表達我方投標意願。

2 We accepts your tender dated _____ [date] for _____ [project name].

我們接受您於〔日期〕對於〔專案名稱〕的投標。

3 The Fee shall be a combination of . . . and . . .

費用將為……和……的合計。

DISCUSSION & EXERCISE 16 — Units 52–53

1 Review the concepts

❶ What is a letter of intent in the context of tenders and bids?

❷ What does RFP mean?

❸ Which document is not part of the tender process? _____
(A) Request for tender
(B) Invitation to award
(C) Letter of intent
(D) Letter of award

2 True (T) or False (F)

❶ ☐ True ☐ False A request for proposal is usually sent to one company.

❷ ☐ True ☐ False A letter of intent is sent to companies to invite them to bid on a contract.

Part 13 投標與出價 DISCUSSION & EXERCISE 16

Units 52–53

327

3 Send an invitation to tender

Imagine you are the Vice President of Operations at the University of Pinney. Write an invitation to tender to Waterfall Gardening inviting them to tender for landscaping work surrounding the university library. Your letter should also include the following information:

✓ A Form of Tender is enclosed.

✓ The Form of Tender includes Tender Conditions that specify what information must be supplied in the tender and how the tender should be submitted.

✓ Mr. David Fisher at (+61) 2 6120 3333, ext. 84 can answer any related questions.

The University of Pinney
NSW 1995, Australia
+61 2 6120 3333

17 August 2023

Waterfall Gardening
95 Cofton Close
Fernbrook, New South Wales

_____

_____

_____

_____

_____

_____

_____

_____

_____

_____

_____

_____

Sincerely yours,

Howard Peterson

Howard Peterson, VP of Operations
The University of Pinney

Enc. (1)

求職書信
Job Hunting Communications

autobiography 自傳

寫作者描述過去經驗的文件；求職用的自傳通常或著重過往學歷、專業經驗和工作成就等能力相關資訊。

benefits 員工福利

在職場上，benefits 指的是員工非直接以現金形式得到的福利。有些福利是法律規定要提供

給員工（每個國家不一樣），有些福利則是每間公司或每個行業都不同。常見的員工福利包括健康保險、不扣薪假期、股票選擇權、退休金等。

candidate 候選人、人選

在求職、徵才過程中，candidate 指的就是求職者（如「a candidate for the job」或「a job candidate」）。其他如「applicant」、

「job seeker」等字亦可用以指稱求職者。

catchy 好記的

指旋律或文字能打動人心，令人難以忘記的特質。寫給未來雇主的求職書信中，可以嘗試寫出好記的文句。

company's mission 公司使命

企業針對自身目標以及提供何種服務的定位表態，有時會包括對於企業和其主要業務的描述，求職者通常可在企業的官方網站上查詢到公司使命的資訊。

commensurate 相稱的

在程度上相同；大小、數量或程度上相當；成比例的。

graduate / undergraduate degree 研究所／大學學位

研究所學位包括碩士學位和博士學位；而低於（under-）研究所（graduate）學位的即是大學（學士）學位。

honorary 榮譽的、名譽的

作為榮譽授予，當事人並不需要完成一般須完成的活動；為肯定其成就或貢獻所授予，當事人不須具一般所需的前提或義務，如 an honorary degree（榮譽學位）。

internship 實習工作

在企業或其他組織中工作一段時間，以獲得經驗或相關知識；實習工作通常提供給在學學生或職場新鮮人。

position 職位

在本章節中，指的就是「工作職位」。

project-based（工作）專案性質的

相較於經常性的（regular）工作職位，專案性質的職缺代表任用時間僅限特定專案執行的期間。

qualification 資格

某一職位或工作所需的特質或技巧，或是指須達到的狀況或標準，如 a qualification for membership（會員資格）。

voluntary 義務的、無償的

在這裡指沒有薪水、義務幫忙的。

Unit	徵人廣告
54	**Want ads**

1 如何撰寫徵人廣告？

　　Want ads 就是**徵人廣告**。公司在徵人廣告中列出需要徵人的職位，目的是吸引符合資格的個人前來應徵。就跟撰寫其他書信時一樣，如果你想要引起讀者的注意，就必須**從讀者的角度去思考**：想想求職者一般會有哪些問題，然後想想你需要在廣告中包含多少資訊，以讓讀者清楚了解這是什麼樣的工作。

2 求職者對於我的徵人廣告會有哪些問題？

　　求職者在閱讀徵人廣告時，一般會在心裡提出下列問題：

❶ **什麼工作？** 徵人廣告至少要把**徵人的職稱**寫出來；如果有個簡短的描述更好。

❷ **工作性質？** 這份工作是**全職**（full-time）、**兼職**（part-time）、還是**短期**（temporary）**的工作**？工作上需要經常出差或搬家嗎？通常固定的全職工作就不用刻意提到這些，但是如果是兼職、短期、企畫專案性質（project-based）等比較特殊的工作，最好在廣告中寫清楚。

❸ **所需資格？** 同樣地，許多職位需要的資格通常大家都有些了解，所以也不需要刻意寫出來，但是如果需要的是具有**特定教育背景或經歷的人才**，最好在廣告中列出重要的工作資格。

❹ **什麼公司？** 在廣告中應寫出**公司的名稱與地址**。如果還有空間，可加上一些公司的資訊。

❺ **薪水？** 有些徵人廣告會寫出**薪水範圍**，有些則會寫「**competitive**」（有競爭性）或「**commensurate with experience**」（視資歷而定）。你也可以完全不提薪水，但是這樣有些求職者可能就不會來應徵。（若在國內招募職缺，依照台灣勞動法規，職位的經常性薪資未達新台幣 4 萬元時應公開揭示或告知薪水範圍。）

❻ **如何應徵？** 這是徵人廣告中最重要的資訊之一。清楚說明**要在哪裡、何時、如何應徵**。寫出應該聯絡誰或哪個部門，並給求職者一個寫電子郵件時可以用的主旨行，寫出你希望求職者連同簡歷一起寄來哪些資料。如果希望求職者以特定的格式寄來簡歷，也寫出來。

❼ **何時應徵？** 如果徵人有截止期限，也寫出來。

3 徵人廣告中應該包含多少資訊？

　　徵人廣告通常會登在報紙或網頁上，這時刊登廣告的價錢往往以**字數**或**版面大小**計價，因此徵人廣告中可以包含多少資訊，便取決於版面大小或預算的限制、工作性質屬於普遍或特殊，以及你需要列出哪些特定資訊。

　　如果是普遍、一般的工作，徵人廣告就可以短一點，但是比較特殊或搶手的工作就需要列出更多資訊，以確保只有真正合適的求職者來應徵。

4 如何安排徵人廣告的內容？

視廣告的長短，徵人廣告的內容有很多種安排方式。短一點的徵人廣告通常會用粗體標題寫出工作職稱，然後用一個段落列出重要的相關資訊；長一點的徵人廣告會以工作職稱作為總標題，然後以小標題分項列舉重要的資訊。所謂「重要的資訊」可能包括：

❶ 職務描述（job description）
❷ 所需資格（qualifications or requirements）
❸ 公司福利（benefits）
❹ 應徵方式（how to apply）

54-1 | A simple want ad 徵人廣告

Mechanical & Electrical Engineers

Award-winning MEP&FP ❶ firm looking for Mechanical & Electrical Engineers w/ at least 4 yrs of exp. ❷ Excellent benefits, salary, & bonuses. Contact: Universal Engineering Solutions, lindas@theues.com, or visit our website at www.theues.com.

❶ 徵人廣告經常採用專業術語，如在這個例子裡就用了「MEP&FP」。符合資格的機電工程師會知道 MEP&FP 是「mechanical, electrical, plumbing, and fire protection」（機械、電子、水管和火災防護）的縮寫，而不熟悉這些術語的人大概也沒有足夠的資格應徵該工作。

❷ 徵人廣告經常採用常見的縮寫以節省空間，如：

- w/ 是 with 的縮寫
- w/o 是 without 的縮寫
- Yrs 表示 years
- exp. 表示 experience

這個徵人廣告包含了幾點求職者會想得到的資訊：公司名稱、職位、所需經歷及基本的聯絡資訊。廣告中沒有進一步說明職務性質和確切的應徵方式，甚至連聯絡人的全名也沒有，有意應徵的人必須主動與該公司聯絡，以得到更多的資訊。

徵機電工程師

榮獲 MEP&FP ❶ 獎項的公司徵機電工程師，需四年以上工作經歷 ❷。福利佳，薪水及獎金優。請與 Universal Engineering Solutions 聯絡：lindas@theues.com 或上網站：www.theues.com。

SENIOR FINANCIAL CONSULTANT WANTED ❶
Granite Financial Services, Inc.

Job Description

To give the client a total investment & wealth protection strategy, a rational and reasonable analysis of the expectations, and the expectations of the return on the investment plan as well as the efficiency of the wealth protection plan.

Requirements

- University graduate
- With drive, initiative, and enthusiasm for financial planning
- Eager to become a sales professional through dedicated training
- Able to identify business opportunities and interact with clients
- Applicants with IFA backgrounds may be eligible for senior grade

> ❶ 徵人廣告通常都會以要招聘的職務為標題，就跟這篇範例一樣。不過有時候徵人廣告也會以描述工作性質，或理想人選的方式設計標題，如「Seeking energetic, motivated sellers」（徵有衝勁、積極的銷售人員）或「Join the fast-paced world of website development」（加入日新月異的網頁開發世界）。

We are offering ❷

- An attractive salary package and support to start your new role here
- Fast-track opportunities for team-building activities
- Extensive product range for all-around financial planning solutions
- In-house professional training on CFP, CWM, FAIQ
- Professional training / attractive remuneration package / medical scheme / study allowance / full CPD training and promising career prospects

> ❷ 「We are offering」這個小標題可以用來描述工作福利。其他的說法還有「benefits」（福利）、「our package」（我們的福利方案）或「you will receive」（你會得到）等。

Application Method

By email, jobnavigator@gfs.com.hk (Please quote reference number FU-27062023 in your subject line.)

All applications will be treated with strict confidence and used solely for recruitment purposes.

Additional Information

Experience:	1–5 years
Job Category:	Banking / Securities / Fund Management
Job Location:	Hong Kong
Key Skills:	Portfolio setting
Job Ref code:	FU-27062023

Role:	• Management Trainee	• Advisory
	• Equities / Capital Markets	• Investment Advisor

這篇徵人廣告比較詳細，廣告中對於職務內容、應徵資格和員工福利提供了充分資訊，此外也跟上一則廣告（54-1）一樣，包含了不少專業術語（CFP 國際理財規劃顧問認證、CPD 持續專業發展等），但是有資格應徵此職位的人應該都能看懂。

徵資深理財顧問 ❶

Granite 財務服務公司

職務描述：
給予客戶全面投資理財保障策略，合理分析客戶期望、投資計畫的報酬期望，以及財富保護計畫之效率。

資格：
- 大學畢業
- 有動力、衝勁、熱忱從事財務規劃相關工作
- 有志透過專門的訓練，成為專業的業務專員
- 能夠掌握商機，善於與客戶互動
- 具 IFA（即 Independent Financial Advisor 獨立財務顧問）背景者有機會獲得資深等級職位

我們提供：❷
- 優厚的薪酬，並協助你融入新工作
- 可隨即參與企業內訓之機會
- 完整的產品系列，全面的理財計畫解決方案
- 專業的內部 CFP、CWM、FAIQ 訓練
- 專業的訓練／優渥的薪酬方案／醫療保險／進修補貼／完整的 CPD 訓練和具發展性的事業前景

應徵方式：
請寄電子郵件至 jobnavigator@gfs.com.hk（請在主旨欄加上參考文號 FU-27062023）。所有的應徵資料都會嚴格保密，僅用於招聘用途。

補充資訊：

工作經歷：	1–5 年	
工作類別：	金融／證券／資金管理	
工作地點：	香港	
主要技巧：	投資組合配置	
工作參考文號：	FU-27062023	
職務：	• 管理實習	• 顧問
	• 股市／資本市場	• 投資顧問

Unit 55　求職信
Employment application letters

1 求職信的功能是什麼？

　　求職信是求職者寄給公司以應徵職位的信，通常會跟履歷一起寄出，因此求職信也常稱為「履歷封面信」（résumé/CV cover letter）。求職信的功能是用來跟求職的公司自我介紹，顯示你非常適合在該公司工作，並且是該職缺的最佳人選，信中包含的資訊應該要能達到以下將介紹的幾個目標：

❶ 文字簡短精要，格式清楚（clear and formatted）

　　求職信不是「履歷表自傳」，不宜長篇大論，要簡短精要，200–400 字尤佳。文字應明確好讀、能打動人，格式清楚，讓你的求職信從人海中脫穎而出（stand out），吸引人資的目光，而有機會打開履歷、自傳審閱。

　　求職信屬正式書信，信件的稱呼語務必正確，可用「**Dear Mr./Ms.＋ 姓氏**」稱呼對方；若不確定收件人姓名，則可**使用對方職稱**，如「Dear Hiring Manager:」。若需使用同一封信當模板寄給多家公司（並不建議此做法），則務必確認有**修改稱謂**。結尾敬辭則可使用「**Sincerely,**」等正式用語，並簽上全名。

❷ 寫出吸睛（eye-catching）的開場白或亮點句（hook），簡短介紹自己

　　求職信的開頭幾行字很重要，是足以讓你脫穎而出的關鍵文句。除了可以精簡提及寫信動機、想要應徵的職位、如何得知職缺相關資訊外，也要簡潔地自我介紹、**說明你個人特質**、**優勢及經驗**，展現個性，強調你**為何比他人出眾**（**outstanding**），展現出寫作與溝通表達的卓越能力。

❶ 簡短說明有意爭取的職位，❷ 並且快速地說明自己的優勢所在，以便吸引審閱者的目光。

> ❶ I am writing with great interest to apply for the sales representative position in your company. ❷ As a capable salesperson with many years of solid experience, I can't wait to help your sales soar, just like I did for the many companies I previously worked for.

❸ 自我介紹，強調個人優勢（strengths）

　　求職者要跟公司自我介紹時，通常會簡述自己的**教育背景**和**工作經歷**。但是如果你把履歷一起寄上，就不需要在信中詳細說明這些經歷了，而可以把焦點放在重要而出色的經歷，像是得獎紀錄、獨特的工作或實習經驗，或是其他的成就。

　　有時候個人資料也很重要，比如說如果欲應徵的工作需要經常出差，那麼你就可以在信中說明你喜歡出門旅行，或是你熟悉哪些以後出差可能要前往的地方。

✅ ❶ 展現過去的求學和工作經驗，如何和 ❷ 應徵中的工作相輔相成。

> ❶ My master's thesis is about the development of artificial intelligence (AI). When I was in college, I also interned at a renowned AI developer in Silicon Valley for six months. ❷ I am sure I am well prepared for your AI engineer position.

❌ ❷ 強調描寫的工作經驗，和 ❶ 應徵的職位需求並無直接相關，可能讓審閱者難以判斷是否適任。

> I am very interested in ❶ working at your café. I may not have much experience in making coffee and sandwiches, but ❷ I worked as a food delivery driver for more than two years after graduating from college. The job was challenging, and I think I have memorized the name of every road in the city.

❹ 表達出你非常適合在該公司工作

應徵前，應先對該公司和該職缺做些研究，找出該公司的經營理念和目標，然後想想如何讓目標公司覺得你跟公司具有同樣的理念與目標。如果你過去曾為類似的目標努力過，或是參與過與該公司所擅長的企畫類似的項目，那就特別強調出來。最重要的目標是**找出你跟該公司與其工作的共同之處**。

❶ 展現已經對該企業進行過研究了解，並且 ❷ 知道未來職位的工作內容、目標與方向。

> ❶ From my research, I understand that your company is trying to develop energy-saving products that help slow down global warming. I appreciate that mission very much. ❷ Environmental protection is where my passion lies too, so I am very interested in taking part in your efforts.

❺ 顯示你是該職缺的最佳人選

找出該職缺的資格要求與職務內容，並強調你符合這些要求，或者可以說明你過去**曾負責過哪些類似的職務**，或有何**相關成就**。如果該職位需要特定的工作態度或工作風格，就可**從你過去的經歷舉例說明**你具有這樣的態度或風格。如果你的工作經歷不多，可以想想你是否在其他的活動中顯示出類似的資格或態度。

❶ 描述先前相關工作經驗，❷ 且指出工作期間所達成的亮眼成就，讓審閱者了解你的專業能力可以如何具體貢獻未來的雇主。

> When I served as ❶ an English tutor for senior high school students during my college years, ❷ their average test scores usually improved by about 30 percent. Many of them eventually got accepted by some of the best universities in the country thanks to their excellent exam results. That makes me believe I will be a great fit for your teaching position.

<u>Jared Lanahan</u>
150 11th Street, NE
Washington, DC 20002

October 15, 2023

Zaftig Creative Communications
1321 Rhode Island Ave, NW
Washington, DC 20005

Attention: Human Resources Manager

Dear Sir or Madam:

> ❶ 這封求職信遵照典型模式寫成，信中前兩句話故意寫得很「搶眼」，以引起讀者的興趣

It appears as though you're looking for a really good writer with the qualities of an illustrious grammarian. Well, look no further; but please read on. ❶

> ❷ 進行自我介紹，簡述背景與能力

My name is Jared Lanahan, and I'm a Canadian living in Washington, DC, where I am currently finishing my master's degree in writing, editing, and publishing at the American University. I have an extensive writing background, and I am capable of many styles; also, I can cater to any sort of creative turn of mind, whatever the project.

In the four years prior to my studies, I wrote for, edited, and published a locally acclaimed literary magazine in Macao called *Bound* (<u>www.bound-literature.com</u>). It is the only publication of its kind ever produced in Macao, and it has found great success, eventually leading to a 5000-copy print run. I have since brought the journal to Washington, DC, and will be launching it here on November 26.

I write constantly and consistently, and I would love to offer you a sample of my creative wares to better illustrate my suitability to your company.

Please let me know if you require any more information besides the attached CV and a sample of my writing. I look forward to hearing from you.

Sincerely,

Jared Lanahan

Jared Lanahan

> ❸ 描述了與此應徵工作有關的經歷，並於下方的最後兩段再簡短提供額外的資訊。

Enc. (2)

經辦人：人力資源部經理

先生 / 女士您好：

貴公司在尋找具有深厚文法基礎的傑出作家。您不用再找了，但是請繼續讀下去。❶

我的名字是傑瑞・拉那罕，加拿大人，目前住在華盛頓特區，於美國大學攻讀寫作、編輯與出版學碩士，具有廣泛的寫作經驗，擅長於各種風格與文體，並能依企畫需求靈活發揮創意。

進入碩士班前四年，我在澳門撰寫、編輯、出版了一本在當地頗受好評的文學雜誌《Bound》（www.bound-literature.com）。這一類的雜誌在澳門只有這一本，一出版就熱賣，最後一刷就是 5,000 本。之後我把這本雜誌帶到了華盛頓特區，今年 11 月 26 日將在這裡出版第一期。

我持續在寫作，隨信附上一篇我的創意寫作，以證明我可成為貴公司的生力軍。

除了隨信附上的履歷和文章樣本，如果您還需要其他的資訊，請不吝與我聯絡。誠心期盼聽到您的回音。

❶ 這封求職信跟上一封稍有不同。寫信人在第一段首先說明應徵職缺的強烈意願，並表示有信心勝任該校的工作。

❷ 第二段寫信人說明相關的經歷與能力。

❸ 第三段描述對於該工作的觀點，這一段的目的是顯示寫信人非常適合從事該工作。

❹ 最後一段再次表達對該職位的興趣，並表示如果有需要，她願意提供更多的資訊。

SAMANTHA HUTSON

88 Shiang Bin 3 Street, Hsin Chu, Taiwan, 300 • samfhutson@yahoo.com
Home (03) 533 1144 • Cellular 0918 824 039

January 15, 2023

Daniel Barton
Saigon South International School
8 An Vuong St., District 4
Ho Chi Minh City
Vietnam

Dear Mr. Barton:

① It is with great interest that I am exploring employment opportunities at Saigon South International School. I am very interested in applying for a primary school position. I am confident that my experience and skill set will be assets to your students' learning and development.

② Since finishing my master's degree in linguistics, I have had the opportunity to work in the field of education in a wide variety of roles. This diversity has given me a well-rounded understanding of education, particularly in language arts and experimental science learning, although I have experience with all of the core subjects. I have devoted considerable time to developing supplemental resources for L2 learners in an immersion environment. In fact, I am interested in pursuing research in this area.

③ Although theory and knowledge are incredibly important aspects of teaching, I strongly believe that the soul of the classroom can be found in the relationship between teachers and students. I am a passionate person, and I strive to foster that same enthusiasm in my students. Moreover, I want to motivate students to think for themselves, and this can only happen if they learn the strategies and skills necessary for independence. In my classroom, these skills and strategies are discovered in a student-centered environment, where children explore and discover through cooperative learning.

④ I am eager to continue growing professionally. I will have completed my teaching certificate by July 2023. I would welcome the opportunity to discuss how my expertise meets the needs of your educational program. I invite you to contact me at your convenience. Thank you for your time and consideration.

Sincerely,

Samantha Hutson

Samantha Hutson

巴頓先生您好：

我非常有意在 Saigon South 國際學校尋求工作機會，我對在小學任職非常有興趣，相信我的經歷與能力，對於貴校學生的學習與發展將大有助益。

取得語言學碩士學位後，我有幸能在教育界參與各種不同的工作。這個廣泛的經歷使我對於教育具有全面的理解，尤其是在語文和透過實驗學習自然科學方面，不過我在所有主要的科目上都有經驗。我花了很多時間研發輔助教材，供第二語言的學生可在沉浸式環境中中學習外語，而我也有意繼續這方面的研究。

理論與知識是教學過程中非常重要的因素，但是我深信課堂的風氣源自於師生之間的關係。我是個熱情的人，而我致力於在學生心中燃起同樣的熱情。此外，我鼓勵學生獨立思考，而這需要學生先學會獨立思考所需的策略與技巧。在我的課堂上，我會打造以學生為中心的學習環境，讓學生透過合作學習去探索和發現知識，習得這些技巧和策略。

我有志在此領域精益求精，並預計於 2023 年 7 月取得教師證。希望能有機會與您討論如何把我的專業知識與能力，應用在貴校的教學課程上。請不吝於方便時與我聯絡，謝謝您的時間與考慮。

Unit 56 撰寫英式履歷
Writing CVs

1 什麼是 CV 和 résumé？

　　「résumé」（亦拼作 resume）和「CV」（curriculum vitae）是求職過程中最重要的文件。Résumé 和 CV 都屬於履歷文件，通常會連同封面信（也就是「求職信」）寄出，目的是讓你得到面試的機會。

　　CV（英式履歷）和 **résumé**（美式履歷／簡歷）非常相似，兩者也經常被當成同義詞使用。兩種文件都列出求職者最重要的資訊，並簡述求職者的教育背景與工作經歷。但是 CV 和 résumé 細分來說其實文件性質不同，主要區別包括含有的資訊量、呈現資訊的方式，以及欲達到的功能。

2 什麼是 CV？

　　CV（英式履歷）會完整列出你至今的成就，包括教育背景、專業經驗、志願服務、榮譽獲獎項等各項成果。**除了美國和加拿大，世界上大多數的國家都採用英式履歷。** 在**美式用法**中，CV 常用來指稱**申請高等學術（academic）**或**教學（teaching）職位，以及獎助學金（grant）**時所需的履歷文件，因此內容會更著重學術成就（如學歷、研究著作成果）和學術相關職位（如教師、期刊編輯等）經驗。

3 英式履歷中應該包含哪些資訊？

　　CV（英式履歷）比 résumé（美式履歷）**更長、更詳細**，同時會包含更多學術和非職場上的成就，像是出版過的論文、從事過的研究、得過的獎項、榮譽學位、義工經驗等。英式履歷通常含有下列資訊：

❶ **個人資訊**：年齡、國籍等完整的個人和聯絡資訊。

❷ **教育背景**：就讀過的學校、取得的成績、學術獎項和研究經歷等。教育經歷通常以**倒敘（reverse-chronological）**的方式列出來，也就是最後取得的學位先寫出來。把重點放在**最高的學位**，例如博士、碩士和學士學位。如果你沒有學士以上學位，才把小學或中學寫出來。

❸ **工作經歷**：英式履歷中要列出所有你在社會上從事過的工作，不管是否支薪。正是由於這個原因，英式履歷有可能會包含**義工或榮譽性質的工作經歷**。工作經歷也是以**倒敘**的方式列出，也就是將現在正從事或最後從事過的工作先寫出來。

❹ **會員資格**：英式履歷通常還會列出求職者所屬於的相關團體，像是學術協會或專業協會。

❺ **出版著作**：英式履歷中會列出**相關的**出版著作，如論文、文章、書籍等。

❻ **獎項**：學術、專業或其他性質的獎項。

❼ **特別的資格認證或培訓**

❽ **興趣**：如果跟應徵的工作**有關係**，英式履歷中可能還會列出求職者私下的興趣。

4 如何安排英式履歷的內容結構？

傳統的英式履歷會詳細列出求職者的資訊，但是現在也出現各種不同形式的英式履歷。

❶ **清單式 CV（inventory CV）**：會完整列出教育背景與工作經歷，但是不把重點放在任何一個時期。

❷ **功能式 CV（functional CV 或 skills CV）**：會把重點放在求職者具有的技能，而非整個工作經歷。這些技能可能來自各種不同的領域，也可以應用於各種不同的領域，因此通常是想要轉換事業跑道的人才會採用這樣的 CV。

❸ **目標式 CV（targeted CV）**：會把重點放在與該職缺有關的經歷與技能。

英式履歷在結構上通常遵守下列原則：

❶ **篇幅**：英式履歷的長度通常為**兩頁**左右，但是如果資訊很多，也有可能長達**三至五頁**，甚至更長。

❷ **項目排列**：傳統的英式履歷有時會按照時間順序呈現資訊，但是新式的 CV 並不常遵守這個模式，例如功能式 CV。

❸ **內容呈現**：英式履歷採用小標題（通常是職稱），下面再以簡短的段落進行說明。

❹ **封面信**：英式履歷通常伴有封面信，封面信上總結 CV 的重點，並強調求職者是該職缺的理想人選。

5 如何撰寫成功的履歷

除了上述各項基本要點，求職者也要打造出自身的品牌價值和特色，才能受到徵才主管的青睞（favor），在廣大勞動市場（labor market）中脫穎而出。求職者可將自己看成待價而沽的商品，**針對企業和職缺要求將履歷內容進行「客製化」**（customize），以吸引對方的目光，讓履歷表使企業一見傾心。

客製化履歷時，需要參考的因素包括：

❶ 企業文化及特性（corporate culture and characteristics）

各家企業都有屬於自己的組織文化（organizational culture）和業務特性，因此撰寫履歷表前，務必**對應徵對象的企業特性有所研究及了解**，藉此決定履歷表寫作的內容與風格口吻，讓審閱者認為你的個人特色與該企業的文化氛圍（atmosphere）可以一拍即合。

❷ 職位需求及內容（job requirements and content）

每項職缺對於應徵者所要求的學、經歷、個人特質和專業技能往往不同，例如業務人員（salesperson）和企劃人員（planner）相比，理想特質就會有所差異，因此寫作履歷表時，**需圍繞在（center on）當下所應徵職缺的要求及工作內容**，避免使用相同履歷應徵不同工作。

Christopher Cohen
12 Hampden Road
0208-948-9011
London
07899-756933
N8 0HT

Date of birth: 10 December 1985
christopher.cohen@herald.co.uk

> 這是一份清單式 CV（inventory CV），列出了求職者所有相關的經歷和成就。頁首的部分寫出了求職者的個人資訊，而第一小節 Summary 並不寫出特定的工作經歷，而是列出了從各項過去職位中習得的技巧。工作經歷（Experience）的部分列出了所有過去就職經驗，包括不同領域的工作，最後幾個部分則寫出外語能力、教育背景和個人興趣。

Summary

- Journalist with 10 years' experience with major international publications
- Newspaper, website and wire service commissioning and subeditor
- Talented writer with sharp, analytical mind
- Excellent written and oral communication skills
- Ability to develop media strategies & creative ideas for generating coverage
- Strong interpersonal and diplomatic skills
- Experienced in managing and motivating teams
- Extensive knowledge of international politics and current affairs
- International sales and marketing management

Experience

The Herald, Edinburgh   2022–present

Assistant foreign news editor (web)

- One of two people managing the integration of international news coverage on the newspaper and the website–the first stage of structural change across the organisation
- Commissioning across platforms of text, images, and multimedia content
- Part of the team responsible for setting each day's news agenda
- Input into strategic decision making at structural, technical and editorial levels
- Forward planning and coordination of major cross-platform projects and future fixed events
- Editorial and technical training of correspondents in multimedia content production
- Other editorial duties: subediting, image processing, editing website's front pages

> 求職者是英國人，所以採用英式英語的拼法。美式拼法為「organization」。

www.herald.co.uk, Edinburgh   2016–2022

Subeditor

- Part of a team responsible for style and content of website's news coverage
- Worked in a team of 10 people in a rapidly changing, time-critical environment
- Filtered, edited and published breaking news while updating non-breaking stories
- Worked with text, images and multimedia content
- Regular editor of the website's homepage
- Specialized in international news

Christopher Cohen
christopher.cohen@herald.co.uk

Freelance journalist based in Manila, Philippines   2011–2012, 2014–2015

- Retained by *The Newsworthy* as local correspondent for the Philippines
- Regular *Newsworthy* contributor in the Southeast Asian, East Asian and Central Asian regions
- Worked extensively with the *New York Times*
- Reported extensively on the international drug trade and Philippines internal conflict
- Filed copy on political, social, economic, environmental and cultural affairs for a variety of audiences, from 500-word news stories to 5,000-word magazine features
- Maintained relationships of confidence with sources from president and senior politicians to paramilitary and guerrilla commanders
- Participated as local producer on a number of television documentaries

Timely Wire Service (TWS), Berlin   2012–2013, 2016
Writer/Subeditor

- Part of a team responsible for style and content of TWS's English news service
- Worked in a team of 10–15 people in a rapidly changing, time-critical environment
- Reported from Hong Kong, Thailand, Iran and the United States

Connections Inc, Halifax, Yorkshire   2008–2011
Export Marketing and Sales Manager

- Responsible for relaunching the company in its neglected Middle East markets
- With local agencies, devised and implemented joint marketing and sales strategies
- Responsible for the recruitment, training and motivation of 15 agency sales staff
- Responsible for monthly/annual budgets and forecasts
- Took turnover from £400,000 to £2.5 million in three years

Vaya (UK) Ltd, Aylesbury, Buckinghamshire   2007–2008
Export Sales Executive – Middle East

Languages

- Fluent spoken & written Spanish, competent French & Portuguese, basic German

Education
University of Sheffield
- BSc (Hons) 2.2 in Chemistry, 2007
- 'O' Levels: 10, 2004; 'A' Levels: Chemistry (C), Biology (B), Geology (C) 2002

Interests

- Travel: Europe, Asia and South America
- History and historical reenactments: a member of the *Battle of Hastings* Players

克里斯多夫・柯恩
漢普頓路 12 號
0208-948-9011
倫敦
07899-756933
N8 0HT

出生日期：1985 年 12 月 10 日
christopher.cohen@herald.co.uk

簡介

- 為各大國際出版刊物擔任記者，10 年工作經驗
- 報紙、網站、新聞電訊任務委託和文字編輯
- 擅長寫作，思考敏銳、善於分析
- 出色的書面和口頭溝通技巧
- 擅長為新聞報導構想媒體策略和創意點子
- 傑出的人際關係技巧
- 具管理和帶領團隊經驗
- 熟悉國際政治和時事
- 國際業務及行銷管理

工作經歷

《前鋒報》，愛丁堡　　　　　　　　　　　　　　　　　2022– 任職中

國際新聞助理編輯（網頁）

- 與另一名同事共同負責統合報紙和網頁之國際新聞——報社內部結構改變之第一階段
- 委派文字、影像與多媒體等多平台內容設計
- 決定每日主要新聞之小組成員
- 在結構、技術和編輯層面之決策上貢獻創意策略
- 主要跨平台企畫與未來固定事件之計劃與協調
- 多媒體內容製作部門同事之編輯與技術訓練
- 其他編輯相關工作：文字編輯、影像處裡、網站首頁編輯

《前鋒報》網頁 www.harald.co.uk，愛丁堡　　　　　　　2016–2022

文字編輯

- 網頁新聞風格與內容之負責小組成員
- 於 10 人小組中，在迅速變化、分秒必爭的環境中工作
- 篩選、編輯與刊登突發新聞，同時更新非突發新聞
- 處理文字、影像與多媒體內容
- 網站首頁編輯
- 專攻國際新聞

克里斯多夫・柯恩
christopher.cohen@herald.co.uk

自由新聞工作者，菲律賓馬尼拉　　　　　　　　　2011–2012, 2014–2015

- 由《The Newsworthy》聘為駐菲律賓外派記者
- 定期為《The Newsworthy》報導東南亞、東亞、中亞地區新聞事件
- 與《紐約時報》密切合作
- 就國際毒品交易與菲律賓境內衝突進行深入報導
- 為各類型讀者投稿政治、社會、經濟、環保、文化議題方面之報導，從 500 字新聞報導到 5,000 字雜誌專題皆有。
- 與重要軍政人物維持互信關係，包括總統、資深官員、準軍事組織領袖、游擊軍隊領袖。
- 於當地參與製作數支電視紀錄片。

即時電訊服務（TWS），柏林　　　　　　　　　　　2012–2013, 2016

撰稿／文字編輯

- TWS 英語新聞風格與內容之負責小組成員
- 於 10 至 15 人小組中，在迅速變化、分秒必爭的環境中工作
- 自香港、泰國、伊朗、美國報導新聞

Connections 公司，英國約克郡哈利法克斯　　　　　　2008–2011

出口行銷與業務經理

- 負責重振受公司忽略的中東市場
- 與當地代理商共同構想與實行聯合行銷與業務策略
- 負責招募、訓練與率領 15 位代理商業務人員
- 負責月／年預算與預測
- 三年內使營業額從 40 萬英鎊成長至 250 萬英鎊

Vaya 公司，英國白金漢郡艾爾斯伯里　　　　　　　　2007–2008

中東部門外銷主管

外語能力

- 西班牙語說、寫流利，熟法語、葡萄牙語，具基本德語能力

教育背景

雪菲爾大學

- 2007 年理學學士（化學系畢），畢業成績 2.2
- 2004 年 O Level 成績 10；2002 年 A Level：化學（C）、生物（B）、地質（C）

興趣

- 旅遊：歐洲、亞洲、南美
- 歷史與歷史戲劇：《黑斯廷斯戰役》劇組演員

Unit 57　撰寫美式履歷
Writing résumés

1 什麼是 résumé？

　　Résumé（美式履歷 / 簡歷）篇幅較 CV（英式履歷）簡短，在結構上也更有彈性。美式履歷長度至多只有**一到兩頁**，並著重在**求職者的技能**、**工作經歷**和**教育背景**，內容幾乎都會按欲應徵的職位量身訂做。

2 美式履歷中應該包含哪些資訊？

　　由於美式履歷的內容簡短，因此所包含的資訊應該要跟欲應徵的工作直接相關。以下為美式履歷中通常會包含的資訊：

❶ **完整的聯絡資訊**：寫出你的全名、地址、電話號碼和電子郵件地址。

❷ **求職目標**：美式履歷中通常會寫出**特定職稱和產業**作為求職目標（也稱「事業目標」）。這並不是美式履歷的必要元素，但可以讓雇主**大致了解你的資格與能力**。這個部分最好與你要應徵的工作直接相關，並突出你的工作技能。

❸ **工作經歷**：寫出重要的**長期工作經歷**，及任何跟要應徵的職位**有關聯的經歷**。工作經歷通常以**倒敘**方式列出，也就是先把現在正從事或最近從事的工作寫出來。

❹ **教育背景**：包括所有的學士、碩士、博士學位，與該工作**有關的學術成就**也可以寫出來。

❺ **特殊資格認證或培訓**：包括與該工作有關的特殊培訓或資格認證。

❻ **技能、職業技能和電腦技能**：例如與該工作有關的電腦程式設計能力或外語能力。

❼ **獎項、出版著作、義工或榮譽工作、興趣**：如果**與該工作有關**，或是有**特別出眾的特殊經歷**，也應該寫出來。

3 如何安排美式履歷的內容結構？

　　美式履歷在結構上一般比 CV 更有彈性，結構可以靈活安排，最重要的就是配合該職缺的需求，顯示出你具備可以勝任的才能。不過美式履歷還是有幾個基本的原則：

❶ **篇幅**：美式履歷的長度只有**一到兩頁**，很少超過兩頁。

❷ **內容呈現**：美式履歷經常採用**小標題**、簡要的**列表**或說明。

❸ **項目排列**：美式履歷通常以**倒敘方式**列出資訊（最近的事件先寫出）；如果你確信自己具有所有該職缺所要求的能力，按照時間倒敘列出資訊為佳。

❹ **重點安排**：美式履歷應該**按照主題或技能調整內容**。如果你想轉換行業或職位，最好把重點放在你如何在不同的領域，累積和應用了該職缺所需的技能，不要只是把工作經歷按照時間順序列出來。

❺ **封面信**：美式履歷通常伴有**封面信**（**cover letter**）。**封面信**中可以用敘述方式寫出更私人的資訊，並強調你是該職缺的最佳人選。

MURRAY WEBB
3132 Mt. Pleasant Ave. NW, Washington, DC 20010
Mobile: 202-495-9206
Email: mtwebb@gmail.com

EXPERIENCE	**Independent Consultant, Research/Organizational Intelligence** 1/2016–Present

- Conduct social and enterprise research projects for public and nonpublic sources
- Design complex projects combining qualitative and quantitative methods
- Conduct and analyze in-depth interviews with experts and executives
- Perform due diligence, peer group, and benchmark research
- Analyze financial, regulatory, and archival documents
- Create and edit complex databases
- Publish reports, articles, copy, and audiovisual material

Selected engagements:
RSP Global, Washington, DC (present)
Gregory Wire Service, Washington, DC
Kim Productions, Seoul, South Korea
ALL TV, Bangkok, Thailand
Building Blocks, Sacramento, California

Visiting Professor of Political Science, St. William's College of Maryland, St. Williams City, MD
August 2018–July 2022
- Taught 6 undergraduate courses in political science
- Advised student research projects and editorial boards for student journals

Lecturer, Graduate Assistant, Research Assistant, University of Kentucky at Louisville, Louisville, KY
January 2012–January 2017
- Taught 9 undergraduate courses in political science
- Served on department governance, hiring, and evaluation committees

Special Assistant to the VP for Academic Affairs, University of Kentucky System, Louisville, KY
February 2014–September 2015
- Managed projects for VPAA during state-wide university system reorganization
- Created and edited speeches, correspondence, and online content for system-wide academic initiatives and special projects
- Conducted peer group, benchmark, and best practices research
- Conducted research for writing and distribution of strategic documents
- Coordinated employment searches for senior executive positions

MURRAY WEBB
3132 Mt. Pleasant Ave. NW, Washington, DC 20010
Mobile: 202-495-9206
Email: mtwebb@gmail.com

EDUCATION	University of Kentucky at Louisville, Louisville, KY Doctorate, Political Science, 2018 Graduate Certificate, International Cultural Studies, 2015 Coursework: international relations, Asian and Pacific politics, comparative politics, and social science methodology University of Maryland at College Park, College Park, MD Bachelor of Arts, International Studies, 2011
LANGUAGES	Intermediate German and Japanese
AFFILIATIONS	American Political Science Association Member Gregory Wire Services Community of Experts Member *Borders* Editorial Referee *Being and Doing* Editorial Referee
COMPUTING	Windows 10/11 and Windows Server Microsoft Office Suite SAP Business Objects / Crystal Reports Intuit QuickBooks macOS OpenProject (MS Project clone) Final Cut Pro, Premiere Pro, and Compressor Adobe Photoshop and Acrobat Pro BlueGriffon (web page design) Westlaw, LexisNexis, and other Web-based research platforms

● 這篇履歷安排內容的方式非常典型：先以倒敘方式列出工作經歷，每項工作以職稱和工作期間為標題，下面再進行簡短的描述。寫完工作經歷後，才寫出教育背景。之後的內容如外語能力、會員資格和電腦技能等，則是求職者依其與應徵工作之相關性選出。

● 除了聯絡資訊外，這篇美式履歷中就沒有其他私人資訊，也沒有列舉義工經驗或個人興趣等資訊。列出會員資格（AFFILIATIONS）的目的，是顯示求職者在不同的機構內擔負了一定的責任。

莫瑞・韋伯
20010 華盛頓特區樂山大道 3132 號
手機：202-495-9206
電郵：mtwebb@gmail.com

工作經歷	**工作經歷：獨立顧問，研究／組織智慧** 1/2016– 現在

◆ 執行公私機構之社會與企業研究計畫
◆ 設計結合質性與量性作法之複雜研究計畫
◆ 執行並分析與專家和主管進行的深入訪談
◆ 執行盡職調查、同儕群體調查、指標研究
◆ 分析財務文件、管制文件和檔案文獻
◆ 建立和編輯複雜的資料庫
◆ 出版報告、文章、文稿和視聽材料

合作對象：

RSP 環球，華盛頓特區（持續合作中）
格里高利通訊社，華盛頓特區
金氏製造公司，南韓首爾
ALL 電視，泰國曼谷
堅石建設，加州沙加緬度

政治系客座教授，馬里蘭聖威廉學院，馬里蘭州聖威廉市
8/2018–7/2022

◆ 於大學部教授六堂政治學課程
◆ 指導學生研究計畫和學生刊物編輯小組

講師、研究生助理、研究助理，肯塔基州立大學路易斯維爾市分校，
肯塔基州路易斯維爾市 1/2012–1/2017

◆ 於大學部教授九堂政治學課程
◆ 政治系教師治理、聘僱、評鑑委員會委員

教務副校長特別助理，肯塔基州立大學系統，肯塔基州路易斯維爾市
2/2014–9/2015

◆ 於全州大學系統重組期間，為教務副校長管理相關計畫
◆ 為系統內學術計畫與特殊計畫撰寫與編輯演講、通訊與線上內容
◆ 執行同儕群體調查、指標研究與最佳表現研究
◆ 執行寫作研究，發行策略文件
◆ 協調高級行政階層職缺招聘

莫瑞・韋伯
20010 華盛頓特區樂山大道 3132 號
手機：202-495-9206
電郵：mtwebb@gmail.com

教育背景	肯塔基州立大學路易斯維爾市分校，肯塔基州路易斯維爾市 2018 年，政治學博士 2015 年，國際文化學研究生證書 修業課程：國際關係、亞太政治、比較政治學、社會科學方法學 馬里蘭大學，馬里蘭州大學公園市 2011 年，國際研究學學士
外語能力	中級德語、日語
會員資格	美國政治學協會會員 格里高利通訊社專家協會會員 《Borders》編審 《Being and Doing》編審
電腦技能	Windows 10/11 and Windows Server Microsoft Office Suite SAP Business Objects / Crystal Reports Intuit QuickBooks macOS OpenProject (MS Project clone) Final Cut Pro, Premiere Pro, and Compressor Adobe Photoshop and Acrobat Pro BlueGriffon (web page design) Westlaw, LexisNexiss 及其他線上研究平台

Franklin Hoosain

15 Orchard Street, Albany, NY 12203
518.903.4303
frank.hoosain@gmail.com

Objective ❶

To obtain an IT position in which I may use my experience as an IT manager with responsibility for all aspects of IT including managing staff and departmental budgets.

❶ 這篇履歷跟上一篇不同的地方在於，開頭有列出「求職目標」簡單自我介紹，以及說明欲應徵的職務性質。後面內容中以倒敘方式列出工作經歷，並按照主題列出重要的工作成就。

Professional Summary

An IT manager with over 8 years of IT experience, encompassing LAN and WAN, training and support, and security. Proven ability to design and implement technology to support large user groups and to manage IT budgets and staff. Highly skilled at supporting company business objectives by clearly translating business needs into technology requirements and managing full-lifecycle IT projects.

Experience

IT Manager, Brightstar, Albany, NY   9/2022–Present

- ✓ Responsible for all computer systems at corporate headquarters.
- ✓ Responsible for the IT department including drafting and managing an annual IT budget of $1.5 million.
- ✓ Brainstorm, implement, and evaluate multiple IT projects ranging from $15K to $100K.
- ✓ Recommend all software for business processes.

Key Achievements

① LAN and WAN

- ✓ Supported a 150 seat LAN and remote users throughout the country using VPN solutions.
- ✓ Designed and implemented a WAN infrastructure.

② Training and Support

- ✓ Created a computer-based training for WordPerfect products, eliminating the need for outside training.
- ✓ Created a central help desk to coordinate support services, thereby increasing their efficiency and improving customer satisfaction.

③ Security

- ✓ Created new information-security committees: Risk Evaluation, Penetration Testing, and Security Engineering.
- ✓ Selected employees to staff the committees and assumed responsibility for their efficacy and budget.
- ✓ Selected and implemented content-scanning software to protect company assets.

Franklin Hoosain
frank.hoosain@gmail.com

Applications Manager, Security Banking, Houston, TX   12/2018–8/2022

- ✓ Managed a staff of three in supporting corporate headquarters.
- ✓ Performed daily administrative tasks including adding and deleting users, controlling data access, setting up shared areas, and managing queues.
- ✓ Configured Cisco AGS+ and 7513 Series Routers using RIP, IGRP, and EIGRP as well as Catalyst 5500 Series Switches.

Consultant, Technology Architects, Albany, NY   8/2015–10/2018

- ✓ Worked with a team to design and implement solutions, including BGP for a WAN/Internet Service Provider.
- ✓ Wrote detailed project plans to apply for management approval of all network projects.
- ✓ Configured PIX firewalls (501, 506, 515, and 525) for new clients.

Technical Proficiencies ❷

Protocols/Standards: TCP/IP, AppleTalk, DECet, RIP, IGRP, BGP, IS-IS, IPsec, VPN, Multicast, RSRB, LANE, HSRP, Token Ring, VLAN, Spanning Tree, ISL, CDP, HDLC, PPP, ISDN BRI/PRI, T1/E1, Frame Relay, Ethernet, DLSw, PIM, IGMP, CGMP, PNNI, ATM, IEEE 802.11b (Wi-Fi)

❷「Technological Proficiencies」是「computer science」（電腦技能）的另一種說法。

Hardware: Cisco AGS+Series Routers, Cisco (Native & Hybrid) Catalyst Series Switches, Cisco PIX Series Firewalls, Riverstone 3000 & 8600, Linksys Wireless Cable/DSL Router, ASX-1000 & ASX-200BX ATM Switches, NET IDNX 10 & 70 Multiplexors, Ascom Timeplex Multiplexors, 3com ONcore and Online hubs, Ascend GX 550 OC-48 ATM Core Switch, NetScout RMON probes (T1, HSSI)

Software: Cisco IOS Releases 11.x - 12.3, Cisco CatOS Releases 4.x - 6.4, Windows 11, Windows 10, SunOS, Solaris, SunNet Manager, SNMPc, BMC Patrol Dashboard, CiscoWorks, ForeView, Visio, MS Project, MS Office Suite

Education
State University of New York, Albany
BS, Computer Science and Applied Mathematics, June 2015

富蘭克林・胡珊

12203 紐約州奧爾巴尼果園路 15 號

518.903.4303
frank.hoosain@gmail.com

求職目標 ❶

有志從事資訊科技工作，應用全方位資訊科技管理的經歷，包括管理員工與部門預算。

資歷簡述

八年多資訊科技管理經驗，經手過 LAN、WAN、技術訓練、技術支援、資訊安全。熟悉設計與執行相關科技，用以支援大型使用者群體，管理資訊科技預算與員工。尤其精通於將企業需求轉換為科技需求、管理資訊科技項目之各階段，以支持企業營運目標。

工作經歷

資訊科技經理，Brightstar，紐約州奧爾巴尼市　　　　　　　　　　　**9/2022 – 迄今**

- ✓ 負責公司總部所有電腦系統。
- ✓ 帶領資訊科技部門，包括編列和管理總額達 150 萬美元之年度資訊科技預算。
- ✓ 發想、執行、評估多項金額達 15,000 美元至 10 萬美元不等之資訊科技計畫。
- ✓ 建議商務過程中所需軟體。

主要成就

① LAN 和 WAN

- ✓ 以 VPN 解決方案，支援包含 150 台電腦主機之 LAN 及全國各地之遠端使用者
- ✓ 設計與執行 WAN 基礎架構

② 技術訓練與技術支援

- ✓ 設計 WordPerfect 產品電腦訓練課程，減少外部訓練的需求
- ✓ 設計中央服務台協調各技術支援服務，由此增進服務效率與顧客滿意度。

③ 資訊安全

- ✓ 新設資訊安全委員會：風險評估、滲透測試、安全工程。
- ✓ 挑選員工擔任委員會委員，負責其工作效能與預算。
- ✓ 挑選與執行內容掃描軟體，以保護公司資產。

富蘭克林・胡珊

frank.hoosain@gmail.com

頁 2/2

應用經理，Security Banking，德州休士頓   **12/2018–08/2022**

✓ 管理三人小組，支持公司總部。

✓ 執行日常管理事務，如加入和刪除使用者、控制資料取得性、設立共享區、管理佇列。

✓ 採用 RIP、IGRP、EIGRP 和 Catalyst 5500 系列交換器裝配 Cisco AGS+ 和 Cisco 7513 系列路由器。

顧問，Technology Architects，紐約州阿爾巴尼市   **8/2015–10/2018**

✓ 與團隊小組合作，設計並執行解決方案，包括為一間 WAN ／網際網路服務業者設計邊界閘道器協定（BGP）。

✓ 撰寫詳細的專案計畫，應用於所有網路專案之管理許可申請。

✓ 為新客戶裝配 PIX 防火牆（501、506、515、525）。

資訊科技專長 ❷

協定／協定標準：TCP/IP, AppleTalk, DECnet, RIP, IGRP, BGP,IS-IS, IPsec, VPN, Multicast, RSRB, LANE, HSRP, Token Ring, VLAN, Spanning Tree, ISL, CDP, HDLC, PPP, ISDN BRI/PRI, T1/E1, Frame Relay, Ethernet, DLSw, PIM, IGMP, CGMP, PNNI, ATM,IEEE 802.11b (Wi-Fi)

硬體：Cisco AGS+Series Routers, Cisco (Native & Hybrid) Catalyst Series Switches, Cisco PIX Series Firewalls, Riverstone 3000 & 8600, Linksys Wireless Cable/DSL Router, ASX-1000 & ASX-200BX ATM Switches, NET IDNX 10 & 70 Multiplexors, Ascom Timeplex Multiplexors, 3com ONcore and Online hubs, Ascend GX 550 OC-48 ATM Core Switch, NetScout RMON probes (T1, HSSI),

軟體：Cisco IOS Releases 11.x - 12.3, Cisco CatOS Releases 4.x - 6.4, Windows 11, Windows 10, SunOS, Solaris, SunNet Manager, SNMPc, BMC Patrol Dashboard, CiscoWorks, ForeView, Visio, MS Project, MS Office Suite

教育背景

紐約州立大學，奧爾巴尼市
理學學士（資訊科學與應用數學系畢），2015 年 6 月

Unit 58 如何撰寫生涯自傳
How to write a career autobiography

1 生涯自傳寫作原則

有時企業會要求在履歷表下方附上求職者的「生涯自傳」（career autobiography），透過文章讓求職者介紹自己的學、經歷背景及個人特質。

自傳最忌諱寫成流水帳（dull description），從家庭成長背景開頭、冗長地介紹與職缺無關的（irrelevant）個人細節，而無法聚焦重點。為了讓自傳內容有效讓主管辨別你的個性和專業能力，可在自傳中著重說明以下幾點：

❶ **個人特質**以及**專業經歷**

❷ 曾經從**過往工作或求學經驗中**，獲得什麼樣的**成長**（growth）或**收穫**（gain）

❸ 過去的**活動**和**職場表現**，曾對雇主或其他人有什麼**主要貢獻**（contribution）

❹ 解釋為何這些個人特質和相關經歷，**足以證明你能適任**（fit）**工作**

除了過去經驗的敘述外，自傳也可以提及自身未來生涯規畫（career plan）。若身為求職新鮮人，不了解所應徵的職缺未來有哪些發展空間，可以多向從事相關工作的親友、學長姐或師長請教，也可以透過報章或網路搜尋相關資訊，作為自傳寫作的參考。

2 自傳常見英文動詞

自傳撰寫時也應使用**強而有力的動詞**，讓審閱者感受到求職者**具備強烈工作動機**（motivation）。以下彙整自傳中用來描述各項個人特質的常見動詞，供參考運用：

❶ 組織企劃與創造能力	organize 組織；establish 建立；formulate 規劃；create 創造；develop 發展；plan 計劃；arrange 安排；launch 發起；introduce 引介；propose 提案；present 做簡報；release 推出
❷ 統整分析與判斷能力	integrate 結合；coordinate 協調；reorganize 重整；restructure 重組；analyze 分析；discover 發現；estimate 預估；identify 辨識；recognize 識別；indicate 指出
❸ 管理領導與培訓能力	manage 管理；lead 領導；guide 引導；assign 交付任務；pilot 帶領；steer 指導；oversee 監督；direct 指導；improve 提升；elevate 提升；inspire 啟發；train 訓練
❹ 溝通協商與諮詢能力	communicate 溝通；negotiate 談判；convince/persuade 說服；collaborate/partner 合作；discuss 討論；resolve/settle 解決；advise/recommend/suggest 建議；consult 諮詢
❺ 目標執行與成就能力	finalize 敲定；execute/perform/conduct 執行；complete 完成；demonstrate 展現；reach/attain 達到；succeed 成功；achieve/accomplish 成就；realize 實現；fulfill 履行

58-1 | An example of a career autobiography
生涯自傳寫作範例

My name is Gary Nielsen, and ❶ I am a qualified and experienced elementary school teacher. I graduated from the University of Michigan with a B.A. degree in education, and then went on to study abroad and obtain a master's degree in English language teaching from the University of Warwick's TESOL program. ❷ I've always enjoyed learning how to become a more capable teacher and a more helpful mentor to students who need my care, support, and guidance.

Currently based in Kenya, I am teaching on a voluntary basis at a local school, but I plan to move to Taiwan by the end of the month. In Kenya, I have taught Grades 1 to 4. I have learned a lot from this overseas teaching experience, and I feel very privileged to be able to devote myself to helping others who are less fortunate than I am. Also, living in another culture has shown me that there is more than one way of seeing the world.

With my extensive training and experience in education, I believe you will not be disappointed if you offer me a chance to help the students at your school to become more confident and competent English speakers.

❶ 從最後一段中,可知作者正在應徵教職,因此開頭著重說明和職缺相當契合的資格和學歷。

❷ 描述個人特質(樂於學習如何提升教學能力)和職缺相輔相成的地方。

❸ 表達過去已經從事過相關工作,並對於職缺有獨到想法,暗示已準備好接下來的職務。

❹ 最後表達可以為未來雇主提供何種幫助,並請求對方給予職缺機會

我名叫蓋瑞 ・ 尼爾森,❶ 目前是合格且經驗豐富的國小教師。我畢業自密西根大學,取得教育學學位,之後並出國進修,於華威大學的英語外語教學(TESOL)學程取得英語教學碩士學位。❷ 我無時不樂於學習如何精進教學能力,希望成為給予學生關愛、支持與指導的良師益友。

目前,我在肯亞一間當地學校擔任志願性質的教職,但我計劃在月底前搬到台灣。我在肯亞指導的對象為一至四年級的學生。我從這個海外的教學經驗中獲益良多,並對於能夠投身幫助境遇不如自己幸運的人們,十分感念在心。此外,在不同文化圈中生活,也讓我體認到看世界的方法不只一種。

我具備扎實的教學訓練和經驗,相信若您能惠予機會,讓我至貴校任職,我定能不負期望,幫助貴校學生成為更有自信的英文高手。

求職書信常用說法
Common phrases in job-hunting communications

1 Phrases for writing want ads: Describing qualifications
徵人廣告：應徵資格

1 Ideally, the candidate should have _____ [desired qualities] . . .
理想的應徵者應該具有〔資格描述〕……

2 We are looking for a candidate with . . .
我們在尋找具備……的工作夥伴。

3 The applicant will have . . .   應徵者應該具有……

4 Only candidates with _____ [type of experience, degree, etc.] will be considered.
具有〔經歷描述、學位要求等〕的應徵者我們才會考慮。

5 Successful candidates should have demonstrated knowledge of . . .
合格的應徵者必須熟悉……

6 Skills required: 所需技能：

7 Desired skills: 所需技能：

2 Phrases for writing want ads: Describing responsibilities 職務描述

1 The _____ [employee or job title] will be responsible for . . .
〔職稱〕將負責……

2 Specific responsibilities include . . .   具體的職務包括……

3 Overall responsibilities will be . . .   總體職務內容為……

4 The _____ [job title] will . . .   〔職稱〕將……

5 Essential job functions: 主要職務：

3 Phrases for writing want ads: Describing salaries and benefits
徵人廣告：薪水與福利

❶ Starting salary depends on education and experience.

起薪將取決於學經歷。

❷ We offer competitive pay and all-around insurance coverage . . .

我們提供優厚的薪酬和全面的保險……

❸ We offer a standard benefits package . . .　　我們提供標準的員工福利……

❹ We offer a complete benefits package . . .　　我們提供完整的員工福利……

❺ We offer an exceptional benefits package . . .

我們提供絕佳的員工福利……

❻ We offer many perks and benefits . . .　　我們提供許多津貼與福利……

4 Common abbreviations found in want ads 徵人廣告常用縮寫

❶ Avail immed ➡ available immediately　　可立刻開始工作

❷ Deg ➡ degree　　學位

❸ Exp ➡ experience　　工作經驗

❹ Exp pref ➡ experience preferred　　具……經驗尤佳

❺ F/t, p/t ➡ full-time, part-time　　全職；兼職

❻ M-F ➡ Monday through Friday　　週一至週五

❼ Min 3 yrs exp ➡ minimum three years' experience

三年以上工作經驗

❽ No exp req ➡ no experience required　　無工作經驗可

⑨	Perm ➡ permanent	長期固定
⑩	Ref ➡ reference	推薦信
⑪	Temp ➡ temporary	短期
⑫	Wtd ➡ wanted	徵……
⑬	$30 p/h ➡ 30 dollars per hour	時薪 30 美元
⑭	$600 p/wk ➡ 600 dollars per week	週薪 600 美元
⑮	$2500 p/mo ➡ 2,500 dollars per month	月薪 2,500 美元

5 Phrases for CVs and résumés: Categories for describing experience 履歷用語：資歷類別

❶	Career History	職涯經驗
❷	Employment History; Work History	工作經歷
❸	Experience; Work Experience; Professional Experience 工作經驗	
❹	Relevant Accomplishments; Selected Accomplishments 相關成就	

6 Phrases for CVs and résumés: Categories for describing technical skills 履歷用語：技能類別

❶	Computer Literacy	電腦技能
❷	Functional Skills	專業技能
❸	Hardware and Software	硬體與軟體
❹	Skills Profile	技能一覽

⑤ Technical Expertise   技術專長

⑥ Technical Skills   專業技能

7 Phrases for CVs and résumés: Other possible CV categories 其他履歷用語

❶ Achievements and Involvements ➡ personal interests and achievements

業餘成就與活動 ➡ 個人興趣與成就

❷ Activities and Interests ➡ nonprofessional hobbies and interests

業餘活動與興趣 ➡ 非專業嗜好與興趣

❸ Other Interests and Activities   業餘興趣與活動

❹ Personal Information ➡ age, date of birth, place of birth, gender, citizenship, visa status, marital status, children, driver's license, etc.

個人資訊 ➡ 年齡、生日、出生地、性別、國籍、簽證狀態、婚姻狀態、子女、駕照等。

❺ Voluntary Work ➡ any nonpaid work

志工經驗 ➡ 任何沒有薪水的志工工作

1 Review the concepts

❶ What information is usually included in a want ad?

❷ What is an employment application letter, or cover letter?

❸ Why should you send a cover letter with a résumé or CV? What is the purpose of a cover letter?

❹ What is the main purpose of a CV or résumé?

❺ How is a CV different from a résumé? Which contains more personal information, a résumé or a CV?

❻ Which information should always be included in a CV or résumé? _____

(A) Outside interests   (B) Contact information
(C) Marital status

❼ Which information is not usually included in a résumé? _____

(A) Work history   (B) Educational history
(C) Ethnic background

2 True (T) or False (F)

❶ ☐ True ☐ False   Résumés are more common than CVs in North America.

❷ ☐ True ☐ False   CVs and résumés are often in reverse chronological order.

3 Write a want ad.

Your company is looking for a new process engineer. Write a want ad using the following information.

> The new process engineer will lead a team in developing a new microchip testing process. He or she must be able to manage a team as well as design, implement, and analyze the results of the testing. Candidates must meet the following requirements:
>
> ✓ A BSc in physics, electrical engineering, or mechanical engineering
> ✓ 5+ years of industry experience
> ✓ Experience with designing, performing, and analyzing experiments
> ✓ Good computer skills
> ✓ Ability to work in a cleanroom environment
>
> Your company offers the following benefits:
>
> ✓ A competitive salary with frequent possibilities for raises
> ✓ A 401(k)
> ✓ A stock option plan
> ✓ Medical and dental insurance
> ✓ Four weeks paid vacation to start
>
> Applicants should send résumés and cover letters as MS Word or pdf files to you at your email address. You do not want phone calls.

_____ **Wanted**

_____

_____

_____

Requirements

_____

_____

_____

_____

_____

_____

_____

_____

_____

_____

_____

_____

_____

_____

_____

_____

Benefits offered

_____

_____

_____

_____

_____

_____

_____

_____

_____

_____

_____

To apply

_____

_____

_____

_____

_____

_____

_____

_____

_____

4 Answer the questions.

Answer the following questions based on the résumé below.

Simon Zoltan   simonz@gmail.com
Date of Birth: 2 May 1991   Hungary – Thailand – Vietnam – Taiwan

Professional Summary
Journalist, photographer, editor, Hungarian and English publications
Educational programming coordinator, NVT, Hungary

MEDIAPOINT, CULTURE.HU, TAIWAN VIEWPOINT, TAIWAN WITNESS, NATIONAL
EXPLORER HUNGARY, LONELY GLOBE HUNGARY, MARIE MAGAZINE
Journalist/Photographer, 2014 to present
- Presently working as foreign correspondent/photojournalist in Thailand and
  Vietnam
- Contributed to various Hungarian- and English-language newspapers and
  magazines (cultural, environmental, and political articles and photography)

NATIONAL EXPLORER BOOKS HUNGARY; LONELY GLOBE HUNGARY; HBTV HUNGARY
Editor/Writer/Photographer, 2015 to present
- Edited written English text
- Worked on books, screenplays, scientific and educational scripts
- Published photographs and stories on Southeast Asia

NTV HUNGARIAN TELEVISION NETWORK, BUDAPEST, HUNGARY
Educational programming coordinator, 2011 to 2014
- Led a team that created the content and managed the production of a live,
  daily education program
- Content formats included panel discussions, short films, and live test sessions

Field projects
*Documentary work for various media (books, magazine articles, videos) and photo
exhibitions*
- Recent exhibition: *In Plain Sight* (2023 ongoing)
- Solo exhibitions included *Vietnam: Land of Dragons* (Budapest, Hungary), *Life in
  the Present: Madagascar; Mountain People* (Budapest, Hungary; Quito, Ecuador)

Education
- Master of Science, ELT University of Natural Sciences, Budapest, Hungary –
  Major in Ecology/Biogeography, 2013

Special training
- NTV Visual Arts Diploma, 2011

Languages
- Fluent in English, French, and Hungarian

Awards
- National Explorer Photography Award for work in Vietnam, 2016
- Japan Prize, International Educational Program Contest, 2010

---

❶ Does this person have a university degree? From where and in what subject?

_____

❷ What is this person's current job?

_____

❸ What awards has this person won?

_____

❹ How many languages does this person speak?

_____

5 Fill the correct information.

Write a draft of your own résumé. In the labeled sections below, fill in the correct information for yourself.

❶ Write your name and contact information, including your address, telephone number, and email address.

❷ Write your major career field or fields (for example, "Software designer, DesignPro, Taipei, Taiwan," or "Freelance programmer, computer companies in Canada, Hong Kong, and the United States").

❸ Begin to describe your most recent job. For items ❸ and ❹, you can choose to list your job title first (in ❸) and then the company (in ❹), or list the company first (in ❸) and then your job title (in ❹).

❹ See item ❸.

❺ Briefly describe the main responsibilities or activities in your job. Use two or more bullets to describe different responsibilities.

❻ Describe your second most recent job (that is, the job you held before your current or most recent job). Keep your description in the same order as the first, meaning if you listed your company then job title for the first job, follow the same order here.

❼ See items ❸ and ❹.

❽ See item ❺.

❾ List your educational history, with your most recent degree first.

❿ For the next three items (❿~⓬) , choose the most relevant category for you and provide details (for example, "Proficient in C++, SQL" or "Certified CPR instructor, Red Cross Certification, 2022"). If no category applies to your history, leave it blank.

⓫ Again, choose the category that is most relevant for you and list details (for example, "Health and Longevity, Aging Magazine, October, 2020" or "Fluent in English and Mandarin, proficient in Korean").

⓬ Again, choose the most relevant category for you and list details (for example "Designer of the Year 2019"; "Web Design United"; or "Founder, Programmers for Clarity in Computing").

① [Your name] _____ [Your email address] _____

[Your phone number] _____

[Your address] _____

_____

Professional Summary

② _____

③ _____

④ _____

⑤ ☐ _____

☐ _____

☐ _____

⑥ _____

⑦ _____

⑧ ☐ _____

☐ _____

☐ _____

Education

⑨ _____

_____

Special training / Computing / Other relevant skills

⑩ ☐ _____

Languages / Publications

⑪ ☐ _____

☐ _____

Awards / Memberships / Affiliations

⑫ ☐ _____

☐ _____

人力資源相關書信
Human Resources-Related Communications

Key Terms

assessment or probationary period 評估／試用期

新員工到任後，雇主或主管觀察其是否能勝任職務的一段時期，以便判斷是否持續僱用。根據台灣勞動法規，試用期可由勞資雙方自由約定，期間勞工勞動權益和一般受僱勞工相同。

appeal 提請重新考慮、提出申訴

用法如「an appeal of a termination」（提請公司重新考慮解僱的決定），即請主管單位重新考慮某一決定。

confidentiality agreement 保密協議

同意將特定企業相關資訊視為機密，未經授權不得洩漏給外部人士知曉的法律協定。有時企業會要求員工簽訂保密協定，以保護商業利益。

decline 婉拒

委婉拒絕。

human resources 人力資源

指公司等機構內的勞動力；公司常會設有「人力資源部」（簡稱 HR），功能為替機構招聘合格員工、甄選求職者、為新進員工計劃和執行適當的新人訓練，以及發展、管理員工福利制度等。

non-compete agreement 競業禁止合約

員工和雇主之間簽訂的合約，員工在合約中同意，離開該公司後，不在同樣的產業中開店創業或任職，與原公司競爭；此類合約通常設有期限。

paycheck 工資（單）

雇主支付員工薪資的支票，也可用來直接指涉薪資。

profit sharing 分紅

公司賺錢或營利增加時，員工可得到的額外獎金或福利。

resign 辭職

辭掉工作。

severance package 遣散方案

企業解僱員工後，給予的補償金或相關措施，通常包括「severance pay」（遣散費）。

stock options 股票選擇權

員工可購買公司的股票，作為一種福利津貼制度。

termination 解僱、終止僱用關係

僱用關係依雇主命令而終止，其原因可能有表現不佳、財務困難、企畫完成、合約到期等。

transition 過渡期

舊員工離職後至新進員工接替該原有職位、熟悉職位業務的期間

Unit 60　錄取通知書　Notification of a job offer

1 錄取通知書

求職過程結束後，公司會依其決定寄**錄取通知書（job offer letter）**或**未錄取通知書（rejection letter）**給求職者。錄取通知書有兩個功能：詳細描述工作內容，並邀請對方簽名承諾接下這個職位。

2 錄取通知書應該包含哪些資訊？

錄取通知書通常比未錄取通知書長，也比較詳細，因為通知書內要詳細描述工作內容與工作福利。錄取通知書通常包含下列資訊：

❶ 工作內容，包括：
　　❶ 工作基本性質（固定、短期、兼職等）
　　❷ 工作時數
　　❸ 主要職責
　　❹ 直屬主管
　　❺ 其他相關細節

❷ 薪酬，包括獎金、加薪、股票選擇權（stock option）等
❸ 員工福利和退休金
❹ 休假制度（假日、病假規定等）
❺ 各項附帶合約（如競業禁止合約〔non-compete agreement〕、保密合約〔confidentiality agreement〕等）
❻ 評估期或試用期規定
❼ 到職日期
❽ 簽約手續
❾ 其他相關資訊，如：
　　❶ 搬家費用
　　❷ 出差費用
　　❸ 必要的培訓

以上當然未涵蓋所有可以寫進錄取通知書的資訊，而其中有些資訊也並不一定總是會寫出來，比如很多工作並不會有試用期（assessment/probationary period），也沒有附帶的合約要簽訂，有些工作則可能需要列出更多的資訊。

3 如何安排錄取通知書的內容？

錄取通知書應該結構清晰，用粗體標題把資訊按照主題分類。通常是先描述**工作內容**，然後說明**薪水**、**福利**等其他資訊。有關如何簽約接下工作，通常則在最後才會說明。下面就來看一封錄取通知書範例。

Jupiter Systems

6 Temasek Boulevard, #8-00 Suntec Tower Four, Singapore 038986
Tel: +65 65299123   Fax: +65 67399124

April 4, 2023

John Manasterli
200 Anson Road
Singapore 079903

Dear Mr. Manasterli:

SUB: JOB OFFER

Jupiter Systems, Inc., is pleased to offer you a position as a senior engineer. We trust that your knowledge, skills, and experience will be valuable assets to our team. As a senior engineer, you will report directly to the VP of Engineering.

■ **Job Description:** Your primary responsibilities will include maintaining accurate bills of materials (BOMs) and parts lists as needed to meet customer specifications; overseeing all new drawings made by the CAD operators; evaluating product change requests; preparing dimensional drawings, assembly drawings, or special instructions needed to ship an order; and providing support to

- CAD operators and PDM personnel with their daily assignments;
- The sales department in helping to answer customers' / sales representatives' questions; and
- The manufacturing department in helping to solve production or testing problems.

Should you accept this job offer, per company policy, you'll be eligible to receive the following beginning on your hire date:

■ **Salary:** Annual gross starting salary of $61,000, paid in monthly installments by your choice of check or direct deposit.

■ **Performance Bonuses:** Up to three percent of your annual gross salary, paid quarterly by your choice of check or direct deposit.

■ **Benefits:** Standard benefits for salaried-exempt employees include a 401(k) retirement account; annual stock options; education assistance; health, dental, life, and disability insurance; profit sharing; sick leave; four weeks of annual vacation; personal days.

To accept this job offer:

1. Sign and date this job offer letter where indicated below.
2. Sign and date the enclosed Non-Compete Agreement where indicated.

③ Sign and date the enclosed Confidentiality Agreement where indicated.

④ Sign and date the enclosed At-Will Employment Confirmation where indicated.

⑤ Mail **all pages** of the signed and dated documents listed previously back to us in the enclosed business-reply envelope, to arrive by Monday, April 18, 2023. A copy of each document is enclosed for your records.

To decline this job offer:

① Sign and date this job offer letter where indicated below.

② Mail **all pages** of this job offer letter back to us in the enclosed business-reply envelope, to arrive by Monday, April 18, 2023.

If you accept this job offer, your hire date will be on the day that you attend new-hire orientation. Plan to work for the remainder of the business day after new-hire orientation ends. Please read the enclosed new-hire package for complete new-hire instructions and more information about the benefits we offer.

We hope that you'll accept this job offer, and we look forward to welcoming you aboard. Your immediate supervisor will be Jane Wu, VP of Engineering. Feel free to call Jane or me if you have questions or concerns. Call the main number in the letterhead during normal business hours and ask to speak to either of us.

Sincerely,

Eleanor Kandadar

Eleanor Kandadar
Hiring Coordinator, Human Resources

Enclosures: 8

Accept Job Offer
By signing and dating this letter below, I, John Manasterli, accept this job offer of Senior Engineer at Jupiter Systems.

Signature:_____ Date:_____

Decline Job Offer
By signing and dating this letter below, I, John Manasterli, decline this job offer of Senior Engineer at Jupiter Systems.

Signature:_____ Date:_____

曼納瑟里先生您好：

主旨：錄取通知

Jupiter Systems, Inc. 很高興能夠通知您，您獲錄取資深工程師的職位。我們相信您的知識、技術和經驗，將會成為我們團隊珍貴的資產。您就任資深工程師後，直屬主管將是工程部副總裁。

■ 工作內容：您主要的職責，將包括維護正確的物料清單（BOMs）和零件清單，以符合顧客需求的規格；審查電腦製圖師之所有新製圖；評估產品變更要求；製成必須的尺寸圖、組合圖，或發貨所需特定指示說明；並

  ◆ 支援電腦製圖師與產品資料管理人員之日常任務；

  ◆ 協助業務部門回答顧客／業務員問題；

  ◆ 協助生產部門解決生產或測試問題。

若您接下這份工作，依據公司政策，從僱用日開始您將享有：

■ 薪酬：起薪年薪 6 萬 1,000 美元，按月支付，依您選擇以支票支付或直接存入。

■ 績效獎金：最高可達年薪百分之三，每季發給，依您選擇以支票支付或直接存入。

■ 福利：給薪的豁免員工之標準福利：401(k) 退休帳戶；年度股票選擇權；子女教育津貼；醫療、牙醫、人壽和殘障保險；分紅；病假；每年四週休假；事假。

欲同意任職：

① 在本信下方指定處簽下姓名與日期。

② 在本信附上之競業禁止合約指定處簽下姓名與日期。

----

③ 在本信附上之保密合約指定處簽下姓名與日期。

④ 在本信附上之同意任職確認書指定處簽下姓名與日期。

⑤ 將所有上述簽名文件，以隨信所附商務回郵信封於 2023 年 4 月 18 日星期一前寄回本公司。每份文件皆為一式兩份，一份供您保存。

欲拒絕任職：

① 在本信下方指定之處簽下姓名與日期。

② 將所有文件以隨信所附商務回郵信封，於 2023 年 4 月 18 日星期一前寄回給本公司。

若您同意任職，開始僱用日即為您參加新進員工培訓之日。當日培訓結束後，您將立刻開始上班。請閱讀隨信所附之新進員工手冊，詳細了解相關指引與公司福利。

Jupiter Systems 誠心期盼您加入本公司。您的直屬主管將是工程部副總吳珍妮。如果您有任何問題或疑慮，歡迎來電與珍妮或與我聯絡。只要於上班時間打信頭上的公司電話，請總機把電話轉給我們即可。

同意任職

本人約翰‧曼納瑟里在此簽名同意任職 Jupiter Systems, Inc. 資深工程師一職。

簽名：＿＿＿＿＿＿＿＿＿＿＿＿＿＿　日期：＿＿＿＿＿＿＿

婉拒任職

本人約翰‧曼納瑟里在此簽名婉拒任職 Jupiter Systems, Inc. 資深工程師一職。

簽名：＿＿＿＿＿＿＿＿＿＿＿＿＿＿　日期：＿＿＿＿＿＿＿

Unit 61 未錄取通知書
Notification of rejection

未錄取通知書（rejection letter）通常會寫得簡潔而客氣，而且**很少會說明為什麼求職者沒有被錄取**。未錄取通知書一開始會先謝謝求職者來應徵，然後說明求職者眾多，且都非常優秀，公司很難做決定，最後表示非常遺憾無法錄取該求職者，但是會留下對方的聯絡資訊，也許以後還有合作的機會。視求職者**是否面試過**，未錄取通知書的內容會稍有不同。

61-1 | Rejection letter with no interview 未面試求職者的未錄取通知書

PROFESSIONAL PR
12 Eunos Road 6
Singapore 408600
Tel: 65 68 394058　　Fax: 65 68 8574965

March 15, 2023

Jordan Kim
34 Pickering Street
Singapore 038986

Dear Ms. Kim:

Thank you for your interest in our recently advertised position.

In light of your background and the available position, it does not appear that an interview would be mutually beneficial at this time. We will, however, retain your résumé for the next year and consider you for any other appropriate upcoming positions.

We appreciate your interest in our company and wish you every success.

Sincerely,

Victoria Seng

Victoria Seng, HR Manager
Professional PR

金先生您好：

謝謝您應徵本公司近期招募之職缺。

基於您的背景與本公司職務需求，現階段面試恐怕並不會對我們雙方帶來多大利益。不過我們會保留您的簡歷一年，也許未來會有其他適合您的職缺。

謝謝您對本公司的興趣，祝您一切順利。

PROFESSIONAL PR
12 Eunos Road 6
Singapore 408600
Tel: 65 68 394058   Fax: 65 68 8574965

March 15, 2023

Thomas Hu
102 Baghdad Street
Singapore 038988

如果求職者面試過，在未錄取通知書中要特別謝謝對方前來面試。

Dear Mr. Hu:

Thank you for giving us the opportunity to interview you for a position with our company. Unfortunately, the position we discussed has been filled.

It is always difficult to choose among the many candidates whom we interview. After careful consideration, we cannot offer you a position at this time. We will, however, keep your résumé in our active files for the next year and contact you should the need for further interviews arise.

Again, we thank you for your interest in our company and wish you every success.

Sincerely,

Victoria Seng

Victoria Seng, HR Manager
Professional PR

胡先生您好：

謝謝您給我們與您面試的機會。可惜我們討論的職缺已找到理想人選。

面試過這麼多求職者後，要做出決定並不容易。經過審慎的考慮，我們必須通知您，此次無法錄取您。但是我們會保留您的簡歷於現用檔案中，未來一年中若有需要，會立刻與您聯絡面試事宜。

再次謝謝您對本公司的興趣，祝您一切順利。

Unit 62 同意任職信
Accepting a job offer

　　同意任職信（acceptance letter）是在收到錄取通知書後，若有意接受，通常要寄一封正式的回信表示同意任職（就算你已經在電話上或當面答應了）。同意任職信的主要功能，是確認錄取通知書上的**工作細節**，並正式接受該職位。這類信件可以很簡短，但是務必：

❶ **謝謝對方給你這個機會**：開頭第一段應盡快表明對於獲得錄取的感謝。若對方在面試等應徵過程中提供過協助，也可以藉此機會表達謝意。

❷ **清楚表示你接受這份工作**：同意任職信目之一的在於確認將會到職，因此應在信中清楚承諾會接下職缺，以便對方公司可以確認開始安排相關事宜。

❸ **簡短覆述該職位的主要內容（薪水和福利）**：可藉由同意任職信，重述職位的主要職務和薪酬福利條件，藉此向對方確認自己對於職位的認知無誤。如果對於該職位的條件仍有疑問，或認為有需要調整之處，不妨也在信中提出和公司討論。

❹ **確認開始上班的日期**：接受任職信中應重述商定的就職時間，若日期需要調整，也可以在此時討論。

　　同意任職信應該寄給寄錄取通知書給你的人。此外，注意信中不要有拼字或文法錯誤。如果你收到的錄取通知書跟 Unit 60 的範例（P. 370–371）一樣，需要你簽名後寄回，那你可以寫一封簡短的同意任職信當作封面頁。工作細節就不用再覆述了，因為都清楚寫在你要寄回去的文件上，不過你還是應該謝謝對方給你這個工作機會。

accepting a job offer

Eli Goh

495 Admiralty Drive
Singapore 038986

April 29, 2023

Victoria Seng
Professional PR
12 Eunos Road 6
Singapore 408600

Dear Ms. Seng:

I would like to express my appreciation for your letter offering me the position of media specialist at a starting salary of $59,000 annually. The opportunity to work with the Professional PR team is an exciting one, and I look forward to adding my strengths to the company's upcoming projects.

As we discussed, my starting date will be May 10, when I will attend a new-hire orientation session beginning at 9 a.m. I further understand that my health insurance is to be paid fully by the organization and that retirement plans and stock option plans are available.

I trust that I have completed all the required paperwork. Please let me know if you need any more information from me before beginning my employment.

I'm eagerly anticipating starting my new position and looking forward to working with you soon. Thank you again for this opportunity.

Sincerely,

Eli Goh

Eli Goh

盛女士您好：

非常謝謝您來信通知本人錄取「媒體專員」一職（年起薪 5 萬 9,000 美元）。對於要加入 Professional PR，我非常興奮，也期盼在即將展開的專案企畫上貢獻一己之力。

如同我們約定好的，我正式開始上班的日期是 5 月 10 日，當天早上九點我會先接受新進員工訓練。健康保險由公司全額支付，此外還享有退休金方案和股票選擇權。

相信我已經完成了所有必要的書面工作。如果您在我開始上班前還需要任何資訊，請儘管告訴我。

我已經等不及展開我的新工作，加入貴團隊。再次謝謝您給我這個機會。

婉拒任職信
Declining a job offer

「婉拒任職信」即求職者收到錄取通知書後，**決定推辭掉這份工作邀約**，於是正式寫給對方公司表示婉拒的回信。婉拒任職的信可以**簡短而直接**。你可以簡短說明拒絕的原因，但是也可以不說明原因。婉拒任職信的主要功能是**謝謝對方給你這個機會**，但是同時**清楚地表示你無法接受這個職位**。

63-1 | A letter declining a job offer 婉拒任職信

George Lim
14 Raffles Street
Singapore 039388

April 25, 2023

Victoria Seng
Professional PR
12 Eunos Road 6
Singapore 408600

Dear Ms. Seng:

❷ 用「unfortunately」這個字顯示寫信人對於被錄取感到很感激。「After careful deliberation」則顯示寫信人並不是看不起這個職位，而是審慎地考慮過。你可以把原因寫出來，例如已經接受另外一份工作、覺得你有不同的事業目標等，但是也可以不寫出來。

❶ 婉拒任職信的第一句話，永遠都應該用來謝謝對方的錄用。

Thank you for offering me the position of media specialist at Professional PR. ❶ ❷ Unfortunately, after careful deliberation, I believe the position is not the best match for my career goals, and I must decline it.

Thank you very much for taking the time to interview me and giving me an opportunity to learn more about your company. I am very grateful for your consideration, and I wish you the best of luck in filling the position.

Yours truly,

George Lim

George Lim

盛女士您好：

非常謝謝您來信通知本人錄取 Professional PR 媒體專員一職。❶ 但很抱歉，經過仔細的考慮後 ❷，我覺得這份工作並不最符合我的事業目標，因此我無法接下這個職位。

非常感謝您花時間與我面試，給我機會更加地認識您的公司。非常感謝您的考慮，祝您能順利找到合適的職缺人選。

解僱通知書
Notification of termination

1 什麼是解僱通知書？

　　解僱通知書（**termination letter**），是公司用來通知員工其僱傭關係已經終止的信。解僱通知書跟辭職信（**resignation letter**）不同：辭職信是員工寄給公司，通知公司將辭去工作的信。

2 如何撰寫解僱通知書？

　　人們常常覺得解僱通知書既傷感情，又不好寫。解除僱傭關係的原因有很多種，有些跟員工的行為或表現有關，有些跟公司財務狀況或企畫的進展變化有關，也許還牽涉到違反工作合約的狀況，因此解僱通知書沒有標準的模式。

　　不過，以下是所有的解僱通知書都應該包含的資訊：

❶ 終止僱傭關係的原因

　　如果是因員工工作表現不佳或行為不檢須解僱員工，簡短說明在決定解僱前公司已採取哪些步驟，嘗試解決問題。如果是基於其他原因須解僱員工，簡短說明該原因。

❷ 薪資支付

- 最後的薪資將如何支付。
- 薪資支付到哪一天。
- 剩餘假日或休假的薪資如何計算。
- 剩下的開銷或其他報帳如何申請。
- 遣散費相關資訊。

❸ 離職程序

- 股票選擇權、退休金（如美國的 401(k)）或其他福利如何處理。
- 歸還公司設備。
- 帶走個人財物。

❹ 法律事項

　　簡短說明任何法律相關事項，如保密協議和員工就解僱一事申訴的權利。

❺ 僱傭關係終止日期

64-1 | Termination for poor work quality
因工作表現欠佳而解僱

The University of Sydney
NSW 2006, Australia
+61 2 9361 3332

17 November 2023

Gene Herrmann
Hirshorn Library
The University of Sydney
NSW 2006 Australia

Dear Mr. Herrmann:

> ❶「I am sorry to inform . . .」的說法,顯示寫信人覺得解僱一事會引起對方不快,因此表示遺憾,但並不表示寫信者在為解僱而道歉。「I am sorry to inform . . .」和「I am sorry.」(對不起)的意義是不同的:如果是具有正當理由而解僱對方,就沒有必要為此道歉,例如有時員工是因為犯法,或其他極端不妥的行為被解僱,此時在信中為解僱而道歉就很不洽當,也沒有必要,只須保持專業語氣即可,無須特別親切友善。但若員工是因為其他外部因素而遭解僱,就該以同情且禮貌的語氣書寫(可參考下一篇範例 64-2)。

I am sorry to inform you that after three work quality counseling sessions with Library Management and three written warning letters about the poor quality of your work, we still have not seen an acceptable improvement in your performance. ❶ As we discussed in our meeting of 5 October, your work quality needed to improve by 16 November in order to justify your continued employment at the library.

I truly feel that we have tried to work with you in every way possible to develop your work skills and to meet our standards of service:

1. After the first warning letter of 20 August, you requested a meeting. We met on 25 August to discuss ways to improve your performance.

2. After the second warning letter of 15 September, we initiated a meeting. At that meeting, we gave you a list of steps to be taken to meet the standards of your position.

3. On 5 October, we held another counseling session to discuss your rate of improvement. The possibility of termination was clearly discussed, and a deadline to meet standards by 16 November was set.

4. Finally, on 16 November, we issued a final warning letter regarding your performance. In this meeting, we discussed your incomplete improvements and the library's policy of terminating employees after three warning letters.

It is evident that your performance has not been up to the standards required for the position of metadata librarian. This leaves me with no choice but to tell you that your employment is terminated effective today. ❷

> ❷ 這是表示「您被解僱了」最專業的說法,不要說「you will be terminated」,因為這表示是「人」被終止,而非「工作」被終止。

Please return all company property to the library, including your employee access badge. If you cannot collect all your belongings today, you are welcome to arrange a time to return with a supervisor and collect them.

You will be paid through today, 17 November 2023. Your final paycheck will be issued on 10 December, the end of the current pay period. It will be mailed to your home. Your one unused paid sick day will be added to your final paycheck. Your medical and dental coverage will continue until the end of the current pay period.

Please feel free to contact me with any questions. According to library policy, you have the right to formally appeal your termination within two weeks of receiving this letter. Your employee handbook has information on the appeals process.

Sincerely,

Brenda Kidman

Brenda Kidman
Human Resources Manager

赫曼先生您好：

很遺憾必須通知您，在與圖書館管理員開過三次工作品質協商會，以及寄出三封工作品質欠佳的警告信後，我們至今在您的工作表現上還是沒有看到足夠的改善。❶ 如同我們在 10 月 5 日所協議的，您必須在 11 月 16 日前改善工作表現，本圖書館才能繼續僱用您。

我深信本圖書館已盡力與您合作，以培訓您的工作技能，並達到我們的服務標準：

1. 於 8 月 20 日寄出第一封警告信後，您要求會面協商。我們在 8 月 25 日會面討論改善工作表現的方法。

2. 於 9 月 15 日寄出第二封警告信後，我們主動邀您會面協商。我們給了您一張列表，列出您應該採取哪些步驟以達到您的職務標準。

3. 我們於 10 月 5 日又舉行一次協商會，討論您的改善程度。我們清楚討論到終止約僱關係的可能性，並將 11 月 16 日設為改善工作表現之最後期限。

4. 最後，我們於 11 月 16 日寄出最後一封警告信。在當天的會議上，我們認定您的進步程度仍未達標準，以及圖書館的政策是：寄出三封警告信後，即須終止僱傭關係。

您的工作表現顯然無法達到後設資料圖書館員該有的標準。這使我別無選擇，只能通知您您的約僱關係將於今天結束。❷

請將圖書館財物全數歸還，包括您的員工識別證。如果您無法於今天打包所有的個人財物，可以另外約定一個時間，在館員同事監督下將個人財物悉數帶走。

您的薪資將支付到今天，2023 年 11 月 17 日。您最後一份薪資將於本月薪資發放日 12 月 10 日發放，並郵寄至您的家中。您還有一天的帶薪病假沒有使用，也將一併算入您最後的薪資。醫療與牙醫保險至本月薪資發放日才終止。

若有任何問題，歡迎與我聯絡。根據圖書館政策，您有權利在收到此信後兩週內提出正式的申訴。您的員工手冊上有申訴程序的詳細資訊。

The University of Sydney
NSW 2006, Australia
+61 2 9361 3332

16 November 2023

Paul McCourt
Hirshorn Library
The University of Sydney
NSW 2006 Australia

Dear Mr. McCourt:

It is with sincere regret that I must inform you that your employment at the Hirshorn Library will be terminated as of Monday, 25 December 2023.

As you know, the Restructuring Task Force delivered its report to the dean of libraries in October. Among the task force's recommendations was the elimination of all temporary and contract positions. Because your position is temporary, you are subject to the task force's recommendation.

I would like to make it absolutely clear that your termination does not reflect any unhappiness with the quality of your performance in your six months at the library. In fact, you are highly regarded as one of our most productive contract staffers. Unfortunately, the decline in enrollment and the general economic downturn are now affecting nonpermanent staff across academia.

We are able to offer you two weeks of severance pay, in addition to your remaining three paid sick days and your two weeks of vacation. Per our request, your medical and dental coverage will remain in effect until the start of the spring semester. If you have any questions about your pay or insurance, please contact Brenda Kidman in Human Resources at extension 21.

I am genuinely sorry to lose such a capable, qualified, and warm colleague, but I am confident that you will be able to find another position in the near future. I would be very happy to write you a recommendation letter to help with your job search.

Best wishes,

Gwen Ulu

Gwen Ulu
Project Manager, Library Relations

cc: Brenda Kidman, Human Resources

這封信的語氣跟前一封非常不同。如果是因為外在因素須解僱員工，而非因為員工本身的問題，最好能表達心中的遺憾，並表示願提供協助以減輕解僱帶來的衝擊（例如延長醫療保險的期限、發放遣散費、撰寫推薦信等）。但是如果是因為表現不佳或行為不檢而解僱員工，採用這種同情的語氣就顯得虛假了。

麥寇特先生您好：

我非常遺憾必須通知您，您在 Hirshorn 圖書館的僱傭關係將於 2023 年 12 月 25 日星期一結束。

相信您也聽說，組織重整委員會已於 10 月分將其報告交予圖書館館長，其建議包括裁掉所有的臨時職位與約聘職位。您的職位屬於臨時性質，因此連帶受到影響。

我想在此特別說明清楚，此次僱傭關係終止絕不代表您過去六個月來，在本圖書館的工作表現不佳。您是本圖書館約聘員工中表現最佳的員工之一，但遺憾的是，新生人數減少與整體經濟衰退，使得整個學術界的非固定員工都受到影響。

我們將支付您相當於兩星期薪資的遣散費，另外您還有三天的帶薪病假及兩週休假，也將折合現金支付給您。我們也爭取到讓您的醫療與牙醫保險持續至下學期初。如果您就薪資或保險還有任何問題，請打分機 21 給人力資源部的班達·基曼。

我非常遺憾失去一位如此能幹、優秀和親切的同事，但是我相信您一定能夠很快找到另一份職位。我非常樂意為您寫推薦信，助您順利求職。

Unit 65 辭職信
Resignation letters

◼ 什麼是辭職信？

　　辭職信（resignation letter）是員工打算辭職時，寫給公司表明辭意的信。就算你已經跟主管說過你要辭職，還是要寫一封正式的辭職信，顯示你對公司與主管的尊重。

◼ 如何撰寫辭職信？

　　首先一定要記住的是，你的辭職信可能會**被公司保存在你的個人檔案裡**，因此會留存很長一段時間，所以不管你對你的工作有多不滿意，千萬不要寫出一封失禮或有失專業的辭職信。

　　辭職信用語應該客氣謹慎，但信中**沒有必要**說明未來的計畫或工作，不過如果你覺得有必要，當然還是可以加以說明。一般說來，你可以這樣安排辭職信的架構：

❶ **第一段**：清楚**說明辭職意願**，並說明從哪一天開始離職。如果你無法及早宣布辭職，給公司留下足夠的緩衝時間，最好也為因此引起的不便道歉。

❷ **中間的段落**：這部分通常用來**感謝雇主**，也可以說明辭職的原因（如果你覺得有必要），或者對於要離開公司表示遺憾。

❸ **最後一、兩段**：最後一、兩段可以用來表示你**願意協助接替你的同事**，讓他更容易進入狀況。也許你還可以提供離職後的**聯絡資訊**，並表示**樂意回答任何相關問題**等。

George Lim
14 Raffles Street
Singapore 039388

April 25, 2023

Steven Lee
Research and Development Director
Jupiter Systems
6 Temasek Boulevard
#8-00 Suntec Tower Four
Singapore 038986

Dear Mr. Lee:

Please accept this letter as notification that I will resign my position as senior engineer with Jupiter Systems on Friday, May 13.

I would like to thank you for the support and the opportunities you have provided me with during my three years at Jupiter Systems. It has been a time of great professional growth. I can assure you that the decision to leave was not easy.

If I can be of assistance during this transition, please let me know. I am happy to help however I can.

Sincerely,

George Lim

George Lim

cc: Victoria Seng, HR Manager

李先生您好：

請容我以此信告知，我將辭去 Jupiter Systems 資深工程師的職位，從 5 月 13 日星期五起生效。

感謝您這三年來給予的支持與機會，我在公司任職期間，在專業領域上成長了不少，離開公司對我來說並不是一個容易的決定。

在過渡期間如果有任何我可以幫忙的地方，請儘管告訴我。我會非常樂意盡力幫忙。

George Lim
14 Raffles Street
Singapore 039388

April 25, 2023

Steven Lee
Research and Development Director
Jupiter Systems
6 Temasek Boulevard
#8-00 Suntec Tower Four
Singapore 038986

> 傳統上，員工會在正式辭職前兩星期就說明辭意，但是現在大部分的工作都會在合約上規定，最晚須於正式辭職日前多少天遞辭呈，或可參考相關法令規定。現在也經常是雇主和員工共同討論出辭職的日期，讓雙方的需求都盡量被照顧到。

Dear Mr. Lee:

My purpose for writing you today is to tender my resignation as senior engineer. I would like to meet to discuss my last weeks here; my last day can be scheduled once arrangements have been made for a replacement.

The decision to leave Jupiter Systems has not been an easy one. My three years here have been a time of great personal and professional growth, and I am deeply grateful for the opportunities that have been presented to me. I have enjoyed my time with the R&D team, and I am proud of our work.

However, I have been offered a position as vice president of engineering at Starburst Enterprise, and I believe I must take this exciting chance to increase my responsibilities and challenge myself.

I would like this transition to be as easy as possible for all involved. If there is anything I can do to help things move smoothly, please let me know.

Sincerely,

George Lim

George Lim

cc: Victoria Seng, HR Manager

李先生您好：

寫這封信的目的是想告訴您，我決定辭去資深工程師的職位。希望能跟您當面討論我在這裡最後幾星期的工作安排；我辭職的日期，可在接替人選安排完成後排定。

決定離開 Jupiter Systems 並不容易。在公司的這三年，我在個人與專業上都有不少的成長，也非常感謝公司給我這份機會。我跟研發部同仁共事相當愉快，而且我非常以我們的成就為榮。

不過 Starburst Enterprise 聘請我去擔任工程部副總裁，而我相信我必須把握這個機會，挑戰自我，更上層樓。

我希望讓這段過渡期間盡量平順。如果有什麼我可以幫忙好讓事情進展更順利，請儘管告訴我。

人力資源相關書信常用說法
Common phrases in Human Resources-related communication

1 Phrases for making job offers 通知錄取

❶ It is my pleasure to offer you the position of _____ [job title] at _____ [company name].

非常榮幸聘請您在〔公司名〕擔任〔職稱〕。

❷ I am delighted to extend to you an offer of employment with _____ [company name] as a/an _____ [job title].

非常高興聘請您在〔公司名〕擔任〔職稱〕。

❸ We are pleased to welcome you to our team.

非常歡迎您加入我們的團隊。

❹ We are excited about the energy you will bring to our company.

對於您將為本公司帶來的新能量，我們感到非常興奮。

2 Phrases for responding to job offers: Accepting the offer 回覆錄取通知：接受任職

❶ I am very happy to accept your offer of the position of _____ [job title].

非常高興能夠受聘進入貴公司擔任〔職稱〕。

❷ I am pleased to be chosen as your new _____ [job title].

非常高興能夠獲聘為貴公司新的〔職稱〕。

❸ I understand the terms of employment . . .　我了解其工作性質為……

❹ I look forward to beginning my work at _____ [company name].

我已經等不及開始在〔公司名〕上班了。

3 Phrases for responding to job offers: Declining the offer
回覆錄取通知：婉拒任職

❶ Thank you for your time and effort in considering me for _____ [job title].

感謝您花費時間和心力，考慮讓我擔任貴公司的〔職稱〕。

❷ Unfortunately, I must decline your offer . . .

很遺憾地，我必須婉拒您的好意……

❸ Unfortunately, I must refuse your offer . . .

很遺憾地，我必須婉拒您的好意……

❹ Unfortunately, I cannot accept the position.　很可惜我無法接下這個職位。

❺ Unfortunately, I am unable to accept your offer.

很可惜我無法接下您的聘請。

❻ Sadly, I will not be accepting the position.　很可惜我將不會接下這個職位。

❼ Sadly, I have decided not to accept the position.

很可惜我已經決定不接下這個職位。

❽ After careful consideration, I must withdraw my name from consideration for the position of _____ [job title].

經過仔細的考慮，我必須撤回當初對〔職稱〕的爭取。

❾ After careful consideration, I no longer wish to be considered for the position of _____ [job title].

經過仔細的考慮，我不再希望成為〔職稱〕的考慮人選。

4 Phrases for responding to job offers: Neither accepting nor declining the offer 回覆錄取通知：暫時不接受、也不婉拒

❶ I am writing to acknowledge your letter offering me the _____ [job title] position with _____ [company]. Thank you for offering me this exciting opportunity. I will give you my response by your deadline of _____ [date].

在此確認收到您通知本人錄取〔公司名〕〔職稱〕的來信。非常感謝您給我這個令人振奮的機會。我會在〔日期〕的期限前回覆。

❷ I thank you very much for offering me the position of _____ [job title]. I appreciate the time you are giving me to consider the position, and I will definitely respond by your deadline of _____ [date].

非常感謝您聘請本人於貴公司擔任〔職稱〕。也非常謝謝您為我留下考慮的時間，我一定會在〔日期〕的期限前回覆。

5 Phrases for announcing your resignation 告知辭職用語

❶ Please accept this letter as my formal resignation . . .

在此謹以此信辭去……

❷ The purpose of this letter is to announce my resignation . . .

本信意在告訴您我決定辭去……

❸ I hereby tender my resignation . . .

在此提出我的辭呈……

❹ With this letter, I officially tender my resignation . . .

在此正式提出我的辭呈……

❺ Please accept this letter as notice that I will be resigning . . .

本信是要告知我將辭去……

❻ With this letter, I give notice that I will resign . . .

本信是要告知我將辭去……

6 Phrases for announcing a termination 告知解僱用語

❶ This letter is to confirm your termination because of poor conduct [poor performance/ budget cutbacks], as we discussed on _____ [date].

此信確認我們於〔日期〕的討論結果，您的僱傭關係將因行為不檢〔表現不佳 / 預算縮減〕而終止。

❷ Please consider this official confirmation of your termination from the position of _____ [job title] . . .

本信正式確認我們將與您結束〔職稱〕的僱傭關係……

❸ Please be advised that we are terminating your employment as of _____ [date] . . .

請注意，我們將於〔日期〕終止您的僱傭關係…

❹ Because we have seen no improvement in [problem], we have no choice but to terminate your employment . . .

由於在〔問題描述〕上沒有見到改善，我們只得終止您的僱傭關係……

❺ I am very sorry to inform you that your position as _____ [job title] will be terminated as of _____ [date].

非常遺憾必須通知您，您的〔職稱〕一職將於〔日期〕終止僱傭關係。

❻ We are sorry to inform you that your services are no longer required . . .

非常遺憾必須通知您，我們不再需要您的服務……

❼ The reasons for your dismissal are as follows . . .

終止僱傭關係的原因如下……

❽ Your termination results from the following . . .

解僱的原因如下……

1 Review the concepts

❶ What is "Human Resources?"

_____

_____

❷ What information should be included in a job offer letter?

_____

_____

❸ When might you write a job offer letter? _____

(A) To offer an applicant a position.

(B) To invite an applicant to an interview.

(C) To apply for a position you would like.

❹ What is the function of a job acceptance letter?

_____

_____

❺ What information does a rejection letter typically convey?

_____

_____

❻ What information should be included in a termination letter?

_____

_____

❼ Why are resignation letters important?

_____

_____

❽ Which is not a way of saying "I resign"? _____

(A) I hereby tender my resignation.

(B) Please accept this letter as notice of my resignation.

(C) I am resigned.

2 True (T) or False (F)

❶ ☐ True ☐ False Termination letters and resignation letters are the same thing.

❷ ☐ True ☐ False You should write a job acceptance letter even if you have already accepted the job over the telephone.

3 Write a professional letter to decline a job offer.

Imagine that you have been offered a job as a manager at Duds. When you interviewed for the job, you were interested in it; however, since then, you have gotten a more exciting offer to be a buyer for another store. You want to take that job instead. Write a professional letter to Marie Somtow at Duds declining her job offer. Use your home address as the sender's address.

4 Write a letter accepting this job offer.

Dear _____[Your name]_____ :

It is my pleasure to extend the following offer of the concierge position to you on behalf of Seashore Resort. This offer is contingent upon your passing our mandatory drug screening and our receipt of your college transcripts.

- Reporting Relationship: As concierge, you will report to the hotel manager.
- Job Description is attached.
- Base Salary: Will be paid in weekly installments of $750, which is equivalent to $40,000 on an annual basis (subject to deductions for taxes).
- Bonus (or Commission) Potential: Effective upon satisfactory completion of the first 90 days of employment and based upon the goals and objectives agreed to in the performance expectation discussions with your manager, you may be eligible for a bonus. The bonus plan for this year and beyond will be based on the formula determined by the company for the year.
- Non-Compete Agreement: Our standard non-compete agreement must be signed prior to start of employment.
- Benefits: The current standard company health, life, disability, and dental insurance coverage is supplied by Seashore Resort. Your eligibility for other benefits, including the 401(k) and tuition reimbursement, will be discussed after completing your first 90 days of work, per company policy. Employee contribution to benefit plans is determined annually.
- Vacation and Personal Emergency Time Off: Vacation is accrued at 5 hours per pay period. Personal emergency days are generally accrued at the rate of one day every 60 working days.
- Start Date: November 16, 2023
- Car/Phone/Travel Expenses: Normal and reasonable expenses will be reimbursed on a monthly basis per company policy.

Your employment with Seashore Resort is at will, and either party can terminate the relationship at any time with or without cause and with or without notice.

You acknowledge that this offer letter (along with the final form of any referenced documents) represents the entire agreement between you and Seashore Resort and that no verbal or written agreements, promises or representations that are not specifically stated in this offer are or will be binding upon Seashore Resort.

If you agree with the above outline, please sign below. This offer is in effect for 5 business days.

Signatures:

_____   _____
For Seashore Resort   Date   [Candidate's Name]   Date

Best,
Miranda Jones
HR Manager

[Your name] _____

[Your address] _____

_____

_____

[Date] _____

Miranda Jones
Seashore Resort
13 Marsden Road
Paihia, Bay of Islands
New Zealand

Dear Ms. Jones:

_____
_____
_____
_____
_____
_____
_____
_____
_____
_____
_____
_____
_____
_____
_____
_____
_____
_____
_____
_____
_____
_____

5 Write a resignation letter.

Imagine that you have worked for three years as a sales representative for the company Tech Solutions. Write a letter to your supervisor, Wanda Duncan, giving your resignation notice. Your contract requires a two-week notice, but offer to stay for four weeks to help the company make the transition. Do not provide a reason in this letter. Use your current address as the sender's address.

[Your name] _____

[Your address] _____

_____

_____

[Date] _____

Wanda Duncan
Tech Solutions
Guangfu Road, Lane 5, #18
Hsinchu, Taiwan 300

Dear Ms. Duncan:

_____

_____

_____

_____

_____

_____

_____

_____

_____

_____

_____

_____

_____

_____

_____

_____

6 Write a job offer letter.

You work for EduTech. You are offering a job to Thomas Hu. Write him a job offer letter using the following details:

✓ The position is curriculum coordinator. He will be responsible for organizing the curriculum for a summer camp for grades 4-6, gathering input from teachers regarding the curriculum, ordering materials, helping teachers implement the curriculum, overseeing the camp program, writing a report on the program, and planning for other programs. He will report to the director of the school.

✓ The salary is $48,000 per year. Salaries are paid by check every two weeks. He may be eligible for a raise after six months.

✓ You offer full medical and dental benefits and three weeks of paid vacation to start.

✓ The start date for the job is November 9.

✓ Before starting work, he must undergo a background check and a complete physical with the company doctor.

✓ To accept the job, he should call Monica Underwood in Human Resources to set up a meeting. Her phone number is (402) 835 0141.

EduTech
323 Bannock Street
Denver, CO 80204

October 26, 2023

Thomas Hu
102 Baghdad Street
Singapore 038988

Dear Mr. Hu:

_____
_____

■ **Job description:** _____
_____
_____

■ **Supervisor:** _____

■ **Salary:** _____
_____
_____

■ **Benefits:** Full medical and dental benefits. Three weeks of paid vacation to start.

■ **Start date:** November 9.

■ **Pre-employment testing:** _____
_____
_____
_____

■ **To accept this job offer:** _____
_____
_____

We hope to hear from you soon.

Best regards,
[Your name]

推薦信
Reference Letters

Key Terms

asset 資產

指對企業有幫助的事物或人才。若員工對公司有重大貢獻，雇主可在推薦信中稱讚該員工為公司的重要「資產」。

employability 就業能力

使個人足以受僱就業的技能和能力。

employment reference 就職證明書

由先前任職公司開出的證明書，證明當事人於該公司的工作日期、薪水等基本資料。

interpersonal skills 人際關係技巧

與人相處的技巧。在商務領域中，尤其指稱個人透過人際溝通與互動在公司內發揮所長的能力。擁有良好的人際關係技巧，表示能夠在不同情境考慮並恰當回應不同的人的需求、感覺和行為，這些技巧包括得體、周到、體貼、細心等。

letter of recommendation 推薦信

由熟識的人所寫的信，通常是老師、雇主或具有相當權威之人士，在信中評估和稱讚被推薦人的能力，並肯定其能夠勝任新崗位。

starting / ending salary 起薪／最終薪資

員工剛到時職的初始薪資稱為「起薪」，而「最終薪資」則為員工離開公司時的薪資。推薦信中可列出起薪和最終薪資，以讓未來雇主推知被推薦人在企業內部的成長能力，並作為未來給薪參考。

<table>
<tr><td>Unit
67</td><td>撰寫推薦信
Writing reference letters</td></tr>
</table>

1 推薦信的種類

推薦信有兩種：一種是**就職證明書**，一種是**推薦信**。兩種推薦信都用來寄給當事人**未來的雇主**，但是目的稍有不同。

❶ **就職證明書（employment reference）**：證明當事人曾於該公司工作，並寫出其工作日期、薪資、職務等。就職證明書並**不是寫給特定個人的**。

❷ **推薦信（letter of recommendation）**：詳述求職者的良好工作習慣、個性、技能等正面特質。推薦信通常是就特定工作而寫，並**寫給特定個人或公司**。

推薦信通常是由求職者的前主管或前同事所寫，但是老師、教授等也常為學生撰寫推薦信。兩種推薦信的寫法不太一樣。

❶ **就職證明書**：**簡短客觀**，有時甚至是當事人自己撰寫，再請主管簽名。

❷ **推薦信**：會就當事人的技能、才能、工作習慣等進行**更詳細的敘述**。

2 就職證明書中應該包含哪些資訊？

就職證明書中應該說明：

◆ 寫信人與當事人的**關係**（例如，主管、企劃經理等）
◆ 當事人於該公司的就職**時間**
◆ 當事人的**職位與職務內容**
◆ 最後離開公司時的**薪資**（通常**起薪**也會一併寫出）

MOOD MUSIC

Elm Corner, Upper Cam Lane
Addlestone, Surrey KT15
United Kingdom

6 January 2023

To Whom It May Concern:

I confirm that Sophia Netzer was employed as a sound engineer with Mood Music from August 2020 to November 2022. Her starting salary was £25,000 annually. At the end of her employment, she earned £29,000 annually.

As a sound engineer, Ms. Netzer was responsible for conferring with performers and producers to achieve the desired sound. She tested and maintained our mixing and recording equipment and recorded, mixed, edited, and reproduced a variety of vocals, music, and sound effects. She is skilled at regulating sound quality during recordings. She also showed herself to be dependable, reliable, and creative in problem solving.

Ms. Netzer was considered a valuable member of the team who consistently achieved good results and met all expectations.

Yours faithfully,

Thomas Brookes-Wolgar

Thomas Brookes-Wolgar
Manager, Mood Music

就職證明書通常不是寫給特定某個人的，所以在稱呼的部分也不會寫出特定的人名。其他的稱呼方式還有：

◆ Dear Sir or Madam:
◆ Dear Sirs:
◆ Gentlemen:

敬啟者：

在此證明蘇菲亞・內澤從 2020 年 8 月至 2022 年 11 月期間於 Mood Music 受僱擔任音響工程師一職。其起薪為年薪 2 萬 5,000 英鎊，離職前薪資為年薪 2 萬 9,000 英鎊。

內澤女士擔任音響工程師時的職務，包括與表演者及製作人進行協商，以達到預期的音效。她必須測試及維護我們的混音及錄音設備，並錄製、混合、編輯、重新製作各種歌唱、音樂及音響效果。她尤其擅長於在錄音期間調整音響品質。在問題解決的過程中，她顯現出可信賴、可靠與創意的特質。

內澤女士在我們的團隊中是不可多得的成員，她持續拿出令人滿意的表現，並達到我們所有的期望。

❸ 推薦信中應該包含哪些資訊？

除了職務、薪資、工作日期等基本資訊外，推薦信還應該就當事人下列特質進行評論：

❶ 優點、技能、天分　　　　　❷ 主動、熱忱、正直、可靠等特質
❸ 工作態度與人際關係技巧　　❹ 團隊合作的能力
❺ 獨立工作的能力　　　　　　❻ 任何其他跟工作方面有關的資訊

67-2 | A letter of recommendation 推薦信

MOOD MUSIC

Elm Corner, Upper Cam Lane
Addlestone, Surrey KT15
United Kingdom

January 6, 2023

Andrew Murn
Sound Systems
30 Leicester Square
London United Kingdom WC2H 7LA

Dear Mr. Murn:

> 推薦信通常是寫給特定個人，因此在稱呼上就可以寫出收件人的名字，就如同這封推薦信，或是至少寫出收件機構的名稱。其他寫法還有：
> ◆ Attention: Admissions Officer, University of Toronto
> ◆ Human Resources Manager, Big Time Computing

I was impressed with Sophia Netzer's proficiency with recording equipment and skill at achieving the desired sound when I hired her as a sound engineer in August 2021. During the two years she was employed here, I continued to be pleased with her technical skills. During that time, I also came to appreciate the many other qualities that make her a real asset to any work group.

Sophia is reliable and unflappable. Her rapport with clients is unparalleled: She guided confused clients to a clear idea of what they wanted to achieve and satisfied even the most fastidious with her attention to detail and commitment to quality. Sophia works well as part of a team, but she really shines in leadership positions. Her knowledge and skills prompted me to make her a lead engineer and put her in charge of several of the biggest productions at Mood Music. With her handpicked team, she achieved fantastic results every time. I received unsolicited praise for her work from several clients. Her work definitely helped Mood Music earn repeat business.

Of particular value is Sophia's dedication to her craft. She is focused on maintaining her technical proficiency and keeping abreast of developments in taste and technology. Her knowledge of the industry and her interest in its development make her a real asset to any organization with a cutting-edge vision.

Sophia Netzer is a hard-working, top-achieving professional in her field. I truly believe that she will improve any organization she is a part of. I recommend her without reservation, and I would be happy to provide more details or to answer any questions about her time here.

Yours faithfully,

Thomas Brookes-Wolgar

Thomas Brookes-Wolgar
Manager, Mood Music

這封推薦信比上一封就職證明書長多了，信中提到內澤女士的任職時間等基本資訊，但是主要的重點還是她的能力與特質，至於職務細節就沒有太多著墨。

穆恩先生您好：

2021 年 8 月我聘請蘇菲亞・內澤擔任我們的音響工程師時，她精通錄音設備的程度與創造預期音響效果的能力，令我印象非常深刻。接下來兩年，她的技術能力從未令我失望。在這兩年間，我也逐漸發現她其他許多的優點，這些優點使她在任何工作團隊中都是珍貴的資產。

蘇菲亞是個可靠、穩定的工作夥伴。她與客戶的關係無可比擬：她引導不知所措的客戶建立清楚的目標，並以追求精確與品質的精神，讓最挑剔的客戶也露出滿意的微笑。蘇菲亞是個優秀的團隊成員，但是她更具有領導的能力。基於她的知識與技能，我們後來請她擔任總工程師，並負責好幾項 Mood Music 最大型的製作企畫。在她和自己精心挑選的團隊的合作下，每一次她都拿出極出色的成果，已經有好幾位客戶主動跟我稱讚她的工作表現。她的優異表現，一定是 Mood Music 一再受客戶惠顧的原因之一。

蘇菲亞最珍貴的特點，就是她對這份工作的熱忱。她非常注意維持自己的技術能力，並留意這一行裡品味與科技的最新發展。她對此一產業的知識與對其發展的關注，使她在任何具有遠見的企業裡都是無價的資產。

蘇菲亞・內澤工作認真、出色、專業。我相信任何一間企業都會因她而受益。我毫無保留地推薦她，也樂於就她在本公司任職期間的狀況，提供更多資訊與回答任何問題。

請求撰寫推薦信
Requesting references

請求撰寫推薦信的方式，取決於推薦信的種類。就職證明書（employment reference）開立起來很容易，因此也很容易請求。推薦信（letter of recommendation）就比較難了，因為你要找到願意、而且能夠抽空為你撰寫推薦信的人，因此本單元重點放在請求撰寫推薦信。**請求撰寫推薦信時，要先考慮以下問題：**

❶ 應該**請誰**幫我撰寫推薦信？

❷ 應該請對方在信中包含**哪些資訊**？

❸ 如何使對方**寫起推薦信來更輕鬆**？

❶ 應該請誰幫我撰寫推薦信？

最好的人選是會幫你說好話的人。一般說來，推薦人的階級越高越好，能夠請高階主管或經理撰寫推薦信當然是很理想，但是記得：**信的內容比推薦人本身的頭銜還重要**。從同事那裡得到一封非常正面具體的推薦信，勝過從高階主管那裡得到一封含糊冷淡的推薦信。

要請誰幫你寫推薦信，也取決於你目前想應徵的職位，最好能找一個**了解你相關技能的人**為你寫推薦信。

❷ 應該請對方在推薦信中包含哪些資訊？

推薦信裡要寫些什麼，當然是由寫信人自己決定，你其實無法要求對方在信中寫出哪些特定的資訊，有時候你甚至無法檢閱推薦信的完稿。不過，你還是可以告訴對方，你正在**應徵什麼樣的職位**，該職位又**要求什麼樣的技能或經歷**。

❸ 如何使對方寫起推薦信來更輕鬆？

對於忙碌的專業人士來說，撰寫推薦信可能很耗時費力。下列的步驟能夠減輕他們的負擔：

◆ 簡短提醒對方你們**曾經有過的合作經驗**
◆ 簡短說明你正在應徵的職位須**負責哪些職務**
◆ 列出你覺得該職位**需要的特質**
◆ 附上**簡歷等相關文件**，列出你最重要的成就

SQL SOURCE

Hamano IS Building, Shibuya-ku
Tokyo 150-0015 Japan
Tel: 03 3661 9088   Fax: 03 3661 9089

June 29, 2023

Attention: Akiko Tanaka

Dear Ms. Tanaka:

I am being considered for the position of software design director at Empire Systems, New York. Would you be so kind as to write a letter of recommendation for me for the position? I know you are familiar with my work, based on our long professional history and the many projects we worked on together over the years.

The responsibilities of the position are similar to yours as director of software development at SQL and, to some extent, the role I have already played as lead designer and project manager on many of our recent projects, particularly the Apache Clone and Lead Click projects. Empire Systems is looking for efficiency, creativity, and stellar management skills in the new software design director. The person in the position is also expected to provide major leadership in the planned overhaul of the company's design process. I have included the job description for your reference.

I would greatly appreciate any comments you have regarding our professional relationship and my service to SQL Source as a whole. I have enclosed a copy of my résumé, and I would of course be happy to provide any other information that will make this task easier for you.

If you are able to provide this recommendation for me, please address your letter to:

Monica Jones
Vice President of Development
Empire Systems
21 Varick Street
New York, NY 10014 USA

The letter should be received no later than September 2, 2023.

Thank you so much for your assistance. Please let me know if I can provide more information to help you with this task.

Sincerely,

Wilson Murasaki

Wilson Murasaki
Lead Designer, SQL Source

Enclosures
(1) Software design director job description
(2) Wilson Murasaki résumé

這封信在第一段先是請求對方撰寫推薦信,然後在後續段落提供相關資訊,以協助對方後續寫信的過程。對於新工作所要求的特質與能力,在信裡寫得越詳細越好,例如在這封信裡,寫信人就還附上了職務描述與簡歷,讓對方寫起推薦信來更輕鬆。

田中女士您好:

我目前在應徵紐約「帝國系統」軟體設計主任一職,能否請您為我撰寫求職用的推薦信呢?基於我們長期的專業合作經歷,及過去幾年在許多專案的合作,我知道您了解我的工作狀況。

該職務內容與您在 SQL 擔任軟體開發主任的職務類似,同時在某種程度上,也類似我在最近幾個專案上擔任總設計師與專案經理之性質,尤其是最近的 Apache Clone 與 Lead Click 專案。「帝國系統」對於新的軟體設計主任所要求的特質,將是效率、創意與優異的管理技能,並在近期公司整體設計過程改造計畫中,展現領導能力。隨信附上職務說明,供您參考。

若您對我們的專業合作關係,與我在 SQL Source 任職期間的表現能著墨一二,我會非常感激。隨信附上我的簡歷,當然,如果您還需要其他資訊以利下筆,我會非常樂意提供。

如果您願意寫這封推薦信,請將推薦信寄給:

莫妮卡‧瓊斯
開發部副總裁
帝國系統
10014 美國紐約州紐約市
瓦瑞克街 21 號

推薦信最晚須於 2023 年 9 月 2 日寄達。

非常感謝您的協助。如果我還可以提供任何資訊協助您,請不吝告知。

附件
(1) 軟體設計主任職務說明
(2) 個人簡歷

推薦信常用說法
Common phrases in reference letters

1 Phrases for writing employment references 就職證明書用語

❶ _____ [Name] was employed in the position of _____ [job title] for _____ [number of years].

〔人名〕在本公司擔任〔職稱〕達〔年數〕。

❷ Over the _____ [period of time], _____ [name's] salary increased from _____ [amount] to _____ [amount].

在〔時間〕期間,〔人名〕的薪資從〔金額〕增加到〔金額〕。

❸ _____ [Name] fulfilled his duties adequately/completely.

〔人名〕的充分／完全達成職務要求。

❹ _____ [Name] fulfilled her duties soundly/impressively.

〔人名〕職務表現無可挑剔／令人驚豔。

❺ _____ [Name's] performance was always up to standard and sometimes above standard.

〔人名的〕工作表現符合標準,有時則極為出色。

❻ _____ [Name's] performance always exceeded standard.

〔人名的〕工作表現一向比標準的還要出色。

❼ _____ [Name's] performance was always up to standard.

〔人名的〕工作表現一向符合標準。

2 Phrases for writing letters of recommendation 推薦信用語

❶ I am only too happy to recommend _____ [name] for the position of _____ [job title].

我非常樂意推薦〔人名〕擔任〔職稱〕一職。

❷ I can wholeheartedly recommend _____ [name] for this position.

我毫不保留地推薦〔人名〕擔任此一職位。

❸ _____ [Name's] performance indicates that he is ready for a new level of responsibility.

〔人名的〕工作表現顯示出他已經準備好擔起更高一層的責任。

❹ _____ [Name] has proven that she is ready for more responsibility by . . .

從……看來,〔人名〕展現她已經準備好承擔更多責任。

❺ _____ [Name] is more than capable of handling the workload of a _____ [job title].

〔人名〕勝任〔職稱〕的工作量綽綽有餘。

❻ In my years of working with _____ [name], he has shown himself to be a _____ [capable manager, brilliant problem solver, etc.]

在與〔人名〕共事的這幾年,他充分證明自己是一個……〔能力出眾的經理、出色的問題解決專家等〕

3 Phrases for requesting reference letters 請求撰寫推薦信

❶ Do you feel we have worked closely enough to write a letter of recommendation for me?

基於我們的合作經驗,您覺得可以為我寫一封推薦信嗎?

❷ I humbly request a letter of recommendation for the position of _____ [job title].

在此想請您為我就〔職稱〕一職撰寫推薦信。

❸ I hope you are comfortable recommending me for the position of
_____ [job title].

希望您樂意為我就〔職稱〕一職撰寫推薦信。

❹ I believe that I can succeed as a _____ [job title]. I hope that you are
able to recommend me for this position.

我相信我能夠勝任〔職稱〕一職。希望您能夠為我就此一職位撰寫推薦信。

❺ I am applying for a job as _____ [job title], and I believe a
positive recommendation from you is vital to the acceptance of my
application.

目前我正在應徵〔職稱〕一職,而我相信一封由您撰寫的正面推薦信對
於我的錄取機會,將扮演非常關鍵的角色。

❻ I was hoping that you could discuss our work together _____ [on a
project, in a department, etc.].

希望您能夠說明我們在〔專案企劃上、同一部門裡等〕的共事經驗。

❼ You are the person who I believe has seen my abilities _____ [in a
particular field, as a manager, etc.], and I would be very grateful if
you could share your thoughts about our work together in a letter of
recommendation.

我相信您了解我〔在某一領域、擔任經理等〕的能力,如果您能夠在推
薦信中就我們的共事經驗分享您的想法,我會非常感激。

❽ The application process for _____ [job title] requires a letter of
recommendation from someone I have worked closely with. I believe
that you are best able to speak to my abilities and the achievements
we accomplished together.

〔職稱〕一職的應徵條件,包括一封由密切共事過的工作夥伴所撰寫的推
薦信。我相信您最能夠評判我的工作能力,及我們共同達到的成就。

1 Review the concepts

❶ What are the two types of reference letters?

_____

❷ Which kind of reference letter is short and factual?

_____

❸ Which of the following details should be included in an employment reference?

(A) Positions held in the company

(B) Dates of employment

(C) Opinions about performance, character, etc.

(D) Salary information

(E) Opinions about the subject's fitness for another position

❹ What information belongs in a letter of recommendation?

_____

_____

❺ Which of these would be a good person to ask for a letter of recommendation? You can choose more than one person from the list.

(A) A close friend

(B) The CEO of your company

(C) A supervisor you have worked closely with

(D) A new supervisor you have not worked with

(E) A colleague you have worked with on many projects

(F) An employee you have supervised

❻ How can you make it easier to write a letter of recommendation?

_____

_____

2 True (T) or False (F)

❶ ☐ True ☐ False A letter of recommendation is usually written to an individual.

❷ ☐ True ☐ False A letter of recommendation is usually longer than an employment reference.

❸ ☐ True ☐ False You should never write your own employment reference.

3 Write an employment reference.

Imagine you work for Sticky Wicket Computer Solutions. Write an employment reference for the individual described below.

- ✓ **Name:** Ken Casey
- ✓ **Title:** Programmer
- ✓ **Dates of employment:** November 2018 to October 2023
- ✓ **Salary:** $45,000 annually
- ✓ **Main responsibilities:** Interacting with clients, visiting clients on-site, providing solutions in time-critical situations, programming in C+, Python, and Flash.

STICKY WICKET COMPUTER SOLUTIONS

www.stickywicket.com 301.930.0394
Rockville, MD

December 30, 2023

Dear Sir or Madam:

_____

_____

_____

_____

_____

_____

_____

_____

_____

_____

_____

_____

_____

_____

_____

_____

_____

_____

_____

_____

_____

_____

_____

_____

_____

_____

_____

_____

_____

_____

_____

_____

4 Write a letter of recommendation.

Now imagine that the same individual is applying for a lead programming job. He has asked you to write a letter of recommendation. Add the following information to your letter of recommendation.

✓ You received several letters from clients praising Mr. Casey's speed, timeliness, and creative problem-solving skills.

✓ You appointed Mr. Casey leader of the Crisis Group based on his leadership skills and excellent performance under pressure.

✓ You recommended a merit pay raise for Mr. Casey in May 2022 based on his performance.

✓ You found Mr. Casey to be a quick learner and dedicated to staying current in his field.

✓ The letter should be addressed to Jill Dunstable, the HR manager at Programming Solutions. The address is 202 Dogwood Boulevard, Richmond, VA 23173.

STICKY WICKET COMPUTER SOLUTIONS

www.stickywicket.com 301.930.0394
Rockville, MD

December 30, 2023

_____

_____

_____

_____

Dear Ms. Dunstable:

_____

_____

_____

_____

_____

_____

_____

_____

_____

_____

_____

_____

_____

_____

_____

_____

_____

_____

邀請函
Invitations

dress code 著裝準則

特定團體或聚會場合所要求的服裝規定。邀請對方出席活動時,若有著裝準則的相關資訊,應一併告訴對方。

formal 正式的

按照正式的格式、傳統、規則。

informal 非正式的

不拘形式或禮儀;在平常、隨意、大家互相熟識的場合中適用。

keynote speech 主題演講

在大型聚會中,用來表達該會議重要議題、原則或方針的演說,以便確立活動的主題,又稱為「keynote address」;在活動中發表主題演講的人則稱為「keynote speaker」(主題演講者)。

launch 創辦、展開、上市

產品或網頁等首次進入市場,也就是顧客第一次看到新產品時。也指展開新企畫或新計畫。

luncheon 午餐(會)

通常指稱正式的午餐聚會,例如為了討論會議事項、或接待賓客所舉辦的餐會。

prior commitment 預定行程

「commitment」在此指必須出席、處理的行程工作;婉拒邀約時,可以用「已有預定行程」(because of a prior commitment . . .)來推辭。

regrets only 若不克出席請回覆

用在邀請函裡,表示如果受邀者計劃出席,就不需要回覆,只有無法出席者需要回覆。

RSPV 敬請賜覆

法文 Répondez s'il vous plaît 的縮寫,表示「請回覆」。這是邀請函中的標準用語,請受邀者回覆是否出席。

showing 展示會

將物品陳列展示給觀眾參觀的活動,目的可包括引起顧客興趣或刺激商品銷售。

<table>
<tr><td>Unit
70</td><td>如何撰寫商務邀請函？
How do I write business invitations?</td></tr>
</table>

在這一章裡，我們來學習寄出和回覆商務領域使用的書面邀請，各單元分別包括以下重點：

❶ 撰寫**正式**邀請函

❷ 撰寫**非正式**邀請函

❸ 邀約**演講**

❹ **回覆**邀請

❺ **感謝對方應邀**演講

1 撰寫正式的邀請函

正式的邀請函遵守所有的標準慣例，以顯示對對方的尊重。那麼什麼時候需要寄發正式的邀請函？其實**幾乎所有的商務活動都需要用到正式的邀請函**；非正式邀請函通常只寄給親朋好友，或熟識的工作夥伴。如果你要舉辦正式的活動（**大部分的商務活動都是正式的**），那就應該寄發正式的邀請函。正式邀請函有兩種形式：

❶ **書信**形式（formal invitations on letterhead）

❷ **卡片**形式（formal invitations on traditional invitation cards）

2 如何寫書信形式的正式邀請函？

撰寫邀請信時，必須將**活動相關的各項重要資訊**告訴受邀人，以便對方可以正確決定是否出席活動。邀請信中必須回答的關鍵問題可分為「**5W**」，詳見以下說明：

❶ **誰是主辦人？（Who is hosting the event?）**

不管主辦人是你的公司、特定個人或團體，務必把主辦人寫出來。

❷ **什麼活動？（What is the event?）**

清楚說明這個活動的功能，例如募款、開會、慶祝新品上市等。如果有特別來賓會演講或出席，或是有任何的特別活動，也寫出來。提供有趣的細節，吸引讀者參加。

❸ **在哪裡舉辦？（Where is the event?）**

在邀請函中告訴對方活動舉辦的地址。你還可以附上交通指南，但是這部分要與邀請函正文分開來，以附件方式提供，不要寫在邀請函上。

❹ **什麼時候舉辦？（When is the event?）**

清楚寫出活動舉辦的日期與時間。

❺ **為什麼舉辦這個活動？為什麼邀請對方？**
（Why is the event being held and why is the reader being invited?）

說明舉辦這個活動的原因，比如說展示新產品，或是討論某個議題。此外，也說明為什麼你決定邀請對方，比如說因為他是重要的顧客，或者因為他對活動相關議題有深入的了解等。

invitation card

除了「5W」的關鍵問題外，信中也需要提供**如何回覆、活動注意事項**等相關資訊。寫作邀請信的其他重點如下：

❶ 說明回覆期限和回覆方式（RSVP information）

在邀請函的末尾，需清楚說明回覆的期限及回覆的方式，如透過郵寄、電子郵件、電話等。邀請函中請對方回覆的標準用語是 **RSVP**，即法語「répondez s'il vou splaît」的縮寫，英文為「please respond」（請回覆）之意，用法例如：

> Please RSVP by phone or email by December 10.
> 請在 12 月 10 日前以電話或電子郵件回覆。

❷ 提供必要的交通、服裝或其他資訊

寄出邀請時，要考量受邀者該如何前來參加你的活動。如果他們可能需要**停車資訊、旅館介紹**或其他**交通協助**，就以**附件**的方式附上。如果你的活動有特殊的**服裝要求（dress code）**，記得在邀請函中寫出來。此外，客人可能還會有其他問題，像是**能不能攜伴（plus one）參加**等。把客人會想知道的資訊盡量提供完整。

❸ 增加親切感（personal touch）

在稱呼的部分**寫出對方的名字**，不要只寫 Dear Sir or Madam。有可能的話，**親自在邀請函上簽名**，甚至稱呼或結尾敬辭的部分也可以自己手寫。

回覆接受 → P. 426

回覆婉拒 → P. 428

Part

17

邀請函

Unit

70

如何撰寫商務邀請函？

70-1 | A sample invitation letter 書信形式的正式邀請函

BLUMENSCHEIN, INC.

Adickesallee 3, 94855
Frankfurt am Main, Germany

20 October 2023

Samuel Potts
Mailander Strasse 4
Frankfurt am Main, 60598

❷ 第二段隨即說明活動在哪裡（where）和什麼時候（when）舉辦，並於本段後方提供停車和交通資訊。

❶ 寫作者在第一段點出為何（why）要邀請對方參加活動，並清楚說明活動名稱和描述活動內容。

Dear Mr. Potts:

Because you are one of our longtime valued customers, we would like to invite you to a private preview of our new Solingen Knife Collection. This new collection includes kitchen knives, hunting knives, and limited-edition decorative and collectible knives. ❶

The showing will be held at our shop on Adickesallee 3, 94855, on the evening of Sunday, 5 November, from 19:00 until 23:00. ❷ Free parking will be available in our lot behind the shop. For your reference, we have enclosed a map and directions to our shop.

We are very pleased to present this new collection to our most valued customers a full month before it becomes available to the public. The artisans and designers of the knives will be on hand to discuss the collection and answer any questions. A demonstration will be conducted at 20:00, followed by a question and answer session.

Please present this invitation for admittance when you arrive. This showing is by invitation only.

To help us plan for refreshments, we ask that you please RSVP to me or Trudi Blumenschein at (49) 60767210 or by email at trudi.blumenschein@blumenschein.de by 4 November. ❸

We at Blumenschein, Inc., look forward to seeing you ❹ at the showing and sharing our new collection with you.

❸ 寫作者在此明確告知讀者要如何回覆（RSVP）邀請，提供明確的聯絡方式和回覆期限，方便讀者進行下一步動作。

Yours sincerely,

Karl Blumenschein

Karl Blumenschein
Operations Manager, Blumenschein, Inc.

Enclosure (1)

❹ 最後一段清楚寫出活動的主辦單位為 Blumenschein 公司，並禮貌地重申邀請之意。

帕特先生您好：

您是我們長年的忠實顧客，因此在此特別邀請您參加我們的 Solingen 刀具組
非公開上市預覽會。這組新系列包含廚房用刀、獵刀和限量生產的裝飾與收藏用刀。

預覽會將於 11 月 5 日星期日晚間 7 點至 11 點於 94855 Adickesallee 3 號，即本公司總店
舉辦。❷ 您可於店面後方的停車場免費停車，隨信附上地圖與交通指南。

我們非常高興能夠在這組刀品新系列公開上市前一個月，就讓我們最重視的顧客們先睹為
快。屆時負責這組系列的工藝師與設計師也會在現場進行說明，並回答來賓問題。產品展
示將於晚間 8 點進行，之後是問答時間。

到達現場時請出示此邀請函。只有受邀者才能出席此預覽會。

請於 11 月 4 日前向我或楚迪‧布魯門欽先生（電話 (49) 60767210 或電子郵件 trudi.
blumenschein@blumenschein.de）進行回覆 ❸，以便我們準備茶點。

Blumenschein 全體同仁誠心期盼您的到來 ❹ ，與我們共享我們的新刀品系列。

🔳 如何寫傳統邀請卡形式的正式邀請函？

　　如果是**非常正式或重要的活動**，就較適合**以傳統邀請卡**的形式製作邀請函，而
不要用書信的形式。卡片形式的邀請函在內容上會與書信形式的邀請函不同，以下
是設計和撰寫邀請卡時應遵守的原則。

❶ **決定樣式與格式（Planning and formatting the card）**

❶ 選擇能夠呈現公司形象與廠牌的卡片。不要用已經事先印好、留有空白讓你填寫
的邀請卡。

❷ 選擇一種字體，不要用好幾種不同的字體。

❸ 以不同大小的字級，凸顯重要的資訊。

❹ 採用與卡片相搭配的信封。

❷ **撰寫內容（Writing the message）**

❶ 邀請卡的內容通常會比邀請信的內容短。

❷ 把活動名稱放在最頂端。

❸ 在活動名稱下方，以正式的語氣邀請對方出席。

❹ 寫出活動舉辦的日期（包括星期幾）、時間和地點。

❺ 用附件的方式提供任何額外的資訊，或是附上網址或電話號碼。

THE 15TH ANNUAL HOPE ANNIVERSARY CELEBRATION

The HOPE Community and Board of Directors cordially invite

Mr. John Smythe

to the 15th Annual HOPE Anniversary Celebration

held this Friday, December 8, 2023, at 8:00 PM
at the Washington Hotel
1294 Independence Avenue NW
Washington, DC

Please use the enclosed response card to RSVP by November 30

HOPE 創立 15 週年紀念慶祝會

HOPE 團隊與董事會
誠摯邀請

約翰・史密哲先生

參加 HOPE 創立 15 週年紀念慶祝會

時間：2023 年 12 月 8 日星期五晚間 8 點
地點：華盛頓飯店（華盛頓特區西北區獨立大道 1294 號）

請在 11 月 30 日前以附上之回覆卡進行回覆。

如果是正式的邀請函，你可以一併附上**回覆卡**，方便對方回覆。
下面就來看一份回覆卡。

The 15th Annual HOPE Anniversary Celebration

Friday, December 8, 2023

Name: _____

Guest Name: _____

> 這裡有一行「Guest Name」，表示受邀者還可以帶一位同伴出席。有時候，回覆卡上並不會要求寫出同伴姓名，但是在勾選是否出席的地方，會有一欄「plus one」（再加一位），這個意思就是受邀者可以選擇帶一名同伴參加。

☐ Will attend

☐ Will not attend

HOPE 創立 15 週年紀念慶祝會

2023 年 12 月 8 日星期五

姓名：_____

來賓姓名：_____

☐ 準時出席
☐ 不克出席

ADELAIDE STEPHANS
Dean, University of Sydney

Invites you to a dinner welcoming
Dr. Meredith Whittaker
Visiting Professor of Linguistics

Sunday, September 17, 2023
7:00 pm

Luhrman Hall, University of Sydney
Sydney, NSW Australia

Please RSVP by September 2   Business attire suggested

✂ -

The favor of your response is requested by Saturday, September 2

M _____

這裡的「M」是回覆者的稱呼開頭：Mr.、Miss、Mrs. 或Ms.。

☐ Accepts
☐ Sends regrets

雪梨大學校長阿戴萊德・史蒂芬

邀請您參加
語言學客座教授美樂蒂・惠特克博士
之歡迎晚餐會

時間：2023 年 9 月 17 日星期日晚間七點
地點：澳洲新南威爾斯州雪梨，雪梨大學勒曼大樓

懇請於 9 月 2 日前回覆。建議著正式商務服裝。

✂ -

請於 9 月 2 日星期六前回覆

M _____

☐ 準時出席
☐ 不克出席

　　非正式邀請函與正式邀請函有何不同？非正式邀請函應用於非正式的活動，像是烤肉派對、午餐會（luncheon）、或其他休閒聚會，寄送對象常為親朋好友和熟識的工作夥伴。非正式邀請函與正式邀請函主要有三點不同：

❶ **邀請的媒介**：非正式邀請函除了可以用書信形式寄發，也可以用**傳真或電子郵件**的形式寄出。

❷ **邀請的範圍**：非正式邀請函可以寄給個人，但是**也可以寄給團體**。

❸ **舉辦的活動**：不妨**依活動的正式程度**決定邀請的方式。

71-1 | A mass-mailed informal invitation 寄給多人的非正式邀請函

Lucky Electronics
33 Eunos Road 8
Singapore 408600
Tel: 65 68 482334 Fax: 65 68 482335

October 2, 2023

John Manasterli
200 Anson Road
Singapore 079903

Dear Mr. Manasterli:

Our records show that you have been a steady customer of Lucky Electronics for the past year. We would like to show our appreciation for your business by inviting you to our preferred customer Fantastic Fall Sale this Saturday, October 7.

All of our stock, including computer accessories, earbuds, game systems, and more, will be marked down 35% to 50%! Doors open at 9:00 AM sharp. We will have complimentary coffee, tea, and fresh fruit plates for our morning customers. The morning's sales event is by invitation only; we will open to the public at noon.

Please accept the enclosed $15 gift certificate to use with your purchase of $75 or more.

We look forward to seeing you at Lucky Electronics on Saturday. Please bring this invitation with you and present it at the door.

Sincerely,

Anthony Han

Anthony Han
Store Manager
sales@luckyelectronics.com

Enclosure: Gift Certificate #56 (not redeemable for cash)

曼納瑟里先生您好：

根據我們的紀錄，過去一年來您一直是 Lucky Electronics 的忠實客戶。為了表達我們的感謝，在此特別邀請您參加我們於本週六（10 月 7 日），為優惠顧客所舉辦的秋季折扣特賣會。

我們所有的存貨，包括電腦配件、耳機、電玩系統等，都將打到 65 折至 5 折！我們將於上午 9 點準時開門，並為上午前來的顧客免費提供咖啡、茶和新鮮水果拼盤。上午的特賣活動僅限受邀的顧客進場，中午之後活動便會開放給一般客人。

隨信附上一份價值 15 美元的優惠禮券，消費 75 美元以上時即可使用。

誠心期盼於本週六在 Lucky Electronics 見到您。到達現場時請在門口出示此邀請函。

附件：優惠禮卷 #56（不可兌換現金）

From:	Georgia Holloway (georgia.holloway@bigorchid.com)	▾
To:	All Staff	
Cc:	Lynne Contra (lynne.contra@bigorchid.com)	
Subject:	Big Orchid's Annual Company Picnic	
Attachment:	picnicdirections.pdf	

Segoe UI ▾ | 14 ▾ | B *I* U A | ☰ ☰ ☰ ☰ | ☰ ☰ ☰ ☰ | — ✎ 🖼

Dear Colleagues,

It's time again for Big Orchid's Annual Company Picnic! Please bring your family and join us this Sunday, July 31 at 12:00 pm at the Sugarloaf Mountain Recreation Center. We will have a BBQ lunch and refreshments galore, plus organized games for the kids, raffles, and sports competitions.

I look forward to hosting this picnic to show my gratitude for all your contributions to Big Orchid. I always remember that it is our staff that makes Big Orchid great.

Directions are attached. If you have any questions, please contact Lynne Contra at 301.252.0888, extension 5.

I hope to see you all on Sunday!

Georgia
. . . .
Georgia Holloway
Founder
Big Orchid Floral Design
www.bigorchid.com
georgia.holloway@bigorchid.com

寄件人：Georgia Holloway (georgia.holloway@bigorchid.com)

收件人：所有員工

副本：Lynne Contra (lynne.contra@bigorchid.com)

主旨：公司年度野餐會

附件：野餐交通指南

親愛的同事們：

又到了 Big Orchid 公司年度野餐會舉辦的時候了！歡迎您於本週日（7 月 31 日）中午 12 點與家人共同前來塔糖山休閒中心，我們會準備豐富的烤肉午餐和茶點，此外還有安排兒童遊戲、抽獎和體育競賽活動。

我期待透過主辦這次野餐會，就諸位同事們對 Big Orchid 的貢獻表達謝意。我一直沒忘記，是員工的付出打造出公司的成就。

隨信附上交通指南。如果有任何問題，請打 301.252.0888，分機 5 聯絡林內‧孔綽。

希望星期日可以看到各位！

演講的邀請函會比起前幾個單元的一般邀請函包含更多的資訊，**如其他演講人姓名、講題**及**預期的參加人數**等，列出這些資訊的目的是吸引對方接受邀請。

回覆接受 → P. 427
回覆婉拒 → P. 429

7Z-1 | Speaker invitation letter 講者邀請信

**OIL INDUSTRY ENVIRONMENTAL
AWARENESS COUNSEL**

88 10th Avenue SE, Calgary, Alberta
Phone: 403-299-8876   Fax: 403-255-6933

August 14, 2023

Mr. Julian Renaud
Executive Director
The Oil Impact Foundation
5756 Westheimer Street, Suite 1-300
Houston, TX 77057 USA

Dear Mr. Renaud:

On behalf of our board of directors, I would like to formally invite you to be the closing keynote speaker at the upcoming 2023 Oil Industry Environmental Awareness (OIEA) Conference.

The theme of this year's conference is "Building Bridges – Connecting Activists and Industries." It will be held at the Big Sky Conference Facility in Calgary, Alberta, on November 9 to 12, 2023. Keynote speeches are expected to be between 40 and 60 minutes long. The closing keynote speech will conclude the conference at 4 p.m. on Sunday, November 12.

We are in the process of compiling our complete draft speaker program. We will forward it to you in the next two weeks to give you an idea of the topics other speakers will be covering. We have already confirmed Tabitha Simpson as our opening keynote speaker. Her presentation is provisionally titled "Strange Bedfellows: The Evolving Relationship of Greengroup and Big Gas." In addition, Dr. Dmitri Safarova of Russia will be presenting a major paper on impact studies involving drilling in Georgia.

We expect high attendance this year, in the range of 900 guests and 15 speakers, in the wake of last year's record attendance. Guests include contingents from Canada, the United States, Russia, and Saudi Arabia. We are already receiving inquiries about the program and presenters.

We would be pleased and honored if you would take part in this year's conference as our closing speaker.

Please feel free to contact me with any questions at 403-299-8876, ex. 13. I will call you next week to follow up.

Yours sincerely,

Peter Tochs

Peter Tochs
Executive Director
Oil Industry Environmental Awareness Counsel

芮納魯先生您好：

在此代表本公司董事會，正式邀請您於即將舉行的 2023 年度石油工業環境影響（OIEA）研討會上，發表閉幕主題演講。

本年度研討會的主題是「搭起橋樑：聯合社運人士與工業界」。舉辦地點為（加拿大）亞伯達省加利市的昊天會議中心，舉辦日期為 2023 年 11 月 9 到 12 日。各場主題演講時間約為 40 到 60 分鐘。閉幕演講將為研討會劃下句點，演講時間為 11 月 12 日星期日下午 4 點。

我們目前正在整理完整的演講排程表草稿，未來兩週內就可以寄給您，讓您了解各演講來賓的演講主題。研討會的開幕演講人已確定是塔必他·辛普森，她的演講題目目前暫定為「不可思議的盟友：環保組織與石油工業的關係發展」。此外，來自俄羅斯的德米奇·沙法羅瓦博士，將發表其就喬治亞境內鑽油工業造成環境衝擊所進行的重要研究論文。

繼去年的研討會達到歷年來參與人數最高紀錄後，我們預期今年的研討將會吸引多達 900 位的來賓和 15 位演講貴賓。出席來賓包括來自加拿大、美國、俄羅斯和沙烏地阿拉伯的代表團。已有不少貴賓跟我們詢問研討會議程與演講人名單。

若您應允擔任本年度研討會閉幕演講人，我們將感到非常榮幸。

若有任何問題，歡迎與我聯絡：403-299-8876 分機 13。我將於下週致電給您進行後續確認。

邀約演講的邀請函應該要比一般正式的邀請函更詳細：受邀者會想知道還有誰會去演講、誰會由此活動中受益、誰會參加此活動等，因為是否在此活動上演講，對演講者的個人和專業生涯都會有很大的影響。

接受正式的邀請
Accepting a formal invitation

　　雖然商務邀請函有時候會附上電子郵件地址或電話，方便對方回覆，但是正式的做法還是要在接到邀請 24 小時內，或是最晚三天之內，寄一封正式的回覆信。但如果邀請函附有回覆卡（response card），那就直接把回覆卡寄回，不需要再寫回覆信。

　　回覆函的形式要配合邀請函的形式。下面就來看兩封回覆接受的信。

73-1 | An acceptance letter 接受正式邀請的回覆信　　邀請信 → P. 415

SAMUEL POTTS

Mailander Strasse 4,
Frankfurt am Main, 60598

23 October 2023

Blumenschein, Inc.
Adickesallee 3, 94855
Frankfurt am Main, Germany

Dear Mr. Blumenschein:

Re: New Knife Collection Showing

Thank you for your kind invitation. It is with pleasure that I accept your invitation to the showing on Sunday, 5 November.

Yours sincerely,

Samuel Potts

Samuel Potts

布魯門欽先生您好：
主旨：新刀品系列上市展示會
謝謝您慷慨的邀請。在此滿心喜悅地接受您的邀請，出席參加於 11 月 5 日星期日所舉辦的展示會。

73-Z | Accepting an invitation to make a speech 接受演講邀約的回覆信

The Oil Impact Foundation
5756 Westheimer Street, Suite 1-300, Houston, TX 77057

August 20, 2023

Peter Tochs
Executive Director
Oil Industry Environmental Awareness Counsel
88 10th Avenue SE
Calgary, Alberta, Canada

Dear Mr. Tochs:

Thank you for your kind invitation to be the closing keynote speaker at the upcoming 2023 Oil Industry Environmental Awareness (OIEA) Conference. I am happy to confirm my participation at the conference.

I understand that I will speak on November 12, at about 4 pm. I will prepare a speech approximately 50 minutes in length on the topic of shared goals between industry and conservation groups. I will send you the final title in the next two weeks.

Please note that I would like to include visual elements in my speech from a laptop and PowerPoint presentation, so I will require a projector and screen. I appreciate your assistance in providing these items. Also, please let me know if there will be time for questions from the audience after the speech.

I look forward to receiving the full schedule of speakers and to participating in this year's OIEA Conference.

Yours sincerely,

Julian Renaud

Julian Renaud
Executive Director
The Oil Impact Foundation

托契先生您好：

謝謝您盛情邀請本人擔任 2023 年度石油工業環境影響（OIEA）研討會之閉幕主題演講人。在此非常高興地與您確認，我將參加此次研討會。

我了解閉幕演講將於 11 月 12 日下午 4 點左右舉行。我將就工業界與環保組織之共同目標，準備一篇 50 分鐘左右的演講。我將在兩週內將確定的演講題目寄給您。

在演講中我會用到筆電與 PowerPoint 呈現視覺資料，所以我需要投影機和螢幕，希望您能夠協助提供這些設備。此外，請讓我知道大會是否會在演講後留些時間讓聽眾發問。

誠心期盼早日收到完整的演講議程，並參加今年的 OIEA 研討會。

婉拒正式的邀請
Declining a formal invitation

婉拒正式的邀請時，你可以簡短說明無法接受邀請的理由，像是：

◆ Due to a prior commitment, I will not be able to attend . . .
由於已預先有約，我將無法參加……

然而，你不需要再進一步說明細節。一般可接受的理由包括已經有預定行程，或是已計劃好要出遠門。**不要用生病作為理由——除非你真的生病了**，而且也想讓對方知道——因為聽到你生病了，對方禮貌上就有義務詢問你的病況。此外你可以加上一句：

◆ Wishing you every success with . . . 祝……圓滿成功

請注意，上面這種句子不適用於婚禮。

74-1 | Declining a formal invitation 婉拒邀約的回覆信　　邀請信 → P. 415

SAMUEL POTTS

Mailander Strasse 4,
Frankfurt am Main, 60598

23 October 2023

Blumenschein, Inc.
Adickesallee 3, 94855
Frankfurt am Main, Germany

Dear Mr. Blumenschein:

Re: New Knife Collection Showing

Thank you for your kind invitation. Unfortunately, because of a prior commitment, I will not be able to attend. I wish you the best of luck with the new collection.

Yours sincerely,

Samuel Potts

Samuel Potts

> 布魯門欽先生您好：
> 主旨：新刀品系列上市展示會
> 非常謝謝您慷慨的邀請。可惜當天已有預定行程，因此無法出席。但還是祝新系列產品大獲成功。

74-Z | Declining an invitation to make a speech 婉拒演講邀約的回覆信

The Oil Impact Foundation

5756 Westheimer Street, Suite 1-300, Houston, TX 77057

August 20, 2023

Peter Tochs
Executive Director
Oil Industry Environmental Awareness Counsel
88 10th Avenue SE
Calgary, Alberta, Canada

Dear Mr. Tochs:

Thank you for your kind invitation to be the closing keynote speaker at the upcoming 2023 Oil Industry Environmental Awareness (OIEA) Conference. Unfortunately, I will be out of the country on business travel from November 1 to November 20.

I wish you the best of luck at this year's OIEA Conference. Please don't hesitate to contact me if I can provide other assistance.

Yours sincerely,

Julian Renaud

Julian Renaud
Executive Director
The Oil Impact Foundation

托契先生您好：

非常感謝您盛情邀請本人擔任 2023 年度石油工業環境影響（OIEA）研討會之閉幕主題演講人。但很遺憾，從 11 月 1 日至 11 月 20 日我將至國外出差。

預祝今年的 OIEA 研討會圓滿成功。如果我能夠提供其他協助，請不吝告知。

感謝對方應邀演講時，要用**具體的細節**說明該演講帶來多大的成效。

75-1 | Thanking a guest speaker 感謝演講嘉賓 邀請信 → P. 424

OIL INDUSTRY ENVIRONMENTAL
AWARENESS COUNSEL
88 10th Avenue SE, Calgary, Alberta
Phone: 403-299-8876   Fax: 403-255-6933

November 16, 2023

Mr. Julian Renaud
Executive Director
The Oil Impact Foundation
5756 Westheimer Street, Suite 1-300
Houston, TX 77057 USA

Dear Mr. Renaud:

I would like to extend my heartfelt thanks for your closing keynote speech at the 2023 Oil Industry Environmental Awareness (OIEA) Conference. The OIEA Board of Directors has also asked me to express its gratitude for your contribution.

Your speech, "Shared Destinations, Different Journeys," had the highest attendance of any presentation at our conference. I have received numerous positive responses to the speech and the topic. I will compile them and forward them to you in the near future. The board members and I also appreciated your handling of the energetic question and answer forum after your speech. We, as well as the audience, learned a great deal from that session.

We are very pleased at the overall success of this year's conference and are thankful for your active participation. As always, please feel free to contact me with any questions or feedback at 403-299-8876, ex. 13.

Yours sincerely,

Peter Tochs

Peter Tochs
Executive Director
Oil Industry Environmental Awareness Counsel

<table>
<tr><td>Unit
76</td><td>發出邀請和回覆邀請常用說法
Phrases for making and responding to invitations</td></tr>
</table>

1 Formal invitations: Making a formal invitation　正式的邀請

❶ We would be delighted if you could attend the launch of . . .

若您能夠出席……的上市發表會，我們將感到非常榮幸。

❷ Your presence is cordially requested at . . .　誠摯邀請您參加……

❸ Mr. and Mrs. Smith request the pleasure of _____ [name's] company to celebrate the wedding of their daughter Samantha . . .

史密斯夫婦誠摯邀請〔受邀人姓名〕參加小女莎曼莎的婚禮……

2 Formal invitations: Accepting a formal invitation　接受正式的邀請

❶ Thank you for your invitation to the launch of . . . I would be delighted to attend.

非常感謝您邀請本人參加……的上市發表會，我將非常樂於出席。

❷ Thank you for your invitation to Samantha's wedding. We will be very pleased to attend.

謝謝您邀請我們參加莎曼莎的婚禮。我們將非常樂於出席。

❸ Thank you for your invitation to . . . I am happy to confirm my attendance.

謝謝您邀請本人參加……，在此非常高興地與您確認我將出席。

❹ Dr. and Mrs. Jones are pleased to confirm their attendance at . . .

瓊斯博士夫婦非常高興地確認，他們將出席……

芮納魯先生您好：

由衷感謝您擔任我們 2023 年石油工業環境影響（OIEA）研討會之閉幕主題演講人。OIEA 董事會委託我就您的貢獻，傳達他們的謝意。

您的演講「共同的目標、不同的旅程」在本次研討會中是聽眾人數最多的一場。對於該演講與該主題，我已經收到許多的好評。我將把這些回饋彙整後，於近日寄給您。董事會成員和我也非常欣賞您從容不迫地處理了演講之後的踴躍問答，我們和在場的聽眾都從中學到了不少。

今年的研討會整體說來非常成功，我們非常滿意，也非常感謝您積極的參與。若有任何問題或批評指教，請不吝照常與我聯絡：403-299-8876 分機 13。

3 Formal invitations: Declining a formal invitation 婉拒正式的邀請

❶ It is with regret that I must decline your invitation to . . .

非常遺憾，我必須婉拒您的邀請……

❷ Thank you for your invitation to . . . However, I regret that I will be unable to attend.

非常謝謝您邀請本人參加……但是很遺憾地，我將無法出席。

❸ Unfortunately, because of a prior commitment, I will not be able to attend.

很遺憾，由於已預先有約，因此我將無法出席。

4 Informal invitations : Making an informal invitation 非正式的邀請

❶ Please come to our party on . . . 請來參加我們於……舉辦的派對。

❷ Would you like to come to dinner on . . . ?

您是否願意出席……的晚餐聚會？

❸ Can you make a meeting at 3 p.m. . . . ?

你能不能在下午三點跟我們碰面聚會呢？

❹ We would love to see you at . . . 希望我們能在……看到你。

5 Informal invitations: Accepting an informal invitation
接受非正式的邀請

• **For a meeting 聚會**

❶ I can attend the meeting at . . . 我可以參加……的聚會

❷ I will be able to make the meeting at . . . 我可以出席……的聚會

❸ Meeting at _____ [time and date] is fine with me . . .

〔日期和時間〕的聚會對我來說沒問題……

• **For another event 其他活動**

❶ Thanks for your invitation.　　　　　　謝謝你的邀請。

❷ I would love to come.　　　　　　　　　我樂意前去。

❸ We are looking forward to it.　　　　　　我們等不及了。

❹ I wouldn't miss it!　　　　　　　　　　我一定會去的！

6 Informal invitations: Declining an informal invitation 婉拒非正式的邀請

❶ We wish we could attend your . . .
真希望我們能夠參加你……

❷ I'm sorry I won't be able to make your . . .
抱歉這次無法參加你的……

❸ Thank you for your invitation, but . . .　　謝謝你的邀請，但是……

❹ I'm sorry I can't come.　　　　　　　　抱歉，我無法參加了。

❺ I'll be out of town.　　　　　　　　　　我屆時人會在外地。

1 Review the concepts

❶ What information should always be included in an invitation?

(A) Where the event will be held

(B) A guest list for the event

(C) The title of the event

(D) The date of the event

❷ What does **RSVP** mean?

_____

_____

❸ What is a **response card**?

_____

_____

❹ Which reasons are appropriate to include in a letter declining a formal invitation?

(A) A business trip   (B) Illness

(C) A personal conflict with another guest   (D) A date

(E) A job interview   (F) A prior commitment

❺ Which of the following words and phrases mean "attend?"

(A) Come to   (B) Make   (C) Create

(D) Present   (E) Participate in   (F) See

❻ What information should be included in an invitation to speak at an event?

(A) The date and time of the event

(B) The cost of the event

(C) People who have declined to speak at the event

(D) Other speakers who will attend the event

(E) The reason for the event

❼ How quickly should you respond to an invitation?

_____

_____

❽ Which is a better opening for a thank-you letter to a speaker?

(A) I would like to extend my thanks to you for speaking at our event.

(B) I would like to thank you for your speech, "Using English in the Working World," at our convention this past May.

2 Write an invitation letter.

Invite Karen Ellis, a client, to the launch party for your new line of gaming systems. The party will be held on Friday, June 2, 2023, at 6:30 p.m. at your store. She may bring a guest. You would like her to RSVP by May 31. She should bring this invitation to the event.

CHANGI ENTERTAINMENT DEVICES

72 Nathan Road, Tsim Sha Tsui, Kowloon
Hong Kong
Tel: 852-36821820 Fax: 852-36821820

May 16, 2023

Karen Ellis
12 Nathan Road
Tsim Sha Tsui, Kowloon
Hong Kong

Dear Ms. Ellis:

_____

_____

_____

_____

_____

_____

_____

_____

_____

_____

_____

_____

_____

_____

_____

_____

_____

_____

_____

_____

_____

_____

3 Write an invitation and response card.

Write an invitation and response card for a farewell dinner for Dr. Phillip Pushton, professor of sociology. Dr. Pushton has worked for the University of Sydney for 10 years. He will be retiring. The dinner will be held at Luhrman Hall, University of Sydney, on July 31, at 7:00 p.m. The host is Sydney Bankfield, dean of sociology. Business attire is suggested, and RSVPs are requested by July 25.

❶ An invitation card

Your presence is requested at a

_____

honoring Dr. Phillip Pushton, Professor of Sociology,
for his 10 years of service to this university

Hosted by Sydney Bankfield, Dean of Sociology,
on July 31 at 7 pm

at Luhrman Hall
University of Sydney

_____

Business attire suggested

❷ A response card

The favor of your response is _____

M _____

☐ _____

☐ _____

4 Write a letter inviting a guest to make a speech.

Imagine that you are an employee at Double Design. You are hosting a conference titled "The Future of Graphic Design in East Asia" on September 18, 2023. Write an invitation to Jane Ko to speak at the conference. Use the following details to write your invitation.

✓ This is the first conference, but you hope it will become an annual event.

✓ The conference will be held at the Mountain Jade Conference Center in Shanghai.

✓ You have confirmed George Lim of Dragon Design as a keynote speaker who will discuss the latest trends in graphic design.

✓ Other speakers include Susan Won of Design Limited, Chen Li-Ping of Studio A, and Boris Huang of East-West Graphics. All speakers will give a 30-minute presentation.

✓ About 300 people from companies in China, Japan, South Korea, and Taiwan are expected to attend the conference.

DOUBLE DESIGN

Room 205, Building 3
Lane 2498, Pudong Avenue
Shanghai, PRC

August 10, 2023

Jane Ko
Founder
Asterisk Design
29 Shuguang Lu, Building A
Hangzhou, PRC 310007

Dear Ms. Ko:

_____

_____

_____

_____

_____

_____

_____

_____

_____

_____

_____

_____

_____

_____

_____

_____

_____

_____

_____

_____

_____

_____

_____

_____

_____

_____

_____

_____

_____

_____

_____

5 Write a letter thanking a guest for making a speech.

Now write a letter to Jane Ko thanking her for her speech "Conservative or Cutting-Edge Advertising" at the conference discussed in the previous exercise. Tell Ms. Ko that her speech was well received and caused a great deal of discussion. Express your gratitude for her contribution and your hope that she will be a part of next year's conference as well.

DOUBLE DESIGN

Room 205, Building 3
Lane 2498, Pudong Avenue
Shanghai, PRC

September 20, 2023

Jane Ko
Founder
Asterisk Design
29 Shuguang Lu, Building A
Hangzhou, PRC 310007

Dear Ms. Ko:

_____

_____

_____

_____

_____

_____

_____

_____

_____

_____

_____

_____

_____

_____

_____

_____

_____

道歉信
Letters of Apology

Key Terms

apology 道歉
承認錯誤或失禮並表示歉意 。

contractual obligation 契約責任
簽訂合約的每一方根據契約內容所應承擔的責任；若有一方未完成契約責任，可能被視為違反契約，並須提供對方相應的賠償。

gift certificate 禮券
可用以在商店兌換面額等值商品或服務的票券；若店家造成顧客損失，可在道歉信中提議提供禮券作為補償。

implication 可能的後果
指從事某個行為後，在未來可能引發的後續影響。若在道歉信中直接承認疏失，須注意是否會引發法律後果（legal implications）。

ramifications 後果
具有關聯或衍生出的主題、問題等，一般也可以用指稱結果、後果、影響等。

rectification 改正
改正錯誤。

sympathy 同情
能體會他人的情緒，尤其是對悲傷或遭遇困境的人；同情、憐憫、惻隱之心。

如何撰寫道歉信？
How do I write letters of apology?

1 **什麼時候需要寄道歉信？**

　　寄道歉信的主要目的，是在你或你的公司犯下嚴重錯誤，或得罪顧客、商務夥伴等其他重要的合作夥伴時，**為挽救雙方之間的關係而寫的書信**。只要你有出錯，不管是送錯貨、送出的貨物有瑕疵、帳目出錯、忘記約定行程（appointment）等，**就應該立刻寄一封道歉信給對方。**

　　寫信道歉顯示你的確知道如何做生意，也知道自己犯了錯。如果不表示道歉，就顯示你不覺得有出錯的地方（以及你不知道如何做生意），或是你不重視雙方之間的關係（因此也不需要或不想要跟對方做生意）。

　　你唯一需要猶豫的時候，是該道歉信可能會引起法律後果（legal ramifications）時。有時候道歉信就如同承認已方有過失或有罪，尤其是當公司為了沒有履行合約義務（contractual obligation）而道歉時。如果你擔心道歉信會引發法律後果（implication），那就先跟律師談一談。你也可以嘗試在措辭上表達同情（sympathy），但避免直接承認責任，例如：

❶❷ 著重在措辭上表達同情；未提及失誤者何人，避免暗示問題是己方的責任。

> **❶** We are sorry that you did not receive your order.
> 很抱歉，您未能收到訂單貨品。
>
> **❷** I am sorry your computer was damaged.
> 很遺憾您的電腦壞了。

❸❹ 直接描述錯誤；坦承自身或公司犯錯，承認問題是我方造成，較可能衍生法律後果。

> **❸** We are sorry that we did not send your order.
> 很抱歉，我們未將您訂購的貨物寄出。
>
> **❹** I'm sorry I dropped your computer.
> 很抱歉，我把您的電腦摔壞了。

2 撰寫道歉信應遵守的原則

❶ 出錯後立刻寄出道歉信：道歉信**越早寄出越好**。

❷ 遵守正式商務書信的原則：這顯示出你對對方的尊重。

❸ 直截了當：**一開始就道歉**，並說明道歉的原因。

❹ 語言簡單誠懇：太過誇張的語言會顯得虛假，語言要**簡單明瞭**。

❺ 解釋出錯的原因：**解釋出錯的原因**，通常會讓對方更容易接受你的道歉，畢竟人非聖賢，誰能無過。但是要確定你的解釋僅是用來說明引發出錯的原因，**不要成為開脫過錯的藉口**，顯示你會為你的錯誤負起責任。

❻ 建議解決或改正的方法：清楚說明你打算**如何解決這個問題**，例如退款、重新發貨、修改你的送貨政策等。但是記住，並不是每種問題都有解決的辦法。

❼ 得體周到：確定你已經思考過這個問題**對對方造成了什麼樣的影響**。建議賠償或解決方法時要特別謹慎：如果是服務上的小問題，贈送禮券（gift certificate）也許就能安撫顧客，但是如果是更嚴重的問題，這種金錢上的補償可能反而會得罪顧客。**每個問題需要以不同的方法解決**。

❽ 在道歉信上簽名：**親自簽名**也顯示出對對方的尊重。

帕特先生您好：

我從紀錄中發現，您於 10 月 30 日所訂購的兩套 Solingen 廚房刀具組到貨延遲了三天，於 11 月 15 日才送達。請接受我的道歉。在此向您保證：本公司一向都能夠準時到貨。

希望此次延遲到貨沒有引起您太多的不便。誠心期盼有再次為您服務的機會。如果還有任何疑慮需要我說明，歡迎來電與我聯絡：(49) 60767210。

Unit 78 為延遲到貨道歉
Apology for a late shipment

　　現代顧客習慣以網路等方式遠距購物，但廠商未必能將貨物準時送達。延遲到貨的影響可大可小，若發生這類錯誤，除了須以道歉信誠懇致歉，並須**視錯誤的嚴重程度**，判斷是否或應該提供**何種補償措施**。

78-1 | Apology letter: A late shipment 貨物延遲的道歉信

BLUMENSCHEIN, INC.

Adickesallee 3, 94855
Frankfurt am Main, Germany

23 November 2023

Samuel Potts
Mailander Strasse 4
Frankfurt am Main, 60598

❶ 本信簡短且直截了當，第一段就說明道歉原因、表達道歉之意，並保證錯誤屬於偶發意外。

Dear Mr. Potts:

It has come to my attention that your order of 30 October for two Solingen Kitchen Sets was delivered three days late on 15 November. Please accept my apologies. I assure you that our company otherwise has a solid record of on-time deliveries.

I hope the delay did not cause you considerable inconvenience. We look forward to having an opportunity to serve you again. Please call me at (49) 60767210 if you have any concerns that I can address.

Yours sincerely,

Karl Blumenschein

Karl Blumenschein
Operations Manager, Blumenschein, Inc.

❷ 然而，或許寫信者認為延誤到貨未造成對方太多損失，因此並未主動提供補償。收信者收到信後，可考量實際狀況，決定是否回信向對方索取補償。

寄出瑕疵品可能使訂貨廠商無法如期提供商品給消費者，造成極大不便，導致對方未來不願意再次向己方訂貨，因此針對此類錯誤，道歉信中須詳加**說明錯誤原因**，並提供**適當的補償**，以期對方重拾信心，往後依然願意再次惠顧。

79-1 | Apology letter: A defective shipment 瑕疵商品的道歉信

CHANGI ENTERTAINMENT DEVICES

72 Nathan Road, Tsim Sha Tsui, Kowloon
Hong Kong
Tel: 852-36821820 Fax: 852-36821820

September 11, 2023

Gregory McMannis
Bleeps and Beeps
17 Talavera Rd
Macquarie Park
NSW 2113

Re: Your PO 91115a

Dear Mr. McMannis:

We are very sorry that the shipment of goods (Purchase Order No. 91115a) that you received on September 10 contained defective items. We understand your disappointment and appreciate the inconvenience this must have caused your company.

There is no question that some of the products we shipped did not meet the very high standards our customers have come to expect and should continue to demand.

We usually adhere to the strictest quality control procedures in our selection, packing, and shipping processes. We are reviewing your purchase's movement through our system to discover where the problem occurred. We value our reputation for the highest-quality products and service, and I can assure you that we are taking steps to ensure this type of mistake does not happen again.

Your replacement order will be shipped free of charge by close of business today. Our shippers will collect the defective items at the time of delivery. I would also like to offer you a 15% discount and free shipping on your next order with us.

We look forward to continuing our mutually beneficial relationship. If we can do anything else to minimize your inconvenience in regard to this matter, please don't hesitate to contact us.

Sincerely,

Julian Zhang

Julian Zhang
Vice President of Marketing
Changi Entertainment Devices

參考文號：貴公司的 91115a 號訂購單

麥曼尼斯先生您好：

非常抱歉，您於 9 月 10 日所收到的貨物（訂單號碼 91115a）含有瑕疵品。我們了解您一定非常失望，也了解這對貴公司一定引起了相當大的不便。

這批貨物中有些商品，無疑並未達到我們的顧客所一貫期望的高標準。

在商品挑選、包裝和運送過程中，我們一般都會遵照最嚴格的品質監控流程。我們目前正在檢查您所訂購的商品，當初在整個流程中的處理經過，以找出問題發生的原因。我們珍惜本公司以優質產品與服務所打造的口碑，而我可以跟您保證，我們正在採取相關步驟，避免類似的錯誤再次發生。

換貨商品將於今天下班前為您免費寄出。換貨送達時，我們的運輸公司將同時收回瑕疵的貨物。此外，我也會提供您下一次訂購商品時，享有 15% 的折扣和免運費的優惠。

誠心期盼能夠繼續維護我們的互惠關係。如果還有任何我們能夠提供協助的地方，以減少這次疏失所引起的不便，請不吝與我們聯絡。

❶ 在信件開頭直截了當地以簡單誠懇的語句致歉，並設想錯誤可能造成對方的困擾，展現體貼周到。

❷ 寫作者表示公司已經著手調查出錯原因，並承諾未來會加以改正。

❸ 提出解決本次錯誤的方法（replacement），並給予後續補償措施（下筆訂單折扣且免運費），以展現致歉誠意。

為帳目錯誤道歉
Apology for accounting errors

　　帳目錯誤由於**具體牽涉金錢往來**，往往觸動雙方敏感神經，因此若發生帳目處理上的錯誤，務必要致歉並**詳加說明出錯原因**，**安撫對方不愉快的情緒**，並保證此類錯誤不會再次發生。

80-1 | Apology letter: Accounting errors 帳目錯誤的道歉信

Exotic Textiles, Inc.

16, Talkatora Road, New Delhi 110001
Ph: 24787040 Fax: 24787042

25 April 2023

Annette Adahl
City Styles
3111 M Street, N.W.
Washington, DC 20007-3705

❶ 寫信者在第一段迅速為近期的帳務錯誤致歉，並表明本信目的：解釋出錯的原因，並針對出錯深表歉意。

Dear Ms. Adahl:

I am so sorry about the recent difficulties with your account. This letter is intended to explain the mistakes that were made and express our deepest regrets.

As you know, it has taken some time to find out exactly what happened. Unfortunately, these matters sometimes take time to fully understand. I hope that you accept our apologies for the delay in this response.

Your payment for your last shipment was indeed received on time. Unfortunately, a new employee in our Accounting Department credited the payment to an account with a name similar to yours. That is why you began receiving overdue notices, which we were sending in accordance with our policy. When we discovered the error, it took some time for the Accounting Department to notify the Credit Department; unfortunately, by then the notices had already been sent and could not be recalled.

I can imagine how aggravating this has been for you, especially with your history of prompt payment. I am deeply sorry that it has taken so long to straighten out this problem. Although we do have procedures in place to prevent this type of error, they appear to have broken down in this case. We are reevaluating these procedures to make them more effective.

You have been a valued customer of ours for a long time, and we appreciate your affording us the opportunity to serve you. Please rest assured that this error will not happen again.

Yours faithfully,

Malika Karmarkar

Malika Karmarkar
Sales Manager
Exotic Textiles, New Delhi

❸ 寫信者在最後兩段盡力安撫對方情緒，表明體會收信者的不滿、肯定收信者是該公司重要的客戶，並且保證類似錯誤不會再發生，以期對方重拾信任。

亞達爾女士您好：

非常抱歉近日發生帳目疏失，這封信意在為您解釋出錯的原因，並表達我們至深的歉意。

如您所知，我們花了一段時間才找出出錯的確切原因。希望您能夠諒解，這種狀況往往需要花上一段時間才能完全釐清，並就這遲來的回應接受我們的道歉。

您為上一筆的訂單所付的款項，我們的確準時收到了。抱歉的是，會計部門的一位新進員工，把這筆款項記入另一位與您名稱相似的顧客帳戶上了。這就是為什麼您後來，開始收到我們依公司政策寄出的付款逾期通知。當我們發現這個錯誤後，會計部門花了一段時間才通知信用部門此事，但是已經寄出的通知當然無法再收回來了。

我可以想像這個狀況對您來說一定非常不愉快，尤其您一向都迅速付款。非常抱歉我們花了這麼久才修正問題。我們一向有固定的流程以預防這類錯誤發生，但是這一次這個流程似乎失效了。我們正在檢討這些流程，並思考改善的方法。

您長久以來一向是我們極為重視的顧客，我們感謝您給我們機會為您服務。請您放心，這樣的錯誤不會再發生了。

❷ 第二段中說明寫信者所屬公司對於找出問題所付出的努力，第三段則詳細說明問題發生的原因，為整起事件提供合理解釋，有助於收信者諒解錯誤。

道歉信常用說法
Common phrases for letters of apology

1 Making apologies 道歉

❶ Please accept our apologies for _____ [overlooking your order, sending the wrong goods, etc.]

對於……〔我們遺漏了您的訂單╱我們送錯商品等〕，請接受我們的道歉。

❷ We apologize for this error. 我們為此疏失道歉。

❸ We deeply regret that _____ [your order was late, etc.]

我們非常抱歉……〔您所訂購的商品到貨延遲等〕

2 Offering explanations 提出解釋

❶ We assure you the problem won't happen again . . .

我們向您保證，這個問題不會再發生……

❷ We assure you it won't happen again . . .

我們向您保證，這不會再發生……

❸ We are looking into what may have happened . . .

我們正在調查可能的原因……

❹ We believe the reason for this mistake was . . .

我們相信發生這個錯誤的原因是……

❺ We have discovered why . . . 我們已經查出來為什麼……

❻ The error was apparently caused by . . . 這個疏失發生的原因據悉是……

3 Offering restitution / suggesting a course of action
提供賠償 / 建議補救方法

❶ We are happy to tell you that the replacement merchandise was shipped today . . .

我們很高興能夠通知您，換貨的商品已於今天寄出⋯⋯

❷ We will be happy to send a technician to you immediately . . .

我們非常樂意立即派一位技師過去⋯⋯

❸ We are prepared to offer you a 25% discount on your next order . . .

下一次訂購商品時，您將可享有 25% 的折扣⋯⋯

❹ We hope you will accept this _____ [coupon, discount, voucher] as a gesture of our goodwill . . .

為表達我們的誠意，特贈送您此份〔優惠券／折扣／抵用券〕，希望您笑納⋯⋯

❺ Please hold _____ [the damaged goods] to be picked up by our agents . . .

請保存好〔損壞的商品〕，待本公司專員收回⋯⋯

❻ Kindly hold the extra shipment for our return agents to collect . . .

請保存好多餘的商品，待本公司退貨專員收回⋯⋯

1 Review the concepts

❶ Why might you send a letter of apology?

_____

_____

❷ Under what circumstances should you avoid sending a letter of apology for making a mistake?

_____

_____

❸ What does it mean to express sympathy rather than responsibility?

_____

_____

_____

❹ In the business context, what is the main purpose of an apology?
(A) To save face
(B) To prevent a lawsuit
(C) To save a relationship

❺ Which of the following should a letter of apology definitely not do?
(A) Offer a clear apology
(B) Point out areas where the reader was to blame
(C) Accept responsibility for the mistake
(D) Explain what is being done to rectify the mistake

2 True (T) or False (F)

❶ ☐ True ☐ False　You should usually send a letter of apology as soon as possible after a mistake has been made.

❷ ☐ True ☐ False　It is always appropriate to offer compensation after a mistake.

❸ ☐ True ☐ False　Letters of apology should be very long and very formal.

❹ ☐ True ☐ False　Letters of apology should be personally signed.

❺ ☐ True ☐ False　Letters of apology should be sent on company letterhead.

3 Read the following apology letter and rewrite it.

Read this apology letter. Identify any problems with the tone, the information, and the structure of the letter. Then rewrite the letter so it is more appropriate.

Exotic Textiles, Inc.
16, Talkatora Road, New Delhi 110001
Ph: 24787040 Fax: 24787042

June 2, 2023

Marie Somtow
Duds
P.O. Box 748
Bangkok 10501, Thailand

Dear Ms. Somtow:

Thank you for your correspondence of May 30. I trust that business is going well in Thailand and that you have received our latest catalog. I look forward to receiving your fall order.

I am very sorry for the damage that occurred to your shipment while it was in transit. Obviously, the damage was inflicted by the shipping company, not by Exotic Textiles. If you had informed us of the damage earlier, we would have replaced the shipment in a more timely fashion.

I look forward to continuing our relationship.

Yours faithfully,

Malika Karmarkar

Malika Karmarkar
Sales Manager
Exotic Textiles, New Delhi

Problems:

1 _____

_____

2 _____

_____

3 _____

_____

4 _____

_____

Rewrite!

Exotic Textiles, Inc.
16, Talkatora Road, New Delhi 110001
Ph: 24787040 Fax: 24787042

June 2, 2023

Marie Somtow
Duds
P.O. Box 748
Bangkok 10501, Thailand

Dear Ms. Somtow:

_____

_____
_____
_____
_____
_____
_____
_____
_____
_____
_____
_____
_____
_____
_____
_____
_____
_____
_____

4 Write a letter of apology (I).

You work for Jupiter Systems. A customer recently complained about a negative experience while having your products installed—the installation technician was rude, he installed the products improperly, and he was not responsive when the customer called him repeatedly to fix the problems. Write back to apologize. Include the following information:

✓ You are sorry for the problems that occurred during the installation.

✓ You have spoken to the employee, who was a contractor, and have terminated his contract.

✓ You understand that the customer's system is functioning now, but you would like to send another employee to check it.

✓ You will refund the customer's installation fee.

Jupiter Systems

6 Temasek Boulevard, #8-00 Suntec Tower Four, Singapore 038986
Tel: +65 65299123   Fax: +65 67399124

April 8, 2023

Penelope Parsons
Parsons, Inc.
200 Anson Road
Singapore 079903

Dear Ms. Parsons:

_____

_____

_____

_____

_____

_____

_____

_____

_____

---

5 Write a letter of apology (II).

You work for City Styles. A customer recently wrote to say that three shirts she bought there were ruined while being washed, even though she followed the washing instructions. Write back to apologize.

Offer to replace her shirts if she would like to exchange them for the same shirts or products of equal value. Explain that your clothes are usually of the highest quality and that you are checking the washing instructions of that whole product line to ensure that they are correct.

City Styles

3111 M Street, N.W., Washington, DC 20007-3705

May 4, 2023

Louisa Ortiz
123 Mount Pleasant Street NW
Washington, DC 20003

Dear Ms. Ortiz:

_____

_____

_____

_____

_____

_____

_____

_____

_____

_____

_____

_____

_____

_____

_____

_____

_____

_____

祝賀信
Letters of Congratulations

anniversary (with a company)
（就職）週年紀念日

指員工任職同一家公司期間，從就職日起算的每週年的日期。不同公司對於員工就職週年紀念的慶祝方式各不相同，有些公司可能會在當天寄發祝賀信。

congratulations 祝賀、恭喜

指祝賀的行為，也可作感嘆詞，用來恭賀他人的成功或好運，如：「Congratulations! You have just won the lottery!」（恭喜！您中樂透了！）

dramatic 戲劇化的；誇張的

用來形容文字時，意為過於誇張而顯得虛偽、不誠懇的。撰寫祝賀信或任何商務信件時，都應避免戲劇化的措辭。

distract 轉移焦點

指使人的注意力從事物的重點移開。寫作祝賀信時，內容應緊扣祝賀的主題，避免提及無關細節，使信件的焦點被轉移。

expand 擴大、擴展

在程度、大小、容量、規模等方面增加，如：「He hopes to expand his company.」（他想擴展他的公司。）

expansion 擴大、擴展

在商務情境中，常指公司增加營運地點，或擴大營運規模。若合作的公司有擴張的行動，可透過祝賀信加以祝福。

fortunate 吉利的、吉祥的

帶來好運或暗示好運的；帶來好結果的。

(mis)interpret（錯誤）解讀

「interpret」意為「解讀」，指分析、理解特定文本中的訊息涵意；「misinterpret」則代表涵義解讀錯誤。撰寫祝賀信時，應避免可能使讀者錯誤解讀訊息的表達方法。

project 專案

為了達成特定目的所從事的一系列任務或活動，通常設有完成期限，由專案經理（project manager）負責管理專案任務分配和時間流程。

sarcasm 挖苦

尖酸刻薄的嘲弄。

sarcastic 挖苦的

尖酸刻薄的，嘲弄的。

Unit	如何撰寫祝賀信？
82	How do I write a letter of congratulations?

1 什麼時候應該寫祝賀信？

祝賀信目的為**恭賀對方的喜事或成就**。有很多時候都適合寄送祝賀信，例如：

- 升遷（promotion）或達成傑出的成就。
- 圓滿完成困難的任務。
- 員工任職週年紀念（anniversary）。
- 銷售量（sales）或生產量（productivity）增加。
- 公司擴展（expansion）。
- 新事業開張。
- 小孩出生。

2 如何撰寫祝賀信？

祝賀信的內容應該**清晰誠懇**，寫作時可以遵守下列原則，以避免對方誤解（misinterpret）你的意思：

❶ **確定你的祝賀是恰當的**：確定對方**不會因為收到你的祝賀信而感到不自在**。如果是對方不想公開的事件，或是同時伴有負面意味的事件，這時寄祝賀信就不恰當了。

❷ **迅速**：聽到好消息後就要**盡快**寄出祝賀信。

❸ **具體**：**開頭就說明**你要祝賀的是什麼事。

❹ **只說好話**：**著重稱讚對方的成就**，不要包含任何負面的評語或消息，也不要講到你自己的近況，以免轉移（distract）祝賀信的重點。

❺ **簡潔**：祝賀信應該**簡短**，長度控制在**一頁**以內。

❻ **把焦點放在對方身上**：絕對**不要**用任何方式，**暗示對方的喜事應該給連帶你帶來什麼好處**，這樣會使整封祝賀信顯得很不誠懇（insincere）。

❼ **注意你的語氣**：使用**簡單而正面**的文字，誇張的文字會使你的祝賀信聽起來語帶挖苦（sarcastic）或嘲弄（mocking）。

恭賀升遷的祝賀信除了要把握上一單元說明的各項原則之外，可以著重說明**為何你覺得對方值得受到升遷**，並**回顧雙方的業務往來關係**，讓對方喜悅之餘還能加深對你的印象。

83-1 | Congratulation letter: Promotion 升遷的祝賀信

Lee Chef Supply

65 Chien Hsing Road, San Min District
Kaohsiung City, Taiwan

December 25, 2023

> 布魯門欽女士您好：
>
> 恭喜您榮升 Blumenschein, Inc. 業務經理！
>
> Lee Chef Supply 全體員工一向賞識您的認真努力，以及對您的工作與雙方關係的付出。您的表現與奉獻對於維持雙方商務夥伴關係，扮演了很重要的角色。我們十分樂見您的成就，也確信 Blumenschein, Inc. 就業務經理的新人選，做出了最佳決定。

Trudi Blumenschein
Blumenschein, Inc.
Adickesallee 3
94855
Frankfurt am Main
Germany

Dear Ms. Blumenschein:

Congratulations on your promotion to sales manager at Blumenschein, Inc.!

We at Lee Chef Supply have always appreciated your hard work and dedication to your job and to the relationship between our two companies. Your performance and commitment play a large part in our continuing business partnership. We are very pleased at your success, and we are sure that Blumenschein, Inc., has selected the best candidate for its new sales manager.

Best regards,

Lee Wen

Lee Wen, Lee Chef Supply

Unit 84 祝賀圓滿完成任務
Congratulations on the completion of a project

恭賀對方圓滿達成工作任務時，除了祝福的話語外，也可以描述對方**至今的努力過程**，以及**任務達成後的正面成果**，讓對方感受到過去的付出是值得的。此外，若可以提供禮品，不妨一併附上。

84-1 | Congratulation letter: Completion of a project
任務完成的祝賀信

OIL INDUSTRY ENVIRONMENTAL
AWARENESS COUNSEL
88 10th Avenue SE, Calgary, Alberta
Phone: 403-299-8876   Fax: 403-255-6933

August 14, 2023

Ms. Claire Purvis
OIEAC
88 10th Avenue SE
Calgary, Alberta

Dear Ms. Purvis:

I would like to congratulate you and the entire OIEA Conference planning team on a job well done. This year's conference was the best attended, best run event so far. All of us at OIEAC know this is due to your hard work.

When we first started planning for the conference six months ago, we knew there would be bumps in the road. You have handled each with grace and poise. We have received numerous positive comments from speakers and attendees about the conference program, which you helped create, as well as the organization and facilities.

Congratulations again on a stellar conference. Thank you for your dedication—I hope you feel, as I do, that it has paid off wonderfully.

Please find enclosed a $50 gift certificate to the Rosewood Spa in Calgary. We are happy to offer you this expression of our gratitude.

Best wishes,

Peter Tochs

Peter Tochs
Executive Director
Oil Industry Environmental Awareness Counsel

Enc. (1)

普必思女士您好：

在此恭喜您和全體 OIEA 研討會計畫小組圓滿完成此次籌辦工作。今年的研討會是歷年來參加人數最多、辦理最順利的一場。OIEAC 的全體人員都知道，這歸功於你們的努力付出。

半年前我們開始規劃研討會時，我們知道過程中一定會遇到不少障礙。你們則沉著自信地克服了每一個障礙。研討會的演講者和與會者，就你們協助安排的研討會議程，以及籌劃和設備給了我們無數的好評。

再次恭喜此次研討會圓滿成功。謝謝你們的付出，而希望你們跟我一樣，覺得這一切都很值得。

隨信附上一份位於卡加利的玫瑰木 Spa 中心 50 加幣禮券，聊表我們的謝意。

商業夥伴擴展業務時，寄送祝賀信可以展現關心和友善。在此類祝賀信中，可以說明你認為**對方公司有何長處，可以達到業務擴展的成果**，並表示**樂見對方持續茁壯發展**。

85-1 | Congratulation letter: Expansion of a business 公司擴展的祝賀信

CHANGI ENTERTAINMENT DEVICES

72 Nathan Road, Tsim Sha Tsui, Kowloon
Hong Kong
Tel: 852-36821820 Fax: 852-36821820

13 August 2023

Gregory McMannis
Bleeps and Beeps
17 Talavera Rd
Macquarie Park
NSW 2113

Dear Mr. McMannis:

Congratulations on the expansion of Bleeps and Beeps. We at Changi Entertainment Devices are very pleased to hear of your growth.

We know you must be proud of having achieved a level of success that few firms reach. Your strong leadership and the company's quality are surely the main factors that brought you to this point.

Please accept our heartiest congratulations and best wishes for your continued success.

Sincerely,

Julian Zhang

Julian Zhang
Vice President of Marketing
Changi Entertainment Devices

麥曼尼斯先生您好：

恭賀 Bleeps and Beeps 擴展業務！ Changi Entertainment Devices 全體員工都很高興聽到貴公司的成長。

貴公司達到的成就實屬不易，令許多其他公司望其項背，我們知道您一定引以為榮。您優異的領導能力與公司素質，無疑是其中的主要功臣。

請接受我們最誠摯的恭賀，並祝貴公司往後也一切順利成功。

Unit 86　祝賀任職週年紀念
Congratulations on an anniversary with a company

若公司員工任職週年，老闆或主管可以藉機寄送祝賀信，以表達對員工付出的重視。信中可以**誇讚員工的工作表現**並**給予肯定**，並表達期許員工未來持續為公司盡力、維持一貫的優良表現。

86-1 │ Congratulation letter: Anniversary with a company 任職週年的祝賀信

Exotic Textiles, Inc.
16, Talkatora Road, New Delhi 110001
Ph: 24787040 Fax: 24787042

24 July 2023

Malika Karmarkar
Exotic Textiles, Inc.
16 Talkatora Road
New Delhi 110001

Dear Ms. Karmarkar:

I would like to congratulate you on your fifth anniversary with Exotic Textiles. On behalf of the entire company, I thank you for your hard work and dedication over these five years!

We know that our superior staff is the reason we are able to thrive. We are so appreciative of your contributions—we would not enjoy the success we do without professionals like you. It is you and your colleagues who make Exotic Textiles great.

We hope that you will remain with us for many years to come. Congratulations on this anniversary and best wishes for your continued success!

Yours truly,

Madhu Jai

Madhu Jai
President, Exotic Textiles

> 卡瑪卡女士您好：
>
> 恭賀您在 Exotic Textiles 任職滿 5 週年，我在此代表公司全體員工，感謝您這 5 年來的努力與付出！
>
> 我們知道優秀的員工，是公司能夠欣欣向榮的原因。我們非常感謝您對公司的貢獻：少了您這樣的專業人才，我們今天就不可能享有這樣的成功。是您和您的同事，使得 Exotic Textiles 能夠成長茁壯。
>
> 希望您還會留在本公司很長一段時間。再次恭喜您在本公司任職滿 5 週年，並祝您往後也一切順利成功！

祝賀信常用說法
Common phrases for letters of congratulations

1 Offering congratulations 表達恭賀

❶ In recognition of _____ [the completion of a project, etc.], I want to commend you for your _____ [hard work, dedication, etc.].

恭喜……〔您圓滿完成此一企畫等〕，您的〔認真努力、付出等〕尤其值得嘉許。

❷ It is our great pleasure to congratulate you on . . .

我們很開心地恭喜您……

❸ Many congratulations on _____ [your new business venture, award, etc.]

恭賀……〔您的新投資、獎項等〕

❹ Please accept the congratulations of all of us at _____ [company name] . . .

請接受〔公司名稱〕全體員工的祝賀……

❺ We share in your happiness at . . .

您在……一事的喜悅，我們都感同身受。

❻ We are taking this opportunity to congratulate you on . . .

我們想趁此機會恭喜您……

❼ We were delighted to hear about . . .

我們非常高興聽到……

❽ We would like to offer you our warmest congratulations on . . .

我們想就……一事，致上最誠摯的恭賀。

2 Offering good wishes 表達祝福

1 I hope to hear of many more achievements in the future.

希望未來能夠聽到您／貴公司更多的成就。

2 We look forward to your continued progress.

祝您／貴公司未來不斷進展。

3 We look forward to your continued success.

祝您／貴公司未來持續成功。

4 We look forward to your continued growth.

祝您／貴公司未來不斷成長。

5 We wish you continued success . . .

祝您／貴公司往後也一切順利成功……

6 We wish you every happiness . . .

祝您順心如意……

7 With all good wishes for _____ [this endeavor, future projects, etc.]

祝……〔此次任務／未來的企畫等〕一切順利……

8 With best wishes for every success . . .

祝一切順利……

1 Review the concepts

❶ What is a letter of congratulations?

_____

_____

❷ Why is it important to choose your vocabulary carefully in a letter of congratulations?

_____

_____

❸ Under what circumstances might it be inappropriate to write a letter of congratulations?

_____

_____

❹ Which of these circumstances might call for a letter of congratulations?

(A) A wedding

(B) The expansion of a business

(C) A restructuring

(D) A promotion

(E) The completion of a long project

❺ Which statement would be a good first sentence in a letter of congratulations?

(A) Congratulations on your achievement.

(B) Thank you for your correspondence.

(C) How are you enjoying your new responsibilities?

❻ Which of these statements is true about letters of congratulations?

(A) They should be sent as soon as possible after the fortunate event.

(B) They should reference how the fortunate event can benefit the writer as well as the reader.

(C) They should be as long as possible.

(D) They should use dramatic language.

2 Write a letter of congratulations.

Imagine that you work for Professional PR. A long-term client of yours, Mr. Mare, has just had a baby boy. Write a letter of congratulations to him.

PROFESSIONAL PR

12 Eunos Road 6
Singapore 408600
Tel: 65 68 394058   Fax: 65 68 8574965

March 15, 2023

Oscar Mare
9 Pickering Street
Singapore 038986

Dear _____ :

_____

_____

_____

_____

_____

_____

_____

_____

_____

_____

_____

_____

_____

_____

_____

_____

_____

_____

_____

_____

3 Mark and rewrite.

Mark what is wrong in this letter of congratulations. Then rewrite the letter so it is more appropriate.

Duds

P.O. Box 748, Bangkok 10501, Thailand
Ph: 66-2-8475934 Fax: 66-2-8470394

May 3, 2023

Attention: Malika Karmarkar
Exotic Textiles, Inc.
16, Talkatora Road
New Delhi 110001

Dear Ms. Karmarkar,

I trust all is well at Exotic Textiles, Inc. Congratulations! We just heard the good news!

For someone of your exceptional talents and incredible business sense, it was only a matter of time before you moved into a top position. We at Duds have seen it coming for a long time. Only the other day, I told a colleague here, "Ms. Karmarkar is sure to be promoted soon." Well, it seems I was right! Finally, Exotic Textiles has seen what a shining star you are.

I am sure that with your new position, the relationship between Duds and Exotic Textiles will be strengthened and improved. I am looking forward to the evolution of our trading partnership.

Again, let us offer our heartfelt congratulations on your achievement. You certainly deserve it.

Best wishes,

Aroon Pradabtanakij

Aroon Pradabtanakij
Manager, Duds Clothing

Problems:

1. _____

2. _____

3. _____

4. _____

Rewrite!

Duds

P.O. Box 748, Bangkok 10501, Thailand
Ph: 66-2-8475934 Fax: 66-2-8470394

May 3, 2023

Attention: Malika Karmarkar
Exotic Textiles, Inc.
16, Talkatora Road
New Delhi 110001

Dear _____ :

_____

_____

_____

_____

_____

_____

_____

_____

_____

_____

_____

_____

_____

_____

_____

_____

_____

_____

_____

_____

其他商務書信
Other Types of Business Correspondence

Key Terms

compatible 契合的；相容的

指兩個或以上事物能夠和諧共存，或能順利和彼此共事及共同運作。在宣布公司合併的書信中，可用此形容詞強調兩家公司彼此契合、合併後可以共存共榮。

correspondence 通信；信函

透過書信或電子郵件等方式的通信，尤其指稱正式的商務通信。

customized 客製化的

根據顧客需求量身打造的，用來形容產品或服務根據顧客特定需求製作、規劃。

entity 實體

獨立存在的個體，在商務情境下可用來指稱各自獨立的單位組織，如企業或政府單位等。

expertise 專業；專才

在特定領域和主題上具有的專門知識、技能等。

merger 合併

兩間以上的公司或組織合併為一間；動詞形態為「merge」。

relocate 搬遷

公司或個人搬到新的地點。當公司搬遷時，為確保合作夥伴能得知新地點的消息，應發信告知搬遷事宜。

Unit 88 公告公司地址變更的信件
Correspondence regarding change of company address

　　如果公司地址有改變，務必要通知顧客和業務夥伴，以便對方能夠以正確地址和己方聯絡。地址更改的消息應在公司**實際搬遷之前寄出**，好讓顧客和業務夥伴有時間更新他們的紀錄，並在**完成搬遷後再寄信**通知一次。以下為通知地址變更的範例信。

88-1 | A letter regarding change of company address 宣告公司地址變更的信

DOUBLE DESIGN
Room 205, Building 3
Lane 2498, Pudong Avenue
Shanghai, PRC

November 30, 2023

National Architectural Supply
29 Shuguang Lu, Building A
Hangzhou, PRC 310007

Dear Sirs:

Please be advised that Double Design will be relocating on December 10, 2023. Please direct all correspondence to our new offices at:

Double Design
No. 106 FuxingDong Road
Huangpu Area
Shangha, PRC 201002

Our phone and fax numbers will remain the same:

Telephone: 21-62288777
Fax: 21-62288778

Thank you for your attention. We look forward to continued prosperity in our new location.

Best,

Xiao Wei Lin

Xiao Wei Lin, Double Design

貴公司諸君您好：

在此向貴公司告知，Double Design 將自 2023 年 12 月 10 日起搬到下列的新地址，往後來信請寄至：

201002 中國上海市
黃浦區
復興東路 106 號
Double Design

我們的電話與傳真號碼將維持不變：

電話：21-62288777
傳真：21-62288778

感謝貴公司留意配合。期盼遷址後，我們依舊能與貴公司共創佳績。

宣布公司合併的信件
Correspondence regarding a merger of companies

　　不同的公司有時候會合併（merge）為一間公司。這時顧客會想知道這對他們會有什麼影響。大多時候公司合併對顧客並沒有什麼影響，因此宣布公司合併的信應該用來告訴顧客，合併並不會影響他們與你從事業務的方式；如果有影響，也是正面的影響。

89-1 | A sample letter announcing a merger 宣布公司合併的信

Quality Training, Ltd

1000 Condor Drive, Suite 4
San Bruno, CA 94066
415.734.9857

January 8, 2023

Arthur Consultants
Metro South, 135 Auburn Ave. NE
Atlanta, GA 30303

Dear Sirs:

We are pleased to announce that Quality Training, Ltd., and Caspar Communication Group, Ltd., have formally merged. Doing business as Quality Training Group, Inc., we will continue to provide you with effective, customized training solutions to your business problems.

This new entity is a synergistic combination of two successful companies. After working together on several long-term projects, we realized how compatible our approaches to training are, even though we each bring unique expertise to our endeavors. Caspar Communication Group's long history of organizational and process-level solutions complements Quality Training's intensive, customized approach. By combining the two, we are able to offer our clients a broader range of services without sacrificing our depth of expertise.

We look forward to continuing to provide you with the service and support you have come to expect from us and to expand both our range of services and their quality. As always, don't hesitate to contact me with any questions or concerns at 415.734.9857 or over email at cooks@qualitygroup.com.

I look forward to hearing from you.

Regards,

Sam Cook

Sam Cook, President of Marketing

貴公司諸君您好：

很高興通知您，Quality Training, Ltd. 與 Caspar Communication Group, Ltd. 已正式合併了，往後我們將以 Quality Training Group, Inc. 的新名稱，繼續為您提供量身訂做的有效培訓計畫，來解決您業務上的問題。

Quality Training Group, Inc. 結合了兩間成功的公司。在幾個長期企畫上合作過後，我們發現雙方儘管各有所長，訓練的途徑卻相當契合。Caspar Communication Group 長久以來提供組織和流程上的解決方案，與 Quality Training 進行密集客製化訓練的做法相輔相成。結合兩間公司的優點，我們現在能夠為客戶提供更廣泛、但是同樣保留專業深度的服務。

誠心期盼能夠繼續不負期待，提供您服務與支持，並擴展我們的服務範圍、提升服務品質。若有任何疑問，歡迎再與我聯絡：415.734.9857 或 cooks@qualitygroup.com。

期盼您再與我們聯繫。

其他商務書信常用說法
Common phrases for other types of business correspondence

1 Phrases about moving 宣布公司搬遷

1 We are now located at _____ [address] . . .

本公司目前地址為〔新地址〕……

---

2 Our new location is . . .　　　　　　　我們的新地址是……

---

3 Our offices have relocated to . . .　　　本公司辦公室已搬到……

---

4 You can now find us at . . .　　　　　　您現在可以在……找到我們。

---

2 Phrases for describing mergers 宣布公司合併

1 We would like to announce the merger of _____ [company name] with _____ [company name] to form _____ [merged company name].

在此通知您，〔公司名〕與〔公司名〕已合併為〔合併後的公司名〕。

---

2 We would like to inform you that _____ [company name] will be merging with _____ [company name], effective _____ [date]. We will do business as _____ [merged company name].

在此通知您，〔公司名〕將自〔日期〕起與〔公司名〕合併，以〔合併後的公司名〕之名繼續營運。

---

3 We believe this merger will allow both companies to . . .

我們相信此次合併，將能使兩間公司都……

---

4 This merger will not affect our _____ [departments, services, etc.].

此次合併並不會影響我們的〔部門、服務等〕。

---

5 The most noticeable aspect of this merger will be . . .

此次合併最大的特點是……

---

6 We will continue to uphold our tradition of [great customer service, etc.] . . .

我們將繼續維護〔完善顧客服務等〕的傳統……

---

1 Review the concepts

❶ What questions might readers have about a company merger?

_____

_____

_____

❷ ☐True ☐False   You should send a change of address announcement only after your company has moved.

2 Write a letter about your company's relocation.

Imagine that your company is moving from 44 Lockhaven Boulevard, St. Louis, MO 63015, phone number (314) 444-7800, fax number (314) 444-7802. Your new address will be 2025 Wildwood Street, Jefferson City, MO 65102. Your moving date is July 18. You will keep the same phone and fax numbers. Write a letter informing partners and clients that you are making this move.

_____

_____

_____

_____

Dear _____ :

_____

_____

_____

_____

_____

_____

_____

_____

_____

3 Write a letter announcing a merger.

Imagine that you work for A Plus Training. Your company specializes in customized corporate management and computer training. A Plus Training has been operating for 10 years. The company has recently merged with Quality Training, Ltd. Quality Training focuses on communications training.

The new, merged company will be known as Quality Plus Training. Quality Plus Training will continue to provide all the services that the two original companies provided but with a larger staff. Send a message to your client, Arthur Consultants, informing them of the change.

QUALITY PLUS TRAINING, LTD

1000 Condor Drive, Suite 4
San Bruno, CA 94066
415.734.9857

January 8, 2023

Arthur Consultants
Metro South, 135 Auburn Ave. NE
Atlanta, GA 30303

Dear Sirs:

_____

_____

_____

_____

_____

_____

_____

_____

_____

_____

_____

_____

_____

_____

_____

_____

_____

_____

_____

_____

_____

_____

_____

ANSWER KEY

DISCUSSION & EXERCISE 1 — Units 1-2 — P. 12

1
1. A functional document is a piece of writing that is meant to help readers do something rather than to entertain them.

   功能性文件是為了協助讀者，而非為了娛樂寫成的文章。

2. They read for information, not pleasure, and they often look for conclusions or recommendations.

   讀者閱讀商業寫作是為了得到資訊，不是為了娛樂；他們通常想立刻就看到最後的建議或結論。

3. Readers oftentimes skim functional documents. Highlighting important information helps readers find it when they are skimming.

   因為讀者閱讀功能性文件時，通常採用略讀的方式，因此清楚呈現資訊將能幫助讀者。

4. By using headers with numbers and/or different-sized fonts and by using bulleted or numbered lists within paragraphs.

   以編號或不同字級大小標示標題，或另外在段落中使用項目符號與數字編號輔助。

5. Use a numbered list when information should be given in sequence.

   如果清單中的內容具有前後關係則，使用數字編號。

2 Formal language:
1. I would like to inform you of . . .
2. I will send a replacement immediately.
3. I am very pleased to hear that . . .
4. I am interested in learning more about . . .

Informal language:
1. Let me tell you about . . .
2. I'll send you another one right now.
3. It's such great news that . . .
4. I want to know more about . . .

DISCUSSION & EXERCISE 2 — Units 3-6 — P. 30

1
1. Flush left means aligned with the left-hand margin.

   「Flush left」是指與左邊的邊界齊頭。

2. Block format (also called full block format).

   在齊頭式中，文件或信中每個部分都從左邊邊界起頭。

3. Indented style and modified block style.

   縮排式與改良齊頭式的寄件人地址會在信件的右半邊。

4. Indented style. 縮排式是老式的書信格式。

5. With the modified block style, all paragraphs start flush left, as in block style, but the return address, date, signature, and closing line are placed near the center of the page, as in indented style.

   改良齊頭式的段落開頭皆齊左，與齊頭式相同；但是寄件人地址、日期、簽名和結尾敬辭都縮排靠近中央，就跟縮排式一樣。

6. The sender's address, date, closing line, and signature.

   寄件人地址、日期、結尾敬辭和簽名。

7. The receiver's address goes in the center of the envelope.

   收件人地址要放在信封的中央。

8. A window envelope is an envelope with a clear plastic pane in the center that shows the receiver's address.

   開窗信封為中央有透明窗口的信封，可從窗口看到收件人地址。

2 1. ❶ The letterhead 信頭
   ❷ The recipient's address 收件人地址
   ❸ The body 正文
   ❹ Title 單位或職位名稱 ❺ Enclosure 附件

2. ❶ Christopher Witte／1234 Main Street／
   Anytown, State, USA 12345
   ❷ May 26, 2023
   ❸ Ms. Emily Harris／567 Grand Avenue／
   Suite 74／Big City, State, USA 67890

❹ Dear Ms. Harris: ❺ Best regards,
❻ Christopher Witte (handwritten
   and typed)

3. ❶ Sender's name and address
   寄件者姓名和地址
   ❷ Recipient's name and address
   收件者姓名和地址

DISCUSSION & EXERCISE 3 [Unit 7] P. 34

1 1. Letterhead is a company's stationery;
   it usually has the company's address
   and logo printed on it.
   信頭是公司的專用信紙，上面會印有公司
   的地址和商標。

2. Use letterhead any time you send
   a business letter, particularly a
   business-to-business letter.
   如果是商務書信，最好可以使用信頭
   （個人書信往來則沒有硬性規定），
   看起來會更專業。

3. The attention line.
   經辦人，也就是信件的指定收件人。
   主旨句（subject line）是信件的標題，有助
   於讀者了解信件的主題。

4. Enc. stands for "enclosure," meaning
   something is included in the envelope
   along with the letter.
   「Enc」是「Enclosure」的縮寫，代表信件還附
   有附件。

5. "Cc:" means "courtesy copy" (or "carbon
   copy"). Names that follow Cc: indicate
   other people who are receiving copies of
   the letter.
   「Cc」指的是「courtesy copy」或「carbon
   copy」，代表另寄副件給某人。

6. It means the letter was dictated or given
   by the writer, EP, to the typist, kn.
   代表信件的作者是 EP，而打字員是 kn。

7. Use Ms. for women unless you are asked
   to use another title.
   商務書信中稱呼女士是「Ms.」，除非對方要求你
   使用「Mrs.」或「Miss」等其他稱謂。

2 1. (E)   2. (C)   3. (C)   4. (A)

3 1. ❶ The sender's address / letterhead
   ❷ The date
   ❸ The receiver's address
      (or the recipient's address)
   ❹ The salutation ❺ The subject line
   ❻ The complimentary close or
      closing line
   ❼ The signature and name of the writer
   ❽ Enclosures
   ❾ Names of people who will get copies
      of the letter
   ❿ The letter was dictated or given by
      the writer, EA, to the typist, pty.

2. ❹ Dear Donald:
   ❺ Sub: Minutes and summary of
      November 2 board meeting

❾ Best regards, / Warmest regards, /
   Yours sincerely, / Yours truly, / Sincerely,
❿ EA:pty

3. ❶ Your reference 1092023 or Reference
      number 1092023
   ❷ Ladies and Gentlemen:
   ❸ Thank you for your letter of August
      28, 2023. I am pleased to enclose our
      latest catalog. or Per your letter of
      August 28, I am enclosing our latest
      catalog.
   ❹ Thank you again for your interest. or
      We look forward to hearing from you
      soon.
   ❺ Yours truly, (Sincerely, or Regards,)

4. A delay in your order, item number S98

1 1. Reader-focused writing is writing that presents information in a clear, concise, and helpful way to help busy readers complete a task.

以「讀者為中心」的寫作方式，是在動筆前與寫作時，隨時想到你的讀者。

2. Who will read this document? What will they use this document to do? What do they already know about this topic? What do they need to know? What questions will they have?

誰會閱讀這份文件？收到文件後，他們會怎麼做？他們對此主題有多少了解？他們需要知道什麼？他們會有什麼問題？等……

3. Connect the product with the reader's needs. Tell a relevant story about the product's impact on a similar company or situation. Show your product's success or your specialized abilities.

將你的產品或服務與讀者的需求連結。可以跟讀者敘述你的產品或服務曾經為其他相關公司或狀況帶來的好處，展示你產品或服務的成功案例，以及你所接受的專業訓練。

4. Concreteness「具體」原則即給予讀者「具體的資訊」，例如具體的對象、事實、數量、日期、時間等。

5. Conciseness「簡潔」指的是省略多餘的字與華麗的詞藻、寫法清楚並強調重點。

6. Concinnity「和諧」原則是指文件各部分彼此協調、內容流暢、安排合理。

7. Use correct titles, spell names correctly, supply the needed information clearly, etc.

使用正確的頭銜稱呼對方（包括注意對方的姓名是否拼對）、提供對方需要或要求的資訊等。

8. Word choice, order of information, formatting, punctuation, and the details you choose to include.

選詞用字、資訊出現的順序、格式、標點符號與決定寫入的細節等因素，都會影響語氣。

9. (B), (D), (E)

10. (C)

2 2. Which laptop offers the best customer service? or The TravelA1 laptop offers the best customer service.

3. Which laptop is the most portable? or The TravelA1 laptop is the most portable.

4. Which laptop is the best value? or The TravelA1 laptop offers the best value.

3 1. a. The passage uses too many long sentences. It is also very wordy.
   b. Passages marked below.

2. Examples of unclear, wordy text are marked below.

> Thank you for the time and effort you put into the proposal **you placed on my desk last Monday** [unnecessary]. **I have very thoughtfully considered your proposal to split the current and continuing Formatting and Design team into two concurrently functioning teams. [too wordy]. I have thought about the positive and negative consequences of making such a split,** [unnecessary detail, should be more concise] and I have come to the conclusion that the team should continue to work together as a unit.
>
> **Allow me to explain my reasons.** [unnecessary] First, although formatting and design are certainly **very distinct, different, and unique processes,** [too wordy] in my opinion the employees function well together as a team. The design of a publication cannot **progress or move forward** without **understanding the limits, boundaries, and barriers** [too wordy] of its formatting. Formatting provides the **organization, hierarchy, and flow that the design team needs to understand in order to create the clear, non-distracting, but beautiful layouts for which we are famous . . .** [should be more concise]

3. **Rewrite:**

> Thank you for your proposal regarding the current Formatting and Design team configuration. I appreciate the time and effort you put into this project. However, after consideration, I believe the team should continue in its current format.
>
> First of all, although formatting and design are different processes, they inform each other and must work together to ensure that projects run smoothly. The designers need to understand the formatting elements of a document to ensure they are reflected in the design. Having the two components on one team ensures constant communication . . .

4 **Tone problems:** Unprofessional salutation; inappropriate abbreviations ("sry," "Tnks"); calling the supervisor "boss" is unprofessional; information is not presented as clearly as possible; contact information is not given; use of a nickname to sign the email.

Rewrite:

> Date: Friday, November 6, 2023
>
> To: All Headquarters Staff
>
> From: Sally Carlin, Office Manager
>
> Subject: Two professional development courses available next week.
>
> Please register this week for one of the two professional development training sessions available next week. All employees are encouraged to attend. The courses are designed for different staff levels:
>
> *Designing Usable Forms is open to analysts and senior analysts.
>
> *Writing for the Reader is open to all staff.
>
> To register, contact me at sally.carlin@company.com or (405) 439-0394, or contact Julia Richards at (julia.richards@company.com) or (405) 439-0394. We will send your information and class schedule to upper management.

5

> Subject: Shortlisted candidates for CEO shadowing internship.
>
> We have selected three candidates for our final short list for the CEO Shadowing Internship: Mira Kumar, MBA student at Harvard University; Barry Enlow, MBA student at Georgetown University; and Brian McArthur, MA student at George Washington University.
>
> **The candidates**
>
> Mira Kumar is a second-year MBA student at Harvard Business School. She has a GPA of 3.9 and has been president of her school's Model World Bank for the past year. In her interview, she was confident and engaging.
>
> Barry Enlow is also a second-year MBA student from Georgetown University. He is focusing on international business development and growth. Previously, he interned with USAID, working on projects to facilitate partnerships in Southeast Asia. Mr. Enlow has a GPA of 3.8.
>
> Brian McArthur is in his second year of an MA program at George Washington University. He is studying international relations, and his GPA is 3.2. He has excellent references and a keen interest in international business.

Recommended candidate: Barry Enlow.

Although all the candidates are well qualified, Mr. Enlow's experience with development in Southeast Asia puts him in a good position to shadow our East Asian marketing team leader. As we promote the international branches of the business, up-and-coming talent such as Mr. Enlow will be key to our continued growth. Mr. Enlow gives every indication that he will be successful in this internship.

DISCUSSION & EXERCISE 5 　Units 13-15　 P. 75

1

1. The contact information, the format of the cover letter, and the information in the body of the letter.

   聯絡方式、封面頁的格式，以及正文的內容。

2. (A), (B), (D), (F)

3. The topic of the fox or email, including any important dates or deadlines.

   清楚傳達傳真或郵件的主旨，包括重要日期或回覆期限。

4. "Transmitting" shows the number of pages in a fax. On the "Transmitting" line, write the total number of pages you are sending, including the cover page.

   「Transmitting」表示傳真的頁數。
   在 Transmitting 一欄中，應打上總共的傳真頁數，連封面頁也要計算在內。

5. Write the email in the Bcc: line.

   在Bcc:（密件副本）這欄輸入的地址，不會被其他收件人看到。

2

1. True 發出的（outgoing）傳真是由你或你的辦公室發給別人的傳真。

2. False 簽名圖文檔設定插入在每封電子郵件的底端。

3. False 商務信件使用正式文字，不要使用表情文字，例如笑臉符號。

4. False 主旨句採用一般標點符號的規則，但是句尾不加標點符號。

5. True 商務電子郵件像商務書信一樣，都要使用稱呼。

3

1. Tilak Ravenu

2. Jens Svenson and Ann-Brit Bech-Nielson

3. Jens Svenson (jens.svenson@global.org) and Ann-Brit Bech-Nielson (a.bech-nielson@usg.edu)

4. A file labeled performancereview.doc

4 **Problems:** Unprofessional email addresses; vague subject line; inappropriate use of smileys; inappropriate salutation; inappropriate personal message included

From:	Annie Mason (annie.mason@nexttech.com)
To:	heather.jones@nexttech.com; sylvia.joely@nexttech.com; clint.brown@nexttech.com; george.kundera@nexttech.com
Cc:	
Subject:	Tomorrow's Expansion Project meeting canceled
Attachment:	

Dear Expansion Project team:

Because of schedule changes, the Expansion Project meeting scheduled for tomorrow has been postponed. I will let you know the new date as soon as it is set. I apologize for the late notice.

Best,

Annie

5 Missing: The sender's name, the receiver's fax number, the receiver's phone number, and the number of pages.

6

Dear Mr. Smith:

I am very sorry, but I have to take emergency leave beginning tomorrow and continuing for the next ten days. My father is critically ill, and I must travel home to see him.

I realize the disruption this causes in my current projects, and I hope to minimize that disruption as best I can. I will work remotely as much as possible. You can reach me at my family's home at (304) 886-4895. I will also be available on my cell phone and will check my email frequently.

I have spoken to my colleague, June Chester, about the current status of all my projects. If I am unavailable, she should be able to answer your questions and continue the work while I am gone.

Again, I apologize for this sudden inconvenience.

Sincerely,

M. Witte

DISCUSSION & EXERCISE 6　Units 16-17　P. 90

1 1. Announcements, descriptions of problems or solutions, and discussions of action to be taken.

備忘錄通常用來宣布事情、描述問題或說明解決方式，也常用來討論如何採取行動。

2. (A), (B), (D), (E)

3. Memos should be as short as possible, one to two pages at most.

備忘錄要簡短，長度至多兩頁。

4. The opening, context/task/problem, and conclusion.

開頭、背景情況（或任務、問題）、結論。

5. Because memos can be sent or forwarded to many people, it is important to be thoughtful when using people's names or assigning blame. This is a time when the passive voice may be better than the active voice.

由於備忘錄可能會寄給很多人，之後又層層轉寄出去，所以盡量避免指名道姓，歸咎於人。這時不妨用被動句，不要用主動句。

6. Bad news should be presented less directly than good news. Rather than stating the key point of bad news up front, provide some context and history to help readers prepare for what is coming. Good news memos may praise specific individuals, but bad news memos should usually not assign blame to specific people.

負面訊息的傳達不同於正面訊息，必須婉轉而間接；不要一開始就把壞消息的重點寫出來，而是先列出原因或證據，讓讀者有時間做點心理準備。正面訊息會直接點出值得獎勵的個人或小組，但負面訊息通常不會指名道姓地歸咎過錯。

2 1. False 備忘錄沒有規定至少三段以上，反而應該要保持內容形式簡短。

2. False 備忘錄的格式包含名稱、標題區，和訊息主文，不用使用稱謂。

3. True 備忘錄幾乎只用在辦公室、公司或團隊內進行溝通，所以不用像一般的商務文件那麼正式。

4. True 備忘錄的寄送對象，通常是辦公室或公司內部的同事。

3

To:	All Moonrise Stationery Employees
From:	Paul Lennard, Office Manager
Date:	[Date]
Subject:	New schedule for employee paychecks

Moonrise Stationery will be following a new schedule for employee paychecks. Starting on February 1, paychecks will arrive on the 1st and 15th of every month. All other employee payment practices will remain the same.

Please contact me at 301-258-0145 if you have any questions.

4

To:	All XYZ Company Employees
From:	Howard Kendal, Office Manager
Date:	November 19, 2023
Subject:	Please complete the "Employee Satisfaction Survey" by December 1

All employees are asked to fill out the attached "Employee Satisfaction Survey" by December 1. Management is looking forward to compiling the results of this survey and using them to review current policies and initiate new ones. Please take this opportunity to make your opinions known to upper management.

Please return your completed survey to the basket on my desk labeled "Completed Employee Surveys."

5

To:	Chelsea Costello, President
From:	Ed Leavis, Vice President
Date:	November 9, 2023
Re:	Problem with London store shipment

The November 7 shipment to the London store (store number 381) contained 500 defective BS99 radios. Replacement radios have been ordered and will be shipped as soon as possible. Customers have been advised that the new radios will arrive by the end of the week.

The reason for the defect is unclear. The factory that supplied the radios has been notified and is conducting a check of all recent output. Radio production has been stopped while an analysis of the assembly line is done. Employee interviews are also in process. Management expects to identify the problem shortly and will inform us of the findings immediately.

DISCUSSION & EXERCISE 7 Units 18-23 P. 112

1 1. The introductory section, discussion section, conclusions section, recommendations section, and references.

報告有前導部分、討論部分、結論部分、建議部分，以及參考資料部分等五大項目。

2. In both the conclusions and recommendations sections.

結論部分是就所收集的資訊發表意見，建議部分是根據前面的結論，説明應該採取什麼行動。

3. The methodology section explains how you gathered your information, including the actions you took to get the information and why you chose them.

   說明研究方法時，需要解釋你是如何收集資料、做了哪些事，以及為什麼要做這些事。

4. Scope refers to the understanding of what is included and excluded.

   一篇報告的內容範圍，指的是報告內容包含與不包含什麼。

2 1. **True** 備忘錄不像一般商務文件那麼正式，其格式只有名稱、標題區，和訊息主文三個基本元素，而一篇報告則包含前導、討論、結論、建議與參考資料五大部分。

2. **False** 摘要濃縮了報告各部分的主要內容，且應該要把重點放在結論與建議，因此需要包含建議部分。

3 1. (B)   2. (A)   3. (C)

4 **Results in paragraph form:** According to our study, patterns of report reading among staff members vary by position. Analysts are most likely to read a report in its entirety; front-line staff are least likely to do so. Front-line staff are also the least likely to read most sections of a report. Executive summaries are worthwhile, as many senior managers and executives read the summary rather than the whole report. Senior managers and executives focus on the introduction (including the executive summary), conclusions, and recommendations. It is concerning that more than one-quarter of senior managers do not read reports at all.

5 1. **Conclusions**

- Although *BigTime* remains popular among those aged 18 to 35, we are losing one of our key readership groups, those aged 14 to 18 years. All readers find our covers dull, and 14- to 18-year-olds are not interested in our content.

- The gaming section does not interest any group. Older readers want more sweepstakes and contests. Readers under 18 want more quizzes and games, and all readers would like more product samples.

2. **Recommendations**

- To increase sales, continue to appeal to our solid base of 18- to 35-year-olds, while increasing *BigTime*'s appeal to 14- to 18-year-olds.

- Research why readers find our covers "dull."

- Research why readers tend to discontinue subscriptions after two years.

- Determine what content would appeal to 14- to 18-year-olds and include more of that content in the magazine and on the cover.

- Include more product samples.

- Include more sweepstakes, contests, quizzes, and games. Make these changes apparent on the magazine's cover.

6 (A)

1

1. Is my request reasonable? What will my reader have to do? How can I help my reader perform these actions?

   撰寫比較複雜的請求信需考慮「我的請求合理嗎?」、「讀者需要做什麼?」、「我如何協助讀者完成這些步驟?」

2. Tell him or her exactly what can be done to accommodate your request, and do everything within your power to ensure that the request is granted. Remove as much of the burden as you can from the reader by including necessary contact information, providing reasons or validations for your request, and enclosing any material he or she might need.

清楚告訴對方你希望他如何滿足你的請求,並盡力讓對方樂於答應你的請求。幫對方把負擔減到最低,例如提供必要的聯絡資訊,並說明對方應該答應請求的理由並提供證明,或是隨信覆上對方可能需要的資料。

3. A letter written by one person who is familiar with another, evaluating and often promoting the fitness of this person for a position.

   推薦信是由熟識的人撰寫的信,目的在評估、肯定被推薦人具有擔任某一職務的能力。

4. (A) 5. (E) 6. (A), (B)

2

1. **True** 如果是給予肯定的回覆,可以盡量簡單扼要。

2. **True** 否定的回覆比肯定的回覆需要給予更多的細節。

3. **True** 如果請求信中的要求屬於常見的請求,信件可能就可以寫得簡短直接。

3

1. The writer apologizes for the request.

2. The writer doesn't provide the name of the illustrator.

3. The writer doesn't provide the publication date of the illustration or other identifying information.

4. The writer could have provided other contact information.

4

Dear Ms. Thomas:

I am writing to request a meeting to discuss a combined marketing campaign.

Our market research shows that consumers who buy our bears are also leading purchasers of flowers online. I would like to discuss the possibility of a holiday marketing campaign in which flower buyers receive discounts on bears or receive free bears with large purchases. We could offer a reciprocal deal for buyers of our bears to receive discounts on your flowers.

I believe this campaign will result in new customers for both of our companies. I hope that you find this idea as interesting as I do.

If you do, I would like to set up a conference call sometime during the week of August 7 to 13. My mornings are free for meetings, but if another time is better for you, please let me know.

In the meantime, feel free to contact me with any questions or comments at a.powers@bearamerica.com or at 913-301-8911, extension 03.

Yours sincerely,

Augusten Powers

Augusten Powers
Vice President of Marketing
Bear America

5 1. **Negative response**

> Dear Ms. James:
>
> Thank you for your interest in FoodSafe Industries. We are proud to enforce the highest standards in food production.
>
> Your résumé is impressive, as is your letter of recommendation. Unfortunately, we are not seeking new food testing technicians at this time. I will certainly keep your name and information on file and contact you if we have any openings.
>
> Thank you again for your interest and best of luck in your endeavors.
>
> Yours truly,
>
> *Rex Hong*
>
> Rex Hong

2. **Positive response**

> Dear Ms. James:
>
> Thank you for your interest in FoodSafe Industries. We are proud to enforce the highest standards in food production.
>
> I am impressed with your résumé and your glowing letter of recommendation. At the moment, we are looking for qualified food testing technicians for our Shanghai offices.
>
> I would like to meet with you to discuss these openings at our office on Pudong Avenue on Mondy, November 20, at 9:00 a.m. Enclosed is a map and contact information for my office. If this time is inconvenient for you, please contact me as soon as possible to arrange another date or time.
>
> I look forward to meeting with you on Mondy, November 20.
>
> Yours truly,
>
> *Rex Hong*
>
> Rex Hong

DISCUSSION & EXERCISE 9 Units 28-30 P. 157

1 1. The event was a big success.

2. Please also pass along my special thanks to Martin Douglas.

3. I will be sure to use your services for any future events we throw.

2 1. Thank you for choosing Chef's Kiss Cookware for your purchase. Your goods are enclosed. We hope they meet your satisfaction.

2. For your information, our 2023 summer sale begins on 1 May. Many of our goods will have a discount of 20% or more.

3. Please visit our website for more details about our sale. Thank you once again for your order.

3
1. We at Chef Mike's Fine Food would like to thank all those who supported us in our first year of business

2. Also, we would like to offer a huge thank you to Millie's Bakery, Bart's Interior Design, and Kitchen Planet, all of whom have played a big part in our first year's success

3. We will continue to provide you all with the dishes you love at affordable prices

4. Again, we thank you all deeply for your support

DISCUSSION & EXERCISE 10 [Units 31-33] P. 179

1
1. A letter of inquiry asks the reader a question. (For example, it asks for information about pricing and work specifications for a certain product or service.)

詢問信是用來跟信件讀者索取資訊的（可以用來跟對方詢價，或要求某項產品或服務工作規格的資訊）。

2. At a minimum, a description of the product or service you want, the quantity you want, and your location.

訊價信裡面至少要說明你想要的產品或服務、你需要的數量及你的地點。

3. (B), (C), (E) 4. (A), (B), (D)

5. (A) 6. (B) 7. (C) 8. (A)

2

First name: Christina	Last name: Jones
Company: ABC Industries	Email: christinajones@abcindustries.com
Industry: Insurance	Job title: Executive assistant
Address 1: 124 Key Boulevard	
Address 2: Suite 16	City: Tallahassee
Country: USA	State/Province: FL
Zip/Postal code: 32301	Phone number: (850) 891-2303

★ Best time to contact you
    Before 1:00 p.m.

★ I would like information about
    ☑Products   ☑Services
    ☐Software solutions   ☑Other
    ☑Pricing

★ Are you interested in a specific 123 product or product family?
    No.

★ Other questions or comments

    I also want to arrange for a technician to look at our current server situation and suggest necessary upgrades or changes. Please let us know if that is possible and how much it may cost.

3

Dear Sirs:

I am writing to inquire about two of your training courses: Writing for Success and Spectacular Sales Writing. My company is interested in enhancing employee communication skills, and your company has come highly recommended. I would appreciate a quote and a description of any work specifications for implementing each course.

There are currently 25 employees who would take the courses, though that number may increase if we include managers. Our employees write a variety of documents for customers and partners. We would like to focus on basic business writing skills and then move on to specialized sales writing.

In your response, please answer the following questions:
- How long do the courses usually last?
- How many people usually attend a course?
- Do attendees have to purchase materials, or do you provide materials?
- What are the backgrounds of the trainers?
- How much time do you need to implement a course?
- How much do you charge for courses?

4

Dear Mr. Lee:

Thank you for your inquiry of March 25. The prices you requested (quoted in US dollars) are as follows:

- **Blumenschein Large Knife Collection** $398
- **Braun Standard Kitchen Line** $214
- **Modern Quality Chef's Set** $200
  subtotal   **$812.00**

For the entire order, expedited shipping and insurance via Globe Ship is $150, bringing the total to $962.00.

Because your order is more than $700.00, we are happy to offer you a discount of 7%, bringing your subtotal to $755.16 and your complete cost to $905.16. The amounts quoted here constitute a firm offer valid until April 31.

Orders are filled and shipped the day after they are received. Using the Globe Ship expedited service, we can deliver an order to Taiwan within three days of the order's placement.

For first-time customers, we require payment in advance, through either an international wire bank transfer or a credit card payment over the telephone. For your future reference, we also offer a 10% discount on all orders over $1,000. Orders over $1,200 are subject to negotiation. We offer discounts for large orders on a case-by-case basis.

If you have any questions or concerns, please call me at +49 69 674561. To accept this order, please fax a completed order form from the enclosed catalog to +49 69 670002.

Sincerely,

Karl Blumenschein

Karl Blumenschein
Sales Director, Blumenschein Inc.
Enclosure: catalog

1. 1. (C)　2. (E)　3. (A)　4. (A)　5. (C)

6. A number assigned to a product by a company to help identify the item. Model numbers are very helpful in ensuring that the correct item is ordered and shipped, especially when there are multiple types of a particular product.

   產品號碼（或商品型號）是公司就產品給予的編號，方便找出該產品；尤其多種產品一起出貨時，可以幫助確認產品和訂單是否無誤並且正確運送。

7. It means the writer wants 3 units of the item called "Chambers indust. solvent hi-concentrate." Each unit is 55 gallons. Each unit costs $122.00, so the total price for three units is $366.00.

   需要 3 桶每加侖 55 美元的 Chambers 高濃度工業溶劑，每桶 122.00 美元，共計 366.00 美元。

8. (B), (C), (D)

9. A customer who orders a product or service is placing an order. Taking an order means accepting a customer's order for merchandise.

   顧客向你訂購商品或服務，是指跟你「下訂單」（place an order）；「接訂單」（take an order）代表你接受顧客訂購商品的訂單。

10. You need the customer's name, address, and phone number; a description of the goods including quantities and prices per item; a shipping address and preferences; and payment information.

    當顧客向你下訂單時，你可能需要的資料包括：顧客姓名、地址、聯絡電話、購買商品描述（數量、單位價格）、運送地址與運送偏好方式、付款資訊等。

2.

Attention: Mr. Charlie Watts

Please supply the following items:

Quantity	Description	Item number	Unit price	Total price
5	Laptop computers	332	$800	$4,000
3	Desktop computers	431a	$500	$1,500
1	Scanner	555	$350	$350

Total: $5,850

Payment terms shall be standard 2%-10/NET 30. Payment will be made at delivery.

Please ship all items using DHL Expedited Shipping.

Please deliver all items by December 10, 2023.

Shipping address: XYZ Incorporated
　　　　　　　　　1650 Mount Pleasant Street NW
　　　　　　　　　Washington, DC 20010 USA

3

Re: Your furniture and equipment order

Dear Ms. Montag:

Thank you for your order of February 15. We are pleased to confirm shipment of the following items:

2 conference desks	HN-33080-WB
2 credenzas	HN-36887-WK
4 executive chairs	HP-56563-SE
2 file cabinets	HN-5344C-K

The total cost of your order is $2492.78, including shipping. I understand that you will pay COD, which will bring your cost to $2422.88, reflecting our 3% discount for payment made within 10 days. If not, the full balance is due within 30 days. We will present you with your invoice at the time of delivery.

Thank you again for your business.

Yours sincerely,

[name]

DISCUSSION & EXERCISE 12 [Units 36-39] P. 230

1

1. Money loaned or the ability of an individual or company to borrow money.

   「credit」可信貸指借來的款項（信貸），或是個人或公司借款的能力。

2. A person or business that can validate or vouch for a credit applicant's ability to pay.

   「信用擔保人」是指保證信貸申請人能夠及時付清款項之個人或公司。

3. Letters seeking information about a company or individual's funds, payment patterns, interest rates on debts, and/or other financial information.

   「信用調查信」就個人或公司的資金、付款模式、債務利息和／或其他財務狀況蒐集資訊。

4. To ensure that any mistakes are resolved quickly. Listing account, invoice, and order numbers in letters requesting payment help customers access the correct records. Reminding them of the payment terms helps them process your payments faster.

   催款信應該寫得清晰明確，因為要避免出錯。列出所有的款項、發貨單與訂單號碼，方便對方找到對應的正確紀錄。提醒對方你們的付款條件，可以加速付款的處理。

5. An explanation or some sort of response.

   除了要求對方付款，也請對方回覆說明（如解釋付款延遲的原因）。

6. (A)

7. (A)

8. (B)

9. True 「outstanding」在此意指「尚未付款的」。

489

2

Dear Mr. Brookes-Wolgar:

Thank you for your interest in Big Sound. We have received your order and are eager to fill it, We are always happy to hear from new customers.

With first-time customers, we routinely ask for a certified bank statement, a credit reference, and the name of your bank in order to open your account. We will offer you our regular terms of 3%-15 days/net 30 as soon as we receive and accept this information. Your financial information will always be kept strictly confidential.

We look forward to receiving your information as soon as possible so that we can process your order and provide you with the quality service we take pride in. Please don't hesitate to tell us how we can be of service to you.

Sincerely,

[name]

3

Dear Ms. Sandusky:

You were named as a credit reference for Mood Music by Thomas Brookes-Wolgar.

We would appreciate any information you can provide on your company's credit and financial history with Mood Music. In particular, we would like to know how long Mood Music has had an account with you, whether the company has any outstanding debts with you now, and whether you have ever had problems receiving timely payments from them. We will, of course, keep any information you send us confidential.

Thank you for your assistance in this matter. Enclosed please find an addressed, postage-paid envelope for your convenience.

Sincerely,

[name]

Enc. (1)

4

Ref: AG0308

Dear Ms. Choe:

Subject: Your order number AG0308

It appears that we have not yet received payment for your order number AG0308, which you placed on August 3 and we shipped on August 5. The details of your order are below:

Order Number: AG0308
Placed: August 3
Shipped: August 5
Items: 50 copies of *Kids and Technology*
Our invoice number: 080315
Amount due: $1000

Our payment terms are 2%-10/ Net 30. We believe that our invoice may not have reached you, so we have enclosed a second copy of the invoice along with a copy of your original purchase order with this letter. Please process the invoice and submit payment through your usual account at your earliest convenience.

Of course, if you have settled the account before this letter reaches you, please ignore this reminder. As always, we thank you for your payment and your business.

Please contact me if you have any questions or concerns.

Yours truly,

[name]

Enc. (2)

DISCUSSION & EXERCISE 13 Units 40-43 P. 250

1 1. Shipping methods, shipping rates, payment options, shipping time frames, return policies, etc.

跟「運送條件」相關的主題可能會有：送貨方式、送貨費用、付款方式、送貨時程、退貨政策等。

2. Rates, exclusions, available countries, types of shipping covered, policy information, types of coverage, etc.

跟「保險條件」相關的主題可能會有：保費、不承保內容、可送達國家、涵蓋的運送方式種類、保單資訊、保險項目等。

2

May 11, 2023

John Doe
Kid Art!
10 Bloor Street East, 5th Floor
Toronto, ON M4W 1A8, Canada

Dear Mr. Doe:

Subject: Order number 23-511a

We are happy to announce that the items in your order number 23-511a have shipped today, May 11, 2023. The package was shipped using FastShip International Parcel Priority. Your shipment's tracking number is IPP0029384112. Your shipment should arrive within four business days.

We thank you for your business and hope you will choose Acme Art Supply for all your future art supply needs!

Order number: 23-511a
Date ordered: May 9, 2023
Date shipped: May 11, 2023

Billing address

John Doe
18 Chestnut Street
Toronto, ON M5G 1R3
Canada

Shipping address

John Doe
10 Bloor Street East
5th Floor
Toronto, ON M4W 1A8
Canada

Items included in this shipment:

Our item number	Description	Price	Quantity	Total
pbm13	Medium paintbrushes	10 NT	50	500 NT
pbl27	Large paintbrushes	17 NT	50	850 NT
e44	Pinewood easels	450 NT	10	4,500 NT
cm34	36"x48" canvases	250 NT	100	25,000 NT
cs12	24"x36" canvases	180 NT	50	9,000 NT
wc30	Beginner watercolor sets	150 NT	100	15,000 NT

Order total: 54,850 NT
Order total in USD: $1805.46

Best regards,

[name]

DISCUSSION & EXERCISE 14 [Units 44-47] P. 274

1

1. A letter written to a company citing problems with goods, services, or other business practices.

   投訴信指的是陳述公司提供之商品、服務或其他商務運作具有的問題。

2. Waiting to receive a response may make an angry customer even angrier.

   盡快回覆投訴信的用意，在於不要讓已經心生不滿的客戶更生氣。

3. (A)   4. (A), (C)   5. (A), (B)

2

1. False 即使是投訴信，也應該感謝顧客來信指教。

2. False 投訴信裡面應該附上的是相關文件的副本（copy）。

3

Dear Ms. Karmarkar:

I am sorry to inform you that there has been a mistake in our latest order. I requested 50 pairs of blue sandals, but the shipment contained 50 pairs of red sandals. Please rectify this error as soon as possible. There is a great demand for blue sandals!

I will hold the box of red sandals to be returned when the replacement shipment arrives.

Thank you for your prompt attention to this matter.

Yours sincerely,

[name]

4

Dear Customer Service Center:

I am afraid that I must report a very negative experience I recently had with one of your service technicians. We called to have someone look at our fax machine, which was malfunctioning. The service technician who came to our office was not up to your usual standard and, I think, not someone who should be representing your company. He took no notice of the mud covering his boots and tracked it all over our office. He spoke curtly and even rudely to the office staff (asking us what we had "screwed up this time," for example. He seemed to take a very long time doing his job and went outside for several long "smoke breaks." Annoyingly, two days later, we are having the same problem with our machine.

Needless to say, I am very disappointed with the service we received, and I am reluctant to use your repair services again. I want our fax machine to work, however. Please send a new technician out to look at it. Also, please speak to the technician who did the original repair. We would not like to see him return to our office, and we can't imagine any other professional office that would tolerate him.

Yours sincerely,

[name]

5

Dear Ms. Choe:

Thank you for your correspondence of August 10, in which you informed us of a mistake in your order. I immediately checked your original order form to confirm our error. Unfortunately, it seems that you did, in fact, order 100 copies of [book name].

We understand how oversights like this can occur. How would you like to handle this situation? You have been charged for the entire 100 copies ordered, so you may, of course, keep the extra 50 books. However, if you would like to return them, we ask that you hold them at your warehouse until our shipping partner can pick them up. We will then credit your account for the returned copies of the book, though we will have to bill you for the cost of return shipping.

Please let me know how you would like to proceed.

Sincerely,

[name]

6

Dear Ms. Wooster:

Thank you for your correspondence of April 1, in which you informed us of the unfortunate problem with your shipment. We are so sorry for the inconvenience this has caused you. I am happy to inform you that your two replacement Wi-Fi routers were shipped today. When the replacement shipment arrives, our shipping partner will collect the defective products for return.

As a gesture of goodwill, we would like to offer you a 15% discount on your next order with us—a coupon is enclosed in this letter. We assure you that we strive for the highest quality standards in our products and services. We are looking into our shipping procedures to help ensure that defective products are not shipped again.

Please let me know if there is any other way I can help you.

Sincerely,

[name]

Enc. (1)

1. Thank you for inviting me to be a speaker at the conference in Tokyo last week. I enjoyed the experience, but I do have a small suggestion about hotel arrangements for your speakers.

2. While my hotel was comfortable, I would have liked a larger room and one on a higher floor.

3. May I suggest that in the future you send out a preferences checklist to your speakers beforehand? I believe this would greatly improve their experience.

4. Thank you once again for the chance to be one of your guest speakers and for your openness to feedback.

DISCUSSION & EXERCISE 15　Units 48-51　P. 307

1 1. (A)

2. To start a partnership, a customer-supplier relationship, or other association with another business.

建立商務關係意指與另一間公司展開合作或買賣等其他商務關係。

3. (B)　4. (B)　5. (A) , (B)

6. Describe the need for your product or service in a way readers can relate to. / Describe your product or service and the benefits it can provide. / Give your product or service snob appeal by listing famous users or describing its elite status or symbolic value.

說明人們為什麼需要你的產品；就產品本身進行描述，比如說該產品能帶來的好處；強調你的產品或服務有哪些名人使用過，或是有什麼特殊的威望或地位。

7. The call to action is a statement describing what the writer would like the reader to do—for example, visit a shop, call a salesperson, use a coupon. It often comes near the end of a sales letter.

「call to action」會陳述你希望讀者採取的行動，例如來店參觀、聯繫銷售員、使用折價券等。由本章所有推銷信範例可得知，含有希望讀者行動的語句往往放在信的最後一段。

8. After a customer has visited your shop, responded to a promotion, or placed an order for the first time. Also, if a customer has placed a big or unusual order, or if a customer has not contacted you in some time.

跟催信的發信時間包括：顧客造訪店面過後、顧客對促銷活動有所回應後、顧客第一次訂購商品後；或者是老顧客訂購大量商品或有特殊訂單，以及當顧客已經有一段時間沒有光顧時。

2 1. Ture「testimonial」意指來自顧客的正面評論，內容說明特定產品或服務對他帶來的好處。

2. True 引用其他顧客的好評，確實可以激起對方購買產品的欲望。

3

Dear Ms. Lo:

I came across your boutique on a Vietnam Exporters website, and I believe I can give you a more competitive price for your shipments than you are currently receiving.

Please allow me to tell you a bit about Air Freight Inc. We have been in business for more than eight years. In that time, we have built a reputation for reliability and speedy service. Our customers trust us because we have never lost a package!

We are also known as one of the most competitively priced shipping agencies, as our unique business relationships with other shippers allow us to combine freight to get the best prices for our customers.

I hope you will visit our website at www.airfreight.vn for more information about our rates and services. Please also feel free to call us at 84 4 3 3849574 at any time to discuss how we can benefit your business.

Yours sincerely,

[name]

4

Dear Sir or Madam:

Every day, we see the power of word of mouth and public opinion. Have you thought about the impact good public relations can have for your company?

Please allow me to introduce you to Professional PR, a superior public relations partner. We currently represent several of the largest companies in Singapore, including Jupiter Systems, Alliance Office Solutions, and the Bank of Singapore. We earned their business because we are the best at providing proactive media relations, strategic counsel, branding and positioning, crisis communications, website launches, and special events planning. Imagine what we can do for you!

At Professional PR, we envision ourselves as your strategic business partner, working with you to establish and promote the right image for your company. As part of the Public Relations Global Network, we handle international as well as national projects—with more than 35 affiliate offices worldwide.

We aren't afraid to promise results. Please take a moment to learn more about us at www.propr.com and discover what we can do for your business.

Yours sincerely,

[name]

5

Dear Valued Big Smoke Customers:

I am so excited to announce the arrival of our new stock of Dominica Viva cigars. These cigars are rated by many as the best cigars in the world! We are the only shop in the United States to stock these cigars, and supplies are extremely limited.

Dominica Vivas are made in accordance with an ancient cigar-rolling tradition. The traditional leaf wrapper gives the cigars their famous chocolaty, fresh taste.

One of our customers said, "This cigar is like none I've ever smoked. I never thought I would have a chance to try a Dominica Viva. I am so thrilled to be able to experience this so close to my home."

Come down to Big Smoke soon to take advantage of this rare opportunity! There's no telling when our supplies will run out, so don't miss your chance to savor a Dominica Viva!

Yours sincerely,

[name]

6

Dear Mr. Dillon:

Thank you again for your April 22 order for ice picks and glacier boots. We are always happy to connect with new customers like you.

I am writing to make sure that everything in your order was satisfactory. At GATHERERS, we know that our customers' happiness is the key to our success. I hope that you are pleased with your order and that you will contact us again if there is any way we can serve you.

Yours truly,

[name]

DISCUSSION & EXERCISE 16 [Units 52-53] P. 327

1 1. A letter informing the requesting organization that a company intends to submit a bid or proposal.

意向書由本章範例看來，是指某組織機構告知有意願要對某項活動投標。

2. Request for proposal
「RFP」是「Request for proposal」的縮寫，指的是「招標書」。

3. (B)

2 1. False 通常招標書會公開邀請所有的供應商。

2. False 「意向書」是用來告知對方自己有意願就特定企畫遞交投標書，並請對方通知任何企畫上的改變。

3

To Whom It May Concern:

Re: Request to Tender—Campus Landscaping

You are invited to submit a tender for landscaping work intended to beautify the area surrounding the university library. If your company is interested in bidding, please find enclosed a Form of Tender. Please complete and submit the form in accordance with the Tender Conditions specified within.

For any questions regarding your tender, please contact David Fisher at (+61) 2 6120 3333, ext. 84.

DISCUSSION & EXERCISE 17 [Units 54-59] P. 362

1 1. The title, terms, and description of the job, the company's name, the requirements for the job, the salary and benefits, and how and when to apply.

徵人廣告中會包含：職稱、工作性質與內容、公司名稱、工作所需資格、薪水待遇、福利、以及如何應徵、何時應徵。

2. A letter sent along with a résumé or CV in order to apply for a job.

求職信通常會和履歷一起寄出，以應徵某個職位。

3. A cover letter helps you introduce yourself to a company, show yourself as a good fit for the company, and present yourself as the best candidate for a particular job.

求職信幫助求職者向公司自我介紹，顯示你非常適合在該公司工作，並且是該職缺的最佳人選。

4. To help you get a job by presenting a clear list of your experiences, accomplishments, skills, and education.

履歷表可以幫助求職者清楚呈現個人工作經驗、相關成就、技能和教育背景等資訊，便於爭取職缺。

5. CVs are often longer and more detailed than résumés. CVs contain more personal information than résumés.

通常英式履歷比美式履歷更長、更詳細。英式履歷也含有較多個人資訊。

6. (B)

7. (C)

---

2 **1.** True 在美國與加拿大，美式履歷使用較為普遍。

2. True 以教育背景或工作經歷來說，會以倒序的方式列出最後取得的學位或從事的工作。

3

Process Engineer Wanted

Seeking an experienced process engineer to lead a team in developing a new microchip testing process. Must be able to manage a team as well as design, implement, and analyze the results of the testing.

Requirements
· BSc in physics, electrical engineering, or mechanical engineering
· 5+ years of industry experience
· Experience with designing, performing, and analyzing experiments
· Good computer skills
· Ability to work in a cleanroom environment

Benefits offered
· Competitive salary with frequent possibilities for raises
· 401(k)
· Stock option plan
· Medical and dental insurance
· Four weeks of paid vacation to start

To apply
Please send your résumé and cover letter as MS Word or pdf files to [name@isp.com]. No phone calls, please.

---

4 **1.** Yes, a master of science degree in ecology/biogeography from ELT University of Natural Sciences, Budapest, Hungary

2. Journalist and photographer

3. The National Explorer Photography Award and the Japan Prize from the International Educational Program Contest

4. Three (English, French, and Hungarian)

5

1. Peter Walsh

pwash@gmail.com
0951368014
153 Jefferson Road
New York, NY 10013

Professional Summary

2. Freelance programmer, computer companies in Canada, Hong Kong, and the United States

3. **Lead Programmer**

4. Programming Plus, Inc.

5. ☐ Handled crisis situations for clients
   ☐ Solved problems in C++, Visual Basic
   ☐ Managed a team of programmers

6. **Programmer**

7. ABC Technicians

8. ☐ Assisted with the installation of hardware and software packages
   ☐ Wrote specialized code for new products
   ☐ Assisted in training clients to use new programs

Education

9. MS, Computer Engineering, 2018
   University of Wisconsin

Special training

10. ☐ Proficient in SQL, C++, Visual Basic

Languages

11. ☐ English, native speaker
    ☐ Mandarin, fluent and literate

Awards/Memberships/Affiliations

12. ☐ Member of Programmers Union since 2019
    ☐ Employee of the Month, August 2022

1

1. The function or department within a business that monitors the availability of qualified workers; recruits and screens applicants for jobs; helps select qualified employees; plans and presents appropriate orientation, training, and development for each employee; and administers employee benefit programs.

   「人力資源」指是企業內部招聘合格員工的組織或部門，功能包括聘用和甄選求職者、協助挑選合格的員工、為每位員工計劃與執行恰當的新人培訓、協助員工培訓與發展，以及管理員工福利制度。

2. A description of the position, salary, benefits, probation period, necessary agreements, or other important details; the date on which the employee is expected to start work; and instructions on how to accept the job.

   錄取通知書應該包含：工作內容描述、薪水與福利、試用期規定、必要的合約條件，或其他重要細節、到職日、如何接受此職缺等。

3. (A)

4. To confirm the details of an offer letter and officially accept the job.

   同意任職信的功能在於確認錄取通知書上的工作細節，並正式接受該職位。

5. It thanks the candidate, perhaps remarks on the difficulty of the decision, and expresses regret at being unable to offer the applicant a job.

   未錄取通知書通常會先謝謝求職者來應徵，然後說明公司是很艱難才做出這個決定，最後表示非常遺憾無法錄取該求職者。

6. The reason for the termination, an explanation of the employee's last payments, an explanation of any legal issues, instructions on how to leave, and the effective termination date.

   解僱通知書會包含幾點內容：終止僱傭關係的原因、最後薪資支付說明、法律事項、離職程序，以及僱傭關係終止的生效日期。

7. They officially declare an employee's resignation, even if he or she has already discussed it. They also show respect to the organization and the employee's supervisor.

   離職信的重要性在於，這是員工正式離開公司的宣布。即使員工之前已經口頭請辭過，一封正式的離職信能顯示你對公司與主管的尊重。

8. (C)

2

1. False 解僱通知書是公司通知員工約僱關係終止的信；辭職信是員工打算辭職時寫給公司的信。

2. True 即使你已在電話上或當面答應任職，還是必須寄一封正式的回信（同意任職信）表示同意任職。

3

[Your name] _____
[Your address] _____
_____
_____

[Date] _____

Marie Somtow
Duds
P.O. Box 748,
Bangkok 10501, Thailand

Dear Ms. Somtow:

Thank you very much for offering me the manager position at Duds. Unfortunately, after much consideration, I must decline the position. I am grateful to have been offered the opportunity, and I wish you the best of luck in your search.

Yours sincerely,
[Sign your name] _____
[Your name] _____

4

[Your name] _____
[Your address] _____
_____
_____

[Date] _____

Dear Ms. Jones:

Thank you for the offer of the concierge position at Seashore Resort. I am very pleased to accept this offer.

I understand that my salary will be $40,000 per year before taxes, that I may be eligible for a bonus after 90 days, that other employee benefits will be conferred after I complete my first 90 days, and that I will report to the hotel manager. I understand and accept the rate of vacation accrual.

Enclosed is my signed offer letter, officially accepting this position. I will see you on November 16, 2023, to begin my employment as Seashore Resort's concierge.

Yours sincerely,

[Sign your name]

[Your name]

Enc.

5

[Your name] _____
[Your address] _____
_____
_____

[Date] _____

Dear Ms. Duncan:

I am writing to officially tender my resignation from the Sales Department of Tech Solutions today, March 15, 2023. Per my contract, I am giving two weeks' notice; however, I am happy to stay for four weeks from today if that will help in the transition process.

I want to thank you for all the support you and the rest of the staff have given me during my three years here. I am very grateful for the experience I have gained and the professional growth I have achieved.

Deciding to leave was not easy.

Please let me know how I can assist you in making this change as smooth as possible for everyone.

Yours sincerely,

[Your name]

6

Dear Mr. Hu:

I am very pleased to offer you the position of curriculum coordinator at EduTech. We look forward to welcoming you to our team. Below are details of this job offer and instructions on how to accept it.

- **Job description:** The curriculum coordinator is responsible for organizing the curriculum for a summer camp for grades 4-6, gathering input from teachers regarding the curriculum, ordering materials, helping teachers implement the curriculum, overseeing the camp program, writing a report on the program, and planning for other programs.

- **Supervisor:** The curriculum coordinator reports to the director of the school.

- **Salary:** $48,000 per year, to be paid by check every two weeks. The employee may be eligible for a raise after six months.

- **Pre-employment testing:** All employees must undergo a background check and a complete physical with the company doctor before beginning their employment.

■ **To accept this job offer:** To accept this offer, please call Monica Underwood in Human Resources to set up a meeting. Her phone number is (402) 835 0141.

We hope to hear from you soon.

Best regards,

[Your name]

DISCUSSION & EXERCISE 19 [Units 67-69] P. 407

1

1. Employment references and letters of recommendation
推薦信包含就職證明書和推薦信兩種。

2. An employment reference
就職證明書簡短客觀。

3. (A), (B), (D)

4. All of the above, plus the writer's opinions about the employee's performance, character, fitness for another position, etc.
推薦信除了描述當事人在該公司擔任的職務、任職時間與薪資狀況外,還包括當事人的工作表現、品行,與對其他職缺的適任度。

5. (C), (E); in some situations, (A), (B)

6. Remind the writer about your history together, explain the responsibilities of the position you want, outline the attributes you believe the position requires, and provide the writer with a résumé or other document that lists your most significant accomplishments.
簡短提醒對方你們曾有過的合作經驗;解釋你應徵的職位所需要負責的職務內容;列出你覺得該職位需要的特質;並且附上如履歷之類的文件,列出自己最重要的成就等,都有助於撰寫者更輕鬆地寫出推薦信。

2

1. True 推薦信通常是就特定的工作、對象(個人)或公司而寫。

2. True 就職證明書通常內容簡短,而推薦信會就當事人的才能與工作表現作出更詳細的敘述,因此長度也較長。

3. False 就職證明書有時事當是人自己撰寫好,再請主管簽名。

3

Dear Sir or Madam:

Ken Casey was employed as a programmer at Sticky Wicket Computer Solutions from November 2018 to October 2023. He earned $45,000 annually. In his time as a programmer, Mr. Casey fulfilled the responsibilities of his position: interacting with clients, visiting clients on-site, providing solutions in time-critical situations, and creating and modifying programs in C+, Python, and Flash. I would reemploy Mr. Casey in the same position.

Yours sincerely,

[Your name]

December 30, 2023

Jill Dunstable
Human Resources Manager
202 Dogwood Boulevard
Richmond, VA 23173

Dear Ms. Dunstable:

I am very pleased to recommend Ken Casey for the position of lead programmer. During Mr. Casey's time at Sticky Wicket, I witnessed his programming and interpersonal skills. I was so impressed with his abilities that I recommended him for a merit pay raise in May 2022, increasing his salary from $41,000 to $45,000 per year. Mr. Casey was the subject of a number of letters from clients who praised his speed, timeliness, and creative problem-solving skills. Recognizing his excellent leadership skills and clearheadedness, I appointed him the leader of our Crisis Group, a work group dedicated to solving high-pressure problems requiring a fast turnaround.

In addition to his grace under pressure, Mr. Casey is also dedicated to his professional development. I found him to be a quick learner. He is keen on staying abreast of developments in his field, making him an excellent addition to a cutting-edge company. I can recommend him wholeheartedly. I am sure his programming skills and demonstrated leadership ability will make him a very capable lead programmer.

Yours sincerely,

[name]

DISCUSSION & EXERCISE 20 [Units 70-76] P. 434

1 1. (A), (C), (D)

2. Répondez s'il vous plaît in French, "Please respond" in English.

   「RSVP」是法語「Répondez s'il vous plaît」，在英語中為「請回覆」之意。

3. A card included with an invitation for guests to use to RSVP.

   回覆卡會附在邀請函中。收到邀請函後可以直接寄回回覆卡，不用另外寫一封回覆信。

4. (A), (F)

5. (A), (B), (E)

6. (A), (D), (E)

7. Within 24 hours or a maximum of three days.

   收到邀請函的 24 小時內，或最晚三天之內需要給予回覆。

8. (B)

2

Dear Ms. Ellis:

We want to show our appreciation to valued customers like you by inviting you to the launch party for our new gaming system. We hope you can attend this special event!

The launch party will be held at our store on Friday, June 2, at 6:30 p.m. All invitees may bring one guest. Please present this invitation at the door. We would be grateful if you could RSVP by May 31.

We look forward to seeing you at the launch party!

Thank you,

[Your name]

3 1. An invitation card

Your presence is requested at a
<u>Farewell dinner</u>
honoring Dr. Phillip Pushton, Professor of Sociology,
for his 10 years of service to this university

Hosted by Sydney Bankfield, Dean of Sociology,
on July 31 at 7 pm

at Luhrman Hall
University of Sydney

<u>RSVPs are requested by July 25</u>
Business attire suggested

2. A response card

The favor of your response is<u> requested by July 25</u>

<u>   Ms. Feng   </u>
☐ <u>Will attend</u>
☐ <u>Will not attend</u>

4

Dear Ms. Ko:

I am very pleased to invite you to speak at our conference "The Future of Graphic Design in East Asia," to be held on September 18, 2023, at the Mountain Jade Conference Center in Shanghai.

This is the first conference, but we hope it will become an annual event. The event is generating a great deal of interest already, with 300 attendees expected from companies in China, Japan, South Korea, and Taiwan.

We have recently confirmed George Lim of Dragon Design as a keynote speaker. Mr. Lim will discuss the latest trends in graphic design. Other confirmed speakers are Susan Won of Design Limited, Chen Li-Ping of Studio A, and Boris Huang of East-West Graphics. All speakers other than the keynote speaker will be giving a 30-minute presentation.

We would consider it an honor if you would join their number and honor us with a 30-minute presentation on a topic of your choosing.

Please feel free to contact me with any questions at [number]. I will call you in the next week to follow up on this invitation.

Yours respectfully,

[name]

5

Dear Ms. Ko:

On behalf of Double Design and all attendees at this year's "The Future of Graphic Design in East Asia" conference, thank you for your enlightening speech, "Conservative or Cutting-Edge Advertising." Your speech was well received by all and generated a great deal of energetic discussion.

We are very grateful for your contribution to our conference, and we hope that you will consider participating in next year's event as well. We are very pleased with the success of our event, and we deeply appreciate your role in it.

Yours respectfully,

[name]

DISCUSSION & EXERCISE 21 | Units 77-81 | P. 450

1 1. To save a relationship after you have made a serious mistake or offended someone.

道歉信是在你或公司犯下嚴重錯誤或得罪顧客後,為挽救雙方關係而撰寫。

2. When you think the apology may have legal ramifications.

當你覺得寄道歉信可能會引起法律後果時,你可能需考量是否寄出。

3. It means that your apology is worded to say that you are sorry the event occurred, not that you are responsible for or had any part in the event. ("I am sorry your coat was lost" rather than "I am sorry I misplaced your coat.")

若擔心道歉信會引發法律糾紛,信中措辭應著重表現「同情」,而不是「責任」,即應該表示你很遺憾某項錯誤發生,而不是表明事情是由你引起並且為此道歉(例如,可以說「很遺憾您的外套遺失了」而非「很抱歉,我把您的外套弄丟了」)。

4. (C)

5. (B)

2 1. True 一般來說,只要發現有出錯,就應該立刻寄一封道歉信給對方。

2. False 某些更嚴重的問題,如果想要用金錢來補償顧客,反而會得罪顧客。

3. False 道歉信的內容應該直截了當、語言要簡單。

4. True 在道歉信上親自簽名能表示對對方的尊重。

5. True 道歉信需要使用有公司信頭的信紙撰寫,以示尊重、禮貌。

3 Problems: 1. The letter waits until the second paragraph to apologize.

2. The word "obviously" creates a condescending tone.

3. The letter does not take responsibility for the problem.

4. The letter blames the reader ("If you had informed us . . .") for the problem.

Rewrite:

Dear Ms. Somtow:

I am very sorry to hear about the damage that occurred to your shipment while it was in transit. Thank you for informing us of the problem in your letter of May 30.

We have looked into the issue and discovered that the damage was inflicted by our shipping partner. We are currently working with the shipper to determine how the damage occurred and to prevent this from happening again.

We shipped your replacement merchandise today. We would also like to offer you free shipping and a 15% discount on your next order with us as a gesture of our goodwill. Please let me know if there is anything else I can do to help you.

I look forward to receiving your next order.

Yours faithfully,

Malika Karmarkar

Malika Karmarkar
Sales Manager
Exotic Textiles, New Delhi

4

Dear Ms. Parsons:

I was very dismayed to hear about your negative experience with the installation of your order. I gathered from your letter that the problems were caused by the technician who worked on your installation. We spoke to the technician immediately and have since terminated his contract. We always strive for the highest standards of customer service, and we are disappointed to hear that we have fallen down on the job.

I understand that your system is functioning now. I would be happy to send another technician to check it, if you would like. I am also refunding your installation fee. We have credited that amount to the corporate credit card used to pay for the installation. Please find the receipt for the transaction enclosed.

Again, I offer my deepest apologies for the problems with the installation of your system. Thank you for your patronage of Jupiter Systems. Please let me know if there is any other way I can assist you.

Yours sincerely,

[name]

Enc.

5

Dear Ms. Ortiz:

I am sorry to hear about the problems you had with our shirts. Thank you for taking the time to inform us of the situation. I want to assure you that our products are usually of the highest quality. We are currently checking the washing instructions on our entire line to ensure that they are correct.

If you would like to return your shirts, we will be happy to replace them with identical ones or with other products of equal value.

Please let me know how we can replace your damaged shirts and if there is any way I can be of more help.

Sincerely,
[name]

DISCUSSION & EXERCISE 22 [Units 82-87] P. 464

1
1. A letter expressing happiness at someone else's good fortune or achievement.

   祝賀信用來恭賀對方的喜事或成就。

2. Dramatic or exaggerated vocabulary can affect your tone, making your letter sound insincere or even sarcastic.

   撰寫祝賀信時，應該使用簡單而正面的文字。誇張的文字會讓你的祝賀聽起來像是挖苦或嘲笑。

3. If the happy event is one the subject might want kept quiet, or if the event could have strong negative implications as well as positive ones.

   如果你祝賀的事情是對方不想公開的，或是該事件伴有負面意味，就不適合寄送祝賀信。

4. (A), (B), (D), (E)

5. (A)

6. (A)

2

Dear Mr. Mare:

Congratulations on the birth of your son! We were delighted to hear about the addition to your family. We could see how excited you were, and we know how thrilled you all must be right now. On behalf of everyone here at Professional PR, I send our warmest wishes to you on this happy occasion.

Yours sincerely,

[name]

3

Dear Ms. Karmarkar,

I trust all is well at Exotic Textiles, Inc.[1] Congratulations! We just heard the good news!

For someone of your exceptional talents and incredible business sense, it was only a matter of time before you moved into a top position. We at Duds have seen it coming for a long time. Only the other day, I told a colleague here, "Ms. Karmarkar is sure to be promoted soon." Well, it seems I was right![2] Finally, Exotic Textiles has seen what a shining star you are.[3]

I am sure that with your new position, the relationship between Duds and Exotic Textiles will be strengthened and improved.[4] I am looking forward to the evolution of our trading partnership.

Again, let us offer our heartfelt congratulations on your achievement. You certainly deserve it.

Best wishes,

Aroon Pradabtanakij
Aroon Pradabtanakij
Manager, Duds Clothing

Problems:

1. The letter does not offer congratulations immediately.
2. The letter takes the focus away from the reader and puts it on the writer.
3. The dramatic vocabulary ("shining star" as well as "exceptional" talents and "incredible" business sense) sounds insincere and unprofessional.
4. The writer implies that the reader's promotion could benefit him as well.

Rewrite :

Dear Ms. Karmarkar:

We just heard the great news about your promotion. Congratulations!

In our working relationship, all of us at Duds have benefited from your talent, professionalism, and business sense. On behalf of all of us, I send you our best wishes for continued success in your new position.

Again, let us offer our heartfelt congratulations on your achievement.

Best wishes,

Aroon Pradabtanakij

Aroon Pradabtanakij
Manager, Duds Clothing

DISCUSSION & EXERCISE 23 (Units 88-90) P. 473

1 1. Which companies are merging? How will this affect me? Where will the new company be located? What products/services will it provide? Will previous products/services be cut? Will new products/services be added?

對「公司合併」會產生的問題有：合併的公司為何？是否影響顧客權益？新公司的地址是什麼？其提供的產品或服務為何？現有的產品或服務是否會停售？是否會增加新的產品或服務等。

2. False 應該在實際搬遷之前就把地址更改的消息寄出。

2

[Your company's name]
44 Lockhaven Boulevard, St. Louis, MO 63015
T: (314) 444-7800 F: (314) 444-7802

July 1, 2023

Dear Sirs:

Our company will be moving to a new office on July 18, 2023. After that date, please send all correspondence to our new office at

[Your company's name]

2025 Wildwood Street

Jefferson City, MO 65102 USA

Our phone and fax numbers will remain the same:

Telephone: (314) 444-7800

Fax: (314) 444-7802

Thank you for your attention to this change. We look forward to providing you with the same great service from our new location.

Best,

[name]

3

Dear Sirs:

We are pleased to announce that A Plus Training and Quality Training, Ltd., have merged to form Quality Plus Training, Inc. As Quality Plus Training, we look forward to providing you with the same dedicated service both companies have always prided themselves on.

Quality Plus Training represents a joining of two successful companies. We first worked together on a long-term training project for a large client. After that positive experience, Quality Training approached us with a plan to expand our capabilities and the services we could offer our clients. After serious discussion, we concluded that this merger could lead to significant growth for both companies—and benefit our clients with increased service options.

Quality Plus Training will allow us to offer all of our customized computer and management training packages, plus a new branch of communications training. Our larger staff will allow us to implement our programs when and where you need them. We will continue to provide the service and support you have come to expect from A Plus Training.

As always, don't hesitate to contact me with any questions or concerns at 415.734.9857 or over email at [email address]. We look forward to serving you in our new capacity as Quality Plus Training, Inc.

Yours truly,

[name]

英文
商業書信
寫作技巧與範例

Business Writing
Skills, Applications, and Practices

作　　者　Michelle Witte / Owain Mckimm（Part 1 部分範例；Part 11 建言信、回覆建言信）

譯　　者　羅慕謙／黃詩韻（Part 6 及 Part 11 建言信）／陳依辰（Part 11 回覆建言信）

審　　訂　Judy Majewski / Helen Yeh（Part 6 及 Part 11 建言信、回覆建言信）

編　　輯　高詣軒／Gina Wang

主　　編　丁宥暄

內文排版　林書玉／謝青秀

封面設計　林書玉

製程管理　洪巧玲

圖　　片　Shutterstock

發 行 人　黃朝萍

出 版 者　寂天文化事業股份有限公司

電　　話　02-2365-9739

傳　　真　02-2365-9835

網　　址　www.icosmos.com.tw

讀者服務　onlineservice@icosmos.com.tw

出版日期　2023 年 3 月 初版一刷 160101

國家圖書館出版品預行編目 (CIP) 資料

英文商業書信寫作技巧與範例 / Michelle
Witte 著；羅慕謙譯 . -- 初版 . -- [臺北市] :
寂天文化事業股份有限公司 , 2023.03
　　面；　　公分
譯自：Business writing : skills, applications,
and practices
ISBN 978-626-300-170-1(16K 平裝)

1.CST: 商業書信 2.CST: 商業英文 3.CST:
商業應用文 4.CST: 寫作法

493.6　　　　　　　　　　　　111018980